Hildegarde Withers: Uncollected Stories

Lost Classics

Hildegarde Withers: Uncollected Stories

By Stuart Palmer

With an introduction by
Jennifer Venola (Mrs. Stuart Palmer)

Crippen & Landru Publishers
Norfolk, Virginia
2002

ISBN (cloth edition): 1-885941-84-6

ISBN (trade edition): 1-885941-85-4

FIRST EDITION

We are grateful to Stephen Leadbetter, B.A. Pike,
Bill Pronzini, and Jennifer Venola for providing photocopies of
the stories in this book.

Crippen & Landru Publishers
P.O. Box 9315
Norfolk, VA 23505
USA

www.crippenlandru.com
CrippenL@pilot.infi.net

Contents

Stuart Palmer, Writer
21 June 1905 - 4 February 1968

My memories of Stuart Palmer begin in September 1965. I was fresh out of college, rooming with friends, and getting my wings dry in the real world.

"Our friend, Stuart, is coming this evening. You'll like him." "Ok," I said. "Do you want me to cook dinner?" "No, we don't know what time, since he's driving in from Eureka."

Well, this debonair gentleman arrived, fussing a bit about San Francisco traffic, and held us spellbound for hours with his deliciously funny stories of highway tie-ups, encounters with folk all over, limericks, and life in general.

I was most flattered with he invited me to dinner at the very tony Sally Stanford's Valhalla Inn in Sausalito the next evening. Two months later we were married. He was 60, I just 21. We had to laugh about the age difference, because too many people wanted to cry. His children, Philip and Penelope, both a few years older than I, were gracious. (I never met the youngest, Jay, who lived in England.) Penelope called me "Mumsie" and she was "Daughter-Dear."

Stuart was a true gentleman, always courteous, always courtly, never abrasive, a gifted raconteur. He took the light side of every question. And loved limericks.

Back in the 1950s, living someplace in the San Fernando Valley near Los Angeles, he had his study in the garage. In the throes of writers-block, he decided to type out his collection of limericks. One to a page, using yellow "second sheets" (this was back in the days of carbon paper). Unfortunately there was a fire, and after it was out, the neighborhood was littered with yellow second sheets, slightly charred at the edges, each with a carefully typed limerick. The parents in the neighborhood took a dim view, and Stuart and his family moved soon after.

When we met, Stuart was working through another bout of writers-block, editing Naturist magazines in North Hollywood, California. In that job he wrote a series of articles about The Nude in fine art. Having been an art major at the University of Wisconsin, he was well versed in art history and the great painters. Plans to republish the collected articles came to naught after Stuart was able to return to writing novels and quit Sun Publications.

Actually, he maintained that he was a writer, rather than a novelist. "I'll write anything for money except poison pen letters and ransom notes," he often said. And did so. Novels, short stories, poetry, film, radio, even a limerick (There was a young couple named Kelly, who got fastened belly to belly, because in their haste they used library paste, instead of petroleum jelly!); mystery, fantasy, science fiction, true crime, art, and how-to-write instructions. Stuart taught writing courses, and worked as a private investigator for various Los Angeles defense attorneys, which gave him a different perspective on crime. He also assisted police departments in investigation, and was allowed into the prison to interview Barbara Graham, the first woman executed in California. That interview resulted in a magazine article which was highly praised by the Chief of Police of Burbank, California, where Miss Graham committed murder.

For five years during the Second World War, Stuart was in the Army Signal Corps, with the rank of major, dealing with film intelligence in Washington D.C. But his sense of whimsy came out even there. Reading a newspaper report about "sporadic rifle-fire" heard from across the Potomac, he generated a memo inquiring as to who had given clearance for media reports about the super-secret "sporadic rifle"! He was proud of having warned his hero General George S. Patton to remove his revolvers and leave them in his car, thus preventing the General from being embarrassed on the steps of the White House en route to a meeting with President Franklin D. Roosevelt.

His working pattern was disciplined. An idea, a twist, and he sat down and started developing it. He worked in longhand first, scribbling notes and developing plot lines. When the typewriter came into play the story was usually fully constructed in his mind. A secretary once complained of his cigars. A one-cigar day meant he smoked one at a time. A two-cigar day was one smoking and one in the ashtray. A three-cigar day meant one in the mouth, one in the hand, and one in the ashtray. That was when things were either really good or really bad. File drawers and boxes overflowed with clippings that might germinate into an idea or provide background detail for some story. His interests were, of course, eclectic: poisons, weapons, writing, ESP, LSD, chess, art, cats, writing, breeding exotic aquarium fish and standard poodles, playing polo, circuses, clowning, education, writing.

When Stuart died, a rational suicide diagnosed with laryngeal cancer, his body went to Loma Linda Medical School for study: he fostered learning even in death. And despite the protests of the authorities, his death certificate says his last occupation was: Writer.

— Jennifer Venola

The Riddle of the Dangling Pearl

Rushing through the wide doors of the Cosmopolitan Museum of Art came Miss Hildegarde Withers, out of the blinding sunlight of Fifth Avenue in August into a hushed, dim world. Pausing for a moment to sniff the musty odors which cling to the vast treasure house wherein men have gathered together the objects saved from vandal Time, the angular school teacher went on, sailing serenely past the checkroom to be halted by a gray uniformed guard at the turnstile.

"Have to check your umbrella, ma'am."

"Young man," she advised him sharply, "can't you see that I need it?" She leaned on the umbrella heavily, and the guard, with a shrug of his shoulders, let her through. She was not lying, even by implication, for this day she was to need her only weapon as never before in all her assiduous, if amateur, efforts at crime detection.

It had been some months since Miss Withers had last found occasion to visit the museum, and today there seemed to be fewer guards and more visitors, particularly juvenile visitors, than formerly. She threaded her resolute way through the crowd, entering the Hall of Sculpture and pushing on toward the staircase at the rear of the building. In this hall the visitors were fewer, and only a solitary art student here and there was copying a painting, lost to the rest of the world.

"You'll find Professor Carter somewhere in the Florentine Wing," the Inspector had told her over the telephone. "You can't miss him, he's a tall, dried-up old fossil with a big round head bald as an egg." But at this moment Miss Withers had no idea how, and where, she was to find Professor Carter, associate curator of the Cosmopolitan. For all her haste, she paused for a moment beside a crouching marble nude labeled "Nymph — by Hebilly West." Using her dampened handkerchief, Miss Withers frowningly removed a penciled mustache from the classic stone face, shaking her head at the laxity of the guards. Then suddenly she looked up.

From somewhere came the patter of light footsteps — the quick steps of a small man or perhaps a woman — fading away down some distant corridor. As they passed, she heard a hoarse masculine scream, thin with surprise, which set a thousand echoes ringing in the vaulted halls. After the school teacher turned and ran on down the hall, turning toward the stairs, she stopped short.

A man was coming, slowly and horribly, down the hundred marble steps — a man whose hoarse scream had almost become a bellow, and who clutched unavailingly at thin air. His body was bent forward almost parallel with the slope of the steep steps ...

Miss Withers was frozen with horror, for at the foot of the stairs loomed a gigantic statuary group upon a granite base. As she watched, powerless to move, the plunging man collided headlong with the base of the statue, and his screaming stopped.

There was no doubt in Miss Withers' mind as to the identity of this man. Inspector Oscar Piper had told her that Carter, the man she had come to see, was a tall and dried-up "fossil" with a head like an egg. And like an egg the round hairless skull of Professor Carter had cracked against the implacable stone.

Almost instantly the hall was filled with gasping, curious onlookers. Here and there a guard began to push his way through. But Miss Withers turned swiftly away, and moved up the stairs. She was looking for something, and when she reached the top step she found it. Then, and not until then, did she rejoin the murmuring, excited group at the base of the stairs.

A small, almost dandyish man in morning clothes was approaching from the opposite corridor, and the guards made a path for him. Miss Withers heard one of them whisper — "It's the curator!"

Willard Robbins, chief curator of the museum, resembled a young and bustling business man more than the custodian of a large share of the world's art treasures. He was not one to waste time upon adjectives. "Quick, Dugan — the canvas and stretcher." He looked around, through the crowd, for a uniformed figure which was not there. "Burton! How did this happen? Where is Burton?"

"Probably studying art again," said one of the uniformed men, softly.

But the curator went on. "Please move back, everybody. Back, out of the hallway. Everybody... "

Miss Hildegarde Withers stood her ground. "Young man, I want a word with you!"

Curator Robbins looked annoyed. Then one of his men whispered something to him. His face cleared. "So you're the lady who saw the accident? Won't you step this way, to my office?"

They faced each other across a bare mahogany desk. "Well?" said the curator.

"It wasn't an accident," said Hildegarde Withers. "Someone tied this"— she produced a loose ball of twine — "across the top step. That was murder."

"Impossible," gasped Robbins. He handled the string gingerly. "And you mean to tell me that poor Carter stumbled over this, and plunged to his death — you expect me to believe that?"

"I expect you to believe what I say," she told him tartly. "Because the police will, if you don't. You may not know that Professor Carter was afraid of something like this. He telephoned Inspector Piper at Headquarters this morning, asking for police help. The Inspector was busy, so he called me and asked me to drop in, because I live just across the Park, and I've been of service to him at times in the past. Now do you believe me?"

Robbins nodded slowly. "All except that Carter phoned for police protection for himself. The old man never thought of his own safety. He lived for the Cellini Cup, which as you perhaps know is the most valuable single art object in the world. He was always dithering for fear bandits would grab it, although we have a burglar-proof system here to protect it. He'd been reading reports from France that a gang of super crooks stole the Mona Lisa from the Louvre, substituting a copy. Why, he even used to spend most of his time in the Florentine Wing, watching over his Cup... "

Miss Withers nodded. "Then there was some reason behind his dithering!"

But the curator shook his head. "Carter had outlived his usefulness here. He had ceased to distinguish between major and minor matters. Indeed, his chief worry was that small boys would do some harm to the Cellini. He used to drive them away from the Florentine Wing religiously, and in turn they teased him... "

The curator smashed his fist against the desk. "That's it! This was no murder plot. Anyone wanting Carter out of the way could have managed it without going to this extreme. Don't you see? It was only a thoughtless prank on the part of some of the little hoodlums who play about here on free days. They tied the cord there to give him a bad fall, as a joke, never dreaming of the possible consequence... "

Miss Withers remembered the light, running footsteps. Yet she was somehow surprised that she could not agree with the curator's easy explanation. Perhaps — yet it was too pat.

"I'm going to find Burton, the guard who was supposed to be stationed near the head of that staircase," explained Robbins. "Then we'll have every child in the building searched to find the rest of that string. It was probably taken off a kite string."

"Probably," agreed Miss Withers. "I have two favors to ask. First, please don't let anybody know that I'm anything but a visitor here. Second, let me go in search of this Burton. I think I can guess where he is."

Robbins bowed, twice. "You'll probably find Joel Burton around a skirt," he advised her. "He's a new guard but highly recommended. Only has this one vice... "

"That you know of," said the school teacher. "What does he look like?"

† † †

Tall, blue-eyed, and Irish as a thatched roof, Joel Burton stood near the end of the second floor corridor which leads to the Florentine Wing of the museum.

"Sure I ought to be getting back to my post," he was saying. But he kept on obediently squirting water from an atomizer upon the clay figure which was beginning to take shape under the slim, deft fingers of the girl.

"Then go," said Dagmar. Her voice was slow and rich and throaty. She looked at the young and handsome guard through lashes as tawny-yellow as her hair. All the same, he knew that she didn't want him to go. It had been five weeks now since Dagmar, one of a dozen art students permitted to copy in the halls, had been at work on her version of Rodin's "Satyr," and for four and a half weeks of that time he had been her slave. The slave of hair and eyes and hands and the tall, smooth body ...

She tweaked a clay ear into pert life. "That's enough water," she said. "Do you want to drown it? Now you can go back to your work."

But Burton lingered. "Just the one trick I'm going to show you," he said. From Dagmar's fingers he took the braided bit of wire with which she cut the damp clay. Then with all his strength he flung it down the corridor. The girl heard it strike tinklingly against a distant window. Then Burton leaned over and neatly extracted it from her curving ear.

She clapped her hands excitedly. "Wonderful!"

Burton persisted. "That's nothing. See this. I used to wow them with this when I was on Pantages time." From his pocket he took a small roll of string, and handed it to her. "Take hold of the end, and pull." He took back the ball, and Dagmar pulled. She pulled until the floor around her was a tangle of string, and then, from his cupped hands, came half a dozen silken flags of the Entente, knotted to the cord, followed by a birdcage containing two celluloid canaries.

Dagmar laughed, and clapped her hands again. The applause was echoed from behind them, and the young couple suddenly became aware of their situation, and sprang apart. Peering benevolently at them was an angular, school teacherish person in a Queen Mary hat. "Splendid, young man!" said Miss Withers. "You've missed your vocation." She came closer.

"If you don't mind an old woman's butting in, you've also missed something else. There's been an accident on the main staircase and unless I miss my guess, the curator is looking for you. You'd better start thinking up an excuse... "

"Huh? Thanks!" muttered Joel Burton, fervently. He scooped up his string and the rest of his props and flew.

"That was a kind-hearted thing to do," said Dagmar, coolly, after there had been a moment's silence.

Miss Withers stared at the lovely art student. "I'm not so old but that I can remember when I was young," she said. She waved a thin yet graceful arm. "Romance... "

Dagmar flushed a little, and bent over her modeling. But Miss Hildegarde Withers was not to be got rid of so easily. "You have talent," she observed, critically. "That's an excellent copy you're doing. The flair, the feeling of the original — and something added... "

Dagmar bowed, almost formally. Then she looked up and faced the intruder with a complete change of subject. "He really isn't meant for this sort of thing, you know." Her tone was almost defiant. "He may be only a museum guard, but he belongs in a different place from this."

Miss Withers cleared her throat. Then — "I'm inclined to agree with you," she said. If her tone was grim, the girl did not sense it. "Then you didn't hear the noise a few minutes ago, either of you?"

Dagmar shook her head. "Oh, yes — I heard a man shouting. But the echoes distort sounds here so much that I didn't pay much attention. I don't know if Joel heard it or not — he was —"

"Oh, he wasn't with you all the time?" Miss Withers noticed the pail of fresh water beside Dagmar's stool. "Did he go on an errand?"

But the girl was quick. "Joel was with me for the last half hour," she announced. "If it makes any difference... "

"It might — who can tell?" said Miss Withers softly, and then withdrew.

† † †

There was a guard outside the door of the curator's office. "You can't go in there," he told Miss Withers.

"I can and I may," she retorted, and plunged through, umbrella clutched firmly in her hand. Inside she found Robbins, flustered somewhat, facing fifteen or twenty youngsters of ages assorted from six to twelve.

"I want the boy who did this wicked thing to come forward and confess!" the curator was thundering. Behind him stood a perspiring and bulky guard. The urchins scratched and shrugged and kept their silence.

"Perhaps," suggested a voice from the doorway — "perhaps you'd let me help, Mr. Curator. I'm used to boys of this age in my own classes... "

But Robbins was out of temper. "Thank you madam," he said, shortly, "but I'm confident that one of these hooligans caused the death of Professor Carter, and I'm going to find out which one it was. Search them, Cassidy."

Miss Withers stood back and watched the process, which was not without its difficulty. "Put everything out of yer pockets here on the table," ordered Cassidy.

One boy hesitated, and Robbins leaped forward. "There! In that pocket. What have you got hidden there?"

He inserted his well-manicured hand swiftly, and withdrew it holding a gummy mass of old butterscotch. The guard continued the search, bringing to light several balls of kite string, but none which matched the sinister cord which lay across the curator's desk. He stepped back, his face perplexed.

Then there came a knock at the door. It opened, and in came Joel Burton, clinging to the arm of a resisting red-headed gamin who had been discovered, he said, lurking in Armour Hall. "This is the last of them," he announced.

The urchin grinned widely, showing the lack of a front tooth. His head was a mass of red curls, and his dress consisted of a ragged sweater and worn overalls. "Leave me alone," the lad insisted. "I done nothing."

"Search him, Cassidy, and see if you find any cord to match this," ordered the curator.

† † †

The prisoner submitted without resistance, his hard, young-old face defiant. But Miss Withers was not watching the boy. Her keen eyes were upon Joel Burton, who stood by the door with his eyes upon the cord which lay on Robbins' table. Automatically his hand went to his side pocket — closed around something —

"What have you there, if I may ask?" said Miss Withers swiftly. All eyes turned on her, and then on the guard.

He never blinked an eye. "Nothing at all," he said. The muscles of his wrist flickered, and then he extended his open palm. "What would I have?"

Miss Withers remembered the exhibition in the hallway. "Never mind," she said. And the search went on, with the result which Miss Withers had known would occur. The boys were released, with a general warning to behave themselves for the good of their souls, and poured out of the office, the red-haired lad in the lead. Miss Withers and the curator looked after them.

"I told you so," said that lady. "No child planned that diabolical scheme." Robbins did not answer. He was smiling at the red-headed urchin, who was walking fast down the hall, away from the others, with his cap perched on one side of his curly poll and his feet turned out, Charlie Chaplin fashion.

"Fathers of men," observed the curator, sententiously.

"Fathers of men and sons of Belial," Miss Withers told him, from bitter experience. Then she faced Robbins. "I still feel that this mystery, if it is a mystery, has something to do with the Cellini Cup you spoke of. I wonder if you'd send one of the guards with me to look at it — preferably one of those whose duty it is to watch it."

The curator hesitated. "That would be Joel Burton. From his post at the head of the stairs he commands a view, down the long corridor, of the Rodin Hall and the Florentine Wing which holds the Cellini. The Cellini case is placed beneath a skylight, so that he could check on it every minute — when he is at his post. He's wandered away once too often, so I've demoted him to the checkroom downstairs, and put Cassidy in his place. Will he do?"

"Splendidly," said Hildegarde Withers. A few moments later she was following the broad gray back of Cassidy down the hall, past the Rodin statues and the pale-haired girl who worked busily in her corner with the mobile clay, and on into a large, airy room whose walls were lined with glass cabinets filled with glittering gold-encrusted glass.

† † †

But she had no eyes for the walls. Set squarely in the center of the room, upon a solid metal pedestal, was a square case of heavy glass. Its base was a polished mirror, and upon the mirror rested an object at once so beautiful and so decadent, so opulent in its color and design, that Miss Withers almost shuddered.

It was small, this Cellini Cup — not more than eight inches in diameter and perhaps seven inches high. But she knew it to be worth the ransom of seven kings.

Its base, resting on the mirror, was a turtle — the legendary tortoise who holds the world upon his back, according to mythology. But this turtle was of crusted gold. Upon the turtle rested a winged dragon of shimmering green and yellow and red enamel, and upon the wings and neck and tail of the dragon rested a wide and richly curving sea-shell of hammered gold.

Crouching on the lip of the shell was a sphinx, with the head of a lovely woman modeled in pure gold, and a serpentine, animalistic body of ardent, opulent greens, blues, whites, and yellows. From the ears of the sphinx depended two miniature pearls, and from her breast, hanging over the bowl in which the Princes of Rospigliosi were wont to keep their salt, hung a great white pearl larger than a pear. This pearl swung back and forth, back and forth, endlessly.

"Vibration of the building," said Cassidy, the guard. "Professor Carter used to say it showed perfect balance."

Miss Withers nodded. "And this cup is left here, protected only by a glass case?"

Cassidy laughed, and then turned to make sure that they were alone. "Not on your life, ma'am. The Professor used to hang about all the time, but he didn't need to. This case is safer than a vault. Look down the hall where we came. See the stair? Well, that's where one of us is always stationed. Now look this way, toward the other end of the Florentine Wing. See Schultz watching us? One or the other of them has his eyes on this case every minute. But that ain't all. Come here."

With a thick finger he traced out the almost invisible wires which ran through the glass. "If one of them is broken, it sets off all the alarms. Instanter, every door and window in the place is double-locked. This wing has no doors and no fire escapes leading out — and the only exit is back through the Rodin Hall to the main stair. What chance do you think a burglar would have, even if the guards did slip? The police would get the alarm direct, and surround the place in two minutes... " He beamed at Miss Withers, proudly.

She was forced to admit that the protection of the priceless treasure did seem thorough. But hadn't she read somewhere that anything one man devised could be out-done by some other man?

Miss Withers thanked Cassidy, and returned to the stair, pausing on her way to note the slow but steady progress of Dagmar's satyr. She found, on reaching the main hall, that she was just in time to have missed the undertakers as they removed the body of Professor Carter, canvas and all. Full well she knew that it was her duty to telephone Inspector Piper that this was a job for the whole homicide squad. But that was one of the advantages of having no official standing. She could do exactly as she saw fit, as long as the results justified the means. For the time being she was content to have the death put down as simple misadventure.

She was surprised to notice that the building was gradually emptying — not because of the "accident" but because it was time for lunch. Thoughts of a sandwich began to fill Miss Withers' busy mind, until she started down the main staircase and saw two white-clad porters mopping the floor around the statuary group at the foot of the stair, and she lost her appetite.

Hildegarde Withers would never have counted this minor loss as an evidence of the good luck which more often than not attended her amateurish efforts as a detective. Yet otherwise she might have stepped out of the building, and missed one of the most exciting hours of her life.

She was sitting on a stone bench in the vast main hall of the lower floor when it happened, trying unavailingly to put in their proper positions the various characters in this mad drama. But she leaped to her feet as there came, from somewhere on the second floor, an unmistakable shot followed by two more in rapid succession.

† † †

The few straggling visitors who remained within sight milled about like cattle, but Hildegarde Withers was going up the stairs three steps at a time. She passed Curator Robbins near the top, and both of them went galloping down the hall toward the American Wing, from which sounds of a scuffle were arising. All the alarms went off hideously.

In the doorway they came upon brawny Cassidy and two other guards, a wiry, swarthy little man grasped firmly in their thick red hands. He was mouthing incoherent cries, and making efforts to regain the cheap nickel-plated revolver which Cassidy had taken from him.

"Nobody hurt, Mr. Robbins," announced Cassidy. "Just a bloody anarchist who wants to destroy the paintings that Mr. Morgan loaned us. All he did was to crack a molding."

The curator drew a long breath. "Good Lord! I thought it was — well, something worse. This day has been a nightmare. Take him downstairs and turn him over to the cop on the beat. I'll prefer drunk and disorderly charges against him later."

Robbins walked back toward the head of the stair with Miss Withers, who was thinking fast. "Funny how things happen all at once," he observed. "Six months go by, and this is the sleepiest place in town. Then in one day we have a fatal accident and an anarchist. I hope this is the end."

† † †

But Miss Withers did not answer him. She was standing stock-still. "Prepare yourself," she advised him. "This is far from the end of things."

Somehow she had known all along that this would happen. She was staring down the Rodin Hall, toward the distant showcase which stood beneath the skylight. Even from that distance, both could see that the light glinted on smashed glass, and that the brilliant, jeweled setting of the showcase was gone.

"Come on," shouted Robbins, unnecessarily, and began to sprint.

Miss Withers followed, but this time she did not run. She walked slowly, staring at the floor. It was too late to hurry. This was the time to be sure and careful. Half way down the Rodin Hall she paused, finding the clue, the discrepancy, for which she was looking.

She could hear the agonized voice of the curator as he came face to face with the shattered case which had held the Cellini. But Miss Withers was bending over the sprawled body of a tall girl in a black smock, a girl who tried weakly to sit up as the school teacher grasped her shoulder.

At least this wasn't another corpse. Dagmar pushed aside the proffered aid and stared down the corridor. "Where did he go?"

"Where did who go?"

"The man in the trench-coat, blast him!" Dagmar's red lips curled in anger. "Slamming into me that way, and knocking me headlong. And look — look what he did to my model!" The satyr did show signs of maltreatment.

Hastily the girl smoothed the profaned clay. "Five weeks work — ruined!"

"It's not ruined beyond repair, child," said Miss Withers. "But this man. Did you see his face?" The curator was coming back, and she beckoned to him. "We have a witness, Mr. Robbins."

"Of course I saw his face," said Dagmar. "It was — well, just a face. No whiskers or anything. About thirty, or maybe forty. He had his mouth open. And he wore a cap, or maybe it was a hat. Anyway, he had on a trench-coat."

"Good enough," the curator told her. "The doors and windows locked instantly when the case was broken. All we have to do is to round up the fellow... "

That was all. It was easy enough. Three men of early middle age were apprehended without difficulty in the lower halls carrying trench-coats. One wore a cap, the other two had hats. Each gave as his only reference the particular relief organization which happened to be maintaining him among the ranks of the unemployed, and none possessed any string or any sign of the Cellini Cup.

Worst of all, Dagmar, when confronted with the trio, was unable to point out any one of them as the man who had crashed into her in the hallway. They all looked familiar, but she couldn't be sure. She tried, desperately, to remember. But, after all, she had got only the briefest glance of the man on his mad flight, and the subsequent crash and its resulting dizziness had erased everything but the memory of the trench-coat. Dagmar thought that the man of mystery had been holding something bulky beneath the coat, but even this was hazy.

Even now the tall, blond girl clung to her satyr, and as soon as Robbins permitted her, she went resolutely back at smoothing out the signs of its rude handling as the vandal rushed by. Miss Withers gave her a long mark for pluckiness.

Outside, the police were already hammering at the double-locked doors to be let in. Three carloads of the burglary squad and four cops from the local precinct station were admitted, and then the doors made fast again.

† † †

"A cup worth at least several millions of dollars has been stolen," announced Robbins. "It's here, in the building. Find it."

From a polite distance, Hildegarde Withers watched, for two hours, while every person in the building was searched, every nook and cranny and corner pried into. Mummy cases were opened, vases plumbed, fountains drained. Bundles of towels were turned out in the wash-rooms. Stew from the building cafeteria was poured out into the sink, and garbage sorted on newspapers. All to no avail.

Robbins and his guards took the lead in the search, but the actual fine-toothing was done by the officers under the leadership of Captain Malone of Centre Street. He recognized Miss Withers, and would have passed her up, but she requested quickly that the matron search her as well as the rest. "The quarry is too important for you to consider persons and personalities," she told him.

But after all, the search finished where it had begun. A snarling, incoherent anarchist languished in handcuffs, loudly advocating the destruction of the paintings which Mr. Morgan had loaned to the museum for an indefinite showing. Three sad, bleary men holding trench-coats over their arms waited hopelessly and patiently in Robbins' office, also handcuffed. But the Cellini Cup, the only remaining creation of the roistering genius of the Sixteenth Century, Signor Benvenuto Cellini, had vanished as if into thin air.

Robbins gave up in disgust and spent twenty minutes in browbeating Cassidy and Schultz, the two guards whose duty it had been to keep the Cellini in view all the time, and who had been lured away by the decoy shots. The police promised to get something out of the self-styled anarchist, but it was Miss Withers' private opinion that he had been hired for the job by an intermediary, and would have little enough to tell, even in a third degree. The crowd clamored to be released; the art students took down their easels and their modeling stands and also demanded their freedom, and still the blond Dagmar smoothed and worked and patted at her satyr. Miss Withers shrewdly guessed that the girl had no intention of leaving until she had seen her young man.

† † †

It was at this stage of the game that Inspector Oscar Piper came battering upon the main doors of the museum until he was admitted. The wiry, gray little man, a dead cigar clenched, as always, in his teeth, made straight for Miss Withers.

"Hildegarde — I sent you here to calm down a fussy old man, and you've set off plenty of fireworks. What's comin' off?"

The spinster who had almost married him once now transfixed him with an icy eye. She told him. Not everything, but almost everything. "That's how matters stand," she finished. "And the Cup has vanished like morning dew."

"Vanished my eye," said Piper, ungallantly. He whirled around and stared toward the checkroom, where poor Joel Burton still stood, with nothing to do. Then the Inspector smashed his right fist into his left palm. "Blundering idiotic numbskulls," he accused, genially. He spoke loudly enough, so that not only the police captain but also Curator Robbins approached.

With his cigar the Inspector indicated the checkroom. "Anybody look there for this wandering soup-plate of yours?"

"But Inspector," protested Robbins. "The checkroom is outside the turnstile. Nobody but a magician could get down from upstairs, cross the wide lobby, and hide a package there without somebody seeing him."

But Piper was already vaulting the barrier. Miss Withers tagged along behind, feeling unnecessary.

"It wouldn't be hidden, it would be in plain view," said the Inspector. He poked at a top-coat or two, tore open a bundle which contained nine packages of flea soap for dogs — Miss Withers often wondered why, afterward — and finally came to a square package, neatly wrapped and sealed, at the end of the package shelf.

It bore the seals of a mid-town drug store, and a label — "Medicines — breakable." A check attached bore the number "41".

He turned on Joel Burton. "When was this box checked?"

Burton shrugged. "It was here when I came to duty at about eleven. Ask Bruce, the regular checkroom man."

Bruce, easily discovered, admitted that the package had been checked early that morning by a man whom he did not remember.

"Rats," said the Inspector. "Are you all blind? This package was checked like fun. One resembling it was brought in here, and while you were all gawping at this so-called anarchist, the Cellini Cup was wrapped up, brought here, and substituted. Maybe the other box was crumpled up as waste paper. Anyway, the thieves planned on your being too stupid to put two and two together — and by heavens, you were!"

"Nobody could have substituted boxes without my knowing it," cut in Joel Burton.

The Inspector stared at him. "That's what I was thinking," he said, gratingly.

The police and guards crowded around as the Inspector took out his pocket knife, carefully lifted off the seals, and opened the box. There was a quantity of tissue paper — and then, to Miss Wither's utter amazement and chagrin, the delicately enamelled sphinx came into view. Beneath were the glowing curves of the shell, the dragon, and the turtle. There were excited cries from the crowd inside the gates.

Curator Robbins exhaled noisily. But the Inspector lifted out the glowing chalice and stared at it. Then he whirled on the curator.

"This the missing cup? Sure of it?" Miss Withers found herself nodding eagerly.

"Of course I'm sure," said Robbins. "There couldn't be two like it in the world. Of course, I don't know the piece as thoroughly as poor old Carter, but it seems genuine to me."

"We'll make sure," said Piper. He beckoned to Captain Malone. "Got anybody here from the Jewel Squad?"

"I was on it for two years," said that worthy. Piper indicated the masterpiece, and Captain Malone bent over it. He tapped the shell. "Twenty-one carat, at least," he said. He ticked at the enamel. "True-blue," he decided. "They don't mix colors like that to day." Last of all, he bent over the pendant pearl which hung from the breasts of the sphinx, and looked up, grinning. "First water, and a real honey," he gave as his final verdict.

"Okay," said the Inspector. He handed the Cellini Cup back to the curator. "Now hang on to it," he said. "As for me, I'll hang on to him."

Moving cat-like across the floor, he suddenly pinioned the arms of the guard, Joel Burton. "And this washes up our case."

† † †

But Hildegarde Withers did not join in the congratulations. "It was easy as falling off a log," Piper told her as they moved toward the stair. "I'll check over this sculptress' testimony just to make sure which one of the three dopes with the trench-coats was hired to play messenger and deliver the Cup to Burton at the checkroom. Then we're through."

"Easy as falling off a log," Miss Withers repeated. That was just the trouble. Something in the back of her mind clamored for attention, but she could not reach it. Something —

"I'd like to know what that fool of a guard thought he could do with the thing if he did get away with it," Piper was saying. "Melted down it wouldn't bring more than a thousand or two. It's the craftsmanship and the associations that make it so valuable. And it would be unsalable. I guess the poor guy just went nuts looking at it day after day."

"Nuts enough to kill poor Professor Carter when it wasn't necessary?" Miss Withers wanted to know. She stopped suddenly. Suppose — suppose it was necessary?

"Wait," she said. "You're holding Burton downstairs until you all leave, aren't you? May I have a word with him?"

"All you want," Piper promised her. He was glowing with achievement. So it was that Hildegarde Withers faced a sullen, handcuffed man across a desk in an anteroom, with a policeman looking out of the window and another at the door.

She wasted no time in beating around bushes. "You're in serious trouble, young man. Attempted grand larceny is one thing, but murder is another. Were you with Miss Dagmar whatever her name is when Carter plunged to his death?"

Burton stared at her, and shook his head. "I was getting a pail of water for her," he said. "But you won't believe me."

"I won't — until you tell me what happened to the ball of string," Miss Withers ventured. But Joel Burton only turned his face away, and refused to answer. There Miss Withers left him.

The Inspector and Robbins were waiting. "Before you go," said the latter, "I'd like to show you something. The electricians have been busy — and the new showcase has been brought up from the basement and installed." He led them up the stairs and through the Rodin to the Florentine Wing. Dagmar had finally given up work, and sat sadly surveying her clay satyr.

She caught Miss Withers' eyes. "I'm going home," the girl announced. "And I'm never coming back. I hate this place and everybody in it!" She bent her sensitive face above her work. This had been a hard day for Dagmar.

As they came into the room containing the Cellini, an urchin or two disappeared through the far door. "Tell the cops that those kids can be released," Robbins ordered a nearby guard. Miss Withers recognized with some amusement the curly red head of the little fellow with the ancient overalls and the toed-out, Chaplinesque feet. This must have been a memorable day in that lad's life.

The Cellini Cup, restored to its rightful place, shimmered as brightly as ever. The turtle held his everlasting burden as cheerfully, the winged dragon hovered as balefully, and the golden lady whose body was that of a reptile smiled forever. Only the pearl which hung from her breast was still.

"This is not the first time that murder has been done for the possession of that Cup," said Robbins. But the Inspector cut him short in his lecture.

"Come on, Hildegarde. A word with the little sculptress outside, and then we'll write finis to this."

"Finis" was very nearly written to another history as the three of them lingered beside the modelling stand in the hall. As Piper questioned the girl in regard to the mysterious man in the trench-coat, and as Miss Withers idly rubbed her fingers against the cool wet clay of the sculptured satyr, a globule of lead came twisting past her head to clip away a strand or two of brown hair and flatten itself against the wall. It happened so simply, and with so little noise, that the four of them stood aghast for nearly a minute before they could move.

There was only one direction from which the shot could have been fired, and to Robbins' eternal credit let it be written that the dapper curator was abreast of the Inspector in the race down the corridor.

Robbins shouted to guards at the stair-head, and in a moment the entire wing was blocked off. From that time on it was only a matter of steady advance until every human being in the Florentine Wing was corralled.

The captives consisted of five little boys, most of whom Miss Withers remembered having seen here and there throughout the building during the hectic day. One of them was the grinning lad with the red hair and the Chaplin feet.

Two of the boys had been found playing with an automatic pistol equipped with a Maxim silencer, though they stoutly denied having fired it at all. They had found it underneath a showcase, they maintained, but a moment before.

"Hold these two, and let the others go," decided the Inspector. But Miss Withers gripped his arm.

"I want to speak to that one," she said. "The little boy with the red hair. Oscar, I've taught thousands of children, but while many of them toe in, I never saw one before that habitually toed out!"

She stepped forward, and suddenly the gamin wheeled and started to run. Miss Withers' lunge missed his shoulder by a fraction of an inch, but caught at his curly red hair. She screamed a little as it came away in her hand, leaving a shiny bald head.

The running figure turned, disclosing the mature, seamed face of a grown man. "Lord Almighty," said Piper. At last he saw the reason for the oddly turned feet. What they had thought was a child of nine or ten was a midget — and a midget whose face was now a mask of hate and defiance! The loose overalls had hidden the bowed legs.

Miss Withers turned away, acutely ill, as the abortive escape was halted and the hideous, frustrated creature dragged back by guards and police.

"Let me go, you canaille," screamed the creature. "Take your hands from Alexius! I would have succeeded but for the fault of that worthless gun. But still you are fools, fools!" Spitting, cursing, the midget was dragged away. His eerie laughter echoed through the place for minutes after he was gone.

The Inspector returned and faced Miss Withers. "The shoe is on the other foot," he said. "I knew there was a master-mind behind this, but it was you who saw through his disguise. I've heard of Alexius — the police of Budapest dubbed him 'the Gnome.' There were rumors that a mad dwarf was the brains of a gang operating in the large cities of Europe and stealing art treasures by sheer black magic, but I thought it was newspaper talk."

Robbins nodded. "I heard the rumors, and evidently so did poor Carter. He feared that the gang were after his pet treasure, and so they were. But why they had to kill him —"

"I can answer that," said Hildegarde Withers. She turned to stare, almost compassionately, at the tall girl who stood behind them. "But, by the way, I think here is a young lady who would very much like to go home, now that she knows her boy friend is innocent of wrong-doing."

"But is he?" cut in Piper. "How about the checkroom?"

Miss Withers hushed him. "Is it all right for Dagmar here to leave, and take her copy in clay?"

"Of course," said Robbins. "By all means."

Gratefully, the girl began to throw wet clothes around the statue. But Miss Withers was quick and cruel.

She wheeled, so that almost by accident, the sharp point of her umbrella slashed into the soft clay. Dagmar cried out, but Miss Withers pointed like an avenging figure of justice. "Look!"

They all looked — and saw, beneath the concealing clay the gold and enamel of the true Cellini! Quickly Miss Withers laid more of the treasure bare.

"It might have been hidden there when I was knocked over... " began Dagmar wildly, but she stopped, for she saw that no one believed her. Her greenish eyes turned a flaring yellow, and she reached for a palette knife, but the Inspector gripped her in time. Silently, like a condemned Juno, she was led away after her master, the dwarf.

"You see," explained Miss Withers later, "I knew that there must have been a real reason for killing Carter. He was the one man who could tell the true Cellini from the copy which had been made by some unknown but marvelous craftsman. The thieves were willing to pay the price of offering a substitute made of genuine gold, jewels, and enamel, in order to have the genuine Cellini. It fooled everybody — even myself — until I saw that the pearl in the spurious cup did not swing back and forth. It wasn't balanced exactly as in the original.

"Carter was trapped. The midget found that the Professor had been annoyed by small boys, so he tied the cord across the stair and then lured the old man into chasing him for some minor infraction of the rules. That got him out of the way. Dagmar, at the time, was taking care that Burton, the guard at the stairhead, was out of the way. She even found opportunity to snip a length of the cord which he carried about with him to do magic tricks with, to further incriminate him."

"The spurious cup, then, was checked in the checkroom and left to be found, just as I found it?" Piper was crestfallen.

Miss Withers nodded. "Exactly, if we hadn't found it, a hint would have been dropped somehow. Alexius, in his role of urchin, kept tabs on that. Then at noon, when the place was nearly deserted, he planted a fake anarchist in the American wing, and while the alarm was on, smashed the showcase, lifted the Cellini, and immediately slipped it into the yawning statue of clay which Dagmar had ready just outside the door. She was thrown flat on the floor to cover her failure to identify the man properly — and probably she noticed the men with trenchcoats and gave us that as a blind."

"Then, with the Cup supposedly found, there'd be no difficulty in her getting out with the genuine one?"

"Not at all," Miss Withers continued. "The only danger was that someone would get inquisitive about the girl's statue. The midget lurked nearby, saw me touch it, and lost his nerve and fired."

"I don't suppose you'd mind telling me where he got the gun?" Piper wanted to know. "Remember, the midget has been twice searched — and the building, too."

"Elementary," quoted Miss Withers smilingly. "The gun was waiting in the receptacle provided under the clay for the Cup. Just in case something went wrong. As something did. He picked up the gun when everything was clear. And very nearly sent me to Kingdom Come with it, too."

They were sitting on a marble bench in the main hall. The three men with trenchcoats were being released, and hopelessly shambled out into the sunlight again. Joel Burton stood unhappily staring after the figure of Dagmar, the girl whose talent had been turned to such strange uses, as she was led away between two buxom police-women. She never glanced in his direction.

Then Robbins rushed up to Miss Withers. "My dear lady," he beamed. "I have just consulted with our Board, and to show our appreciation we would like to give you as a souvenir of this day the imitation Cellini, provided the police do not want it to try and check up on its artisan... "

"I hope I never see it again," said Oscar Piper fervently.

"Nor I," said Hildegarde Withers.

"Instead, I wonder if you'd grant me just one thing — let me have the remains of the clay satyr which Dagmar copied so painstakingly from the original Rodin?"

That crumbling clay satyr leers today from Miss Withers' living room table, the marks of her umbrella still gouged deep in the smoothly molded body. Strangely enough, the thing has about its eyes and mouth something of the twisted malevolence of Alexius, the red gnome.

The Riddle of the Flea Circus

For the tenth time that afternoon, the stocky man in the gray suit walked past the entrance of General Orloff's Original Flea Circus, a block from busy Times Square. His air of casualness did not deceive Elsie, the faded blonde at the ticket window. She eyed him suspiciously. Not for a long time had the reformers made any trouble about the scanty costumes of the girls in the Marble Venus show inside, but this might, she thought, be a self-appointed Anthony Comstock, all the same.

The stranger finally seemed to make up his mind. There was a letter box on the nearby corner, and he took from his inside pocket a long white envelope and dropped it inside with a clang. Then he came to Elsie's window, paid his dime, and passed inside. Elsie watched him go, wondering if it was her duty to tell Max Jurgen, the manager and spieler of the show, of her suspicion that this person was John Law.

He did not linger above the low canvas booth in the corridor where the Snake Prince, Texas Joe, was dozing peacefully with the nest of fat sluggish rattlesnakes. Nor did he show any interest in the penny peep-shows which lined the long walls, each labeled discouragingly "Passed by the New York Board of Censors."

The man in gray plodded on toward the large hall in the rear, whence was coming the booming voice of the spieler, now drowned out by loud and raucous blasts of music. As he joined the nondescript crowd of tourists and idlers which faced a platform whereon two girls played accordions with more vigor than skill, the act came to a speedy close. Marie and Mary, the famous "Hartford Twins," bowed in unison at the smattering of applause, and stepped a little awkwardly down from the platform in the direction of the dressing-room door behind them.

Marie, the prettier of the two, tried to hold back as a brawny, dark-haired young giant in a leopard skin came up toward the platform, but Mary pushed forward. While the sisters had different tastes and desires, they happened by an accident of nature to share eight lower vertebrae, and Marie was dragged along willy-nilly.

The stocky stranger in gray stood a little apart from the crowd, turning his keen and calculating eyes from the Hartford Twins to the man in the leopard skin, and then toward the lanky person who was acting as master of ceremonies.

† † †

"Ladies and gentlemen," spieler Jurgen was shouting. "Introducing none other than Ajax, the Wonder Man of strength and sinew! Never before have I had the pleasure of presenting an attraction like this, the toast of the crown' heads of Europe, imported at great expense for your amusement and edification. Come up closer, and meet Ajax!"

The spieler had a broken nose and a mouth like a letter-drop. But there was no resisting his voice.

"Look at him, ladies and gentlemen!" The spieler rumpled Ajax's hair, kneaded the mighty muscles of his shoulders, prodded him in the ribs. "Six feet six of sinew and bone — especially here." He tapped the wide forehead. "He eats, he sleeps — and they call him the Wonder Man because it's a wonder that a man can live to be twenty-eight without a single thought."

The crowd guffawed. "Look at those feet," demanded the spieler, pointing to the size fourteen sandals. "Lift your foot, Ajax, and show the ladies and gentlemen that you're a man of understanding." Ajax stood still, and received a sharp kick in the shins from the spieler. Then he lifted his foot, as might a patient performing elephant, but his smile set like concrete.

"Ajax will now tie an iron horse-shoe into knots," announced the spieler. He leaped down from the platform, and lit his cigarette with a match which he scratched across a poster depicting a dignified and undressed fat lady.

Ajax had no eyes for the crowd. He tied his horseshoe into knots, and then untied it. He borrowed a half dollar from a man in the crowd, and bent it into a cup. Finally he tossed around a pair of dumb-bells marked "Five Hundred Pounds."

Ajax set the weights down with a mighty crash, and the crowd gasped. Only one member of the audience was unimpressed. "It's a trick," he announced loudly. "They do it with mirrors. For ten censh I'd lift that m'self."

† † †

Nobody accepted his offer, and the drunk subsided, muttering. Ajax stood there, waiting for his cue. The spieler took his cigar from his mouth and shouted, "And now, ladies and gentlemen, Ajax the Wonder Man will give you a demonstration of skill and daring never before equaled on any stage."

From beneath the platform Jurgen drew a small table and a box containing a dozen or so glittering butcher knives. He arranged these beside the strong man, who immediately chose a knife and then tossed an apple into the air. His wrist barely flickered, and the apple descended in two semi-spheres, one of which Ajax immediately swallowed.

"As his assistant in this feat of daring, Herr Ajax will have that beautiful and fearless little lady, Miss Annabel Lee, whom some of you just saw as the star of our special art attraction, The Marble Venus. Come up here, Annabel... "

After a long pause, there appeared in the doorway of the dressing-room a figure all in white. Annabel Lee wore only a scanty white rubber bathing suit, which matched the smooth whiteness of her well-built body. Only her lips, full curving red, bore any sign of color.

As she passed the platform where the strong man stood, he turned and stared at her. For the first time that day, Ajax looked alive. But she suffered herself to be led to a similar platform about thirty feet away, where Jurgen proceeded to fasten her waist and wrists, by means of leather straps, to a heavy wooden shield. Her piquant face turned toward Ajax provokingly, and then away. A white silk handkerchief was tied across her eyes.

The spieler came back through the crowd toward Ajax's platform, and reached for a light switch behind him. "Let her go!" he shouted — and every light in the long hall went out, with the exception of a single red bulb above Ajax's head, and a white spot above the girl who waited there, spread-eagled.

Ajax took a knife in either hand, hefted them, and blinked twice. "What you waiting for, you big palooka?" shouted the drunk, edging closer. Somebody hushed him.

Ajax took a good grip on the blades, by thumb and finger of either hand, swung them back over his shoulders, and let them go.

Two dull plunks against the shield — and a knife quivered beneath either armpit of Annabel Lee. She winced a little.

"You missed her!" said the drunk. "Gimme the knife, I'll do better... "

"Quiet, please," came Jurgen's voice. There was a strained tenseness in the room, which was felt even in the far corner where the chess players — (Nothing to pay unless our experts win) — had left their interminable games. One of them rose to his feet and came softly across the hall. The boy at the soda-pop counter forgot to polish glasses with his dirty rag.

Again Ajax let the knives go — and on either side of her platinum hair, two more blades quivered near Annabel Lee. She winced again.

"Never touched her," complained the drunk.

Ajax seemed to have something on his mind, if that thick skull contained such an organ. He fingered the knives nervously, chose another pair, and finally brought them to his shoulders. But he did not let them go.

"Ach, Anna! Will you hold still?" he cried.

Then there came an interruption. In spite of hands that tried to hold him back, the drunk lurched up to the platform where the strong man stood. "You couldn't hit anything," he was saying hoarsely. "Get off there and let somebody else try." Somehow he managed to leap up beside Ajax. "Go on, you big fake!"

Then, to the awe and horror of the crowd, the inebriated gentleman leaned back and swung with all his force on the point of Ajax's iron jaw. The strong man blinked.

"He'll kill the drunken fool!" screamed a woman in the audience. "Police — help, help — Police!" There was the sound of running footsteps.

"Lights!" shouted someone else. Max Jurgen fumbled for the switch, but instead of turning on the house lights, he pulled out the plug, and the room was plunged into total obscurity. A woman screamed, horribly.

Then there was pandemonium, an interminable nightmare of muffled voices, of scurrying footsteps and flying fists as men turned in the pitchy darkness to run from nothing or anything. "Ladies and gentlemen —" Jurgen attempted. But these were no longer ladies and gentlemen. They were animals, insane with panic.

Then Jurgen managed to force his way through to the lights again. "Quiet, quiet — for God's sake, quiet," he shouted. The lights snapped back. "Only a slight accident," the spieler went cheerily on. "Just a mistake... "

Ajax the Wonder Man still stood, foolishly clinging to his knives. The drunk who had sought to do battle with him was fiercely shadow-boxing at the other end of the platform, daring them to come one at a time. As they watched, the mood of the crowd already swinging from panic to amusement, he lost his footing and fell headlong among them.

Then somebody noticed Annabel Lee, who hung transfixed against the shield. She had fainted ...

Swiftly they let her down, and she opened her eyes. "Give me a drink," she begged. They brought her water, and she pushed it away.

The show must go on, in spite of hell and high water, and this had been neither. The spieler was in full cry again before Annabel was halfway to the dressing-room. "Ladies and gentlemen, now that the disturbance is over — (the drunk had been started on his way out) — our next and final attraction will be presented in the booth across the room. There the genial General Orloff in person will present his world-famous trained fleas. See the insects with university educations as they dance the polka, play football, and race with miniature chariots! This way, ladies and gentlemen — the Flea Circus will conclude our show for this afternoon." But he was wrong. "Okay General!"

But the General was not on duty at the entrance to the flea tent, to take the dimes of the crowd. At that moment he was leaning over a police alarm box, pounding on the metal door.

† † †

It was the pleasant custom of Inspector Oscar Piper, of the New York homicide squad, to call at the close of the day for his very good friend and occasional partner in crime detection, Miss Hildegarde Withers. Jefferson School is only a few blocks north of the grim police mansion at Centre Street, and the two strangely assorted friends would often share a taxi northward toward their homes and dinners.

They shared one now, rocketing up toward the bright lights of the theater section of Manhattan; but, suddenly, Miss Withers was amazed to see the

Inspector leap from the cab as it paused for a light, and go at a surprisingly good pace down the street.

If he gave her a farewell, it was lost in the din of the city. Hildegarde Withers rescued his hat, her own brief case and umbrella, and paid off the driver. Then she followed after the fiery little man whom she had once almost married — an old-fashioned sailing vessel in the wake of a bouncing tug.

She arrived at the alarm box in time to hear a small, round gentleman, whose curly hair rose like a soft nimbus around his face, as he incoherently gasped of riot and bloody murder down the street. "Oi, it's terrible!"

"You stay here," the Inspector told her. But there was one direction in which the authority of Oscar Piper did not extend. The angular spinster followed close behind as the little man led them down the street and into the Flea Circus.

Elsie stared at them through the ticket window, but they did not pause. Texas Joe, the Snake Prince, was stirring up his pets with a stick, and turned to gaze after the newcomers as they hurried past.

But for all their hurry, there was no riot in the main hall of the Flea Circus. Max Jurgen, the spieler, hurried toward them. "Manny, it's time for your show," he greeted their guide.

"But I thought — Ajax —"

The spieler grinned, and gestured toward the platform where Ajax was putting away his knives. The crowd was peacefully spending nickels at the soda-pop stand, peering into the peep-shows and at the various two-headed calves in formaldehyde which decorated the room, and otherwise whiling away the time.

"We did have a slight interruption," admitted Max Jurgen. "A drunk took a sock at Ajax, and some dame got scared. But the big fellow wouldn't hit back — he's timid as a lamb." He stopped, and looked at Piper through appraising eyes. "You a policeman?"

"I'll do until one comes along," said the Inspector. He showed the spieler a badge of solid gold. "Happened to be passing, and saw our friend here trying to break into an alarm box."

Max Jurgen nodded. "Well, sorry you had your trip for nothing. I see your lady friend is interested in our little place here. Too bad the show is about over..."

Miss Hildegarde Withers, who had been making a cursory survey of the hall, came toward them. The Inspector knew by the flaring curve of her nostrils that something was up.

"The show isn't over," she said softly. "It's just begun." She clutched the Inspector's arm, and spoke lowly enough so that only he could hear. "Look, Oscar — underneath the platform where the strong man is standing." She pointed into the shadows.

Oscar Piper looked. Then he whipped a pocket flash from his coat, and looked again. "Somebody under there, I can see the soles of his shoes," he said slowly. "Say —"

With Miss Withers close behind, the Inspector walked straight toward the platform. As they approached, the school teacher took a wide step to avoid a trickle of bright scarlet which was running out along a crack in the floor. She drew back, but the Inspector dropped to his knees. Suddenly, every eye in the room was on him.

Slowly and carefully he drew from the recess beneath the platform the body of a stocky man in a gray suit. From between his shoulder blades protruded the wooden handle of a butcher knife, and there was a dark splotch on the rough woolen material. He was quite dead, but when they turned him over his eyes were still narrow and thoughtful.

The Inspector sprang back to block the rush toward the doorway. "No you don't! Nobody leaves!" He sought his ally. "Miss Withers — get to a phone and turn in an alarm — precinct, headquarters, everybody!"

He unbuttoned his coat. "Who was the guy who said I'd had my trip for nothing?"

† † †

The sallow-faced assistant medical examiner straightened up and closed his black bag with a snap. "I'm through," he announced cheerfully. "Death was instantaneous, caused by seven inches of steel rammed through his trapezius muscle, glancing off the backbone and into the heart. No chance of suicide, even if he'd been a contortionist. And no need for a banquet, if you ask me."

That was Dr. Levin's pet name for the gruesome formality of the autopsy. He bade Miss Withers a polite good evening and withdrew, followed almost immediately by the two official police photographers.

A little circle of precinct detectives and finger-print men still swarmed about the body, like flies in a summer pasture. Sergeant Peters, grim and methodical, turned to his superior.

"No prints on the knife, Inspector. But it's a dead ringer for the ones in the strong man's set."

The Inspector nodded. He was staring down at the dead man. "Funny there wasn't a piece of paper or anything in his pockets to identify him. And doubly funny that nobody here admits knowing him."

Miss Hildegarde Withers, who had been roaming idly about the empty hall, rejoined him. "Unusual haircut, don't you think!" She stared, fascinated, at the corpse.

"You mean cut short with the clippers above the ears? Yeah, I noticed that. He must be a hick from the tall grass somewhere," hazarded Piper.

"But he isn't tanned," objected Miss Withers. The Inspector did not hear her. Detective Sergeant Moran was approaching.

"I got statements from everybody who was here when the lights went out," said that worthy. "None of 'em told us anything we didn't know. I let the visitors go, like you said, after we'd got their names and addresses. D'you want to talk to the people who work here regular?"

"Might as well," said the Inspector. "Send 'em out one at a time — this guy who calls himself General Orloff has his name outside, so send him here first."

The frightened, fuzzy-haired little man who had first sounded the alarm was let out of the crowded office. The voices of the other inmates followed him, demanding freedom.

"Any place we can talk quietly?" asked the Inspector. The General led the way into his own precinct, the canvas-walled booth of the flea show. The walls, Miss Withers noted, were covered with colored and enlarged portraits of fleas engaged in playing the piano, dancing a waltz, and even meeting with pistols upon the field of honor.

In the center of the small enclosure was a marble-topped table, with a brass rail to protect it from the public. Upon this table stood six or seven large mother-of-pearl boxes.

Miss Withers was ready with her pencil and notebook, while the Inspector fussed with a match at the dead end of his cigar. Suddenly he wheeled on the little man.

"What's your real name?"

"Manny Silver," was the prompt reply. "The 'General' — that's just sort of honorary, y'understand."

"You own this dump?"

"Not exactly. Max Jurgen and me, we run it for the General — the real General. He lives in Paris. But there's four troupes of trained fleas, one at the Fair in Chi, one in Phillie, and this — each has to have a General Orloff, see?"

"I see. Suppose you tell us just what happened when the lights went out. Unless you were in here and didn't see anything."

"I saw all there was to see," said Silver. "Between shows I make a little extra by working as a checker expert, outside at the table with the other two experts. Sort of doubling in brass, y'see. So when it happened, I heard a dame scream, and I ran out to get the cops. Only first the drunk tried to sock Ajax... " The little man gave a sketchy account of the events leading up to the tragedy.

Finally the Inspector halted him. "And so you never saw the stiff before, eh? Well, somebody did."

"And that somebody is the murderer," put in Miss Withers.

"Okay, Silver, you can go." The Inspector leaned across the rail and touched the cover of one of the mother-of-pearl boxes. "By the way, what's in here?"

A frenzied hand seized his wrist. "Oi, Inspector! Not that box! You must not open it — the trained fleas are in there. They'll get out!"

The Inspector hastily withdrew his hand. "Okay. I'll take your word for it. My dog already has trouble enough without my bringing home any trained ones. Beat it, now — and on your way out ask Sergeant Moran to step in."

"One moment," interposed Miss Withers. "You might ask the — er — General, if he has ever made a trip to Germany, or contemplated such a trip?"

The little man paused in the doorway. "Germany? Sure, I was there with a touring freak show once. But now" — he made a wide gesture — "now I got reasons why I keep away." He left them with alacrity.

"Check him off the list of suspects," said the Inspector. "Wrong type for homicide. He might chisel a little, but never use a knife."

Piper went to the doorway. "Moran! Where in blazes are you?"

After a long interval the Sergeant appeared. "Sorry, Inspector, but I just was talking to Elsie, the blonde who works the ticket window."

"Business or pleasure?"

"In the line of duty, Inspector. And she remembered one thing — when the guy who got murdered walked in here he hung around outside a while first. And he dropped a letter in the letter box!"

† † †

The Inspector's eyes widened. "A letter! Why, that'd tell us his name! Hustle outside and camp beside that letter box until the collector gets there to open it. Hurry, man!"

"That's what I did," confessed the Sergeant. "He came just a moment ago. And when I tried to look at the letters he said I was interfering with the United States mails. He said that unless I showed him another envelope addressed like the one we wanted I couldn't get it anyhow..."

The Inspector snapped into action. "Under the law, a letter is the property of the sender until it reaches its destination. Well, that letter is the property of the dead man, and as such is under my jurisdiction. Besides, I know the postmaster. You follow that collector down to the Post Office, and I'll see that when you get there you have permission to bring back postman, bag and all..."

"I might suggest that you save a lot of trouble by looking for a letter addressed to Germany, or written in German script," said Miss Withers. Inspector Piper stared at her, and then nodded. The Sergeant left at a trot.

"The dead man wore, not a hick hair cut, but a German military style trim," Miss Withers pointed out. "A farmer would have been tanned by wind and sun."

The Inspector hurried away to call the postmaster, leaving Miss Withers alone. She made sure that no one could see into the canvas enclosure, and then that impulsive and curious lady leaned across the rail and seized upon the largest of the mother-of-pearl boxes.

She had a moment's trouble with the catch, and then gingerly lifted the lid. She almost dropped box and all as eight sinister and long-bodied fleas leaped high into the air from their bed of soft cotton, failing to alight upon her inquiring face only because each was bound around the middle with a microscopic gold wire which connected with a heavier one, slave-galley fashion. Miss Withers squeaked a little. Then, forcing her courage, she lifted them out of the box, cotton and all.

Underneath the packing was a nickel police badge, a German passport issued in the name of Otto Krall, and a crumpled letter of credentials requesting that the police of America cooperate with Ober-Polizist Krall in any possible manner. There was also a hotel key, labeled Room 607.

Soberly Miss Withers replaced the cotton and the hysterical dancing insects. Then she closed the cover of the box. She knew that in her hands she held the personal papers of the man who had come into the Flea Circus to be killed that afternoon. The one who had put them here had taken no chances of the corpse being identified.

As soon as the Inspector hung up the phone he was besieged with pleas for freedom, with questions and threats and demands.

"I'll take you one at a time," he told them.

† † †

The Hartford Twins were standing impatiently. "I don't see how you're going to question us one at a time," said Mary acidly. Her sister cut in. "I didn't stab anybody, and if Mary had stabbed anybody I'd know it, wouldn't I?"

"Never mind that," said the Inspector, a little out of his depth. He beckoned to Max Jurgen, who had waited with a patience and a silence quite foreign to his nature. The spieler eagerly rose to follow them, but the way to the door was barred by a small and pleading girl in a white rubber bathing suit beneath her flimsy wrapper.

"Listen," demanded Annabel Lee. "You got to listen to me now. Take me instead of him, and let me get out of here!"

There was something oddly appealing in the girl's face. Miss Withers turned toward Piper, but he shook his head.

"Take your time," he told the girl. "You'll have your chance in a minute." And he led the way out of the office and across the empty hall to the booth at the farther side. Miss Withers was very near to telling him of what she held in her handbag, but there was no chance for that now.

"Just one or two things I want to ask you," began the Inspector. "You're the manager of this place, and you ought to know something of the people who work here. Who could have pulled this job?"

Jurgen shook his head. "It was an outside job, Inspector. Just because somebody worked off an old grudge on a man who happened to wander in here, we get blamed for it."

"Anybody among the performers who was ever in Germany?" asked Miss Withers.

Jurgen flashed a glance of recognition for a moment. "I know what you're thinking," he said. "Ajax comes from Germany. But that's nothing — every one of us has been over there on tour at one time or another. The Twins, Texas Joe, the General — even the soda-pop boy. I been there twice. But just because the stiff looks Dutch... "

The Inspector drew a blood-stained knife from his pocket. "Ever see this before?"

Jurgen nodded. "It's one of Ajax's knives. But anybody could have got hold of it... "

"Not everybody would have had the strength to drive it seven inches into the back of a man," said Piper.

Jurgen still shook his head. "I know you're suspecting Ajax," he said. "Just because he had the weapon and the opportunity. But for anybody who knows Ajax, that's a laugh. There never was a gentler guy in the world. He's such a coward that he'll jump if you yell boo at him. That's why Annabel won't give him a tumble. The drunk could have hit him a dozen times, and Ajax wouldn't hurt him... "

Jurgen lowered his voice. "You see, I happen to know why Ajax is so afraid of using his strength. He killed a man once — a French waiter named Dupuy in a Dresden cafe a couple of years ago. It was a fight, but Ajax forgot his strength and broke the fellow's neck. He got off, but ever since then he's been scared to death for fear he'll do it again. Why, Ajax would be the last guy on earth to commit murder."

"Got that, Hildegarde?" asked the Inspector. She nodded, thoughtfully.

Piper rubbed his chin. "All right, Jurgen. Thanks for the information. I'd appreciate it if you'd stick around, though... "

Jurgen grinned. "Even if the place is closed, I usually sleep on a couch in my office," he said. "Besides, Annabel might need me for something... "

As he left them, Piper saw Sergeant Moran, red-faced and puffing, coming down the corridor.

"I see you're empty handed," he observed as the man came up to them.

"Yes, sir, I mean, no, sir." Moran fumbled in his pocket, and produced a long white envelope, stamped but not cancelled.

"Is this the one, sir?" It was addressed to Herr Franz Holm, Polizei Haus, Dresden, Germany. Piper tore it savagely across the end, puzzled over the single sheet of paper for a moment, and then handed it to Miss Withers.

"Remember any of your German?" he asked.

She studied it for a moment. "Not much — but enough to get the meaning of this. It's a daily report of one Otto Krall, detective, to his superior officer. 'I have traced the murderer of Dupuy to a Fliege-Circus ... (that means fly, by the way) in this city, and shall make an arrest as soon as I can arrange ex–tradition...' "

The Inspector whistled softly. He whistled again as Miss Withers showed him documents which she had unearthed at the bottom of the mother-of-pearl box.

"I wonder," he said slowly, "I wonder if Ajax the Wonder Man had an opportunity to sneak across the room after the murder and before the discovery of the body, and hide these here?"

"I wonder, too," agreed Miss Withers. But the Inspector was already half way across the room.

"Moran," he called. "Peters! Get what uniformed men we have, and come with me." He paused outside the door of the office, and gave hurried instructions to his force. Then he opened the door.

"All right, everybody," he announced cheerily. "That's all for tonight. You can all of you go — but don't try to leave town."

The mob surged past him — the Twins first, then the two girls from the Marble Venus act, Elsie the ticket blonde, Texas Joe, Annabel Lee and finally, the brawny bare shoulders of Ajax.

"Now," said Piper softly.

As the blond giant passed through the doorway, steel gripped his thick wrists, steel that clicked tight about them. He turned his mild blue eyes down in consternation to see himself handcuffed to Officers Burke and O'Hara.

"You're under arrest for the murder of Detective Otto Krall," intoned Piper. "Go along easy with the boys, and if you're wise you'll make a statement as soon as you get to the station."

† † †

The two detective-sergeants had their service pistols ready, but there was no need for them. Ajax blinked, shook his head, and tried to hold back. But the officers manacled to his wrists pushed on.

The shrill laughter of a girl cut through the tensity of the scene. Annabel Lee had stopped to stare.

"You!" she gasped. Then her laughter rang out again. She turned to Miss Withers. "Him! For the love of —"

Piper was still in command. "Take him down to the precinct station, boys. Don't wait for the wagon, better put him in a cab. I'll be along directly."

Staring back at the girl as if even now he expected her to perform a miracle and save him, Ajax went meekly along with his captors. It was Max Jurgen who remembered to throw an overcoat across the bare shoulders.

"General" Silver appeared from somewhere to rub his hands together sadly. "Such a good knife-thrower he was, too," he complained. "Such trouble we'll have to get another like him!"

"Who'd want another like him?" the Inspector queried.

Miss Withers noticed that Annabel Lee had left off laughing, and was looking down the hall with a strange expression, a look almost of admiration, in her eyes. "To think that big dumb sheep had nerve enough —" she was saying.

He disappeared into a taxicab, with an officer on either side, and a sergeant on the running board. The Inspector handed over the knife, the dead man's papers, and the letter in German to Morgan. "Take these along downtown," he ordered. "If there are any newspaper men outside, tell 'em I'll give out the story down there in an hour or so."

The crowd was rapidly thinning out. General Silver shook hands with Piper and hurried off to his dinner. Annabel Lee disappeared into the dressing-room to remove the whiting which covered her body, and Miss Withers stood, very thoughtfully, watching the Inspector.

"It was clear enough to me after what you told me about Ajax's little trouble in Dresden two years ago," Piper was saying to Max Jurgen. "I wonder if you'd mind running through the details again, just to refresh my memory? I'm going to hand over the case to the District Attorney's office to night. Miss Withers here will take it down in shorthand."

Jurgen nodded amiably, but Miss Withers shook her head. "You'll have to excuse me a moment," she said, and disappeared into the dressing-room.

Annabel Lee was sitting on a bench, smoking a cigarette with trembling fingers. Miss Withers crossed to the mirror and began to tidy her hair. She turned, to see the whitened girl watching her.

"That looks like terrible stuff to get off," observed the school teacher.

Annabel shrugged. "You get used to it. I don't mind when I only work in one act, but doubling between the Marble Venus and the knife act is tougher. I usually stand under the shower for a while, and then use cold cream for the rest of it." She slipped out of her bathing suit, pulled a rubber cap over her hair, and climbed under the spray.

† † †

When she came out, Miss Withers was washing her hands at the basin. Annabel's young body was streaked with dirty white, and she sat down with a towel and a jar of cream.

"When I toured in Germany," said the girl conversationally, "it was just after the war, and cold cream was three dollars a jar. I had to use soap and elbow grease."

"Did you meet Ajax over there?" Miss Withers wanted to know. Annabel shook her head.

"Listen," she began. "Do you —"

"Do I what?" Miss Withers was very casual.

"Oh, nothing."

"Do I really think Ajax committed the murder?"

Annabel looked up, startled. "Yes, that's what I was going to ask. But —"

"Yes, they seem to have a tight case against him," said the school teacher. "Why do you ask? Don't you think so? He had time to leap off the stand when the lights were out, knife the man, throw the body underneath, and be back in place when they went on. The drunk could have been a plant."

"He could have been an accident," said Annabel. "It happens often enough in this dump. But if Ajax did do the murder, then why" — she was plainly puzzled — "why did he want me to chuck this job and go back to the old country with him? If he knew they were looking for him over there… "

Miss Withers shrugged. "Maybe Ajax wasn't bright enough to think of that?" But Annabel shook her head, and applied another gob of cream to her shoulders.

"Ajax isn't always as dumb as he looks," she said. "Once in a while he surprises you."

"How did he get along with the other men in the show?" Miss Withers asked confidentially. "I mean, with Jurgen and the General and the others?"

"He was friendly enough with Jurgen, except where I was concerned," said Annabel complacently. "They were both on the make for me, but I didn't give either of them a tumble. Ajax has the looks and Jurgen has the brains, but I want a man with both. As for the General, Ajax was always having an argument with him. They used to fight like cats and dogs. Ajax believed in some German named Hitler, and the General couldn't stand him."

Annabel started to climb into her clothes, and Miss Withers moved toward the door. "Child, you've given me the germ of an idea," she said, and went out.

She found Piper with his feet on the desk in Jurgen's office. The spieler was putting his signature to a typed statement.

"Well, Hildegarde," said the Inspector as she entered, "Mr. Jurgen has given me everything we need. This whole business can go before the grand jury next week. This is one case that was broken according to the rules, eh?"

"Indeed, yes," said the school teacher. She was praying desperately for a break. A wild fantastic plan was forming in her mind, needing but one completing link in the chain.

And then the telephone rang. Max Jurgen reached for it and the Inspector slid his feet from the desk, but Hildegarde Withers was ahead of both of them.

It was Detective Sergeant Peters at the other end of the line. "Quick — is the Inspector there?"

Miss Withers was averse to lying, but she ignored her conscience and answered — "Busy — but I'll take the message."

"Tell him Ajax escaped when we were taking him out of the taxi," came Peters' excited voice. "Snapped the cuffs and then threw both cops at me. When we got up he was gone — for God's sake, ask the Inspector what do we do now?"

"Thank you very much," said Miss Withers politely, and hung up the phone. Avoiding the eager eyes of the two who watched her, the spinster school teacher stared for a moment at the opposite wall, where there hung an unpleasant lithograph of Roscoe, the Three Legged Boy, in the act of kicking a football.

She licked her lips. "We have to start all over again," she said. "That was the precinct desk captain. Ajax has proved that at the time that Dresden murder was committed he was in jail in Munich! So they've turned him loose."

"What! They couldn't have... "

The Inspector's voice trailed away as he saw the glare in Miss Withers' bright blue eyes. Perhaps it was his imagination, but he thought he saw one of her lids drop, and lift again ... She turned toward the spieler.

Max Jurgen was tasting this news. He licked his wide lips, but he did not speak.

"So whatever Ajax told you about killing a French waiter named Dupuy was pure fiction," continued the school teacher. "He couldn't possibly have been there."

Max Jurgen nodded, thoughtfully. "But you see, he didn't tell me, exactly. I got the information from a newspaper clipping... "

"You haven't the clipping, I presume?"

Jurgen shook his head. "I'm afraid not ... why?"

† † †

"I just happened to think," said the school teacher sweetly, "that it was about time that you explained how you knew so much about the murder of an obscure French waiter in a little Dresden cafe two years ago. Unless —" Her meaning was unmistakable.

Max Jurgen looked at the Inspector, who was frowning at his dead cigar. Then his face brightened. .

"Wait a minute!" he said. "I think I did put that clipping away somewhere —" He pulled out a lower drawer of his desk, and fumbled among ledgers and old photographs. "It ought to be here... "

Then the honey went out of his voice, and he turned on them with a squat black automatic in his hand. "Get over against the wall, both of you!" he rasped.

Drops of perspiration were running down his forehead, and a grayish-yellow film seemed to obscure his eyes. "Quick!" he ordered. "I won't hang any higher for four stiffs than for two. And keep your hands up!"

Oscar Piper hadn't carried a gun since he laid aside his uniform. He backed over beside Miss Withers, his teeth meeting in the butt of his cigar.

Jurgen was edging toward the door, but he paused long enough to jerk the telephone wire from its box.

† † †

Miss Hildegarde Withers realized that she had bitten off a good deal more than she could chew. This was no problem in criminology, no case in deduction and reasoning. Here stood a man, twice-trapped in murder, and desperate.

His hand was on the door-knob. "I'm standing outside to count thirty," said Max Jurgen. "If anybody comes through, I'll blow him to hell and gone."

Miss Withers felt Oscar Piper tense his muscles. "You can't get by with it," said the Inspector through clenched teeth. "We'll get you sooner or later."

He drew a breath, and the school teacher realized that he was about to spring forward in the dive that is taught to every rookie copper by jiu jitsu experts imported from Nippon. But the murderer still held the gun steady.

"*No*, Oscar!" cried Miss Withers, and clung to his arm. At that moment there came the sound of light, clicking footsteps outside, and a tap at the door.

It was the voice of Annabel Lee. "Ready to eat, Maxie?" she called, Jurgen fumbled for the key, but before he could lock it, the girl swung it open. "What's the — Max!" Her eyes were wide as saucers.

His hand caught her neck, and jerked her into the room on her hands and knees. Then he sprang swiftly through and the key turned on the outside.

Annabel rose to her feet, bewildered. "Why, of all the —"

But the Inspector thrust her savagely to one side, and threw his weight against the door. It burst outward, and he sprang through the opening. The two women followed him, clinging to each other. They rushed to the corridor ...

† † †

There was supposed to be a uniformed man on duty at the far entrance. "Toole," shouted the Inspector. "Toole, stop him!"

The footsteps echoed down the long corridor, as Max Jurgen sprinted for freedom. Beyond him, the three could see a blue-clad figure. But Officer John Toole was in no position to stop anybody. A blow from the brawny fist of Ajax the Wonder Man put him out of the picture.

Ajax was coming on, his brawny bulk blocking the passage. Annabel shrilled above the Inspector's hoarse orders. "Ajax — Ajax — stop him!"

Ajax simply stood there, a bewildered, incongruous figure in leopard skin and an old overcoat. From his wrists dangled broken manacles, and there was blood on his forehead.

"Ajax, *do* something!" There was infinite pleading in Annabel's voice.

Jurgen had paused only a second. Now he was plunging on. His gun roared twice — and glass tinkled in the ticket booth. He fired again, but Ajax did not fall.

The strong man plunged, swifter than one of his own flung knives, and the two men met head-on.

"Hold him," yelled Piper, and sprinted for all he was worth. He saw Jurgen twisting, fighting ... and the heavy gun came down again and again on Ajax's skull.

† † †

Then the strong man got his hold. Bracing his mighty frame, he lifted Max Jurgen high into the air and then flung him, blindly, down the hall.

There was a sickening crash of wood and wire as the murderer plunged head first into the low square of canvas where Texas Joe, the Snake Prince, kept his loathsome pets. Miss Withers stopped, and turned her head away, for from three smashed containers poured forth the mottled, muddy rattlesnakes, twining their thick bodies around this invader. There was a buzz of angry rattles, and a tapping of padded, stinging hammers against his body, his throat, his face.

Max Jurgen screamed once, and then was oddly silent. The Inspector brought Toole, still dizzy from the crack Ajax had given him when he tried to bar the entrance, and together they managed to lift the inert man from his resting place among the disturbed snakes.

He was stretched out on the floor, and the Inspector bent over him with a pocket mirror. There was no film across the glass ...

"Why, the man's dead!"

Miss Withers, frightened and breathless as she was, had not been able to tear herself away. She approached closer now.

"But Oscar — these snakes are supposed to have had their venom removed. It says so on the sign. And besides, rattlesnake poison can't kill as quickly as that."

All the same, Max Jurgen was dead. The assistant medical examiner, dragged back from his own fireside for the second time that evening, pronounced it *cardiac failure.*

"Which means exactly what?" Miss Withers asked him.

Dr. Levin shrugged. "Heart failure can mean anything," he admitted. "My own personal opinion is that he was scared to death."

† † †

Ajax the wonder man lay in a private room at Bellevue, with fourteen stitches in his scalp and two forty-five caliber holes through his shoulder, neatly bandaged. Beside him, where she had been during the long ride on the ambulance and the long half hour in the emergency room, was Annabel Lee.

"And you did it all for me!" she told him tenderly. Ajax nodded, a peaceful smile on his placid face. His hated leopard-skin hung in the hospital closet, but he knew he would never don it again.

"We go back to the old country when I get up — maybe tomorrow," he promised.

The Inspector and Miss Withers tiptoed out of the room. They had come to tell Ajax that no charges would be brought against him for having attacked half a dozen cops. After all, none of the boys was seriously hurt.

"I don't want it in the papers that a murder suspect cleaned up half the force, even if Ajax is a strong man," the Inspector told Miss Withers. They were riding down in the elevator. "All's well that ends well," he went on. "But all the same, dear lady, your somewhat theatrical methods came very near going wrong and making me the laughing stock of the town."

"It was that or nothing," Miss Withers offered tartly. "You were sending an innocent man to jail without a shadow of doubt crossing your mind. And I had nothing on Jurgen except a suspicion, and he knew it. His defense of Ajax, you see, was just a little too pat. He only offered it, you remember, when he had already heard you phone to the postmaster, and knew that we would eventually read the letter written by the German detective. We were supposed to be convinced then — and you were.

"But, Oscar, he overplayed his, hand. The rumpus with the drunk could have been an accident and probably was. But the lights went out and stayed out for quite a long time. Ajax could not have arranged that from where he was standing in full view of the crowd. But nobody was watching Jurgen... "

"Anyway," said the Inspector as he hailed a cab, "the snakes saved the sovereign state of New York the expense of a trial and execution, with the help of Ajax. Just why did the big fellow come tearing back, anyhow? Did he suspect Jurgen, and get worried over leaving his girl there with the murderer?"

† † †

Hildegarde withers shook her head. "I don't think such an idea ever occurred to him until he came into the corridor and saw Jurgen with the gun and us screaming after him. But he didn't come back for that, I'm pretty certain."

"Too bad you didn't ask him what he did come back for, then," said Piper.

Miss Withers smiled. "That's just what I did," she confided. "When Annabel went to get him a glass of water just now. I came right out and asked him why he broke away from your men and fought his way back to the Flea Circus."

"Well, what did he say?" demanded Piper.

"You see," she went on, "the poor fellow was arrested so suddenly that he had no chance to change from his leopard-skin costume. 'Lady,' he admitted to me, 'I came back for mine pants.' "

The Inspector whistled. "What a man!" he said.

"What a night!" retorted Hildegarde Withers. "I'm worn to a frazzle. And I suppose the newspapers are already setting up front page stories about how the brilliant sleuth Inspector Oscar Piper tracked down the Fiend of the Flea Circus!"

Oscar Piper patted her shoulder admiringly.

"What a woman!" he said softly.

The Riddle of the Forty Costumes

Miss Hildegarde Withers knew that something was afoot as soon as she came into the Inspector's outer office and saw that his door was closed. It was a chill wet morning, raw as only Manhattan in late December can be. Unwilling either to go back into the drizzle or to interrupt one of her friend's official "conversations" with some unlucky suspect the good lady proceeded to cool her heels.

She pricked up her ears as the sound of excited feminine voices came faintly through, and then the door opened and Inspector Oscar Piper appeared. He was ushering out of his office three attractively dressed and scented young ladies, visitors who fitted very strangely indeed into this center of the grimmest police activity. They were very young, muffled in fur coats of civet, squirrel, and seal respectively, and they teetered upon ridiculously high heels. They were alike as three peas in a pod except, perhaps, that the girl in seal was a little younger and prettier and more distraught than her companions.

"Last door at the end of the hall," the Inspector was saying. "Tell the Sergeant I sent you."

The girls passed on down the hall, and Piper held the door for Miss Withers. "Well," observed that lady, eyeing a trayful of red-smeared cigarette butts, "your clientele seems to be changing its tone."

The Inspector grinned sheepishly. "They didn't belong here," he confided. "Got in by accident. Some sort of a wild, hysterical story about the disap—pearance of their dance teacher up at Carnegie Hall last night. Seems that this woman, name of Carla Monterey, popped off into thin air, leaving her clothes on a chair. She even left the shower running in the bathroom to steam a velvet dress, so these kids say. I sent them up to the Bureau of Missing Persons."

† † †

There was a light in Miss Withers' eye, and her long nose began to twitch. "Just what good will that do them?"

"Not much," Piper admitted. "The Sergeant will fill out a blue slip, and the clerk will put it in a file. Then they'll be sent home."

"But, Oscar..."

"There's nothing in it for the Homicide Squad. We have rules, you know."

"Fiddlesticks," Miss Withers retorted. "Rules are made to break. What's the rest of their story?"

A little nettled, the Inspector faced her. "Just that they are all students in the school of this Monterey woman, who teaches Spanish dancing in a big studio up at Carnegie. Sometimes she books herself and her advanced pupils for exhibitions and professional engagements. Last night they were having a late rehearsal, which ended in some sort of a row between the Monterey woman and her manager, an Argentine named Valentine. The Inspector showed his disgust with the name. "Anyway, Valentine and the girls went out for supper, and when some of them came back to get a forgotten handbag, the dame was gone. Studio on the twelfth floor, and the elevator man hadn't taken her down. This morning she didn't answer her phone, so the girls came down here. I figure it as just another case of artistic tantrums. Ten to one the woman will show up presently."

"So you think she walked out and left her dress to steam," said Miss Withers thoughtfully. "You might have gone up there and looked around."

"I'm up to my ears as it is. But if you're so all-fired interested, why don't you —"

"I believe I will," decided Miss Withers suddenly. "School closed yesterday for the holidays, and I've nothing useful to do... " She rose to her feet.

"If you hustle, you may catch the girls up at the Bureau —" began the Inspector.

But already she had started to her feet, and with her cotton umbrella grasped in her hand went out of the door like some grim, ungainly bird of prey.

† † †

She was lucky enough to catch the three disconsolate dancers on the stairs. "The man says a person isn't missing until after forty-eight hours," the girl in civet complained to Miss Withers, after that lady had identified herself. "They think she will show up —"

"I can imagine what and how they think," the school teacher admitted. "Suppose we do a little sleuthing ourselves? And while we're in the taxi, let me hear all about it. One of you start at the beginning, keep on until you get to the end, and then stop... "

The girl in seal smiled, showing that she recognized the quotation from Miss Withers' bible — *Alice in Wonderland.* The older woman immediately loved her for it.

This one was Lou Jeffers, and the others were Sally and Babs Dell. The name Jeffers meant little to Miss Withers, who avoided the society pages.

Lou Jeffers obligingly started at the beginning, as the four of them rolled northward from Centre Street. She spoke slang with a careful finishing-school accent.

"We were all at the studio last night, Sally and Babs and I and some others rehearsing. The *senorita* had been teaching us the swellest Andalusian peasant dance, and she promised a long while ago that if we did it well she'd let us perform it as part of her professional performance at hotels here during the holidays. But —"

"Everything was going BEAUTIFULLY," cut in squirrel-clad Sally, who spoke in capitals and italics. "Until VALENTINE came in about eleven o'clock —"

"With a telegram offering *Senorita* Monterey a chance to bring her group and dance New Year's Eve at the Corals Hotel in Florida," finished her sister Babs, a high soprano.

"I understand that started an argument?" Miss Withers inquired.

"Well, maybe. You see, all the girls are crazy to dance professionally. But most of them knew that their families wouldn't let them go so far from home, and the others wouldn't give up their New Year's Eve dates here in town," continued Lou Jeffers.

"All but you, darling," cut in Babs Dell.

"All but me, because my mother is in Europe and my aunt doesn't care. Besides, I'm crazy to take the trip! Anyway, the *senorita* was furious with the girls because they wouldn't go, and furious with Valentine for having wired an acceptance. He wanted her to go alone, and just do the solo, or perhaps a duet with me — but she wouldn't listen... "

"And POOR Emile tried to talk her out of it while we were dressing, but she WOULDN'T listen, so he left her in her room, and came out to supper with us... "

"Miss Monterey, I mean the *senorita*, usually has supper with us when we dance late," explained Lou. "But last night she wouldn't come. So Valentine called good-night to her and we all called good-night to her, and she sort of slammed the door."

"But you went back?" Miss Withers queried. "After you ate?"

"Yes, because I'd left my purse. Emile went with me," explained Lou Jeffers. "The door was locked, the lights were all on, and the water was running in the shower where the dress was being steamed. But Carla was gone."

"You're sure she wasn't hiding?"

"Where could she hide? Emile Valentine and I went through the place together, even looking into the closets. She hadn't taken the elevator, and she knows nobody in the building, and I don't believe she'd walk down twelve stories."

"What about windows?" Miss Withers asked.

"They open out above the street, with no fire escape. There's one from the bathroom onto the air shaft, but it's tiny."

"What about Miss Monterey's clothing? Did she dress before she left?"

"Her practice clothes were on the chair, and I think all her street dresses were in the closets, although I can't be sure because the place is so full of costumes. Anyway, it was after midnight, so we turned out the lights and Emile took me home. This morning we girls got together, and we thought that perhaps something dreadful had happened and the police ought to know... "

"Babs and I thought so," corrected Sally.

"I thought so, too," insisted Lou. "Only — only if *Carla* had wanted to go away for a little while, I couldn't help thinking how furious she'd be if we turned in a false alarm."

"I'm afraid," Miss Withers decided, "that this is not a false alarm." The three girlish heads were cocked at her.

"You mean — SUICIDE?" But Miss Withers wasn't tipping her hand.

† † †

The taxi drew up before the entrance to the studios of Carnegie Hall, one door east of the venerable portico beneath which three generations of music-lovers have stood in line for symphony tickets. There was a long line there now, but the three girls and the inquisitive schoolteacher pushed past and made their way into the little raised foyer.

Here an ancient and solitary darky dozed inside an ancient and solitary elevator. They entered, and it rose beneath them, haltingly and painfully, first one floor and then another ...

Miss Withers was amazed to notice that the sixth and eighth floors came on the same level, with the seventh above them!

"Buildin's powerful old," said the darky as he noted her surprise. "Sort of scrambled here and there, and easy to get yo'self lost in."

The steel cage faltered to a stop, and Miss Withers followed the girls out upon the twelfth floor. Then she hesitated to make sure that the elevator man had not seen Miss Monterey this morning. "No, ma'am, nor the night man neither!"

Then they set off down a narrow hall, turned left and right and left again, went down three steps and up seven, and came finally to a gateway and grille in heavy Moorish style, beyond which they saw a thick oaken door bearing the sign "Carla Monterey — Home of the Spanish Dance" ...

Lou fumbled for a moment in the maze of grille work, and withdrew a key. "She showed all of us where she keeps it," explained the girl. Then she unlocked the door.

Miss Withers found herself in a gayly tiled hallway, hung with shawls, Moorish armour, and photographs. At one side was a massive writing desk, its drawers awry.

The air was thick and stuffy, as if all the windows had been closed for a long time. "Carla!" called Sally hopefully. "Carla ... have you come back, Miss Monterey?"

Walking on tiptoe, for no particular reason, the four women passed through the tiled foyer and came into the tremendous expanse of the main practice hall, a long, high room with a glistening parquet floor and unfurnished except for practice bars along the wall and an upright piano.

At the right, a door opened into two additional practice rooms, smaller in size, each with its little dressing-room and shower. Directly across the main hall stood the curtained doorway leading to the dancer's private quarters. Miss Withers walked slowly after the others, noting every detail.

They came into a living room, bright and cheerful in spite of its one narrow window, for brilliant scarfs and shawls covered furniture and most of the walls. There was a Murphy wall-bed, two large closets overflowing with costumes, shoes and the like, as well as a small but modern bath and a kitchenette and dining alcove bright with blue oilcloth.

This was where Carla Monterey had last been seen. Now there were only pictures of the dark-eyed Spanish beauty — pictures in every pose and style of dress and undress. From each wall Carla Monterey stared at the intruders ...

Miss Withers penetrated the bath, and studied the velvet dress. It was of fine plum-colored velvet, but sadly ripped at the seams.

The window onto the airshaft, she discovered, was barely large enough to get her head through, but she peered out of it, seeing nothing at all.

Nowhere were there any signs of bloodshed or violence, although at that moment Miss Withers would have staked her life upon the fact that Carla Monterey was dead. The girls, back in the studio, were chattering excitedly. Nowhere was there any sign of the wearing apparel which had been strewn upon the chairs last night!

"Then she *has* come back," cried Lou Jeffers.

"Possibly," said Miss Withers. She was prowling about, aimlessly. It seemed strange to her that there was no picture of a man in the apartment.

"Was there a love interest?" she inquired slyly. "*Cherchez l'homme...* "

Lou Jeffers started to say "No," but Sally interrupted. "Not since Valentine!"

"*Since* Valentine?"

"They used to be very close," Lou said, with the sophistication of her years. "But they broke up months ago, and Emile stayed on as her tango- partner and manager."

"Naturally!" said Miss Withers. But she looked thoughtful. She led the way back into the practice studio. In spite of her suspicions, this case seemed to be falling to pieces. If she only had something to get her teeth into!

Then the hall door opened, and a young and dapper gentleman stepped into the foyer, a key in his hand. He was exquisitely dressed, with pearl-gray hat and spats.

"Excuse me," he said. "I really didn't... "

"Mr. Valentine," said Lou Jeffers, with what seemed unnecessary quickness. "This is Miss Withers, of the police. She's going to help us find Carla Monterey."

† † †

"Of the police?" repeated the Argentinian. His face was clear-cut and pleasant. Miss Withers changed her opinion of him — this was no gigolo. He walked swiftly toward them. His hand was outstretched.

But he did not want to shake hands. "If you are of the police," he announced, in a smooth voice almost free from accent, "then it is right that you should see this." He extended an envelope to Miss Withers. "I found this last night in Carla's desk," he explained, "when Miss Jeffers and I were looking around. I opened it, naturally — and under the circumstances I am afraid I had better turn it over to the authorities."

"To the police," was written in scrawling, childish hand across the envelope. "*If anything happens to me arrest Emile Valentine!*" was the message. It was unsigned.

"That's Carla's writing," gasped Babs, looking over Miss Withers shoulder.

Miss Withers drew a deep breath. "Well, Mr. Valentine... "

He bowed. "I confess that I could not easily bring myself to show this. Do not credit me too highly for turning it in. There are probably others which will come to light."

Miss Withers folded the letter and tucked it into her handbag. She found herself beyond her depth, and the frightened, amazed girls gave her no support.

Emile Valentine extended his hands. "For the er — bracelets?" he inquired cheerfully.

Miss Withers stared at him for a long time, and shook her head. "I'm not that kind of a policewoman," she said. "And I'm not convinced that this is the time for handcuffs." She tapped her teeth with the handle of her umbrella. "Rather, we ought to be looking for Carla Monterey." She placed her bag on the table, and her umbrella upon it.

"We could ask at the neighboring studios?" suggested Lou Jeffers eagerly.

"And we shall," the schoolteacher pronounced. "I'll take the left of the hall, and you take the right. Perhaps Babs and Sally will divide the floor above?"

Valentine waited patiently. "Would you care to aid us?" asked Miss Withers casually.

"Delighted!" His handsome face cleared. "I'll choose the floor below. As a matter of fact —" his face was rueful — "I have more reason than any of you to find Carla now." Thinking of the letter, Miss Withers was inclined to agree with him.

The ringing of doorbells began in real earnest. During the next fifteen minutes, Miss Withers interrupted one class in tap dancing, four singing lessons, one luncheon party, and got an elderly violin teacher out of bed. The sum total of her discoveries was that none of them knew Carla Monterey except by sight and reputation, none had ever entertained her, and none had heard anything unusual in the studio last night.

There was only one studio left, and that was the one which, though entered from another hall, abutted directly upon the wall of *Senorita* Monterey's living room. Here lived two little old maidens of sixty-odd, who had, Miss Withers soon discovered, devoted their lives to each other and to the raising of Angora kittens for the pet shops. They lived in Carnegie because it was convenient and cheap and lively.

"We dearly love young people and life around us," one explained. It had taken Miss Withers no time at all to gain their confidence and to share a cup of tea. Miss Withers could heart from where she sat upon an ancient hair-cloth sofa, a cacophony of piano lessons, voice culture, and stringed instruments filtering through the paper-thin walls. She raised her eyebrows.

"Did you hear anything out of the ordinary last night?"

"You mean, late last night?" The little old ladies chimed in together. "Why, we went to bed about nine, as usual... "

"There was nothing unusual, except that about eleven... "

"Grace dear, it was nearer twelve... " cut in Miss Wanda.

"Between eleven and twelve we heard the girls leave the dancing place next door, chattering and laughing with a man. Then it was quiet."

"That's the Monterey studio?"

"Yes, indeed. And if you ask me, that Monterey woman is no better than she should be, with that man calling at all hours!"

"He hasn't been there late at night these last few weeks," corrected the other. "And if you ask me, it wasn't so quiet after the girls left. I could hear the Monterey woman or somebody playing castanets."

"It wasn't castanets," argued Grace. "It was tap dancing."

"You're positive of that?" Miss Withers prodded. The little old ladies were positive. Finally the sounds had died away, and then later someone had gone through the studio calling "Carla" — a girl and a man, she thought. "You know, that's the first time we've ever heard sounds of dancing in that studio," Miss Grace concluded.

† † †

Miss Withers left, very thoughtfully. For a moment, the mystery had seemed to clear, and now she was faced with a fog ten times denser than before.

She came back to the studio, although there was something uncanny and unwholesome about it, something that made her feel like walking softly and speaking in whispers. Perhaps that is why she opened the door very softly when she entered.

Then she stopped, immobile. Across the main hall, the door of the living room stood half open, the tall dressing mirror outlining a distant but distinct picture.

There was reflected the image of lovely Lou Jeffers. As Miss Withers watched, her coat slipped from her shoulders, revealing her slender figure wrapped in a man's arms — the arms of Emile Valentine. Their lips met in a passionate, interminable kiss, and Miss Withers backed hastily out of the door and leaned against it.

That was the secret which she had sensed, in the depths of Lou Jeffers' warm eyes! Or was it? Miss Withers walked up and down the hall, pondering.

Her meditations were shortly interrupted by the sisters Dell, who announced clearly and loudly that they had discovered a violinist upstairs who had heard some one beating a wooden drum last night, shortly before twelve. But that was the sum total of their findings.

With the girls leading the way, Miss Withers went back into the studio. They found Lou Jeffers smoking a cigarette in her dance teacher's big armchair, while Emile Valentine walked nervously up and down behind her.

Both announced that their searches had drawn a blank, which did not surprise Miss Withers a particle. She did not offer to pool results with them.

She looked at her watch, and found that the afternoon had slipped swiftly past. The Dell girls hinted that they were expected home for dinner, and that they had dates for the evening. They were obviously tired of playing sleuth.

"Run along," Miss Withers told them. She reached for her bag and umbrella. Strangely enough, while she had purposely left them with the umbrella handle at right angles to the monogram on her handbag, it now lay parallel! This was a trick that she had used in the past to test the honesty of a suspected pupil, and she felt strangely and wonderfully elated. This puzzle could be broken — and she was getting close, or someone would not have burgled her bag!

She rode down in the elevator with the others, and in the lower hall scribbled her telephone number upon several cards. "If any one of you hears anything, please phone me at my home," she instructed them. "I have a strong notion that this evening will bring word from Carla Monterey!"

Lou Jeffers gasped. "Then you don't think she's ... dead?" Miss Withers shook her head noncommittally, and summoned a taxi. After a moment she opened her bag, but as she had known, the envelope marked "To the Police" was gone.

† † †

Across a white tile table Miss Withers was consulting with Inspector Piper. Painstakingly, point by point, she gave him the developments of the case. "If you see through it, you're smarter than I am," she finished.

"It was this sheik Valentine who lured her off somewhere and bumped her," suggested Piper. Then he shook his head. "He's got a pretty good alibi, and besides, how could he dispose of a body?"

Piper crumpled his cigar into the tray. "Wait — suppose the Monterey dame took a run-out powder and left the note to throw suspicion on her former boy-friend?" His face fell. "That isn't so good, and it doesn't settle how she left the building."

"You forget the sounds of dancing that came from the studio after the others left that night," Miss Withers told him. "You forget the rips in the seams of the velvet dress, and the letter which Mr. Valentine produced and which some one filched… "

"Never mind, I have a duplicate," the Inspector sprung on her. He showed her a long legal envelope, with a smaller one inside. "Come this afternoon. The law firm that sent it refuses to talk. Same message as yours, only the Monterey woman signed this."

Miss Withers studied it carefully, and nodded. "Valentine was right," she said.

"Perhaps you'd better let the Homicide Squad handle this after all?" said Piper.

"Over my dead body!" The school teacher had come to a decision. She wrote busily upon the back of a menu for a moment, and then showed the result to her friend.

Piper whistled. "Spanish Dancer Disappears," she had written. "Leaves poison pen letters attempting to implicate manager, but proved false by police investigation. Nation-wide search for Carla Monterey is on!"

"Will you see that this gets into the newspapers, immediately?"

"But—"

"But nothing! This is important, Oscar."

"There's barely time to get the early editions of the morning rags," he said. "But I'll try. After all, this is your funeral. Now what?"

"Get that into the papers, and then go home and go to bed," she told him. "As you said, this is my funeral."

Miss Hildegarde Withers hastened home to her little apartment in the neighborhood of Central Park West, and rocked placidly back and forth while the long evening ticked away. She was anxious to be up and doing, but this was not the time for action.

The early editions of the tabloids, she knew, came on the streets about eight-thirty, with the Herald-Tribune and the Times an hour or so later. As calm as a country boy who has just baited his hook with an angleworm, Miss Withers sat by her telephone and waited for a nibble.

It came, shortly after eleven. She lifted the receiver and heard Emile Valentine's suave voice.

"Madam, you are a genius," he announced, much to her pleased surprise. "A true genius! I just received a message from Carla — from the missing Miss Monterey!"

"Where are you now?" Miss Withers wanted to know.

He hardly hesitated. "I'm at Miss Jeffers' home. I simply had to tell her the good news as soon as I got the message. It was filed at The Corals, Florida — and reads, 'SORRY CAUSED WORRY EXPLAIN EVERYTHING WHEN I SEE YOU I AM GOING AHEAD WITH ENGAGEMENT HERE PLEASE FOLLOW AT ONCE WITH COSTUMES AND LOU IF SHE CAN COME — CARLA'."

"Gratifying," said Miss Withers. "Are you going to follow instructions?"

"Why not? After all, I'm her manager. And I expect anything of an *artiste* like Carla."

"Naturally," Miss Withers told him. "May I speak to Miss Jeffers, please?"

"Hello!" came Lou's throaty contralto. "Isn't it wonderful? It must have been all just a silly joke of the *senorita's*!"

"Or a joke *on* the *senorita*, said Miss Withers softly. "I hope you enjoy your trip to Florida."

"Why —" the rich voice raised a note. "How did you know I was going?"

"I didn't until just now," said Miss Withers sagely. "Good-bye," and she hung up.

She hustled into her coat, and ten minutes later was climbing the steps of Carnegie Hall again. A different darky was on elevator duty, but after a certain amount of persuasion he consented to take her to the twelfth floor.

It was late, very late, but Miss Withers had no mercy at all. She pounded upon the door of the two little old ladies until they came tottering in bathrobes and slippers to see if the building was on fire.

"I wanted to ask you," she demanded of Miss Wanda. "Have you ever really heard a Spanish dancer playing castanets on the stage?"

Miss Wanda falteringly admitted that she had not. The invader turned to Miss Grace. "And you — did you ever see a tap-dancer on the stage?"

"I never cared for vaudeville much," that lady ventured tremulously.

"I thought so!" Miss Withers triumphed, and leaving them convinced of her utter madness, she went resolutely down the hall.

† † †

When she woke early the next morning she knew that, except for one important detail, the puzzle had been completed by her subconscious while she slept!

She knew what it was up to her to do, but first there remained the necessity of toast and orange juice and coffee. As leisurely as if her next few hours were not to be perhaps the most thrilling and dangerous in all her forty years, Hildegarde Withers prepared and ate a leisurely meal. Then she strolled southward through the crisp December morning toward Fifty- seventh Street and the ancient grimy pile of Carnegie Hall.

She rode up to the twelfth floor, passed down the hall, and searched for the cached key, but it was gone. The door was locked, but at her knock a cheerful voice responded — "Just a minute, please!"

The door was swung open, and there stood Emile Valentine, his coat and vest off and his smiling face dusty and perspiring.

"Oh, it's you!" he said, a little disappointed. "I was expecting —"

"Miss Jeffers, I presume?"

He nodded. "She promised to come down early and help me pack the costumes." He motioned toward the two great wardrobe trunks which stood against the wall. "I had the elevator man bring them up from the basement," he continued, "and the job is nearly finished."

"Perhaps I can help?" said Hildegarde Withers gently. She followed the handsome Argentinian into the studio. One trunk was closed, completed, and the other stood gaping amid a litter of scarfs, castanets, shoes, and brilliantly colored silks.

"You are very kind," said Emile Valentine. "But I am nearly through. Excuse my appearance, but it is a big job to pack forty costumes and their accessories."

"What? Good heavens, how long is this Florida engagement to last?"

Valentine stared at her, as if he would very much like to ask why she had come, and why she was interested in such minor matters.

"It is for New Year's Eve only," he said. "But the *senorita* is temperamental. She never decides what to wear until curtain time, and she always takes her entire wardrobe. Only this time, adding insult to injury, she leaves me to pack it... "

He stuffed a wad of chiffon into a drawer. Then, as Miss Withers sought for a way to voice the question that was in her thoughts, he turned. There was something on his mind.

"Tell me, as one who knows of detective matters, is there any way of being sure that this telegram came from Carla, and is not a hoax?"

Miss Withers found the wind gone from her sails. She took the message that he offered her. It was a genuine Western Union form, she recognized that. Strips of yellow paper from an automatic typewriter spread their message across the page as they had been pasted. According to the data at the top, the message had been filed at the Corals Hotel, Coral Beach, Florida, at ten-fifteen the preceding evening. It was verbatim as it had been, read to her over the telephone.

"I'd feel foolish if I carted this stuff and Lou Jeffers all the way down there and found this telegram was a hoax along with the letters," he said.

"It looks all right to me," Miss Withers told him. "But I want some information. Carla Monterey was prodigal with money, extravagant like most artists, was she not?"

He shook his head. "She was not. Carla knew the value of a dollar and she never wasted one in her life. Anybody who knew her will tell you that."

"I see." Miss Withers roamed about the room as he continued the packing. She fumbled with the telephone, straightened a picture, and then sat down on the piano stool, knowing to the bottom of her boots that this young man would like to have her go.

He finished the second trunk, and slammed it shut. Then he looked impatiently at his watch. Miss Withers was watching him closely. "Miss Jeffers seems to be late?"

He nodded. Then he came over to the piano. "You're not at all satisfied that the case is settled, are you?" he challenged. "What's on your mind? Is there anything I can do before the expressmen come for the trunks? They'll be here at ten... "

Miss Withers consulted her watch, and then told a bare-faced lie. "Why, it's almost ten-thirty now!"

Emile Valentine looked again at his watch, shook it and put it to his ear, and then turned toward an electric clock which graced the desk in the foyer. Its hands pointed to twenty after ten; Miss Withers had already seen to that detail.

"I've got to telephone," cried Valentine. He hurried to the instrument, dialled furiously, and then emitted a string of soft Latin oaths. "The thing's dead," he said.

"There's a pay phone at the drug store up the street," she suggested.

"I'll go to the express office myself," he decided. "We can't afford to miss that eleven-thirty train. Would you mind waiting here and telling Miss Jeffers where I've gone if she comes before I return?"

Miss Withers wouldn't mind. She gave him time to get to the elevator, and then began a survey of the closets. To her amazement, they were empty. The man *had* packed all forty costumes! She poked at the trunks, but they were all tightly locked.

Then heavy knocks came on the door, and the expressmen came in trundling rollers. They seized upon the trunks before the agitated school teacher could make up her mind. "Okay," said the foremost. "Here you are lady." She shoved two red tickets into her hand, and they departed with much shouting.

Miss Withers chanced to notice that the kitchenette door was open. The place looked cheerless, but that was because the gay blue oilcloth had been stripped from walls and dining alcove, leaving only bare rough boards! She came back into the foyer, with an eye on the phone. Suddenly the door opened.

Miss Withers whirled defensively, and looked into the youthful face of Lou Jeffers, dressed for traveling and bearing a wardrobe suitcase in her hand.

"Whatever are you doing here?" demanded the girl. "Has anything happened?"

"Never mind." Miss Withers was trembling with excitement, but she drew the girl in and closed the door. Then she ran across to the telephone. She slid her fingers along the cord to the point where a common pin had been inserted to break the connection (she had also seen to that little detail), and removed it with a little jerk. She lifted the receiver and was rewarded with a buzz.

"S — P — 7 — 3 — 1 — O — O," she dialed, while Lou Jeffers watched with wide and frightened eyes.

"Piper's office, and hurry," she begged. Then — "Oscar! Could you and some of your friends hurry here and help me? I'm at Carnegie, and the beans are spilled. But I'm sitting out on the limb... "

She had hoped that the girl would not catch her meaning, but in an instant Lou tugged at her sleeve.

"What's happened? What have you done to Emile?"

Miss Withers looked down at the girl, and shook her head. "You've got to listen to me," she said.

"Listen nothing," burst forth Lou. "Haven't you eyes to see? Don't you realize that this is all a frame, a plot to incriminate Emile? She hated him, I tell you. They were lovers, and then they broke up. And she hated him for it. If she's dead, she killed herself to make him suffer, and if she isn't, she's in hiding hoping he'll be arrested."

"If that is true," said Miss Withers kindly, "I know a way to prove it. I think something incriminating was hidden in the trunks ... suppose we open them?"

Lou couldn't know that the trunks were out of the place. She nodded. "I see — to pin more suspicion on poor Emile! Of course I'll help you clear him. If they're locked, we'll use a hammer... "

Miss Withers caught the girl by the shoulders and swung her around. "Never mind the trunks," she said, her voice lighter. Somehow she had known that a girl who quoted Lewis Carroll could not be a murderess. "I know what I needed to know," she finished.

"But you said —"

"Never mind that. We haven't a moment to lose. You've got to get out."

Lou Jeffers was stiff as a ramrod, her young body tense and quivering. "Not without Emile!" she cried.

"You must," said Miss Withers. "Do you care for him so terribly?"

"Care for him? Of course I care for him! I'm of age in another three weeks, and I'm going to marry him in spite of what anybody says!"

Miss Withers was saddened. But she did not soften. "You must not stay here, and you must not go on this trip to Florida," she insisted. "Believe me —"

"I won't believe a thing against Emile!" the girl almost screamed.

Hildegarde Withers knew what she must say. "But if you go that will only play into the hands of whoever plotted this diabolical thing," she explained. "If you travel with Mr. Valentine, even in separate Pullmans, he can be arrested for violation of the Mann Act. Suppose that came to the mind of somebody?"

Lou Jeffers' face was a mask of loathing. "That! Would anybody do *that?*"

"You'd be surprised what people are capable of doing," the schoolteacher said. "Trust me, and come. Your life may depend upon it."

Clinging to the young girl's arm, Miss Withers hurried her out of the place and down the hall. Her carefully laid plan was going to pieces.

† † †

Her thumb pressed upon the elevator button, and she held it there until the cage started up. Somewhere at a lower floor it paused, and the cables ceased to swing past. "Can't you hurry?" she called down. There was a long wait, and then it came on again, more swiftly than ever.

The door clanged open, and Miss Withers pushed the girl through. She followed, and the man in the uniform cap slammed the door shut.

"Down!" gasped Miss Withers, and then, as the cage started to drop, she caught a glimpse of the face of the man who huddled at the controls. Instead of the sleepy fat face of the colored man, she saw the handsome Latin mask of a face she had seen before.

"Emile!" cried Lou Jeffers, but the man did not answer her. He faced Miss Withers, and Valentine's eyes were like those of a dead toad.

"Down there," he coughed — "Down there the street is full of police! You did that, you *hija d'perro!*"

"Emile!" cried Lou Jeffers again, "Emile, what has happened?" She was unbelieving.

He caught her by the shoulder and flung her out of his way. He leaned back his head and laughed. "Happened? This daughter of a dog has tricked me, my sweet. And I have tricked her by flinging the fool who runs this elevator out on a lower floor and taking it myself."

There were shouts in the hall below, and running footsteps on the stairs. "Oscar!" screamed Miss Withers. She kept on screaming the name, endlessly.

Valentine stopped the elevator so suddenly that she was catapulted to her knees, and it shot upward again.

Miss Withers saw that Lou Jeffers had fainted quietly in the corner where her adored one had flung her.

The footsteps mounted steadily below them as Valentine, his face twisting with the excellence of his practical joke, sent the elevator to the top of its shaft. He turned to face the frightened woman who cowered against the side of the cage.

"Stop your howling," he told her. "Perhaps nothing will happen to you."

Below them a shot was fired, perhaps as a signal to those in the lower hall. But Emile crouched down.

"*Aguard!*" he shrieked. "Hold your fire or I cut your woman into bits and fling them down to you — yes, both the women! Do you hear?"

The feet pounded steadily upward. Valentine was holding a long and shining knife in his right hand, and holding the control with the other. He looked frantically to the right and to the left ... but the car was on the level of the fourteenth floor, and once the police reached it, they could fire into the cage above the waist-high metal siding.

He crouched lower, and then, as the foremost bluecoat came up the last flight, Valentine sent the cage hurtling downward.

"I speak only with your leader," he screamed, as the speed slackened.

"I bargain — my life for these two women. If I give them to you unharmed, I get my life. Is it yes?"

There was no answer from the staircase. "Can't you hear me?" wailed Valentine. "I give you a bargain." The weird hide-and-seek went on ...

He sent the cage down another floor, and then another, slobbering, begging for his life from the invisible, implacable guardians of the law who swarmed up from below.

Miss Hildegarde Withers, her terror subsiding, never took her eyes from the knife to which the madman clung. She weighed the chance of seizing it, but knew it to be a desperate one. If only the Inspector were here! A thousand times he had chided her for her foolhardiness in getting into grips with situations unsuited to her sex and age. Again her life was in the hands of a mewling madman.

Then she heard a sentence — perhaps the sweetest words she had ever heard in her life. It came, strangely, through the top grille of the cage from above where a man peered down the shaft from an open door.

"Stoop a little lower, Hildegarde," said Inspector Oscar Piper. In his hand, the first time that she had ever seen him armed, he held a police automatic. As she flung herself down on the floor beside the limp figure of Lou Jeffers, the gun spat ... once.

The knife tinkled to the floor of the car, and Emile Valentine ceased to laugh. He collapsed slowly, his hand still clenched on the controls.

The weight of his body swung the handle toward him, and the car shot down suddenly.

Steadily it increased speed, hurtling like a plummet. Miss Withers knew what she must do. Painfully she got to her feet, tugged at the limp and bloody thing that had been a man before soft lead had splashed down into its skull, and as the daylight of the first floor hall came rising like a comet to meet them, she cleared the bar and swung it over.

The car stopped dead, and she was flung painfully to her knees again. Then, with infinite pains she hitched it downward the few remaining feet. Her strength sufficed to fling the door open, and then Miss Hildegarde Withers joined the little Jeffers girl in womankind's ancient prerogative, and fainted dead away in the extended arms of her rescuers.

† † †

"Must you drown me?" Hildegarde Withers inquired, as she opened her eyes and received another sprinkle of water from the glass in the Inspector's hand.

She tried to rise, for she saw that someone had brought her back to the studio. "Take it easy," the Inspector advised. "You've been out for more than half an hour. Take it easy."

"I'm perfectly all right," she retorted. "But —"

"When you feel well enough," the Inspector advised, "I wish you'd tell me what all this is about. I've sent a darky to Bellevue to have stitches taken in his scalp, and a little girl to Park Avenue with a broken heart, and a dead Argentinian to the morgue. Suppose you let me in on it?"

She sat up straight in her chair. "It was Valentine who did away with La Monterey," she began. "But I wasn't sure of it until this morning. Everything that happened seemed to make it more confusing." In a high monotone, she ran through the events which had transpired.

"I didn't know until Lou Jeffers was willing to help open the trunks that she was innocent of complicity," she said. "That completed my case."

"I know what happened, but I don't know why," objected the Inspector. "You say Valentine killed the dancer. But why, and how ... and when?"

"His alibi was perfect," Miss Withers admitted. "You remember, the girls testified that he came out of the room where Carla Monterey was dressing, and called good-night to her. She didn't answer — but that was because she could not."

"Dead? But they said she slammed a door."

Miss Withers nodded. "There are portieres between the hall and the living apartment," she pointed out. "You cannot slam a portiere. But I'll cover that point later. Anyway, Carla Monterey was dying then. As the handsome young Argentinian took the girls out to supper, the woman who had loved him strangled to death here."

"Strangled? But —"

"They had a row, and he decided to kill her. He thought fast, Oscar. And things played right into his hands. It was even a lucky break for him that Lou Jeffers forgot her handbag, because that gave him an excuse to come back and make sure that everything was well under cover.

"He wanted to marry the girl from Park Avenue, Oscar. She's of age in a few weeks, and she has a pretty considerable fortune. And she's fifteen years younger than Carla Monterey.

"But he couldn't let Lou know, or even suspect. He wanted her to think that the disappearance was a phoney, a frame, devised by Carla to injure him. Therefore the smoke screen."

"But the velvet dress?"

"He tied and gagged Carla, and then turned on the shower to drown out any noise she might make. The dress was to explain the shower — but it was torn so badly I knew the Monterey woman would not have bothered to steam the wrinkles out of it."

Piper nodded slowly. "Valentine thought he'd clear himself by producing the letter," he suggested.

"Carla had probably been threatened by him before, and had told him of the letters," Miss Withers said. "He knew there'd be others, so he beat us to it. Clever of him.

"Then the two little old ladies told of the noise they'd heard. Each one picked a different cause for it — and upstairs someone thought it was beating on a wooden drum. But I'll cover that point later, as I promised.

"It was Lou Jeffers who took that letter from my handbag, not Valentine. She thought he was being framed, and before he joined her in the studio she did it. That convinced me that she loved him, and that she was not entirely in his confidence.

"Then I set a trap," continued Miss Withers. "Or rather, I had you set one for me. The announcement in the newspapers that the police took no stock in the 'poison-pen' letters ... that gave Valentine confidence, and also a new idea. In his attempt to make the case seem like an attempted hoax, he thought that if he received a wire from Carla in Florida, everything would be dropped. The idea was that she had read the New York papers, seen that her plot had failed, and had decided to pass it off."

"But you can't get a New York paper in Florida as soon as published," said Piper.

"Exactly. I knew the wire was a fake, if only because it so conveniently offered Valentine an excuse to get out of town and take Lou Jeffers with him. Heaven knows what he expected to tell her when they arrived at The Corals."

"But you saw the wire, with a Florida filing address... "

"That puzzled me," the schoolteacher admitted. "Until I realized that Valentine had received a telegram from the hotel in Florida offering the dance engagement. He simply went out and sent himself a message signed Carla, and then soaked off the typed strips and pasted the fake date and message on the genuine superscription!"

She paused for breath. "Of course he was mad, mad as a hatter. But he was clever as sin. He almost convinced me that Carla Monterey, who was careful about her money and who saved seven hundred dollars in small bills, was in the habit of paying excess fare on trunks containing forty dance costumes — for one night's performance!"

"But the costumes are gone!" objected the Inspector. "Why should he send them?"

Miss Withers stood up. "They're not gone," she said. "Get me some fishhooks and line, and I'll show you the finish of this case."

"There's a regular grappling iron in the car downstairs," said Piper. "But it's not heavy enough to lift a dead body up the airshaft... "

"There's nobody down the airshaft," she told him. "But you'll find forty dance costumes there, if I'm not mistaken."

"Then — then where's the body of Carla Monterey?"

She handed him two red baggage checks. "Look in the larger of the two trunks down at the B & O Ferry," she advised. "You'll find Carla Monterey wrapped in blue oilcloth... "

† † †

Piper turned and ran for the telephone. He returned almost instantly. "I've started the boys," he said. "And I've also discovered the motive of this murder. They've discovered at the morgue that Valentine is really a bigamist named Ramez, wanted in all the Americas. Suppose the Monterey woman threatened to tell the Jeffers girl of his marrying habits?"

Miss Withers agreed. "But," continued Piper, "I see it all except one thing. Where did he hide the body until he could put it into the trunk?"

The schoolteacher led the way into the studio living room. "It just occured to me," she admitted. "He left her where she died — in this!"

She tugged at the Murphy bed, and finally it swung down to the floor.

"Good God! You mean he shoved her in that?"

Miss Withers nodded. "Still alive, but gagged and tied; with her own scarfs he left her there to die — head down in a tangle of bedclothes. Strangling brings muscular spasms, and that accounts for the noises — the slammed door the girls thought they heard, and the castanets and dancing and drum playing the neighbors fancied. They heard Carla Monterey's last dance — her shoes tapping against the door in a true Danse Macabre!"

"Let's get out of here," said the Inspector. And they did.

The Riddle of the Brass Band

"By Killarney's lakes and dells ... boom, boom-boom!" blared the marching band.

Bravely the slender trumpets sent echoing from skyscraper to skyscraper a tune which has run through the green valleys of Erin for hundreds of years. The heavier brasses of the band were throbbing close behind, and the drums boomed their ageless provocative rhythms. It was no wonder that the crowds which lined lower Fifth Avenue pressed closer to the curb, bodies swinging in step with the marching thousands.

The Finest looked the part today, from the Commissioner in a cutaway and gardenia that put His Honor to shame, down to the newest rookie who marched twenty blocks back at the tail of the parade, with the price tag still on the band of his uniform cap.

Everybody admitted that it was the best St. Patrick's Day parade in many a year. More than one disillusioned citizen paused to see those thousands of scrubbed honest faces above scrubbed honest shields, and realized that whatever was wrong with the city could not be traced to the Finest.

Rain had threatened all the morning, but now the skies were clearing and a fine April sun beamed down on the broad blue backs of the marching men. Steadily the column marched uptown in the wake of the band, twenty thousand polished brogans tramping as one upon the asphalt.

The band passed Thirtieth Street, and struck up "It's a Great Day for the Irish... " It was a great day, with only one shadow to mar the event.

That shadow came hurtling down out of the sky, and it was only just in the nick of time that horrified passers-by threw themselves to the right and left to avoid its path.

Directly before the main doorway of the Rance Building a man struck the sidewalk, and ceased to be a man. Women screamed, men fainted, and everybody pressed closer to the unsightly relic, with the typical desire to see everything and anything which marks the true New Yorker.

This man had fallen fifteen stories, and he was not a pretty sight to see. The lilting music of the band was strangled and the parade halted uncertainly.

† † †

Inspector Oscar Piper was not in a good mood. While his department consisted mostly of plainclothes men and other specialists and thus was not actively required to participate in the parade at noon, the event had caused an unusual amount of department upsets, and dozens of matters usually outside the field of the Homicide Squad were being routed through his busy desk.

Worse than that, the Inspector had sat through a Gridiron Club dinner on the preceding evening, and had listened to a talk by an amateur criminologist which sent him away boiling in sulphurous silence.

He gave Miss Hildegarde Withers a resume when she dropped into his office that morning, as was her custom whenever Jefferson School had a holiday. "Who's this fellow Leverer anyway?" demanded Piper. "Suppose he is a chemist and an expert in poisons! Suppose he does have the biggest library of crime books in the world? He's got a lot of nerve to stand up there and say that dozens of perfect crimes are being pulled off all around us, crimes that no one ever suspects to be such, and I'd like to tell him —"

"I know what you'd like to tell him," Miss Withers comforted. "Go on, this interests me."

"Leverer says," continued the Inspector, grinding his teeth into an already mangled cigar, "that the perfect crime is a murder wherein the murderer is never suspected and where the police never bother to investigate because the whole thing passes off as an accident. Why, he has the unmitigated gall to say that out of the supposedly accidental drownings and falls from windows that are listed every year, three-fourths are homicides!

"If he wanted to kill anybody, Leverer says, he'd wait until he was alone with them, call their attention to something in the street below, and then up with their ankles. No finger-prints, no investigation. Of course the man is crazy."

"Of course," agreed Miss Withers thoughtfully. "But why don't you show him up?"

Oscar Piper stared at her. "Huh?"

"Why don't you investigate the next 'accident' of the kind? Do it quietly, and then announce your findings when the Gridiron Club has another meeting."

Piper put down his cigar. "By heaven, I'll do it — if I can spare the time."

"And if you cannot, perhaps I can," finished his old friend and rival, sweetly. A few minutes later she left Centre Street, strolling lazily through East Side tenements until she reached Washington Square. Her plan had been to continue home by bus, but the parade had already started, and the busses were crawling northward on a detour via Fourth and Madison. She finally hailed a taxi, but even that usually dependable conveyance, trying to make a crosstown dash, came to a sudden halt. Traffic on Thirty-first Street was jammed fender to fender.

The driver, glad of a chance to stretch his legs, slid out into the street leaving the school-teacher to watch the whirling wheel of the motor. In a few moments he was back, raising his voice above the howl of an ambulance.

"Some guy jumped out of a window and spoiled the parade," he announced. "Splashed himself all over the sidewalk — I guess he was just another stock broker. Last year, they say the Wall Street men were standing in line for a chance to jump off the East River piers... " He paused as he saw the effect on his passenger.

A dollar bill fluttered into his lap. "Never mind the change," gasped Miss Withers, afire with a sudden determination. She was out of the cab in a moment, forcing her way through the jammed cars in the direction of the Avenue. Here was a tragedy made to order, exactly fitting the requirements of the Inspector. Only Oscar Piper wasn't on hand, and she was.

† † †

Order had been resolved out of chaos by the time she arrived. After all, when ten thousand policemen are already on the scene, there would seem little enough for one snooping, inquisitive schoolma'am to accomplish.

The parade was under way again, its spirit undampened. Half a dozen officers had been detailed from the ranks to take care of the remains and to keep the crowd back. The ambulance was screaming away empty, and a canvas from somewhere had been drawn over the thing on the sidewalk.

Luckily for Miss Withers she recognized the wide shoulders of Patrolman Tolliver braced against the hysterical crowd. Tolliver had shared swift adventure with her during the memorable murder investigation known to fame as "The Blackboard Murder," and he knew her to be the left if not the right hand of Inspector Oscar Piper.

He pushed a buxom stenographer rudely aside to let the school-teacher inside the circle, a somewhat surprised smile lighting his hot red face. "'Fraid it's outa your line," he greeted her. Miss Withers was inclined to agree as she stared down at the murky smears which spread from beneath the canvas.

Kneeling beside the blanket was another familiar figure — a small, sallow Hebrew with a black bag. It was Levin, chief assistant to the medical examiner.

"No mystery about this, my lady," said Dr. Levin cheerfully. He arose. "Okay, boys. When the Public Welfare truck gets here, they can take it away. So long."

Miss Withers caught his arm. "Wait!" she counselled. "Doctor, I don't want to interfere... "

"Not much you don't," said Levin wearily. "Well, what is it?"

She told him what she wanted. "Unofficially, you understand. But will you do it for me and then ask the questions afterward?" He sensed the intensity in her words. "Why, I suppose I can insist on it, if you have some reason."

"I haven't," she admitted. "But I'm going to find one." She looked at the lump beneath the canvas. "Does anybody know who he is, or is identification impossible?"

"Face isn't bunged up much," the doctor told her. "He lit feet first, I guess. But it isn't my job to identify him. Maybe the Sergeant here found something in his pockets."

Miss Withers looked inquiringly at a short, fattish man who squinted back at her. "Nothing personal in his pockets," growled Sergeant Halloran. "Initials T-W in gold on his fountain pen. And nobody saw where he fell from."

"Naturally — with ten thousand trained observers, not one of you noticed anything," the school-teacher retorted, with the veiled sarcasm which had so endeared her to all the members of the Force who knew her.

She caught sight of a little man who stood on the fringe of the crowd, nearest the building entrance. He was a smudged sort of person, with jet-black hair and eyes, and in his grimy hand was the padded box and brush which proclaimed his vocation.

"Get that man — the bootblack!" she cried. When no one obeyed, she forced her way through and seized his arm.

"Do you shine shoes throughout this building?"

He nodded, proudly. "My name's Tony Pappas. I shine this building ten year."

She dragged him back inside the police lines. "Then look under that canvas and see if you know that man's name!"

Halloran drew back the covering, showing the face of a plump young man with thin brown hair and wide cheekbones — a face which bore a mildly puzzled look.

All eyes were upon Tony Pappas. But he shook his head. "Lady, I don't know his name," he denied. "Sorry." And he slipped away.

White-clad men from a Department of Public Welfare truck were pushing up with a wicker basket slung between them. Miss Withers turned away from the gruesome sight, and on an impulse she followed the bootblack into the lobby.

"Wait," she called. In her fingers was an engraving sample. "If you don't know the name of the dead man, do you happen to know where in the building he works?"

Tony Pappas smiled with many teeth. "Sure! Nobody ask me that. I shine his shoes every morning. He's the boss in the book place on the top floor. He owe me two dollar —"

His blackened finger was pointing toward a name on the directory over their heads — "The Lehigh Press — 1501."

Without a backward glance at the circle of police outside, Miss Hildegarde Withers dashed for the elevator. She had one chance in a hundred of being first on the scene ... Up she went.

"The Lehigh Press" — there was the legend, in heavy gold letters, on the door halfway down the hall. But the hallway ended in an open window, and Miss Withers hurried to steal a glance at the scene below.

Almost directly beneath her she saw the wicker basket — like some thing through the wrong end of a spy-glass. It was being shoved unceremoniously into the truck, and the crowd was moving on.

She wondered suddenly if it was over this low sill that the man had plunged to his doom. There were no marks on the sill except where the print of her fingers showed plainly on a film of black dust.

A moment later she opened the door marked "The Lehigh Press" and found herself in a small reception room. There were a number of deep red leather chairs, a lounge, and a table bearing half a dozen popular novels fresh from the binders. In the farther corner a platinum-haired stenographer was rattling unconcernedly at a typewriter, and on the lounge a heavily jowled woman of Miss Withers' own age was noisily shuffling through a litter of galley-proofs.

It was all too evident that the tragedy had not echoed here as yet.

There was a young man in one of the red leather chairs, a crisp and pleasant young man of perhaps thirty, with a clipped toothbrush moustache, a well-brushed derby, and a silver-topped malacca stick. He was emitting clouds of villainous cigarette smoke, and the tray beside him was overflowing. He was staring at the right of the two inner doorways, at a panel which bore the name in gold — "Thomas E. Wright, President." The young man sat in the leather chair as if he had been waiting for a long time, and as if he expected to continue waiting.

Miss Withers looked at the name on the door, and spoke the initials to herself. "T-W ...!" She finished taking stock of the room, and faced the pale-haired receptionist. "I'd like to see Mr. Wright, please."

The young lady inspected her scarlet nails. "If you haven't an appointment, you won't be able to see Mr. Wright this afternoon. There are two ahead of you... "

Miss Withers sank down in a chair, more to collate her discoveries than for any other reason. Had she made a fantastic mistake, or was this entire office oblivious to the death of its chief?

The lady with the jowls rattled her proofs. "Miss Hink," she called out suddenly. "Will you please tell Mr. Wright that I cannot wait any longer?"

"He'll be so sorry to have missed you," lied the platinum blonde. "But Mr. Wright simply can't be disturbed now, while he's — while he's busy. If you'd care to speak to Mr. Orcutt or Mr. Shutts, Miss Terwilleger, I'll be glad to —"

She made a motion toward the inner door on the left, but Miss Terwilleger rose abruptly. "I have never in all my life —" she began. Then — "It seems to me —" She stalked toward the door. "If people have no regard and no respect —" Then the door slammed behind her, galley-proofs and all.

† † †

Miss Withers judged the time about right for a momentous announcement, but as she drew a deep breath the young man in the other chair rose abruptly. "I've been here since eleven this morning," he said softly. "Now, Gertrude, be a nice little girl and tell Tom Wright that if he doesn't come out I'm coming in after him!"

Gertrude, shocked into immobility, watched the young man stride past her and rap heavily upon the door with his stick.

"But, Mister Orchard — you must not —"

The young man paid no attention. He rapped again. "Tom! Will you come out?"

There was no answer from the inner office. Somehow Miss Withers had known that there could be none. The young Mr. Orchard swore softly, kicked the door, and then jammed his derby down over his head and went out of the place.

"Well!" Gertrude decided to be human, when she caught the calm blue eyes of Miss Hildegarde Withers staring benignly. "Aren't our authors getting temper'mental these days!"

The school-teacher turned her gaze toward the new books on the table, and noted that the brightest and most garish of all was *Ace of Vamps* — by Paul Orchard. Then she understood, or thought she did.

"It's quite important that I see Mr. Wright," she offered.

But Gertrude shook her head. "He isn't seeing any more authors just at present."

Miss Withers was vaguely pleased at the compliment. "I'm not an author," she said. "I — I'm his aunt from Boston."

"Oh," said Gertrude. "I didn't know he — you see, I had strict orders not to disturb him. But if you're his aunt from Boston... " She looked suddenly suspicious. "You're not from the Morris Plan people?"

"Heavens, no." Miss Withers rose. "Please send in my name."

Gertrude fiddled with the switch board, snapping a plug again and again. She looked surprised. "He doesn't answer," she said.

She tried again. "I'm sure he didn't go out! The boy came from downstairs with his lunch at twelve, and I've been sitting here ever since!"

"Something may be wrong," Miss Withers cut in. She tried the door and found it locked.

"We'd better —"

But at that moment the hall door burst open to disclose the bulk of Patrolman Tolliver. "I'm goin' through this building to identify a guy that fell out of the windy," he boomed. "Anybody missing in this office?"

He spoke his piece before he saw Miss Withers — and saw that the school-teacher was tapping her lips with her bony forefinger. His eyes widened, and he nodded slightly. "This guy had the initials T-W."

Miss Withers was pointing toward the name on the door and Gertrude was beginning to sense that something had happened. "But Mr. Wright is in there," she cried.

"We'll soon see," said Tolliver, and he threw his shoulder against the door. It crashed inward, and the three of them came into a luxurious and completely untenanted office. On the desk stood a container of stale coffee, and the wreck of a sandwich, but the wide open window gave the only clue as to the possible whereabouts of Tom Wright.

Gertrude ran to the window to stare down at the dark spot on the side walk where a janitor was wielding a mop, and then stretched out on the floor, dead to the world.

The cat was out of the bag. While the rest of the office force crowded around, Miss Withers drew back and took stock of them. The two other partners in the little publishing house were Mr. Orcutt and Mr. Shutts — the former a lean, unhappy Scotchman who served as treasurer and whose resources, she learned, had largely financed the venture, and the latter a dumpy little man whose eyes twinkled through rolls of fat, and whose duties, he announced, were the reading of manuscripts and the translation of foreign works.

These two shared the smaller corner office, while Abe, a gorilla-like office boy with a stubble of beard on his prognathous jaw, had a little cubicle with a mail desk and a storeroom at the rear.

† † †

They had all been too busy, they announced, to pay any attention when the sounds of the parade and band music drifted in the window. Orcutt had been checking accounts, and Shutts writing letters of application for a job as instructor in German. Miss Withers did not need this to tell her that the Lehigh Press was at the point of dissolution.

"But poor Tom wouldn't have been too busy," Orcutt told her. "He was always crazy about band music. Told me that he'd had lots of trouble at his hotel because he played Sousa records on his victrola late at night."

"Some one of ye will have to go down to the morgue and identify him," Tolliver finished. "Unless he had a wife or a close relative."

"He had a wife," said Shutts, and then stopped short.

"Well, where is she?" Tolliver had his notebook out.

"She sailed for Europe four o'clock Sunday afternoon with his best friend," Orcutt announced. There was a long silence, and Miss Withers wondered about suicide.

Gertrude had been revived, and appeared none the worse for her collapse. "As Mr. Wright's aunt," she suggested to Miss Withers, "you'll probably want to identify him?"

The school-teacher was wishing that she had never become Tom Wright's aunt. "I haven't seen him in years," she said quickly. "Someone else had better take my place."

"I'd be delighted — I mean, I'm willing to oblige," said Ralph Orcutt. Miss Withers made a mental note of that.

† † †

She made a lot of mental notes before she found herself closeted with Inspector Oscar Piper later that afternoon.

"It looks like an accident, and I don't see how you can make anything else out of it," the Inspector was saying. "After all, the door of the office was locked on the inside. This Wright fellow went to the window to hear the band, got dizzy, and fell out."

"Probably," said Hildegarde Withers. "And yet — the stenographer was leaning out of the window when she fainted, and she fell back into the room."

"Doesn't prove anything," Piper retorted. "Besides, he may have bumped himself off. Financial troubles — and losing his wife... "

"It wasn't suicide," said Miss Withers tartly. "As for the wife, he was lucky. Because she seems to have caused most of the financial troubles. Her name was Golda, and that's what she was after. She'd been Dr. Frey's mistress for years before she married Wright, and as soon as she found out that the millionaire publisher hadn't a dime, she went back to the doctor, and they sailed for Majorca together. Wright should have been relieved at getting out of it so easily — and he owed the doctor money, too. Besides, suicides never endanger other people's lives. Only the other day I read of a man who was about to jump off the Brooklyn Bridge, and who climbed fifty feet further than he needed to do, just to avoid striking where a number of children were playing... "

"All right," grinned Piper. "But if you try to make this a murder, what about the doctor fellow? Or the dame?"

"They are out on the Atlantic," Miss Withers told him. "And they had no motive, either. The only approach to this case is via the motive!"

"Motive or no motive," Piper pronounced, "I don't see how a man can be thrown out of his office window when he's alone in the office."

"Nor I," said Miss Withers. "But that doesn't prove that it can't be done." She was interrupted by the shrill jingle of the telephone. The Inspector grabbed it.

"Piper speaking — put him on. Hello Levin. What? Who asked you to make one anyhow? Oh. Yes. Yeah. Uh-huh." He replaced the phone.

"That's funny," he observed. "That's damn funny. Levin says you begged him to make an autopsy, so he went ahead and did a preliminary one. Death was instantaneous, due to a fall from considerable height... "

"I know that!" the school-teacher told him.

"Maybe you don't know this," said Piper. "Lower part of the body crushed to pulp, but the skull was intact — except for an oval indentation at the base as if he'd lit on a stone. All the same, Levin reports it as death by misadventure."

"I'm still looking for a motive," said Hildegarde Withers. "You might start looking for a stone on Fifth Avenue. They're rare enough, I understand."

Although it had always seemed a little like cheating, Miss Hildegarde Withers purchased a copy of Friday's *Times* late on that Thursday evening, and spread it out beneath her desk light. She found a sober and comprehensive report of the accident upon page three, beneath a modest headline "Accident Mars Parade."

It continued — "At exactly two minutes past one o'clock yesterday afternoon, when the police parade was passing Thirty-first Street on Fifth Avenue, spectators narrowly escaped being crushed by the hurtling body of a man, later identified by his business partner Ralph Orcutt as Thomas E. Wright, youthful founder of a new publishing house, who had fallen from the window of his office on the top floor of the Rance Building..."

There was a paragraph giving some details of Wright's marriage some months before to Golda Green, ex-show girl, and of the subsequent separation, and information relative to his living at the Hotel Chesterfield. The news story concluded with this — "The remaining partners in the new firm, The Lehigh Press, announce that the business will be continued as usual, and that invitations for a literary tea this Saturday introducing Lehigh authors to the critics and the press will not be recalled. 'Tom Wright would want us to carry on,' said Emil Shutts, editor of the firm. 'The party will be held in our offices just as he planned before his untimely taking-off!' "

Miss Withers digested that for a moment. She finally came to the conclusion that perhaps, after all, the party would not be held just as Wright had planned it.

She rose bright and early the next morning, arranged for a substitute to take her third-grade class at Jefferson School, and then, as the good lady herself would no doubt have misquoted, she "set her shoulder to the grindstone."

† † †

Her first call was at the offices of the Yankee Merchant Lines, where she had little difficulty in ascertaining that Dr. and "Mrs." Otto Frey had actually set sail upon the *S.S. Yankee Realtor,* bound for the Mediterranean, some four days before that fickle lady's real and legal husband had plunged to his death on the sidewalk. That seemed to eliminate two suspects. "I shall have trouble enough pinning this murder — if it is a murder — upon anyone who was in town today," she told herself. But all the same she paused at a Postal office and sent a wireless message, carefully worded. Then she hastened on to the offices of the Morris Plan, Manhattan's largest home-loans firm.

She immediately found her thin ankles wound in red tape, but a telephone call to Spring 7-3100 finally rectified that. Late that afternoon she wormed her way inside the doors.

Mr. Ticheborne, a southerner with an accent that suggested south Chicago, was at her service. Yes, Thomas E. Wright had borrowed five hundred dollars from the Morris Plan late last August. Mr. Ticheborne referred to a file. The payments had been made for September and November and then, he assured her, "the account was placed in the hands of our legal department."

"Does that mean that you lost the balance of your five hundred dollars?" Miss Withers somewhat innocently inquired.

It did not. "We always require two responsible co-signers on these personal notes," said Mr. Ticheborne. "In this case we required three, as literary people are, ahem, well — not always financially responsible. In case of default, the co-signers are liable for the full amount, in order. If one defaults, we sue the next."

"And these were —?"

Mr. Ticheborne studied the contract. "Dr. Otto Frey was the first to sign," he informed her. "Then a Mr. Paul Orchard, and finally Mr. Ralph Orcutt."

"Well!" said Hildegarde Withers. "Who paid up, finally?"

The other shrugged. "I understand that it was taken care of a few days ago, by means of a legal process," he said. "But I shall have to refer you to the legal department for further information."

It was five minutes after five, and the legal department had shut up shop and hustled off to its respective lairs in the suburbs. But after all, Miss Withers had no reason to be downcast. She had got a whiff of the scent, and it did not smell like a red herring across the trail.

† † †

Saturday found the streets of Manhattan driven with wind and wet — a fit setting for a literary tea, or at least for such a literary tea as was thrown by the Lehigh Press that afternoon.

There had been twenty invitations sent out, and this was the result. The tragedy had brought them, and the tragedy had caused a strained note in the laughter, an added loudness in the voices, and unusual inroads on the mixture of gin and grapefruit juice which flowed from the spigot of the conveniently mounted ten-gallon keg in the middle of what yesterday had been Miss Gertrude Hink's desk.

The school-teacher found her hand grasped by the fishy palm of editor Emil Shutts. "So glad you could come!" he announced, with a whiff of gin. "As Tom's aunt — there ought to be some relative of his here to see how his memory is respected."

Miss Withers overheard snatches of conversations on either side — and she had little difficulty in discovering just how much Tom Wright's memory was respected. "Come on, I'll introduce you to some of the critics," urged Shutts. He paused. "I'm afraid I don't remember your name, is it Wright, also?"

"I am on the other side of the family," she told him. "My name is — er —"
... she hesitated, and then gave the right one. After all, someone here might
know her. "But I'd rather not meet any critics," she confided. "I'm more
interested in the authors."

In the next few minutes she was introduced to the entire string of Lehigh
authors, all of whom expressed themselves as delighted to meet the aunt of their
deceased friend and publisher. Miss Withers shook hands with Paul Orchard,
who seemed not to remember that they had crossed paths before; with Miss
Emma Terwilleger, the poetess, who did remember; with Rosalie Loos, a
flashing-eyed damsel of thirty who, it seemed, wrote novels of purple passion;
with Horace Feets, whose epic was a life of the Adolf Hitler whom he had never
seen, and with some four or five others.

Mr. Shutts then pressed a tall cold glass in her hand and deserted her. Miss
Withers stalked through the merrymaking, like a skeleton at the feast, waiting
for her opportunity.

She came upon Gertrude, the platinum stenographer, standing alone in a
deserted corner. "How Tom would have loved to be here!" she observed
pleasantly.

The girl nodded slowly, and set down her untasted drink. Miss Withers
remembered that Gertrude had fainted dead away when she knew of her
employer's death, a more sincere tribute than most stenographers would have
given.

"You know," confided the schoolteacher, "an idea just came to me — Tom
was publishing books for all these people here. Yet his primary interest was in
writing. He used to send me his poems from time to time, and I saved them all.
Wouldn't it be nice if we'd all band together and contribute toward publishing a
deluxe edition of his poems — not for the trade, but just for private distribution?
As a sort of memento?"

Gertrude turned toward her. "Oh — oh, yes! I'd like to be the first... "
Her voice died away. "I'd make a contribution, only —"

"Only what?"

"Only Tom — I mean Mr. Wright — borrowed my salary checks back from
me as soon as I got them for the last three weeks," confided Gertrude. "And I
haven't any money. But I think it's a wonderful idea!" Gertrude hesitated. "I
wonder if any of the authors would do it?"

"Dear me," said Miss Withers. She threaded her way through the crowd
with a paper in her hand. Her own name headed the list, with an imaginary
subscription of one hundred dollars.

She found the poetess, Miss Terwilleger, wrapt in contemplation of the
dummy prepared for her forthcoming book, *Cloud-thoughts*. After an inter-
change of remarks complimentary to the departed, she brought forth her
suggestion.

Miss Terwilleger hedged. "Why not?" demanded Miss Withers.

"I'll tell you why not," said the lady with the jowls. "You may not know it, but I raised the money to finance my own book of poems. Tom Wright told me it would cost seven hundred dollars to publish my poems in morocco, and after he got the money he went ahead and ordered them bound in cheap linoleum. He charged me fifty dollars for author's alterations, and then had the book set in plates with all the mistakes left in!" She went on to insinuate that it would be a very cold day indeed when she would subscribe to a memorial for Tom Wright.

† † †

That was that. Miss Withers plunged merrily on, button-holing first one and then another. All were loud in praise of the dead man until she mentioned the memorial. "Tom Wright gave me an advance of five hundred dollars on my book," blurted out Rosalie Loos when pried away from the male critics, "and then he borrowed it back, and more, too. I'd be likely to write you a check!"

Orcutt, still worried, shook his head. "Tom was my partner," he said. "He had the experience and I had the money. He spent the money and now I have the experience. No, thanks."

Miss Withers was learning things. Little Mr. Shutts gave her another negative. "I'm afraid I can't afford what you ask now," he told her. "Though I'd like to."

"You mean — because you're leaving the firm?"

She was thinking of the letters of application he had been writing. But he shook his head. "I'm not leaving the firm now," he said calmly. "With Tom gone, we have a chance to pull through, on a less grand scale than he planned. Tom Wright had grand ideas, you know."

"I know," said Hildegarde Withers. She was beginning to. She got hedging negatives from several other Lehigh authors, from two members of the printing firm which had largely subsidized printing and paper bills for the new venture, and finally she passed on into the little room where Abe, the ape-like office boy, sat on guard over the copies of new novels in the store room.

"I want you to do a little errand for me," she told the boy. He protested, but went. Miss Withers wandered back into the reception room, and then on into the crowded office which had been Tom Wright's.

She paused beside Gertrude again. "In case anybody should ask, do you remember when it was that Miss Terwilliger arrived in this office day before yesterday, asking to see your employer?"

Gertrude remembered, vaguely. "It was some time around one o'clock." She nodded. "Yes, it was just about one, because I remember that Mr. Orchard was getting impatient. He said two hours was enough to wait for anybody, and he flounced out of the office and then came back. I guess he changed his mind."

Miss Withers nodded, and pushed on through to the window from which Tom Wright had plunged to his death. It was closed, but she raised it, and leaned out.

As he had been instructed, Abe the office boy was leaning from the window at the end of the hall. Strangely enough both windows opened upon Fifth Avenue, with only a short gap between them.

Was there room for a thrusting hand to have bridged the gap? Miss Withers called to Abe to try, but he could not come within two feet of touching her shoulder. And that seemed to be that. She was glad to close the window from the inside.

† † †

Back in the office the party was breaking up. It had been somewhat of a frost due to the unseen presence of a spectre whom everybody seemed to hate — everybody except Gertrude and Abe the office boy. Tom Wright was every-where ...

Paul Orchard was the only author whom she had not approached with her idea for the memorial edition of the works of Tom Wright. She caught sight of him passing out the door with his silver-topped stick in one hand and four copies of his novel under his other arm. She came up with him at the elevator, and he noticed her glance.

"I hooked them from Abe's storeroom," confided the author cheerfully. "It's about all I'll ever get out of the book, what with the way Wright and those other stupid incompetents have mismanaged the whole job."

"Oh," said Miss Withers. The elevator was slow in rising, and she asked Orchard about his part in the Wright memorial.

The young man tugged at his wispy moustache. He showed more hesitance about disclosing his real feelings than had some of the other literary lights that afternoon, and Miss Withers admired his delicacy.

"You're his aunt," said Orchard. "I don't like — I'd better think it over. I'm in a hurry now, because I've got to get down to the paper with a report on this tea. I'm a slave on the *Herald Trib*, you know. Suppose you phone me — I'm in the book —"

The elevator door opened, and he followed her inside. "I'll do that," promised Miss Withers. "So you're a newspaperman as well as an author, eh?"

"I was an author for about two weeks," Orchard told her. "Then Tom Wright commandeered my book — sold it off for ten cents a copy to the junk men. But it was nice while it lasted, and I suppose Tom did need cash."

They were in the lobby, and Miss Withers held out her hand. "So glad to have met you."

He shook hands, incidentally letting the stick fall from under his arm. He retrieved it quickly.

"I'm always dropping it," he said. Miss Withers noticed a deep indentation in the soft silver knob.

"So I see." She leaned closer. "A very beautiful piece of malacca."

Orchard brightened. "You like it? I got it up at Umbrella Sam's, off Sixth. He makes Chaplin's whangees, too... "

"Dear me," murmured Hildegarde Withers, as he turned to depart. "I shall have to buy one for a friend of mine."

†††

At dinner time that night she presented a silver-topped malacca stick to Inspector Oscar Piper. He surveyed it, speculatingly. "But, Hildegarde, you know I never carry —"

"Never mind," said Miss Withers. "Put it away as Exhibit A. I've spent half an hour dropping it on the sidewalk, to dent the silver knob."

"But it isn't dented, barely nicked!" objected the Inspector.

"I noticed that, too," said Hildegarde Withers.

When she arrived home that night she found a wireless message in answer to her own. That, too, did not surprise her, though it was collect.

"Sorry cannot join in memorial to Wright," Dr. Frey had wired, "as I am leaving the country to avoid court judgments."

Suddenly a new thought struck her. She leaped into a taxicab and hurried down to the Public Library, which was still luckily open. In the newspaper reading room on the first floor she called for copies of each morning news paper for the day of the tragedy, seeking for a report on the Gridiron Club banquet of the night before.

She drew a blank on the *News* and *American*, found a tiny paragraph in the *Times* and half a column in the *Herald Tribune*. But there was little more than a list of the distinguished guests, and no resumé of the speeches. Then no one had got an evil inspiration from the speech of Mr. Leverer ... unless he had been a guest at the proceedings. She read over the long list of distinguished names, and did not find the one she sought. Well, she told herself, that would have been too much of a good thing. The case was almost perfect without that tiny detail.

Tomorrow would see the finish, she told herself triumphantly, and went home to bed.

†††

But tomorrow, a damp April Sabbath was not to be as simple as she had imagined. An hour before noon, when the streets of Manhattan were as deserted as Timbuktu, she took a trip southward to the apartment on West Tenth Street, in the northern part of the Village, which was listed in the telephone directory as that of Paul Orchard.

Orchard's apartment was on the second floor rear. A sleepy young man, his hair standing up in all directions, opened the door.

"You keep late hours," she suggested. "I'm awfully sorry for intruding, but —"

"But you had to know whether or not I'd contribute to this memorial for Tom Wright?" Her host sat on the edge of a desk and lit a cigarette. "For an aunt you take a lot of interest in his sacred memory."

Miss Withers made a bold play. "I'm not Tom Wright's aunt," she said.

Orchard nodded. "I know you're not," he admitted. "He used to be a close friend of mine, and I happen to know that his mother's maiden name was Klein. I'm not inquisitive, but... "

"But you'd like to know why I woke you. That's simple. I'm connected with the police," she told him. "And I've got a hunch that Wright was murdered."

"What makes you think that?"

"The fact that everyone who knew him, except the office boy and the stenographer, hated his — hated him."

Orchard nodded. "Sounds reasonable. Tom Wright was a four-flusher, with a smooth tongue and delusions of grandeur. I'm not pretending that I loved him. But as you say, everybody had a motive for bumping him. Even —" he laughed shortly — "even myself, if you come to that."

His eyes traveled to a picture above the fireplace. It was the picture of a girl, a very pretty if haughty girl. The picture had been torn into small pieces, and then pasted back together again.

"Who is that?" Miss Withers asked. She usually got an answer, and this was no exception.

"That," said Paul Orchard, "is — or was — the girl I intended to marry. She lives down in Bermuda, and I was to have sailed this weekend to cinch it. Tom Wright got me to sign a Morris Plan note for him in the days when I thought he was a big-shot publisher. Some other friends of his signed it, too, but one of them got out of the country and the Morris Plan smacked a judgment against my bank account. Ergo — no Bermuda. I wired the lady fair — and when she heard that I'd postponed coming to Bermuda for the second time, she wired back that she'd amuse herself otherwise."

He butted his cigarette, and lit another. "I'm telling you this because you'll find it out anyway," he said. "But after all, I don't see how I or anybody else could be suspected of bumping off Tom Wright, for all that he deserved it. Because his office door was locked on the inside when he fell out of the window."

Miss Withers felt horribly uncomfortable. She nodded slowly. "By the way," she suggested, "who covered the Gridiron banquet for your paper?"

Orchard's eyes widened. "Why — I did, as a matter of fact. I usually get those assignments, because of my supposed literary background... "

"I see," said Miss Withers. She saw everything now, and she did not like what she saw. Worst of all, she did not like the part that she must play in the forthcoming drama. She had been so sure of herself — and now she realized that perhaps she was terribly, horribly wrong. Not from the Inspector's point of view, but from her own. If only there were some way to be sure — not of the obvious questions of fact, but of the deeper maze of motives and causes and circumstance.

† † †

The telephone shrilled, and in that instance she made up her mind to a daring plan, a plan which would settle once and for all the problem that filled her mind. She had spent half an hour arranging things with the Inspector — this call was part of the plot. But she reorganized it all.

Orchard put down the phone. "It seems to be for you," he said.

She nodded. "I told them at Headquarters where I'd be if they needed me." She picked up the instrument, and heard Piper's baritone.

"Well, are you all set? Do we surround the place and make the arrest?"

"Um —" she hesitated. "No, decidedly no. I had no idea. Put her on the wire, will you?"

The Inspector gurgled at the other end of the wire. "What in hell?"

"Oh, yes," said Miss Withers. "What? What? Good heavens, yes. Yes, of course. Why didn't you speak sooner?"

"Have you gone nuts?" inquired the Inspector. "Or are you putting on an act?"

"Yes," she told him. "What's the address? Just a minute, I'll write it down. One-seven West Seventy-sixth — yes — it's the second floor front apartment —"

She scribbled busily, while Paul Orchard watched in wonderment. Then she spoke into the phone again. "No, I can't get up there right away. It will take an hour or so to communicate with the proper authorities today, because it's a holiday. Suppose we meet you there, say, at one o'clock? In the meantime you might write out a statement of just what you saw last Thursday. Yes, that's right. Good-bye."

She looked up, her face alight with excitement. "I was right!" she announced. "There was something fishy about the death of Tom Wright. That call was from a man who works in the building across the street. He was at the window, watching the parade, and caught a glimpse of something. He won't tell what it was over the phone, so I've got to get down to Centre Street and start things rolling. I'm so excited!"

Miss Withers fumbled for her handbag and her umbrella, while Paul Orchard lit another cigarette. He had two already burning in the tray, but he did not notice that. His eyes were very sad and sleepy.

"So sorry to have troubled you," Miss Withers told him, and flounced out of the place.

She walked leisurely toward the subway, but at the corner dashed into a drug store and called the Inspector. She did not bother to explain, but implored him to hurry. Then she trotted northward a block, and back along Eleventh Street to Fifth. It was hardly three minutes later when a green squad car careened northward and skidded up the curb.

The Inspector and a Sergeant were inside, and she joined them instantly. "My apartment — and hurry!"

According to the laws of the state, mail trucks and ambulances have the right of way over all vehicles, but no mail truck nor ambulance ever went northward through Manhattan's arteries in half the time that was made by that green squad car. Cutting through red lights, dashing eastward on odd numbered streets and westward on the even, hurtling up through Central Park against the arrows, they reached Miss Withers' modest brownstone apartment house in a little over seven minutes. The siren died away.

"Get that thing out of sight," ordered Miss Withers hastily, and the bewildered Sergeant drove around the corner at the Inspector's nod. Piper followed Miss Withers into the lobby and watched her remove a card engraved "Miss Hildegarde Withers" from the bell-rack. "Mr. Ralph Jones" was the legend printed hastily upon a substitute.

"What in God's holy name does all this mean?" demanded the Inspector.

"Nothing," said Hildegarde Withers, almost tearfully. "Pray with me that it means nothing at all. I'm giving some one a chance —"

She led the way up one flight of stairs, and unlocked her door. Leaving it ajar, she drew the Inspector into the room.

"If I can only find it!" she gasped. Bewildered, the Inspector watched while she rummaged in a deep closet, and finally appeared with a strange wire contraption which he recognized as one of those old-fashioned dressmakers' forms.

"Help me!" implored Miss Withers. She was forcing an old coat over the wires. Then, while Piper gave awestruck aid, she snatched from a bureau drawer a thick strand of hair, and cut part of it off.

"I had it made into a switch when I had the fever," she informed him. She was everywhere at once, and under her direction the dummy began to take on a rude semblance of life.

Luckily the day was cloudy. "Draw the shades!" demanded the school teacher. "If only we could bend this wire... "

The wires were bent, and, at last the two surveyed their handiwork. "But I'm still praying that I'm wrong," Miss Withers said breathlessly. "Here — behind the sofa —"

She drew the Inspector down beside her, and they peeped out at the darkened room.

† † †

One light burned above the desk where a figure having a vague resemblance to a man in the dim light was leaning over scattered sheets of paper. "Put out that cigar!" demanded Miss Withers — in great excitement — "Yes, on the rug if you must."

They waited interminably. "Thank heaven I was wrong," Miss Withers whispered. "Thank —"

There were light footsteps in the hall, and she caught Piper's arm. Another long silence, and the door-knob began to turn. Miss Withers could just see it around the arm of the sofa.

The door swung slowly open, an inch at a time. Still nothing happened. It came completely open, and a man tiptoed into the room. He was wearing a hat pulled over his eyes, and a coat buttoned high to hide the fact that he still wore the top to his pajamas.

His hand was in the pocket of his coat. He paused, not two paces inside the door, and drew a gun from his pocket. The gun spat once — twice — red flame that leaped toward the wire frame. Acrid odors filled the room.

He turned, and was gone, but not before Miss Withers had recognized the pleasant face of Paul Orchard. It was just as she had seen him last, except for the fact that the mouth under his small moustache was working, mumbling, with an independent life of its own ...

Piper ran to the window, threw it open, and blew a police whistle. There was an answering blast from the street below, and the Sergeant ran up the steps to collide with a plunging madman.

Piper turned to Miss Withers, and saw her dabbing at her eyes. "Well," he said. "Do we arrest him for the attempted murder of Mr. Jones the dressmaker's dummy?"

† † †

The school-teacher shook her head. "For the murder of Thomas Wright," she said. "This theatrical last act had to be, Oscar. Don't you see — I had to find out whether Orchard was really a murderer or not! He hated Wright, and he had reason enough. I didn't know whether to turn him in or not — though the case was clear enough to me when I realized that Orchard had been in the hallway of the building when the parade went by. He went to the hall window to look down, and happened to notice Wright leaning out of the office window, a few feet away. He didn't plan it, Oscar. But he'd heard Leverer's talk on murder, and it came back to him. In his hand was the silver-topped stick — and there was the man whose financial chiseling had taken his savings, lost him his girl — the man who kept him waiting outside while he listened to the band music. It was enough to make anyone kill, Oscar — and if it happened like that,

I wasn't going to turn him in. At the worst it was only second-degree murder. But this was a test. I make him think that someone had seen him strike Wright on the back of the head with his stick — and if he was a murderer at heart I knew he'd try to kill the mythical Mr. Jones. And he did —"

The Inspector resurrected his cigar from the floor behind the sofa, and lit it. "I'll be a such and such," he said fervently. He moved toward the door, and then paused. "You know, the District Attorney will have a time for himself trying to make a case stick against this Orchard fellow."

Miss Withers was undressing the dummy. "That," she told him firmly, "will probably worry me."

The Riddle of the Blueblood Murders

"Who's afraid of the big bad wolf? Big bad wolf, big bad wolf?
"Who's afraid of the big bad wolf? dum diddy dum di dum… "

Emilie Vail had sung the one about "Fairies at the Bottom of My Garden," and "Birmingham Bertie," and she had her audience, as was her wont, in the hollow of her hand. Now, as she concluded a spirited rendition of another classic of yesterday, an angular lady who sat in the fourth row of the mezzanine turned to her somewhat grizzled companion and said, "Oscar, aren't you sorry that you didn't take me to the Philharmonic, after all?"

But Inspector Oscar Piper preferred the Palace for his evenings of relaxation. "Watch her," he told Miss Withers. "She's good."

As the song ended, Emilie Vail took a quick step backward and locked arms with two charming if somewhat plumper young ladies who suddenly appeared from the wings. All three cavorted about the stage to the catchy tune, now and theft displaying enough of their backs to show that each wore, over her evening gown, a gaily twisted tail affixed behind.

"Three Little Pigs," said the Inspector Joyously. At that moment the three gaily dancing figures stopped short. From behind a "prop" tree there bounded on to the stage a grotesque creature wearing black trousers and an insecure silk hat. It was a *Borzoi*, a Russian wolfhound, looking fearsome and tremendous except for the fact that his tail was, naturally, wagging. But Ivanitch was a fair actor. He approached the three terrified women stopped short facing them, and braced himself upon his haunches. He barked, hollowly, and then a wind machine offstage began to roar.

"He's supposed to be blowing their clothes off," the Inspector confided.

The Three Little Pigs wept and begged and pleaded, but off went their hats in a wild swoop to the wings, followed by the van-coloured silken coats. With exaggerated ripping sounds, a dress gave way, and the plump little girl on the right stood arrayed only in make-up and a lacy wisp of French underwear. The crowd roared.

The *Borzoi* barked obediently once more, and the dress of the plump girl on the left gave way and flew off in two pieces. She, too, was huddled in fragile nothings. More frantic applause.

Then a hush fell over the audience. It was Emilie Vail's turn. When the wolfhound barked a third time, she let out a wild scream, and the audience gasped as the wind whipped off her shimmering gown — leaving her in a suit of red flannel underwear.

The Big Bad Wolf tucked his tail between his legs and scrambled for the wings as The Three Little Pigs took up their ditty again and gambolled in a circle around the stage. The audience applauded wildly as the curtain fell.

In a matter of a few seconds it rose and, remarkably, there stood Emilie Vail, her gown on as if it had jumped back on her body, and not a hair of her magnificent coiffure loose from the "huffing and puffing" of the wolf. She leaned triumphantly on the neatly groomed head of the Borzoi, her diamond bracelets sending bright pencils of reflected light over the faces of her audience.

Her follow-through was every bit as professional as her actual performance. She bowed three times, then held out her graceful, bejeweled hand to several eager attendants, and stepped down into the auditorium, where she marched triumphantly up one aisle, across the rear of the house, then down the other aisle. Admirers reached out to touch her gown as it swept by, with Ivanitch trailing obediently behind as he'd done after each performance during the week.

But this time, as they were about to step back upon the stage, the big animal faltered. Emilie turned to him, a look of puzzlement on her face, and snapped her fingers. But Ivanitch remained where he stood, rocking as though drunk. The audience sensed that this was not part of the act.

Suddenly the wolfhound keeled forward, his forefeet buckled, and he collapsed and rolled over on his side. A distressed murmur went through the throng. A woman sitting on the aisle rose and screamed.

Though it was said that Emilie Vail smiled coldly when unrequited lovers shot themselves for her sake, there was nothing heartless in the way she threw herself to the carpet and lifted the dead wolfhound's head into her lap.

"Well, if it's a publicity stunt we'll read all about it in the papers tomorrow morning," said the Inspector, as he took Miss Withers home. Yet strangely enough, there was no mention of the scene in the theater in any New York daily. A human stooge took the place of poor Ivanitch in the act at the Palace, and the show went on.

Miss Hildegarde Withers and her old friend Inspector Oscar Piper were in the habit of meeting once a week for a mild orgy of spaghetti and the theater. She entered his office at Centre Street one rainy afternoon some days after the tragedy aforementioned, and found him deep in a telephone conversation.

He waved to her, and went on talking. "But it's not up to the Homicide Squad! Your friend would do better to see a vet, or get in touch with the S.P.C.A."

Miss Withers was graced with a long and inquisitive nose, and for most of her forty-odd years she had been completely unable to keep it out of other people's business. Her nostrils widened a bit now, as she scented a faint suggestion of the adventure for which she had secretly longed for weeks.

"See him!" she said tersely.

The Inspector looked up at her. "But it's not in my line!"

"It may be in mine," said Miss Withers.

The Inspector shrugged his shoulders and returned to his telephone. "Sorry, Tomlinson. Had a crossed wire. Yes, tell your friend I'll see him. How about Monday?" There was a pause. "Why — yes, I suppose so. He's in the city, you say? Very well, I'll stick around for half an hour, if he can get here by then. Name's Neville, you say? Right you are. G'bye."

He swung around in his chair. "See what you've done? That was Chief Tomlinson of the Bronxville force. Wants me to see a man about a dog. Now we've got to stick around here until dark."

Miss Withers was fumbling in her capacious handbag. She finally found the clipping for which she sought and handed it to the Inspector. He read aloud: "For sale, very cheap to good home, pedigreed 18-months-old terrier, wonderful pet, female, must sell, as dog poisoner in neighborhood, phone — Prospect: 6-4435."

"I clipped that out of the *Times* last Sunday," she told him.

"Looking for a mate for Dempsey?" asked Piper.

He smiled, remembering his spinster friend's one unwilling venture into dog-breeding, which had transpired at Catalina Island a year or so before. At the climax of a thrilling series of adventures in murder, the good lady had discovered herself the guardian of a pedigreed wire-haired fox-terrier, the most effervescent, roguish, combative puppy that ever gnawed a slipper.

"I was not," she answered him shortly. "But what do you make of this — and of what happened in the theater the other night?"

"Nothing," said the Inspector. "It happens every now and then that some misbegotten crank takes it into his head to sneak about, poisoning his neighbors' pets because their barking annoys him. This can't have anything to do with the trouble in Bronxville — the phone exchange mentioned is in Brooklyn."

Miss Withers opened her mouth to say something, but closed it again as the office door opened and the uniformed man in the outer office ushered through a quiet gentleman who announced himself as Henry Neville, president of the Knickerbocker Kennel Club. He wore a pince-nez and a worried look.

"I'll wait outside," suggested Miss Withers. The Inspector said nothing, knowing full well that wild horses could not have dragged her from her chair. Neville looked at her through his glasses, and the Inspector motioned him to proceed. "This lady is my unofficial assistant, Miss Withers."

"Assistant!" muttered the school teacher indignantly. But Neville was getting right down to cases.

"Inspector," he began, "you may not be aware of the fact, but in the last six weeks more than a hundred dogs have been murdered within a radius of fifty miles of this city. This is not the usual matter of a neighborhood crank. With those the S.P.C.A. is quite capable of dealing. But these animals are mysteriously killed, sometimes in broad daylight, by a poison which leaves no traces that veterinary surgeons can discover in the stomach. Sometimes they are even stricken while being walked on a leash by their owners... "

"The Big Bad Wolf," said Miss Withers cryptically. She was listening eagerly.

"I came to you," Neville went on, "because I happen to know the chief of police in my home town, and he promised to use his influence."

"Yes," objected Piper, "but what has the Homicide Squad got to do with suburban dog poisoning?"

"The squad knows poisons," said Neville. "And this may not be a suburban matter very long. Three weeks from today we are holding, or planning to hold, the annual dog show of the Knickerbocker Kennel Club in Madison Square Garden. It has occurred to many of our members that perhaps this fanatic, who has largely confined himself to ordinary mutts on the street, may seize his — or her — opportunity to do wholesale murder among the thousand or so canine bluebloods that will be gathered there. I've talked to private detectives and found them totally incapable of protecting us and our exhibitors. So I ask your advice."

"Here it is," said Piper, biting his cigar. "Call off the show."

Neville shook his head. "Not as easy as that, Inspector. All over the country — in England, even — breeders of fine dogs are depending upon this show. Handlers and trainers, skilled men who sadly need the work, are beginning to train and condition the elite of dogdom for the bench. A booming dog show means increased business for the kennel men, who have been raising dogs mostly for the love of it these last years. It means that the public will be moved to invest a few dollars in a lifetime friend and companion when they're proud to be seen leading on a leash; it means —"

"You've got me sold," said Miss Withers softly, thinking of Dempsey.

"If we call off the show, it not only admits failure, it means disappointment, and worse, for hundreds," finished Neville.

"And it also means," the Inspector agreed, "that you'll be knuckling under to a madman who'll go right on murdering harmless, friendly pooches on the street."

"Blast him!" Miss Withers said fervently. Neville sensed an ally in this surprising lady.

"Hmm," said Piper. "I might detail a couple of plain-clothes men to cover your show. Or give you a squad of reserves to keep order, if need be."

"Excuse me a moment," broke in Miss Withers. "I've got a better idea even than that." Her angular face was alight, and her nostrils wider than ever. "Just suppose —"

For the next half hour the two men listened.

The Henry Neville leaped to his feet. "I'm convinced," he announced. "If you're willing to run the risk. Naturally, the Club will stand all costs." He scribbled an address on a card. "Send your dog to this man, and he'll put him in such shape that you won't know him." He paused — "I do believe that you're going to be our Guardian Angel, ma'am."

"With a guardian flatfoot or two in the background," amended the Inspector.

† † †

Miss Withers, out of breath from hurrying, showed her badge to the man at the door of Madison Square Garden, and was immediately admitted. It was not, this time, the borrowed badge of the New York detective squad, but only a brass-bound ribbon bearing the gilt letters "Owner."

There was a fair crowd passing in toward the amphitheater, and she followed where they led. Sounds of distant barking came to her ears, and in her nostrils was the pleasant mingled odor of disinfectants, sawdust, and canine personality that is so characteristic of a dog show anywhere.

The rows of seats in the Garden itself were more than half filled with spectators. Half of the big oval in the center was bare except for a small square platform where officials congregated — the rest of it was taken up by rows upon rows of high boxes with wire-screen fronts, placed like the houses and built-up blocks of a city. Indeed, this was a city — a veritable metropolis of dogdom.

An usher moved to direct her, but relaxed again when he saw her badge. Miss Withers passed down into the arena, and was almost immediately greeted by Mr. Henry Neville, resplendent behind a gold badge marked "President." He was in a highly nervous state, with his pince-nez slipping from his nose, but he left the group with which he seemed to be arguing, and joined her.

"Everything going well so far," he whispered quickly. "But I feel better now that you're here. We can't talk now — but we'll have a chat later on. Now go ahead and play the part. You're a fond owner, and your dog is in number — let me see — number 82. Excuse me, I have to see a man... "

He turned and bustled off. Miss Withers saw him seize the arm of a tall, saturnine person who looked like a character actor for British colonel roles. "See here, McGrath... " he began, angrily, and the two of them passed from sight. Miss Withers went on toward the kennels, trying to look as dog-wise as her fellows. She would have liked to stand in admiration before almost every one of the cages. But tonight she had other fish to fry. Whatever the villain of this place, it was not one of the bored, four-footed aristocrats behind the wire.

She passed on, trying to find number 82 without much success. She tried all the main avenues, growing slowly warmer, and then stepped into a little blind alley nearest the barrier that separated the seats from the arena, shut off from view of the crowd. This, too, was lined with wire-fronted boxes.

A dog ahead of her was barking furiously. She paused beside a small fat man in modish knickerbockers, who was engaged in staring through the netting of a cage almost at the end of the line.

He whirled toward her, and she found herself staring into a strange and tremendous instrument which looked like a twisted megaphone. The little man was smiling pleasantly.

"Did you speak?" he asked. He wore a badge similar to her own.

She shook her head. "I am slightly deaf," he continued. He put away the ear-phone. "But I read lips rather well. Beautiful animal, isn't he?"

She agreed that the beast inside was magnificent, in spite of the barking that assailed her ear-drums. The name on the card above the box was "Surefire Scout." He was a wire-haired terrier, this immaculate beast, and as she glanced at his eager face Miss Withers realized that her own poor Dempsey would look sad indeed beside such a perfect specimen of his kind.

Her companion was rattling on, evidently glad of somebody to talk to who did not interrupt. The dog behind the wire whined and cocked his head first to the left, then right, and Miss Withers noticed his eyes. Good heavens — this was Dempsey! Sure enough, the box bore the figures "82" — there was no mistake.

His furry hair had been plucked from his body except on face, forelegs and chest. He had been conditioned so far as to lose several pounds. His tail was held more erectly, his neck was upright at a strange and classic angle, and his ears hugged his skull as they had never done in real life. But it was Dempsey, all the same. For a moment the schoolteacher forgot her mission and rubbed the shiny black button of a nose that was pressed to the netting. "*Surefire Scout* indeed!" she said.

The little man was beaming. "And to think," he said bitterly, "that there are people in this world who can poison a little fellow like that!"

Miss Withers looked up suddenly. The man had voiced her innermost thoughts. Her companion pointed to the wire netting. "Ought to be glass," he said. "Why, any one of the thousands of visitors who walk past these cages could toss a bit of poisoned meat inside, and be on his way before the dog was dead."

She agreed that it was possible. The little man introduced himself as Peter A. Holt, of the Holt Color and Eye Works, Hoboken, and said that he was very glad to meet Miss Hildegarde Withers. "Now I've admired your dog, you'll have to have a look at mine," he said, leading her down the alley a short distance. "Devonshire Lad's his name."

Devonshire Lad was a collie, a great tan and white creature with a long, pointed muzzle. As his master approached, the collie looked up, and then dropped his head on his paws again.

Miss Withers praised him, but Holt shook his head. "I'm afraid Lad is out of his class here. You're going to be luckier than I. That terrier of yours ought to go into Winners. Yes, ma'am, I have an idea that the great Mr. McGrath will pin a red, or even a blue ribbon on that dog of yours."

"Oh, is he the judge?" Miss Withers asked, and could have bitten off her tongue.

"The judge? Of course he is. Why everybody knows that Andrew McGrath has judged terriers and Alsatians at every show in the last ten years." Holt stared at her not unkindly. "You must be as green at this as I. I've only had Lad a few weeks, and this is my first show, too. Don't be ashamed to admit it, we all have to start."

They were shoved aside by an incoming crush of visitors. A family stopped to admire the eager Dempsey, under his *nom de Guerra*, and then surged toward the bored collie, who finally condescended to approach the wire and permit his white muzzle to be touched by the smallest child.

"I'll see you later," said Miss Withers, into the gaping ear-trumpet. Then she passed on, leaving little Mr. Holt admiring his collie and gently whistling the universal tone of "The Big Bad Wolf."

She was looking for Mr. Neville, but he was not to be seen. Finally she asked someone, and was told that she might be able to find the president in the offices which were located down the runway and beneath the tiers of seats.

She found a door marked "office." Voices came from within, but there was no answer to her gentle knock. She pushed the door open, and saw a tableau which she was never to forget.

A whiskey bottle lay smashed and reeking in the middle of the floor. Beyond it two men were confronting each other, their faces almost touching. One was the quiet, mild-mannered Henry Neville, and the other she recognized as the colonel-ish man whom he had called McGrath.

"You can mind your bloody business," the latter was saying, in a voice that was like breaking sticks. "I'll do what I please."

"You'll make an effort to act like a gentleman," said Neville. "I've made all the allowances for you that I'm going to make. I don't care who you are, you'll conform to the rules of the Club... "

Miss Withers, as yet unnoticed, began to withdraw. But she still had time to see the larger man extend a mighty palm and press it full against the face of Mr. Henry Neville. He shoved — and the president of the Knickerbocker Kennel Club, dignity and all, went over backwards.

McGrath turned, and came out of the office, his face strangely contorted. He pushed past Miss Withers without seeing her, and she heard him utter, "Damn all dogs and fools who breed 'em!"

Miss Withers saw that this was not the time for her to have a chat with the pleasant Mr. Neville. She tiptoed softly back toward the amphitheater.

† † †

She spent the rest of the evening patrolling the avenues between the dog cages, keeping a sharp lookout for any signs of the mysterious murderer. The crowds were thick, and extremely innocent-seeming. She met several other owners and was inevitably introduced to their precious exhibits. Every time she passed the cage wherein her own Dempsey was confined, the dog forgot all the manners that had been impressed upon him in three weeks of rigorous training, and bounced up and down in eagerness to get out.

Closing time arrived, and she saw the odd little Mr. Holt saying goodnight to his collie who evinced no interest in his master. The crowd thinned out, and Miss Withers, glad that nothing had happened, moved toward the doors. She was intercepted by Henry Neville, whose face was very red, and whose lips were gray.

"Won't you come back to my office?" he invited. "Things seem to be going along quietly, except for a little trouble we're having with one of our judges. All the same, I'd like your ideas on the other situation."

He led the way back to the little office, which had been straightened since Miss Withers saw it last. The broken whiskey bottle was gone.

Miss Withers plunged at once into her own suggestion for safeguarding the situation, which was to have plate-glass installed instead of wire netting in all the cages. Neville seemed only half listening to her, but he shook his head. "Think of the cost," he said. "Besides, the public would object, and the owners be unduly alarmed at the necessity for the scheme."

The talk dwindled. Miss Withers looked at him, playing a wild hunch. "I wonder," she said, "if you'd tell me just what is the trouble in regard to Mr. Judge McGrath?"

Neville looked at her sharply. "Trouble? Nothing at all, really. The man is an excellent judge of dogs. His wife and he used to have a big kennel themselves, and he is the last word on disputed points. But he's taken to drinking himself to death, and it's bad for the Club. I wish we'd never hired the gentleman for this job ... There's plenty others who'd do anything to get in his shoes."

Neville shrugged his shoulders. "He'll probably be all right tomorrow, though. The judging starts at nine o'clock and terriers come first."

"I know that," said Miss Withers. "I was just wondering. Am I not likely to show that I know nothing of handling a dog when the time comes to lead Dempsey up to the stand? I'd like to take him myself, but still —"

"Simple enough," said Neville cheerily. He reached for a telephone on his desk. "The dogs have been fed and exercised by now, and I'll get one of the kennel men to bring your pooch in here, and demonstrate how you should act." He rattled the receiver, and got no answer. "Must be that the boys are gone for the night," he observed. "Wait here, I'll fetch him myself."

In something over ten minutes he was back, with a wriggling Dempsey under his arm. "It's almost pitch dark in there," he announced. "I had trouble getting the key to the boxlock. Somebody must have turned out the wrong lights."

He searched in his desk for a light whip-leash and loose collar, and the next half hour was spent in technicalities. Miss Withers learned facts which had already been well impressed upon her pet by the trainer in Westchester who had labored with him for weeks. Finally, Neville said that she would pass muster.

They went back into the arena, dimly lit by a cluster of tiny bulbs high in the ceiling. Far ahead of them exit lights gleamed dully, like evil red eyes in the gloom. As their eyes became accustomed to the darkness, they managed to make their way between the high-ranked cages, with Dempsey growling at every sleeping occupant. Finally they came to the last alley-way ...

Suddenly Dempsey wriggled out of his mistress' arms, and dropped to the sawdust. He plunged forward as if hot on the scent of something, and then stopped short, his legs braced wide and a salvo of barks issuing from his mouth. The noise died away to a nervous, unsteady whining. The hair on his back was bristling ...

"Who's there?" cried Neville.

Nobody answered. Dempsey huddled against his mistress' stocking.

Miss Withers produced a tiny affair of polished nickel from the depths of her handbag, and cast its beam ahead of them. The alleyway was empty. They went softly forward.

"Something is wrong here," Miss Withers decided suddenly. She sniffed, and found that there was an odd, sweetish bitterish odor above the smells of dog.

Something was very wrong. The two humans realized at last what Dempsey had known from the beginning — those eight cages contained the bodies of seven dogs. Some of them appeared to be sleeping, but it was the long sleep that knows no waking.

Neville was shouting for the night-watchman. "Clyde! Where are you?"

There was no answer. Neville pressed against the wire-netting which screened the nearest cage. "Dead — all of them, in torment! It's happened while we were wasting our time in the office. What insane devil out of hell could do a thing like this?"

Miss Withers did not think that his question required an answer. She was staring at Devonshire Lad, the big bored collie of which little Mr. Holt had been so proud. Devonshire Lad was only a tumbled pile of fur now.

Neville was still shouting for "Clyde." Finally there came an answering hail from the distance. But Miss Withers paid no attention to the breathless and perspiring night-watchman, when he trotted into the scene. She was watching Dempsey, who was walking stealthily forward, his nose pointed into the shadows beneath the cage of Devonshire Lad.

He was sniffing, and seemed to be stalking something. Miss Withers sent her flash ahead and saw what it was. The circle of yellow light fell upon the gaunt face of Andrew McGrath, reputed to be America's best judge of terriers. He was dead, quite dead. Clutched firmly in his right hand was a large bottle more than half full. Through the loose cork came the tell tale odor of bitter almonds ...

Neville was demanding to know where Clyde had been. "Didn't I tell you to keep your eyes open?"

"You told me to see to the doors, and that's what I was doing," said the old man belligerently.

"But the lights? They're supposed to be on all night. Who turned them out?"

"So help me," said the watchman, Clyde, "I thought you did."

Miss Withers, not without a qualm, put Dempsey back into his cage and snapped the lock. "Where's the nearest telephone?" she then demanded.

† † †

It was four o'clock in the morning when Miss Withers finally left the Garden. The Inspector's myrmidons had descended upon the place with flashlight powders, cameras, and fingerprint apparatus, but their general opinion was that they were wasting their time on a snipe-hunt.

Medical Examiner Bloom himself condescended to put in a brief appearance in full evening dress, and the wagon from the Department of Justice finally carried away the body of the dead man and the bodies of the seven dead dogs.

The Inspector led Miss Withers to a little all-night lunch counter on Eighth Avenue, and ordered ham and eggs and coffee for two.

"Don't take it so hard," he said. "You did all you could. But you were looking for an outsider and not a judge of the dog show himself."

"Oh, that," she said. Then — "Oscar, in spite of what Dr. Bloom says, do you believe that McGrath was the dog poisoner, and that he killed himself in remorse?"

"I'd like to know how you could give any other explanation," Piper retorted. "He had that bottle of prussic acid gripped in his hands, tight as a vice. No one could have put it there. Besides, with his wife dying a few months ago from blood poisoning that she got through the bite of a dog she was buying, he had reason enough to hate the whole canine tribe. Neville told me the whole story. Says that McGrath has been queer ever since the tragedy. Tonight he must have had one last orgy and then finished off himself." The Inspector looked pleased with such a facile explanation.

Then Miss Withers stuck a pin in his balloon. "You think that McGrath took a sip from the poison bottle, carefully recorked it, then died?"

"By George!" the Inspector wagged his head. "Cyanide of potassium, especially in liquid form as prussic acid, is the strongest and quickest known poison. He wouldn't have had time to recork it — a few drops on his tongue would have knocked him out." Piper stopped. "Yet, look here. Bloom swears that he doesn't need an autopsy to know that McGrath died from the stuff in that bottle."

"When you answer my first question," Miss Withers cruelly went on, "I wish you'd tell me how the poisoner got the dogs to come up to the wire netting and take a sip from his bottle, in the first place. He had no meat, nothing to dope with the acid... "

Piper shook his head. "Then it wasn't suicide. And we're right back where we started." He looked at the school teacher for guidance, which was unlike him.

Miss Withers was grim. "The dog show must go on tomorrow as usual," she insisted. "I'm going to have another try. I believe that a madman was loose in the Garden tonight and with nearly a thousand dogs gathered there, he won't be able to keep away. I think I'm beginning to see something, but I'm going ahead as planned. Do me a favor, and have the newspapers hush up this 'suicide' as much as you can."

He nodded, and went to the wall-telephone. He gave some instructions to his office, and then called another number. He listened for some time, and then came back. "Bloom and three assistants are almost finished with the autopsy on the stiff," he told the school teacher. "He says it's prussic acid all right. Each of the dogs had a trace of it around the mouth, but none in the stomach. The man must have choked to death on the stuff, for there's a good bit of poison in the nasal passages. Bloom says he never ran across that before. He still holds out for simple suicide."

"Things are seldom what they seem," quoted Miss Withers wearily. "I'm for home and bed. Tomorrow I've got to play a lone hand, and outbluff this murderer."

She was not so confident when, shortly before nine o'clock the next morning, she was back at the Garden, after a few hours of fitful slumber filled with dreams of the little dog Dempsey in which he wore a silk hat and drank prussic acid from a silver flask.

Yet he was safe and sound when she came to his lonely cage among the seven empty boxes. Indeed, he was carrying on a long-range verbal battle with a terrier somewhere in the next row — a dignified, nettled terrier whose deep growls befitted an aristocrat named Champion Million-dollar Highboy.

There were not many spectators at this early hour, Miss Withers noticed. What people there were had been firmly ushered to the front tiers of seats nearest the platforms, from which they could overlook the judging. A goodly crowd of owners and experts stood in a semicircle around the platform, evidently waiting for things to begin.

She had a look around for poor little Mr. Holt, seeking to commiserate with him for the loss of Devonshire Lad, but the man was not to be seen. Mr. Neville she noticed in the center or a circle of indignant dog-owners, and she heard him wearily explaining that the club had taken out insurance against just such a tragedy as had occurred last night, and that they would be reimbursed for the loss of their pets. She tried without success to catch his eye.

The work of judging terriers was beginning with a brisk, self-satisfied young man — somebody said his name was Kearling — as the substitute for the great McGrath. He looked extremely pleased with himself. "It's an ill wind that blows nobody good," she observed.

A trainer brought Dempsey to her, and the little dog looked the part of "Surefire Scout" for he had been well brushed, dusted with chalk, and otherwise prepared for the supreme test. Miss Withers took the leash, and wondered if, after all, she was really fooling anybody as to her real mission here. One after another she saw magnificent specimens of dogdom circle around the sawdust, mount the "bench," and come under the sharp eye and exploring hands of Judge Kearling.

Some he quickly motioned away, to be grouped forever among the goats. Others went into a smaller grouping, while Champion Million-dollar Highboy stood alone, sure of his blue ribbons and looking like a painted, calendar dog.

Her turn came, and in full view of the crowd Miss Withers led a sober and sedate Dempsey around a bit, and then to the bench. He was almost, but not quite, wagging his tail.

Kearling bent down, dictating swift, nervous sentences to an aide who kept score. He patted Dempsey's rump. "Stern, ten points," he said. "Hind legs, eight. Barrel and shoulders, nine. Ears —"

His practiced hands felt of the cocked ears, and Dempsey immediately forgot all that had been so patiently drilled into him. This was a very nice man, thought Dempsey, a man who smelled charmingly of dog. Rising swiftly on his hind legs, he licked Kearling across the face. The crowd gasped. It was as if a debutante being presented at Court had kissed the King.

Kearling jerked erect and frowned. He raised his hand and started to say the word "Disqualif —" But for some reason he thought better of it. He knelt again, avoiding Dempsey's friendly red tongue, and completed his examination. "Ears — zero, because surgically dropped. Skull, two points because of overwidth. Jaw..."

It was soon over. Dempsey went, as Miss Withers had feared, among the goats. Not even superb preparation and conditioning would conceal the fact — his skull differed tremendously from the narrow brain-pans of the over-bred elect. Surprisingly enough, the little dog seemed to realize the slight, and when the blue ribbon went to the bored and beautiful Champion Million-dollar Highboy he growled deep in his throat.

As required by rule, the judge passed cheerfully among the disgruntled owners, explaining his findings. When he came to Miss Withers he stroked Dempsey kindly. "I'd rather own him than the Champ," he comforted her. "But show dogs are being bred for narrow skulls, because they don't need brains."

"Do judges?" Miss Withers almost said aloud. She glared suspiciously at the brisk young man. Was his soft-soaping her an evidence of some feeling on his part that she was a person to be placated? Did he guess her real mission here? She remembered that Neville had said that there were those who would do anything to get in McGrath's shoes.

Miss Withers led a subdued little dog back toward his cage, as a procession of Aberdeens trotted forward to face the judge. She noticed that the Garden management, no doubt taking advantage of the smallness of the crowd at this hour, had set two singularly inept looking carpenters to work repairing a slightly damaged step leading to the tiers of seats.

As she entered the alley-way, she stooped short and very neatly disgraced herself by screaming. For one horrible moment she thought that her mind had given way and that she was seeing things — witnessing a ghastly repetition of the tragedy of the previous evening.

For Henry Neville was tearing down beneath the empty cage that was Dempsey's and dragging something forth from the shadows, just as the body of McGrath had been dragged only a few hours ago. Yet this was, at any rate, not a corpse.

It was Peter A. Holt, and the little manufacturer was spluttering and bubbling with wrath. "Take your hands off me! Let me go!"

Neville's glasses were slipping from his nose, but he was tightly holding on. Dempsey, who loved a fight of any kind, barked encouragingly and fought to get out of Miss Withers' arms. The two men stopped struggling, as they looked up and saw the spinster approaching.

The president of the Knickerbocker Kennel Club was rosy with triumph. "Got him!" he announced ungrammatically. "Here's the little rat who was lurking underneath your dog's cage — no doubt waiting for a chance to poison him, and complete last night's work."

Miss Withers frowned. There was more in this than met the eye. "Lucky you happened to be here," she said. "By the way, just how *did* you happen to be here?"

Neville flushed, but he still kept a grip on Holt. "Why shouldn't I be here? I was keeping an eye on the cages, just to make sure that nothing more went wrong. And I saw a movement under the cage."

Mr. Holt still clung to his ear-trumpet. "He's mad, mad as a hatter," he confided to Miss Withers, when he got a chance to speak. "Or else crazy drunk. And he has the colossal nerve to say that I was lurching!"

"Not lurching — lurking," repeated Neville angrily.

"He thinks you're the dog-poisoner," Miss Withers shouted into the ear-trumpet. Holt's round little face tightened.

"He thinks I'd kill my own prize collie?" The man laughed ruefully. "Then he *is* mad! Why, I came down here this morning and hid myself under the cage hoping to catch the person who was responsible for what happened last night. I thought he might come around again, and I'd nab him."

Miss Withers looked thoughtful, but Neville laughed jeeringly. "Yeah? Well, we'll just have in the police, and see what they find on you, mister."

Holt looked worried, for the first time. "If you cause me any unpleasant publicity," he promised, "I'll see that you have a lawsuit on your hands inside twenty-four hours. But if searching me is all you want, go to it here and now."

He held his arms away from his body. Neville searched him, wrathfully, and found nothing. There was no trace of anything that could have caused death to a dog or a human being.

Miss Withers remarked casually that something might have been dropped beneath the dog-cage. But Neville only drew another blank. There was no use going further.

He drew himself up stiffly. "Mr. Holt, I apologize most sincerely. But if you knew how the events of last night had worried and upset me... "

Holt took it well. He offered to shake hands. "I know," he said. "I felt the same way. Our intentions were both of the best."

Neville, still feeling embarrassed, rushed away to his proper place beside the judging stand, and Miss Withers drew a little nearer to the ruffled little manufacturer. He stroked Dempsey with a hand that trembled. "Nice fellow," he said. Dempsey seemed still subdued by the ill fortune that had attended his efforts at passing as a show dog. He drew away.

Miss Withers murmured proper condolences to the man who had lost his own pet. "I'll get the one who did it," promised Holt tensely, "if it takes the rest of my life. McGrath was no dog-poisoner, and he did not commit suicide. I know — he has been in the middle West judging shows for a month or so, and he could not have been responsible for the poisonings in the metropolitan area here. We must look closer to home."

Miss Withers spoke the word "Exactly" into his ear-trumpet.

"I was just thinking," said Holt. "Neville and McGrath have been at cats and dogs lately ... and they had a fight yesterday, so I hear. I wonder —"

So was Miss Withers wondering. She put Dempsey back into his cage, and carefully snapped the lock into place. According to her orders, a close wire screen had been tacked up inside the wide wire netting, and she knew that he was safer there than anywhere else in the building. Yet, somehow, she felt that she was doing the wrong thing.

She turned to Holt. "Going to keep on with the sleuthing?"

He nodded. "But not here. I've got a hunch — a real clue." He drew closer to her. "Is it true that you've got some connection with the police?"

"Er — yes, and again, no," she answered.

But Holt went on. "I know you have." He looked quickly around. "We may be watched. Meet me in Neville's office in five minutes and unless I miss my guess I'll be able to show you something that will surprise you!" The little man was quite evidently under the strain of intense excitement. "I see it!" he cried. "I see it all — will you help me?"

"I'd like to know what it's all about," said Miss Withers.

"I'll show you," he promised. "I'll convince you, sure enough."

"Very well," she spoke into the trumpet. "I'll meet you." The little man darted away, in the direction of the judging stand, and she watched through narrowed eyes while he engaged Kearling in close conversation.

Then Miss Withers walked slowly down the runway which led under the stairs toward Neville's office. The door was unlocked, but she did not enter. She stood thoughtfully outside for a moment, and then on a wild impulse turned around and hurried back whence she had come.

The thought had just occurred to her that perhaps, even behind the barrier of fine screen, Dempsey was not as safe as she had thought him. He had been trained never to take food from an unknown hand — but the little dog was most over-friendly with all humankind ... And suppose poisoned food was not the means used by the poisoner.

Miss Withers came scurrying past the rows of kennels, noticing as she came that not even a kennel boy or a handler was about. In the ring they were judging Alsatians, and everyone was clustered close to see the beautiful big tawny police dogs, with their wolf-like heads.

"Who's Afraid of the Big Bad Wolf —" Miss Withers found the silly tune running through her head. As she turned the corner leading to the alley-way in which Dempsey was confined, she stopped short, knowing the truth.

The whole puzzle arranged itself swiftly in her mind — even before she saw the little figure of Holt leaning against Dempsey's cage. His ear-trumpet was in his hand, and he was gaily whistling the little tune, as she had heard him whistle it before.

Terror gripped her as Holt looked up, with a wide smile on his face.

"Get tired of waiting?" he asked. "Something delayed me. I was just having a look around."

Miss Withers tried to control her face and could not. She stared at the wire, and saw that Dempsey stood watching her, wagging his tail. It had not happened — yet. Then she noticed that a tiny hole had been torn in the wire which protected the little dog.

Holt saw her glance turn in that direction, and he stopped whistling. "you noticed that, eh?" He came closer to her. "Too bad."

Miss Withers tried to scream, but as in a nightmare her voice failed her. Only Dempsey heard the gasp, and leaped frantically against his cage in an effort to come forth to the rescue.

Holt walked toward Miss Withers, who moved falteringly backward. She was out of the alley-way, crossing the main avenue of kennels. Here and there a dog, disturbed by currents which he could sense and not understand, whined a little.

She still moved away from that smiling face, from the hand that was sliding within the ear-trumpet. Then she found her back against a barrier.

Peter A. Holt, manufacturer of colors and dyes, drew a fat hypodermic needle from its place of concealment — within the ear-trumpet. "If you want to know who killed McGrath, go and ask him in hell," said the madman.

And still nobody came ...

Miss Withers gasped, and knew that he had been waiting for just that. He thrust the needle within a foot of her face, and his thumb touched the plunger ...

She waited for the thin, stinging stream of prussic acid to strike her face.

† † †

High on the steps leading to the rows of vacant seats above, a white-clad carpenter snatched from his tool-kit a pair of powerful binoculars. He handled them more cleverly than he had been using his saw and hammer.

"My God!" he cried. "What are you waiting for?"

His companion sighted along the barrel of a blue-black police target pistol, and pulled the trigger with a soft and loving squeeze.

A leaden bullet mushroomed against the madman's chest, and he was thrown back. He staggered, but did not fall. Nor did he lower the hypodermic needle, though his hand trembled.

He rammed the plunger home, with a wild shriek. But the delay had given Miss Withers time to regain her paralyzed senses, and to turn. She felt a thin splattering of liquid against her hair at the back of her neck. At the time she thought nothing of it, but as long as she lived she was to wear a bald spot there, as large as a dime.

The two erstwhile carpenters were racing over the sawdust, and they arrived on the scene to find both parties to this fantastic finale lying stretched out on the ground. Miss Withers regained control almost at once, to find Inspector Oscar Piper bending over her.

"I'm afraid I wasn't much of a success at playing a lone hand this time," she confessed weakly. "Oh, Oscar, why didn't you tell me that you were planning to double-cross me?"

The Inspector was surveying what was left of Holt, crumpled on the sawdust floor.

"Rotten shot," he said accusingly, to Detective-Sergeant Georgie Swarthout. "I told you to wing him, didn't I?"

"I aimed for the wing and got the wish-bone," said the young marksman cheerfully. "And I saved the State several thousands of dollars incidentally. Shall I ring up the boys at HQ?"

† † †

"Of course," said Miss Withers later in Neville's office. "I didn't have the wit to see that all the killings must have been done in some such manner. Only from a hypodermic needle could poison have been sprayed on all those dogs who have been killed during the past month or so. Remember how it happened in the theater — and yet nobody saw anything? Prussic acid is the only poison that can cause death that way when it touches the tongue or the nasal passages."

"The needle's been used by racketeers recently to spray acid through keyholes and thus to ruin clothes in rival tailor shops," Piper told her.

But she was proceeding. "Who but a maker of colors and dyes would have had access to unlimited amounts of prussic acid, which is the main ingredient of Prussian blue, as every schoolboy knows? Holt had such success with his poisonings in the streets that he got the idea of entering the dog-show as an owner, and bought his collie to carry out the illusion."

"How could he, if he hated dogs, as you say?"

"Well, he killed his own dog first. Psychologists call such men caniphobiacs, Oscar. McGrath must have come along and caught Holt in the act. They struggled, and McGrath got hold of the poison bottle from which the madman had been refilling his syringe. Holt saw he was getting the worst of it, so he pulled out his needle and sprayed cyanide in the other man's face. McGrath naturally gasped — and that did for him."

"That might explain the poison in McGrath's nostrils that puzzled Doc Bloom so much," agreed Piper.

"Of course. I should have guessed at the truth from the way Holt's dog ignored him. The beast was neither friendly nor afraid — he simply had never got acquainted with his master. Probably just purchased, before the show."

The Inspector was puzzled. "But why should Holt endanger himself by trying to continue today what he started last night?"

"He was mad, Oscar. Last night Neville and I came into the place talking, and our voices warned Holt away before he had time to do more than tumble the body of McGrath out of sight. He ran off and forgot his bottle of poison, so all he had was whatever was left in his syringe. He may have come back here looking for the bottle this morning. At any rate, he could not resist sending me on a fool's errand when he saw that I was interested in the case, and it must have appealed to a madman's sense of humor to think that while I waited for him in the office here, he was putting the finishing touches to my own dog. That would make his crimes dramatically complete in his warped mind."

Henry Neville knocked on the door of his own office, and entered with a glass of water for Miss Withers. She drank it gratefully.

"And all the time," the lady concluded, "there was a fine, fair clue staring us in the face. Holt carried an ear-trumpet but it was only to conceal the needle. He wasn't deaf, not very. For I heard him whistling, Oscar."

"Whistling?" Neville looked surprised. "I don't see —"

"Neither did I until it was too late," Miss Withers admitted. "But did you ever see a blind man using tobacco?"

The Inspector nodded. He guessed what she meant.

"They seldom do, because they can't see the curling smoke. Same reason — a deaf man *couldn't* hear himself whistle. All through this affair, something has been bothering me, and it was that. I made a mess of things, and you only saved my life by playing Sherlock Holmes and double-crossing me, Oscar."

Piper grinned. But Henry Neville looked very weary. The Inspector turned to him. "Well, you may rest easy now, my friend."

"Only because the show is over," confessed Neville. "There was no hushing up this second killing, even if it was to save a life. I've had to call off the last day of the show, and let the owners take their animals home. It's just as well. I'm going to take my own setters and go down to Maryland for a week's shooting. Anyway the poisoning scare is nipped in the bud."

"In the flower, rather," said Miss Withers. The Inspector led the way toward the kennels, where at last there was a scene of bustling activity. They collected Dempsey and crowded toward the doors, amid a throng of dog fanciers, each with one or more precious bluebloods at the end of a leash.

"Poor old Dempsey was out of his class," Miss Withers remarked. It was not exactly true. At that moment the pugnacious little terrier jerked his leash from the hand of his mistress and threw himself upon the nearby Champion Million-dollar Highboy, whom he set about whittling down to size.

They were dragged apart almost instantly, but Dempsey took his punishment without sadness, and capered cheerily homeward. He had bitten off about two thousand dollars worth of blue-ribbon dog flesh, and regained his self-respect.

The Riddle of the Forty Naughty Girls

The staccato roar of sub-machine guns rose to a deafening climax and then broke off short as down the deserted street there sounded the oncoming wail of the sirens. The mobsters turned and fled, the smoke of battle cleared, and Little Augie knelt alone on the sidewalk, clutching his vest.

Squad cars screamed to a stop beside him, pouring forth bluecoats. McKee was foremost. He knocked the empty gat from nerveless fingers. "I always said we'd nab you some day," he rasped triumphantly.

But Little Augie only grinned. "As usual, Copper, you're just too late." And he died.

As the screen went dark, the twelve men who had just crept into the orchestra pit struck up a few bars of "The Stars and Stripes Forever," and then without pausing broke into "Did You Ever See a Dream Walking?"

Footlights flared on, and the audience roused itself. All through the picture, which filled in between shows at the Diana, they had been drifting in by ones and twos. But the several hundred — mostly masculine — who made up the audience had not left the garish lights of Forty-second Street and paid their half dollars at the box office to see a movie.

It was the first day of a new show at the Diana Burlesque — its title was one of those Rabelaisian affairs designed to catch the masculine eye. Last week it had been something equally raucous, although except for the change in the big electric sign outside, few could tell the difference. Dapper Max Durkin, who acted as house manager of the Diana, often thought that the long hours he spent working out new gag titles was a waste of time.

He wasn't wasting his time now, though he lounged in the wings and idly watched the "Forty Naughty Paris Girlies" as they rollicked onto the stage in their opening dance number. He leaned forward and caught a ribbon which formed an essential part of the costume of a handsome, red-haired girl who was waiting for a cue.

It was the ribbon which, if tugged hard enough, would leave Janey Vere de Vere attired in little more than what she had first worn into the world. She whirled suddenly, drawing the ribbon from his fingers, and frowned.

"How about dinner and a little bottle of gin after the show?" he asked.

"Oh — it's you. Ask me later, will you? I — something's happened."

He saw that the big brown eyes were glazed with fear. "What? Spill it, girlie."

She came closer. "You've got to get me a new lock for my dressing-room door, Durkin. I tell you —"

"Lock? Say, what have you got that anybody could steal?"

"If you want to know, somebody got into my dressing room while I was out to dinner and stole a gun I kept in my trunk, and that's what!"

Still Durkin didn't see anything in this to upset her. "I'll buy you a dozen pop guns if that's all you're worrying about. Now listen, baby —"

His fingers caught the soft flesh of her upper arm. Then came an inopportune interruption. "Say, boss, what lighting goes with the cafe scene?"

The hulking, ape-like form of Roscoe, stage electrician, came between them. Durkin stared into the little pig-like eyes and wished for the tenth time that he had enough on this gorilla to fire him. "You know damn well it gets amber foots and a pair of baby spots from up above, why come busting —"

But Janey Vere de Vere was going out on the stage, as all twenty-four of the Forty Naughty Paris Girlies kicked their way off. Her hand was on her hip, and her throaty contralto voice picked up her song.

There was a little smattering of applause from the darkened house, for Janey was possessed of charms notable even among strip-artists, and she was a newcomer to the Wheel. She went into a slow hip dance as a purple spotlight struck her, body twisting, wide hips surging back and forth beneath the wispy evening gown of revealing black lace — one of those slashed affairs especially designed for dancing.

As the cash customers agreed later, Janey was at her best that night. Which showed that she was a real trouper, for the people backstage knew that she had something on her mind.

"What's eating Vere de Vere?" Durkin demanded of Murphy, a slapstick comic who approached in a costume composed of a silk hat and a long flannel nightshirt. "She looks scared of something."

"Her?" The comic grinned. "Must be she's scared of you, you sheik. Janey ain't used to this racket yet. She's been accustomed to better things, says she."

"Yeah?"

"Yeah. And she moves with a classy crowd, Maxie old thing. Why last week out in Brooklyn there was a dude in a tuxedo came into a box every night, just to see her act." The comic peered through the wings, past Janey's gyrating body on the stage, and squinted. "Say, it looks like the same guy — see him, alone in the right front box? Maybe it's him that she's scared of."

Max Durkin took a long greenish-brown cigar from among the half dozen which graced his vest pocket. Murphy also helped himself. "Thanks," he said. But the manager wasn't listening.

"So," he said. "Vere de Vere has got herself mixed up with the Park Avenue crowd. Somebody ought to do something about that."

"Maybe somebody will," agreed the comedian. "Me, I'd do anything short of arson if it would get me to first base with her."

He stared admiringly out onto the stage. Janey's song was only four minutes long, and at the first encore, when stage lights flared on, her costume was due to go off.

Durkin turned and went through the door, placed just beside Roscoe's switchboard, which led to the left side aisle and the front of the house.

At that moment Janey Vere de Vere, without breaking the pagan rhythm of her dance, began to fumble with the ribbon at the rear of her costume. A round knee and thigh began to disclose themselves. She was still singing — "... he may have the manners of a country lout, but who wants politeness when the lights are out? ... he's my —"

But that was all anybody was to see of Janey Vere de Vere's knee that night. Her song was interrupted by a tremendous bang! and a burst of flame which came from the left front box.

A woman screamed somewhere in the audience, and the acrid smell of powder drifted out over the house.

From somewhere came Max Durkin's voice. "Hit the lights!"

Then the crowd knew that this was not meant to be part of the show. "Roscoe, hit 'em!" shouted Durkin, from the aisle. "Everybody keep their seats!"

Still Roscoe fumbled with his switches, so that instead of casting a flood of brilliance over the auditorium, even the red exit lights went dark. Only the purple spotlight remained, slanting down from the film booth in the balcony. Janey Vere de Vere, her red mouth open wide, stood frozen in the center of the stage. The orchestra died away in a confusion of strings and brass.

Then the spotlight left the girl on the stage, sliding eerily past the white frightened faces of the girls who were crowding into the wings, sliding over the orchestra and the people in the front rows, and finally pouring its soft brilliance into the box from which the shot had come. But it stood empty and bare.

"House lights," roared Durkin again. This time the house lights came on. The audience straggled into the aisle, staring at each other and muttering questions. There was a long moment of this, and then the forgotten girl on the stage made a throaty, whimpering noise. She pointed — and then suddenly collapsed like a sack. But she had been staring at the right front box — the box in which a little man in a white shirt front was sitting, slumped down in his chair.

He was staring at the stage, but his stare was sightless — for everyone in the audience could see that there was a small round hole in the center of his forehead.

† † †

"Hell, on my first night off duty in three weeks," complained a bulky man who sat in the middle of the house. He forced his way to the aisle and ran back toward the rear of the house. "Leave nobody out!" he commanded as he ran past the ticket-taker. Then he went down the side aisle toward where Max Durkin stood. "I'm Fogarty, Eleventh Precinct!" he said. One hand was fingering his service gun. "How do you get into that box?"

There was a short flight of stairs opening from the aisle. Up these steps the two men plunged.

Except for four chairs and a litter of cigar and cigarette butts the box was empty. Patrolman John Fogarty bit his tongue as he saw, on the floor, a small calibre target pistol, with a long and wicked barrel. This he swiftly picked up with his handkerchief, and dropped into his pocket.

Then he whirled on Durkin. "You the manager? Who sat in this box tonight?"

Max Durkin shook his head. "Nobody. We don't have many customers for these dollar seats."

Fogarty was staring across the auditorium, in which the crowd still muttered and milled about, to where the man in the dinner jacket sat slumped in his chair with a hole in his forehead. "Well, you had one customer, while he lasted," said Fogarty grimly. "Come on."

They crossed the house. "None of you gets out of here, so you might just as well sit quiet," Fogarty told them. He climbed to the right front box, an exact duplicate of the one opposite, and bent briefly over the man in the tuxedo. He was a small, flabby man of perhaps forty, and there was no doubt at all that he would never grow any older.

"Croaked deader'n a codfish," pronounced Fogarty. That ended his sleuthing. He folded his arms and became a bulwark of the law. "You get to a phone and notify Headquarters," he commanded. "Scram, now." Max Durkin scrammed.

† † †

In a wide attic room at Centre Street, a sergeant leaned over a vast and glass-topped map of the city of New York. He chose a brass tag, read its number aloud, and turned it upside down to show that the car it represented was on a call.

Across the room another sergeant snapped a switch, and the place began to hum. "*Calling car eleven seventeen, car eleven seventeen,*" he said. "*Go to Diana Burlesque, Forty-Second near Eighth, Forty-Second near Eighth, code number five, code number five, that is all.*"

That was enough. The wheels of the world's second most famous murder machine had begun to turn.

Oscar Piper, gray and grizzled inspector of the Homicide Squad, climbed out of a green roadster perhaps twenty minutes later, and stared up with distaste at the flaring sign on the Diana facade. Then he stalked toward the theater entrance.

Inspector Piper was prepared for almost anything, knowing the setting. But he was not prepared to see the angular figure of Miss Hildegarde Withers before him. The meddlesome school teacher was engaged in a furious argument with the uniformed officer at the door.

"I tell you the show's over for tonight!" he was protesting.

"Young man, the show hasn't even begun!" Then Miss Withers saw the inspector, and brightened. Which was more than can be said for Oscar Piper.

"Hildegarde — how in blazes —?"

"Don't be profane, Oscar! I guess I can own a short wave radio set just like anybody else — and it was you yourself who told me what code number five means." She pointed to the brass buttons. "But this man won't let me in."

The inspector smiled wearily. "It's all right, she's my secretary," he told the guardian of the portal. That was the old fiction which had served so many times to cover the old maid school-teacher's meddling in crime investigation. They passed into the lobby, and Miss Withers wrinkled her nose at the mingled odors of humanity and stale tobacco.

Piper paused. "Now see here, Hildegarde —"

"I know. This is no place for a woman." Miss Withers pointed with the handle of her umbrella toward the stage, where were grouped most of the scantily-clad ladies of the ensemble. "All the same, there are a number of women here beside myself. Perhaps I'm not dressed for the party, but —"

The inspector was already half-way toward the right lower box, where detectives and photographers were grouped around the assistant medical examiner and his grim *piece de resistance*. Taking his silence for passive permission, Miss Withers hurried in his wake.

"Hello, folks," Dr. Levin greeted them. "Nice business, this. You can move him whenever you like." He scribbled an order. "Nice shot — smack on the frontal ridge. Slug is still in him — we'll find that it came from the little .32 the boys found in the opposite box. He went out without knowing what hit him."

Piper scrutinized the revolver, and Miss Withers peered over his shoulder. "Prints?"

"Not a print," he was told. "One shot fired."

The inspector broke the gun, and sniffed. "Old-fashioned black powder, eh? That ought to give us a line." He dropped the gun into his pocket and leaned over the dead man. "Got any dope on who he is?"

Cards in the dead man's pocket informed them that his name was David M. Jones, proprietor of the Loop Autosales Agency, Chicago. "I know that place," cut in a sergeant. "A half a block of show windows near Halstead Street. Probably in town for the auto dealers' convention — Say, this is a bigger case 'n I thought."

"Yeah," agreed Piper. "Get the manager of this place up here." He drew Miss Withers into the rear of the box, where hung a heavy pair of ancient red plush curtains. "Well, here's a shot fired in front of several hundred people, and we can't get a lead. The opposite box was empty — so anybody on that side of the audience could have sneaked up there and fired the shot, and then got back to his seat before the lights went on. Ditto, anybody backstage could have sneaked through the door and got back the same way —"

She nodded. "You've narrowed your suspects down to just about everybody who was here tonight, haven't you?"

"Everybody but the girl who was wiggling on the stage when the shot was fired," said Piper sadly. "And she's —"

He broke off as Max Durkin appeared. "Look here, inspector," began that worthy gentleman. "Isn't there some way you can fix it to let the audience out of here? We can't keep them here all night... "

"*We* can't, but I can," said Piper. "I've got something to ask you. Do you keep a gun in the theater?"

Max Durkin denied that the Diana Burlesque had ever needed such a protection.

"Well," said Piper, "Anybody else in the theater pack a rod?"

Max Durkin shook his head. "As far as I know, nobody in the place ever owned a gun." But Miss Withers' noticed that his eyes blinked twice before he spoke. There were few better signs that a man was lying.

"Excuse me," she cut in, "but from what I hear, Mr. Durkin was somewhere in the opposite aisle when the shot was fired from the box. You didn't hear anyone pass you in the darkness?"

"I was practically in the front of the house," cut in Durkin. "When I heard the shot I ran back. I thought — I thought somebody had shot the girl on the stage."

"*Did* you?" smiled Miss Withers in her usual sweetly sarcastic tone.

The inspector, who had turned his back for a moment, held out his hand. "Thank you for your help, Mr. Durkin."

Instead of a friendly grasp, the manager felt his wrist caught and held. A wet swab of cotton was pressed swiftly against his index finger. "What the hell —"

Piper smiled. "It's all right. I just made sure that you hadn't fired the shot yourself. A solution of sulphuric acid and waxed diphenylamine crystals brings out the nitrate flecks — if there are any. You don't happen to have a pair of gloves here, do you?"

Durkin shook his head. "Search the place if you want to."

"We did," Piper told him. "Well, we're right back where we started. You can go now."

† † †

Max Durkin departed, and the inspector turned to Miss Withers. "Well, that's that —" But he was all alone.

He caught sight of the resolute figure of the school teacher going up the aisle, and hurried after her. "Wait a moment — what do you know that I don't?"

"Nothing — yet," she snapped. "Suppose we have a look at the box from which the shot was fired."

Together they climbed the stairs, and Miss Withers turned up her nose at the untidy condition of the box. "Sherlock Holmes would have told you the middle name of the killer just from one flash at those cigarette butts," said Piper. "And ten to one they mean nothing more than that the boys up above in the gallery use this as a target. Come on, let's get backstage. I haven't had a talk with the cootch dancer yet, and you'd better come along as a chaperone."

They descended to the aisle and walked forward through the little door which led past the switchboard. "Hm," observed Miss Withers. "If anybody from among the performers did the murder they'd have had to walk right past the electrician."

The inspector nodded. "But it's no help, unfortunately. Because he admits that, being soft on this Vere de Vere dame, he was watching her strip-number from the wings instead of being at his board."

"And that's why he was so long in putting on the house lights?"

The inspector shook his head. "He claims that somebody screwed up his switchboard by dropping a piece of tin behind it and shorting the wires. It took him time to get his flashlight and lift it out."

Miss Withers digested this as they walked through the weary crowd of show girls — in temporary guard of two delighted detectives — and down to the basement dressing rooms.

There was a cop on duty outside the door. "She's still under," he informed them. "Must have been a terrible shock to her."

"Yeah?" Piper pushed open the door. The dressing room was small and stuffy, holding little more than a stool, a bench, a mirror and a coat rack. The voluptuous figure of Janey Vere de Vere lay stretched out on the bench, which had been padded with her coat. Beside her sat the ministering figure of Murphy, the comic, still attired in his nightshirt costume, over which he had thrown a topcoat. He held a glass which was half full of something which looked like water and smelled like juniper juice.

"You're the guy who caught her when she fainted on the stage?"

The comic nodded. "Ran out from the wings. Y'see, we're engaged to get married, and I got a right here."

"Yeah? Well, did she say anything as she fainted? Did she cry out?"

Murphy shook his head. "Nothing... "

"Except what?" prompted Miss Withers, on a hunch.

"Except she said something, sort of mumbling, about — 'My husband!' " He put down the glass. "But that don't mean anything, because she's been divorced for years."

Piper leaned over the prone figure. "Out cold, eh? Well, she certainly can't help us any... "

"Neither can Mr. Murphy, right now," suggested Miss Withers. The inspector took the hint. "Outside," he ordered. The comedian went out.

"It's more than an hour since the shot was fired," Miss Withers pointed out. "It's a long faint that lasts an hour."

Piper snapped his fingers. "Right! Say, that's one of the reasons we knew Ruth Snyder was lying. She claimed to have stayed in a faint all night. You think —"

"She's either dead, or —" Miss Withers took up the glass of gin, and suffered a few drops to trickle down the arched nostril of the girl on the bench.

Janey Vere de Vere was not dead. She sat up, coughing and gasping wildly. "What — where am I?"

"You're in a bad spot — unless you tell us plenty," said Piper gruffly. "What do you know about this?"

Janey Vere de Vere blinked. "About — about the shooting? I only know that I used to be married to him. I mean Davey. I still am, I guess, because they tell me those correspondence Mexican divorces aren't legal. But I hadn't seen him for four years until I saw him with that black hole in his forehead — I mean, not seen him really —"

Miss Withers gave her the gin. "Steady, young woman," she advised.

"I'll talk," the girl hurried on. "I'll tell you everything. I walked out on Davey, and I wrote him that I had a divorce. Then I found that it was a phony, and the lawyer took my money and didn't even register the papers in Mexico City. So I wrote Davey, and he was sore. He came to New York and all last week he sat every night in a box and just stared at me — I was afraid of him, and I got a gun that I'd had for years, and kept it in my dressing room. Tonight while I was out to dinner it was stolen —"

"This the gun?" Piper showed her the .32. She nodded, without being able to speak. "Got a permit?" She pointed toward her handbag.

"You usually go to dinner while the moving picture is being run?" inquired Miss Withers. Janey Vere de Vere nodded.

"Who do you think might have known that you kept a gun here?" She shook her head. "The lock on my dressing room door is broken. I told Durkin about it tonight, when I told him the gun was gone. But he didn't —"

Miss Withers and the inspector exchanged a glance.

"Well, we've got to be getting on with it," said Piper. "You better stick around, young woman. Don't leave town. By the way, you haven't any idea of any enemies your late husband had — anybody who might have wanted to see him bumped off?"

"Nobody in the world," said Janey Vere de Vere. But she looked intently at the buttons of the inspector's vest when she said it, and Miss Withers made another mental note.

† † †

They went out of there. Piper called his myrmidons. "As soon as you finish searching the audience and get the house cleared out, go backstage and give everybody the nitrate test — on both hands. We ought to get a positive reaction or two."

To Miss Withers: "Funny about the old-fashioned black-powder cartridges in that gat. They haven't been on sale since smokeless powder caught on. Looks like the girl had been sitting on that gun for years and years."

"She didn't sit on it quite long enough," Miss Withers told him. There were sounds of violent trouble behind them, and both ran across the stage. An ape-like figure in overalls, with long swinging arms, collided suddenly with the inspector, and both went down.

"Got you!" cried Piper. He rose with a hammer-lock on Roscoe, the stage electrician. Miss Withers looked surprised.

The man ceased to struggle, and stared at his forefinger. It was rimmed with black. He gasped and muttered.

Detectives surrounded them, and someone slapped handcuffs on Roscoe. "A *positive*, the first crack out of the box," somebody said. "Here's the rat that fired the gun. He hit McMann over the head with a slug... "

"I tell you I went to a shootin' gallary during the dinner hour tonight!" Roscoe was insisting. "I only shot at the brass ducks —"

Nobody listened to him. The detectives had torn from his pocket the "blackjack" with which he had sent into unconsciousness the sergeant who daubed diphenylamine on his finger. It happened to be a neo-Maxim silencer.

"Well, for the love of —" Inspector Oscar Piper straightened his tie. "There's our case, boys. Roscoe what's-his-name — sweet on the cootch dancer — bumped off her husband when he got the idea that she might go back to the guy. He'd probably hopped — but he was smart enough to have a silencer handy in case things didn't work out right for popping the guy otherwise. Take him away."

He turned to Miss Withers. "As easy as that!" he said. But the look on her face sobered his joy.

"Suppose," she said softly, "suppose that Roscoe is telling the truth?" Suppose he spent his dinner hour at the shooting gallery across the street? Where's your case?"

"Suppose the moon is made of Camembert?" retorted Piper. All the same he turned to his men. "Go on, give the nitrate test to the rest of the performers. Just in case somebody asks. But it's the ape, all right."

He saw that she frowned. "Well, why else should he have a silencer? They don't carry them for pocket luck-pieces, you know."

"I know," said Hildegarde Withers.

"He was going to use the silencer, and then he got a better idea. He'd shoot Jones from the box, with the house lights off, and then get back to his board and give himself a swell alibi, see?"

"I see," said Hildegarde Withers. "I see, said the blind man, I see clearly. By the way, Oscar, where's the stage door?"

They discovered that the Diana, like many theaters on crowded and alley-less Manhattan Island, had no regular stage door. The performers left and entered the place through the side aisle down to the front of the house.

A few minutes later Sergeant Twist reported that the performers had a clean bill of health as far as the nitrate test was concerned. None of them had fired a gun within forty-eight hours. "We even tested the dame who's downstairs in the dressing room," Twist reported.

"See? I told you so," said Inspector Piper. Miss Withers nodded.

"I'll be back in a minute," she said. She hurried downstairs and knocked on Janey Vere de Vere's dressing room. The girl was smoking a cigarette, having dressed for the street. "I just thought," said Miss Withers. "Wasn't it in an act — a dancing act — at the Palace that I saw you?"

Janey Vere de Vere confessed that she had never risen in vaudeville to the heights of the Palace. "More likely the Hippodrome," she said.

"It must have been two other fellows," Miss Withers agreed, and took her departure. She came out on the stage fired with a new energy. "Shall we leave, Oscar?"

"See you out front," he said. "I've got to have a word with the manager if I can find him. I want some more information about this electrician."

But it was Miss Withers who found Max Durkin. He was sitting in his office, which opened off the foyer, glaring morosely at his smouldering cigar.

"Bad for business, this sort of thing," he told her.

"I've got just one question," she told him. "About the gun. You're sure that you never saw it before, and that you never knew of anyone in the theater owning one — or losing one?"

"Positive!" said Max Durkin. "And if anybody says anything different they're lying."

"Thank you so much," said Hildegarde Withers, and left. Durkin stared at his empty ash-tray, and then at the floor.

"Hey!" he began, but the school teacher was gone. Max Durkin shook his head. "That woman is either nuts, or else —"

Then the inspector arrived to tell him that his presence would be required at headquarters next morning. Durkin agreed with a willing smile. "But I still don't see why poor old Roscoe would run wild —"

"You can't fool the nitrate test," Piper told him. Then he was gone.

Janey Vere de Vere came up the aisle beside Murphy, in the center of a crowd of relieved and still excited girls. She saw Durkin in the office door.

"Wait outside, will you?" she asked the comic. He protested, and finally drew away a little. The red-haired girl, looking a little bulky and big in her street clothes, crossed to where Durkin waited.

"How about dinner and a bottle of gin?" he asked, grinning.

"Max! After all that's happened —"

"It's over, and you're well out of it," he said. "Never mind Murphy. You've got eight more weeks of the Wheel to eat with him, but you're only here till Sunday."

"Yes," said Janey Vere de Vere. "But —" She wore one glove, and dug in the pocket of her modish sport coat for the other. "Say! I've dropped a glove somewhere... "

Durkin stared at her. "It's probably the old dame who hunts with John Law," he said lightly. "She just hooked one of my cigars — a lighted one. I figure her for a souvenir-hunter. Did she get any fillings out of your teeth?"

But Janey Vere de Vere wasn't listening. "See you tomorrow, Max," she told him, and hurried out. Max Durkin lit another cigar, and then he too left the darkened theater to its guardian cops. He had no appetite for his usual late supper that night, for an idea had just begun to occur to him ... an idea which spoiled the taste of his cigar.

† † †

Miss Hildegarde Withers rode northward in a taxi which she shared with the inspector. "A pleasant and illuminating evening," she said, as they drew up to her door. It was barely eleven o'clock.

"If you're not too tired, Oscar," she continued, "I wish you'd do something for me. You have your travelling laboratory kit at home, have you not?" She handed him a parcel wrapped in a sheet of newspaper. "Suppose you give this your famous nitrate test, and let me know how it comes out?"

"What? Why, of course, but —"

Miss Withers slammed the door and went up the stairs. "If that doesn't put a bee in his bonnet nothing will," she said to herself. Lighting the lamp above her study table, she proceeded to arrange upon it a surprisingly incongruous exhibit consisting of half a dozen cigar butts.

For a long time she stared at them. They ought to make sense, but they didn't. At the extreme right she placed the fresh green-brown cigar, its tip barely burned away, which she had stolen from Max Durkin's ashtray.

The relics which had been left in the littered theater box she one by one discarded. Only one of them showed any trace of dampness where it had been chewed by the smoker. Surprisingly enough this one — like Durkin's — had been cut, rather than bitten off, and it was rolled of the same green brown tobacco as the first.

Yet there was little more than a quarter of the cigar remaining — instead of ash on its end there were only shreds of blackened and acrid smelling tobacco.

"In the best tradition of sleuthdom," she told herself. "Sherlock Holmes could spot a *Trichinopoly* miles away, and he published a monograph on heaven knows how many kinds of cigar ash. Now I wonder what Holmes would deduce from this?"

For nearly an hour she puzzled over the two remnants of cigars, all the time listening with one ear for the buzz of the telephone. If Oscar Piper found what she expected him to find, he would lose no time in communicating with her. His case was going to be sent sky-high, or else she was very much mistaken. All the same it was still a mystery to her how a person could manage to be in two places at the same time.

The night was a hot one, and Miss Withers mopped her face. Through the open window little black gnats came to buzz around her lamp. Though a fly swatter and an insect-gun stood nearby on the sideboard, the lean and worried school teacher pored over her booty and let the gnats buzz.

"I wonder why Oscar hasn't let me know how he came out with his nitrate test?" she finally asked herself.

It was at that moment that her bell rang — three long impatient rings.

Miss Hildegarde Withers lived at that time in an old-fashioned brown stone on West 74th Street, remodelled from one of the mansions of the eighties. She hurried to the door and pressed the buzzer which unlatched the downstairs door. There were hurried steps on the stair — and she nodded to herself. The Inspector had come instead of phoning.

"He's found it!" she cried ...

†††

When Oscar Piper arrived, shortly before one o'clock, at Miss Wither's apartment he peered eagerly from the taxi window. Yes, her light was on and he could bring her the news without being inopportune. He hurried into the lobby, pressed the bell beneath her name, and finding the door ajar, ran up the stairs.

He knocked excitedly on the door. "It's me, Hildegarde!"

There was a long pause, and he knocked again. Miss Hildegarde Withers, her long Bostonian face unusually grave, swung open the door. He displayed "exhibit A," and then stopped short as he entered the room and saw that a handsome red-haired girl was sitting in a chair near the window.

"Miss Vere de Vere —" he began.

"Nobody else," she said evenly. "I believe you have my glove."

He was holding it in his hand. "I —"

"Oscar," said Miss Withers quickly. "I'm afraid you and I have been making a grave mistake about Miss Vere de Vere. Circumstances —"

"Circumstances fiddlesticks," said the inspector, bracing his feet. "I gave this glove the nitrate test for powder marks — and look at it." There was nothing to look at until he turned the glove inside out, and then the forefinger bore a telltale brown stain.

"You fired a gun in the last forty-eight hours," he accused the girl who watched him so calmly. "Fired it while wearing your glove inside out. Never figured we'd be smart enough to try it both ways — even though you had read of this nitrate test."

"You're crazy," said Janey Vere de Vere. "I've got five hundred witnesses that I was doing a dance on the stage when my husband got bumped off. You can't bust that... "

Piper thought he could try. But he suddenly realized that the red-haired girl was covering him with a gun which peeped over the arm of her chair. He suddenly understood Miss Withers' hesitancy in opening the door, and the look on her face ...

"You can't get by with this," he said.

"One way or another," said the girl. "Don't forget I learned to shoot in a Wild West show, and I can cut the buttons off your vest. I came here to get my glove. It's my property."

"And the cigar — you'd like that, too?" Miss Withers hazarded. She nearly got a bullet through her mouth.

"You'll clown once too often," said the girl. She had risen in her chair. "I'll bargain — that glove for both your damn lives. How about it?"

"Clowning!" repeated Miss Withers, foolishly. "*Clowning.* That's it! That's —"

"Shut up!" snarled the red-haired girl. She looked her age now. "Sure I killed Dave Jones. He was a rotten husband, and I left him because I wanted to show him I could get somewheres in show-business. I got into the Follies, too — and then times got bad and I had to take this burlesque job. He found out about it, and came to New York just to sit in a box and give me the ha-ha. But it wasn't his auto business nor his lousy insurance I wanted, see?"

She left off her hysterical outburst, and her mouth closed like a trap. "I take that glove with me, or I leave two more stiffs here," she said. "Without it you'll never pin anything on me. Not with my alibi anyhow."

Piper was waiting his chance, poised on his toes. But the hard brown eyes never wavered, and the gun still swung between the two of them.

† † †

For all the inspector's poised readiness, it was Miss Withers who acted. She suddenly broke into shrill, high-pitched laughter. Head thrown back, eyes wild, she screamed mirthlessly.

"Shut up, or I'll —" Janey Vere de Vere backed away from the inspector, watching his every move. "If she goes nutty I'll have to knock her out... "

Miss Hildegarde Withers gave every evidence of having gone completely insane under the strain. Her laughter choked off, and her eyes followed a single black gnat which circled around the overhead lamp.

"Hildegarde!" cried the inspector. He knew that her brain had snapped, for she had picked up the flit-gun from the sideboard, and was threatening the gnat with it.

"Go away, you nasty thing!" Then more hysterical laughter ...

"By God," cried the amazed girl who held them at bay, "I'll —"

She said no more, for a stream of murky white liquid struck her full in the face. The revolver fell from her fingers as she clawed at her eyes in agony.

The inspector snatched it up. But Miss Withers still pumped the flit-gun.

"Ammonia," she told the inspector. "Think she's had enough?"

Janey Vere de Vere's voluptuous big body was huddled in a shuddering heap on the floor. The room was thick with the strong astringent.

"Cease firing," said Oscar Piper.

† † †

It was hours later, and dawn brightened in the sky over Brooklyn, when they finally were alone again. The inspector was still weak in the knees, and Miss Withers was halfway between tears and laughter — genuine laughter this time.

"I'm a rotten actress," she confessed. "But the Vere de Vere woman had her attention divided between us."

"Bother that," said Piper. "Start at the beginning. I'm hours behind you."

"Nice of you to admit it," said the school teacher. "Only you're weeks, not hours. You see, Janey was ashamed of her job in burlesque, even though she was good at it. It was particularly tough for her, in spite of the admiration she got from the men who recognized something better in her than the usual strip-artist, when she saw that her husband, from whom she had separated but not legally divorced, had come to give her the laugh. She suddenly remembered that he had property and insurance — and she wanted to get out of the racket she was in.

"Well, she started in a Wild West show, you know. She must have clung to one — no, two — of the guns she'd used in a shooting act. She got a silencer, and attached it to her .32, which was still loaded with ammunition of the old type. Last night she came back from dinner, saw that her husband as usual was alone in an opposite box, and shot him through the forehead during the wind-up of the gangster picture. There was noise enough then so nobody would notice the tiny spat that a silenced gun makes. She took the silencer off the gun, still wearing her gloves inside out as an extra-smart precaution, and left the gun in the box. That was to make it look as if someone had planted it to point to her."

"But the second shot —"

"Wait. The house was dark for the movie — but she was a crack shot. The dead man slumped in his seat, and wasn't noticed by anyone. Just as she'd planned. She hurried backstage, dropped the silencer behind the switchboard — that was the 'piece of tin' that poor Roscoe removed and put in his pocket — and after changing into her costume came upstairs again and planted with Durkin the story of her gun's having been stolen.

"She knew the gun could be traced to her. She wanted to be involved — because she knew her perfect alibi would free her. She didn't mean the silencer to be found, but then she was ignorant of the switchboard. It all worked out better than she had planned, and while she was in her dance, the audience heard the sound of a shot in the box from which she had already killed a man. That puzzled me for a long time, Oscar. I brought home a cigar stub trying to find out if perhaps Durkin had not, after all, fired the shot and accidentally dropped a cigar butt, incriminating himself. There was a cigar butt in the box, still damp, which matched his. But he had not left it there. Just as I stole out from his office, Janey Vere de Vere got hold of one he'd smoked. I saw the whole thing when she accused me of 'clowning'! Don't you see — practical jokers and would-be clowns have used exploding cigars for years."

"You mean she left a *trick* cigar burning in the box?"

Miss Withers nodded. "She must have timed it by trying experiments at home. She put in a much bigger load than the usual trick cigar has. Probably she used powder from her old cartridges, for the cigar butt smelled faintly of it. The cigar went off, the lights went on, and she pointed at the box to make sure that the fake shot and the dead man would be connected. No medical examiner in the world can set a death closer than twenty minutes or so, and it was certain the stunt would take in the doctor and the police.

"Thus, when the 'shot' went off, she was under the spotlight. She had to have an alibi like that, because she was the natural person to be suspected and she knew it. There would be nothing left to show in the box except the cigar butt — and I suspect that she had sense enough to strew several there so it would not stand out."

Piper nodded slowly. "Then Roscoe was an accomplice? Because he must have seen her come through the door after she fired the real shot."

"Not a bit of it. It was during the movie, when he was off duty. When he was across the street at the shooting gallery, as a matter-of-fact. The cigar burned quietly for ten or fifteen minutes — it wouldn't go out, particularly if she had remembered to sprinkle a faint bit of powder in with the tobacco when she rewrapped it"

The Inspector heaved a sigh. "Good heavens, what a woman!" He was not praising Miss Withers. "One thing," he asked finally. "Why did Max Durkin deny that she had mentioned her gun's being stolen?"

Miss Withers smiled. "Simple," she said. "Durkin was sweet on her, and only trying out of loyalty to keep her name out of it. He was positive, like everybody else, that she was innocent because of that perfect, cast-iron alibi. The alibi was so cast-iron I couldn't resist trying to crack it."

"You nearly cracked me with that scene in your apartment," he admitted. "I thought you had gone clean crazy with the flit-gun... "

"An invention of my own," she admitted proudly. "Heaven knows I need some protection now that I'm mixing myself up continually in other people's business. And I can't abide guns. *I* didn't get my start in a Wild West show, you see."

The Inspector was thinking of Janey Vere de Vere. Miss Withers stared at him, coldly. "Oscar! Don't start admiring the woman. It will make it all the harder for you to send her to the electric chair."

He smiled. "The chair? With her brains and her looks? You don't know juries, my dear Hildegarde. They'll never give her a death sentence."

But a chill March evening, nine months and five days later, showed Miss Withers was right, as usual.

The Riddle of the Hanging Men

History was changed, and the city of Rome saved, by the screaming of a flock of geese. Therefore it was in the best of tradition that the entire course of Miss Hildegarde Withers' life was altered by a turkey.

The turkey was dead and roasted, and it reposed in the show window of Pugh's Star Delicatessen on lower Sixth Avenue, New York City. At two o'clock of a soggy September morning, Patrolman John Duncan came along the avenue, swinging his nightstick. He looked in the delicatessen and saw the turkey in question. With the keen eye of one ambitious to become a plainclothes detective, Patrolman Duncan likewise noted, in the full glare of the lighted show-window, that the turkey was being rapidly devoured by a large and apparently very hungry tortoise-shell cat.

There was nothing unusual in old Pugh's keeping open until two in the morning, for much of his business came in the shape of late calls for sandwiches from the big apartment houses of lower Fifth Avenue, one block to the eastward. But it was unusual to see the best behaved cat on Duncan's beat thus engaged in open unabashed felony. The young cop struck the window with his night-stick, but the cat only eyed him insolently and went on voraciously chewing turkey.

The cop opened the door and yelled "Hey!" but nobody answered. Slowly Duncan went on back through the shop, past counters loaded with cold meats and canned delicacies. He was eager, alert — filled with a strange certainty that something was up.

He came into the rear room, where a door stood slightly ajar admitting the moist September air mingled with odors typical of a Sixth Avenue alley. Slowly the alley door swung shut, as if closed by the wind. But Duncan had no eyes for the alley door and whatever dark secrets might be concealed in the shadows beyond. He was staring through the glass door of the big refrigerator room at the face of Herman Pugh.

It was greenish-black, and unpleasant in the extreme. This was caused by the fact that Pugh, along with numerous hams and dressed poultry, hung by his neck from a hook in a high oak beam.

Anybody could see that the man was dead. But Duncan had been trained to seek confirmation of first impressions. He had his knife out in a moment, and slashed the necktie which served as a noose. He eased the body down to the floor, and then dragged it out of the icy chill of the cold room.

Then he freed the neck from its tight band, and attempted brisk artificial respiration. After a moment he realized that he had come in time. The horrible grayish-green had ebbed from the face of the delicatessen keeper, and his heart pumped very faintly ... erratically ...

Duncan knew his instructions. This was a case for the emergency squad. Leaving Pugh where he lay, the young cop hurried into the front of the store and snatched up the telephone.

It was a dial phone, and in his haste the young officer twice put his large forefinger in the wrong hole. Then he got through to Spring 7-3100, and gave his message. "Emergency squad and pulmotor — ambulance — precinct notified —"

Then John Duncan went back to the man whom he had rescued. He had not been gone more than six or seven minutes at the outside — but Herman Pugh, whom he had left sprawled out on the floor in a death coma, had completely disappeared.

The alley door was open again, and Duncan ran to it and cast his flash into the areaway. It was empty and deserted.

"Well, I'll be —"

Whatever Patrolman Duncan may have been about to say was forever lost as he happened to glance toward the refrigerator. Through the glass door he could see the contorted face of Herman Pugh, greenish black again. The incredulous young officer clutched the cold-room door with trembling fingers, and saw that the man hung from a hook in the high oak beam by his necktie — which had been neatly tied at the point where his knife had cut it!

There was now not the slightest doubt of the fact that Herman Pugh was thoroughly and completely dead. Duncan drew his gun, and made a cautious but thorough search of the place. He hadn't the slightest idea what he expected to find, but he found nothing. Then he sat down on a tin cracker box, and chewed his finger nails until the squad car arrived.

† † †

Men piled out, bearing pulmotors, clinical teeter-totters, oxygen tanks. A gray old man with the stripes of a Captain waved them back. He was staring through the glass of the ice-box door.

"Lord God Almighty!" he breathed. "Another one!"

Grizzled Oscar Piper, Inspector of New York's Homicide Squad, chewed savagely upon an unlighted cigar as dawn began to show itself that morning. He stared at a typewritten sheet which a sleepy desk sergeant had just placed before him.

"Nord, Donald M.," he read. "Tried before Judge Milton, Criminal Courts of General Sessions, November last ... charges first degree murder of Customs Agent George Bates. Sentenced January fourth to die week of March fifteenth suicide in cell at Ossining, using own suspenders, March second. Jury list as follows —"

For a long time the Inspector studied that jury list. Here were twelve ordinary names drawn from Manhattan's melting pot — but through three of them had been drawn heavy lines in black pencil, with grim notations added.

"Mark Taylor, bookkeeper, (strangled with own silk scarf in boarding house hallway, March tenth) ... Frank C. O'Toole, janitor Regent apartments, (strangled with own belt in basement, June thirteenth) ... P. N. Jones, bank clerk, (strangled with necktie in automatic elevator, July thirteenth) ... Herman Pugh, delicatessen-keeper —"

The Inspector drew a line through the name, and added "strangled in icebox with own necktie, September fourth —" Then he threw the pencil across his desk.

He rose wearily and went over to a file case at the other end of his office. After a moment's search of the newspaper clippings kept there, he returned to his desk. He pressed a button on his desk, and spoke into a black box. "Give me Lieutenant Walsh," he snapped. "Walsh? Get this! For immediate questioning in my office, these persons —"

The name of Miss Hildegarde Withers was not on the list, but all the same that good lady was announced not long after by the uniformed lieutenant who guarded the Inspector's portal. She entered bearing an armful of morning papers, with which she beat vigorously at the eddying cigar smoke. "You keep your office like a pool-room, Oscar," she told him.

There were times when the Inspector wished that his old friend had taken up stamp-collecting or welfare work instead of criminology, as a hobby.

He glanced wearily at the newspapers, with their headlines — "Police Powerless in Widening Death Circle" — "Suicide Club Has New Member" — "Another Nord Juror Dies"

"The newspapers," said Miss Withers caustically, "don't seem to feel that the long arm of coincidence could stretch far enough to make four jurors take their own lives in remorse for having sent a man to Sing Sing."

"Newspapers!" growled Piper. "A lot they know. Suicides always go in circles — the suggestion works on the minds of others. And when a jury is exposed to the tremendous publicity and pressure that was brought to bear in the Nord case, with the public sympathy on the side of the accused, I don't think it's so impossible that they could get to brooding —"

Miss Withers looked at him quizzically. "You're not convinced of that yourself, Oscar."

"Well, what if I'm not?" The Inspector lit a fresh cigar. "If the deaths aren't suicides, they've got to be murder. And what murderer could mesmerize his victims so they'd let him take articles of their own clothing to strangle them with? Not one of those dead jurymen showed a sign of chloroform or of a blow on the head. They must have done it themselves — yet I don't see how that fellow Pugh, after the cop had cut him down and begun to revive him, could have had the strength to get up and re-hang himself!"

"Nor do I see," put in Miss Withers, "how anyone but a madman would have nerve enough to creep back and hang his victim up again while the policeman who had cut him down was in the next room telephoning."

The lieutenant stood in the doorway. "Gentleman to see you, Inspector. Name of Lindst. And Walsh is on his way up with a dame."

Piper frowned. "Tell Mr. Lindst, whoever he is, he'll have to wait. Send Walsh and the girl in when they arrive." He turned to Miss Withers. "Hildegarde, you'll have to excuse me. I've got a bit of questioning to do."

The school-teacher nodded, but she did not rise. "If the girl you expect to question happens to be Sheila Thorne. I'm sitting in," she said. "That's why I cut a faculty meeting to come down here. School starts next Tuesday, but I've a more important job, Oscar. A lawyer named Abe Radin telephoned me this morning and asked me to take up this case in behalf of his client, Miss Thorne."

Piper stared. "Hildegarde! After all these years we're going to be on opposite sides of the fence?"

"Not necessarily," she told him. "But this is the first time I've ever realized my ambition to be called in as a private investigator. I told him that I'd try to get to the bottom of this mystery, but that I'd play no favorites. If this Sheila Thorne —"

The door opened, and a tall, almost Junoesque young woman came into the office. She was possessed of a curving body, curls which peeped from beneath a smartly tilted hat, and a full and scornful mouth.

Behind her came a very short, very fat little man who was dressed like a fashion-plate. Behind them stood Lieutenant Walsh and two detectives. Piper waved them away, and the door closed.

The little man spoke. "Inspector Piper? Delighted to meet you. Of course you have no objection to my being present while you question my client?"

"Not at all, Radin," snapped the Inspector. "Sit down, will you? You already know Miss Withers, I understand... "

† † †

Both newcomers turned to stare at the school teacher. "I'm on the job already," she told them. "Now can't we all have a friendly discussion —"

But the Inspector wasn't in a friendly mood. "Miss Thorne, you were Don Nord's girl, weren't you?"

"We were engaged to be married," said the girl. Her voice was unusually rich and vibrant. "But I never had anything to do with his — his business, if that's what you mean."

"You loved him! Anyhow, you made violent efforts to save him from the electric chair, didn't you? You even raised the money to get Abe Radin here, New York's greatest theatrical lawyer, to defend him?"

Sheila nodded. "I knew Don Nord wasn't guilty of murder. If he did throw that Customs man off a ship in the Bay, it was self-defense. Only the jury were too stupid to —"

"That jury," put in Abe Radin, "was the worst, and the lowest in mentality, that I ever encountered in twenty years at the bar, so help me!" He seemed to feel very strongly about it, Miss Withers thought, but she kept her own counsel.

Piper nodded. "Anyway, when the jury, after four days of disagreement, found your boy friend guilty, you felt pretty indignant about it, didn't you? As I remember, you talked somewhat violently at the time."

"Any fool could have seen that Don Nord, while he may have been a jewel-runner, wasn't a murderer," the girl said. "I did my best on the witness stand to make them believe Don was with me that night. I thought I had convinced them, but I was wrong. They found him guilty, and he was sent to Sing Sing. They murdered him — though he did take his own life. Don Nord was a jewel-smuggler, but he was worth ten dozen of the mangy, stupid jury which condemned him… "

Piper nodded. Abe Radin was making signs to the girl, but she went on. "I know what you think. But no matter how much I hated the jury, do you suppose that a girl could kill four able-bodied men? Do you think I'd be insane enough to try —"

Piper held up his hand. "You're way ahead of me. I just want to know where you were at, say, two o'clock this morning?"

"I was with a friend, in his apartment."

"And the name of the friend?"

"Well, if you really must know, I'll tell you it was Sven Nerd, Don's brother!"

There was a long silence. "Not the best alibi in the world," observed Piper sagely. "And where were you on the night of March tenth, and June thirteenth, and July thirtieth… "

"I was with Sven Nord!" said the girl defiantly. "And a lot of other nights, if you must know. We — you wouldn't understand, but we're in love!"

"You seem to have it all worked out," said Piper. "Now if anybody asked me, I wouldn't be able to remember that far back."

"It's just possible that Miss Thorne has been searching her memory since she knew you wanted her to come down here," Miss Withers put in.

They were interrupted by a knock at the door, and the lieutenant put in his head. "Excuse me, Inspector, but Mr. Lindst says he simply must see you."

"Tell him to cool his heels," growled the Inspector. His morning was not going any too well.

He turned toward the girl again. "Miss Thorne, you're not planning any trips, are you?"

The girl almost smiled. "Why — I was, as a matter of fact." Then her face hardened. "But not out of the state of New York, Inspector."

"Well, you'd better not go out of the city of New York until I tell you," he returned.

Abe Radin stood up. "If that's all, Inspector, we'll be running along."

Miss Withers thought it time to put in her oar. "Mr. Radin, I wonder if you'd send Miss Thorne up to see me this evening. There are one or two things she might be able to tell me."

Sheila Thorne looked at the lawyer, who nodded. "I'll be there," promised the girl. "I'll come to your flat between shows." But she was decidedly not eager, Miss Withers could see. The door closed behind them.

"That girl is concealing some thing!" said Piper slowly.

He went to the door. "I'll see this guy Lindst," he barked. But much to his surprise, Mr. Lindst had vanished.

"Said he couldn't wait," the lieutenant said. "And he wouldn't tell me what he wanted."

Miss Withers was leaning over the Inspector's desk. "I can tell you that," she said. Her long forefinger pointed to the list of the Nord jury, with its four blackened-out names. Toward the bottom of the list was the name "Jonas Lindst."

Piper scratched his head. "Wonder if I ought to send out and have him brought in?"

Miss Withers smiled. "I'd think you would be wiser to send out and have your minions produce Sven Nord, brother of the jewel-runner. He would have just as much motive to avenge his brother as Miss Thorne... "

The Inspector was amused at this. "I looked into that," he said. "But naturally you wouldn't happen to know that Sven Nord lost his left arm two years ago, and wears an artificial one tipped with a glove. He got blood poisoning in a fencing match, in the course of his job as a fencing instructor. And if the impossible happened and these four deaths were murders, they certainly weren't pulled off by a one-armed man."

"In this world," said Miss Withers sadly, "nothing is certain but death and taxes."

† † †

She spent the next half hour in mollifying the Inspector, who still felt vaguely injured at having her allied on the other side. But he let her make a copy of the jury-list. "Four down, and eight to go," he told her. "But you can cross off three more. One of the jurymen sailed for a visit with the old folks in Italy the first of June, and if he's wise he'll stay there. One of them is in Flower Hospital as a result of a fall from a step-ladder, and a third is in Denver for his lungs. That leaves only five who are likely to be found hanging in odd spots, if this madhouse continues."

"I have a feeling," Miss Withers told him, "that this madhouse is barely under way."

Her feeling was even more strongly entrenched that evening when she received Sheila Thorne in her little brownstone apartment on West 74th Street. The young woman was all too evidently uneasy, and eager to go. Miss Withers tried vainly to get on friendly terms of understanding with her "client."

Sheila Thorne admitted that she had said, at the conclusion of the trial, that it was the jury who ought to get the death sentence for their stupidity in finding a man guilty of first degree murder when at the worst it was only manslaughter. She had no idea of any one who could have been mad enough to act upon her words.

Miss Withers left off fencing. She decided upon a desperate stroke. That afternoon she had come across one salient fact in the course of her search of the back newspaper files, and she decided to try it.

"Mr. Radin asked me to help you," she began, as the girl moved restlessly in her chair. "I suppose, like many other people, he thought that I might prove a back-door to the police department, and secure a little gentler handling for you."

Sheila did not answer, but she hurriedly lit a cigarette to conceal what Miss Withers read in her eyes — that the thrust was true.

"But the best way to help you, if you're innocent," Miss Withers went on, "is to find out who is guilty of those four deaths, provided they were not suicides. That will promptly stop the publicity which, Radin tells me, you are afraid will hurt your career as a singer." The school-teacher cleared her throat. "Young woman, you are — er — friendly with Sven Nord, are you not?"

Sheila nodded without speaking. She did not tell Miss Withers that the handsome young fencing-master waited, at the moment, in the hall downstairs. But Miss Withers already knew that fact, having been looking out of her front window when they arrived.

"You and Mr. Nord have joint alibis for the times when those four jurymen were killed," she continued. "I shan't probe into the genuineness of your claim. But has it occurred to you that Mr. Nord may not be as close a friend as you think?"

Sheila sat up straight in her chair. "What?"

"Perhaps he didn't tell you that almost two months ago Sven Nord was married at City Hall to a Miss —" the school-teacher consulted her note book — "a Miss Sally Thompson of Yonkers?"

For an instant a strange emotion flashed across the face of the blonde girl, and then she managed a smile. "Really?"

"That doesn't make you want to tell me anything?" Miss Withers was disappointed. "If you and Nord were not together on those nights, and if you had nothing to do with the murders, then don't you see —"

"I see that I'd better get back to the club before I lose my job," cut in the blond singer. "We go on the air in an hour. She displayed her wrist-watch, which pointed to ten o'clock. Miss Withers bade her good-bye, and closed the door. Then she rushed over to turn on her radio, and snap a button on the dial. Only a few weeks before it had occurred to her that the much-advertised "home-broadcasting" principle might be put into application to give her an insight into the minds of her departing and arriving callers. A microphone costing only a dollar-fifty now stood concealed in the overhead light fixture of the entry inside the door, with a wire running to her own little radio.

As the tubes warmed up, she heard the clatter of descending high heels on the stair, and then a quick masculine voice. "Sheila — does the old maid know?"

Sheila's only answer was a carol of hysterical laughter, cut short by the closing of the door. From her window Miss Withers watched them hail a taxi, watched without her usual sympathetic smile for young lovers.

"I'm going to enjoy this case," she said grimly, as she turned off the radio.

† † †

The house was small, and for forty years the dust and soot of New York had been settling upon its red brick until all was of a sombre gray with darker streaks of black. Miss Withers had already sniffed dubiously as she came up the little side street on the outskirts of Greenwich Village, toward the roar of the Ninth Avenue El. As she pressed one neatly gloved finger on the bell beneath the card which read "Jonas Lindst, Notary Public," she sniffed again.

"Perhaps I should have waited until morning, after all!" she told herself. But she had never been addicted to waiting, even of the watchful variety. The police were doing enough of that sort of thing, she thought. And there was no telling what might happen before morning. That was why, a few minutes after that strange and exotic personality, Sheila Thorne, had hurried away from Miss Withers' apartment, the school-teacher had hailed a taxicab and given this address. It had not been hard to find out the residence of the man who had tried, and failed, to see Inspector Oscar Piper that morning. And he must have had some reason for making the attempt. That reason Miss Withers was out to discover.

She rang again, and then beat upon the door with the handle of her umbrella. Surely the man was at home, for there was a light in an upper window.

After a long wait there was the rattling of a chain, and the door opened a few inches. A pale and frightened face peered through the crack, and then the door was flung open. She looked upon a small, almost wizened man of fifty-odd years, dressed in a bathrobe of musty brown. Beneath it showed shapeless trousers, a shirt without a collar, and old slippers.

He held himself very erect, though his hands trembled a little. Miss Withers apologized quickly for disturbing him at this hour.

"It is not yet midnight," said Jonas Lindst. "I am a public servant, and it is my duty to be at the service of my public... "

Miss Withers followed him into an ancient hallway furnished with three horsehair chairs and a towering object which was at once bureau, mirror, and hatrack. As pegs for the hanging of hats, there had been fastened to this prehistoric object several deer antlers.

They passed down the hall, and Lindst led the way into a small room in the rear which had been furnished, in some bygone day, as an office. There were plans on the wall of buildings which had gone down under the wrecker's crowbar these many years, photographs of houses for sale or rent, and large calendars illustrated with photographs of the home offices of various insurance companies.

From a drawer of the desk, the little man took a rubber stamp and a round seal. Miss Withers watched him, mildly surprised.

"Sign the document, please," he told her. "You must sign it first... "

Then she understood. "I didn't wish to consult you as a notary, Mr. Lindst," she told him gently. A flicker of disappointment went across his face, which changed to a wondering suspicion as she explained her presence.

"You were a member of the jury which found Donald Nord guilty of murder last November, were you not?"

He nodded. His eyes widened, and he panted a little. It was evident that his fling at jury duty had been an event of the most tremendous significance in the life of little Jonas Lindst. "The poor fellow killed himself in jail," he told her. "Capital punishment is a terrible thing. The responsibility which rests upon a jury called upon to send a man to the gallows or save him — the newspapers, the crowds, the shouting voices of the attorneys, the eyes, eyes, eyes everywhere... "

His voice had risen to a shrill crescendo, and then suddenly he regained control. "We could do nothing but find the man guilty," he continued more calmly. "Although I must admit that since that time I have spent many and many a sleepless night —"

"You haven't contemplated suicide, by any chance?" Miss Withers pressed on.

"Suicide! It is the escape of a coward. I would not commit suicide. The deaths of the four who have been found strangled —"

He hesitated, and Miss Withers said "Yes?"

"They were not suicides, either!" He was confidential. "That was why I tried to see the police today. Someone is trying to murder us, all of us Jurors! I wanted protection."

Miss Withers felt that she was getting warm. Her experience had taught her never to ignore the suspicions and imaginings of even such a strange and erratic character as the pompous little man before her.

Her own suspicions were justified. "Tell me," she cried, "have you any idea who that someone is?"

Jonas Lindst looked at her. "No," he said. But he was staring oddly.

"No idea at all — not even a wild guess?"

He smiled. "I have a wild guess, yes. In fact, I think I know. But you will laugh at me. You will think me mad. You see — the death circle started a short time after the newspapers reported than Don Nord had killed himself up at Sing Sing, and thus beaten the chair. If I were asked the truth of this affair —"

"You are!" said Miss Withers.

"I think —" he smiled almost apologetically — "I think that Nord is the murderer, the avenger! Yes, Nord, the man we found guilty, the man who was sent to Sing Sing. You do not believe in reincarnation, no?"

Miss Withers sniffed. "No," she said.

"Nor do I. But there was money behind Nord's defense. Money can do anything in this city. Money could spirit Nord out of his cell alive and substitute a body, strangled, there. Money —"

† † †

Miss Withers thought of this dubiously. "You mean you think Nord is alive, and perpetrating this series of crimes to punish the jury who found him guilty?"

Lindst shrugged his shoulders. "Who else would have the motive?"

"His sweetheart?" inquired the school-teacher softly.

Lindst laughed gratingly. "Miss Thorne? A lovely girl like her? You must be crazy to suggest it. She did her best to save Nord, but the other fools on the jury didn't listen, didn't believe her. I —" He stopped short. "She is not, and could not be, the one you seek. Go back and tell the police —"

"I am not working for the police," said Miss Withers. "I'm working in behalf of Miss Thorne. I want to clear her by finding the real murderer, the fiend who is perpetrating this series of outrages… "

"Look for Don Nord!" declared her surprising host. He rose suddenly from his chair. "Listen! I hear someone or something at my back door. Wait!"

He scuttled away, leaving Miss Withers alone. She shivered, involuntarily. It was approaching midnight according to the old-fashioned watch which ornamented her old-fashioned bosom.

"And I had this trip for a false alarm!" she told herself. There was no thought in her mind of putting any faith in the last surprising suggestion of the dignified little notary. Money might do many things in New York, but she had seen the walls of Sing Sing and talked with the quiet man who is warden of that grim vacation spot, and she was not inclined to think that money, any amount of money, might move one or the other.

Lindst rejoined her, carrying a flash light. "It was nobody," he confessed. "Perhaps a cat … but I am nervous, you see. Living alone as I do, and with this danger hanging over my head, it is enough —"

"Enough to drive anyone mad," suggested Miss Withers. "Nightmares like this make us all doubt our sanity."

But Jonas Lindst insisted that he was sane as could be. He seemed eager to talk, eager to hold his caller as a shield against the loneliness and worry which must close in upon him as soon as she went.

Miss Withers finally arose. "It is clear that something must be done to protect you and the others of that jury who are in the city," she said. "The police may or may not be of help, but it seems to me that we ought to call a meeting of the survivors, and discuss ways and means."

Lindst squinted at her. "To get us all together? Have you thought what a chance that would be for the murderer — if he found out?"

She smiled. "I think I could take care of that danger," she said. It was at that moment that a bell rang in front of the house. "One minute," gasped Lindst. He dashed out of the room, closing the door carefully behind him. She heard his footsteps in the front hall, and a creaking of the front door chain followed by a low voice. That was all. No further sound came to her, at least for a long time.

She pressed her ear to the door, but could hear no voices. She dared not open the door, for she knew that the lighted crack would show down the darkened hallway. But a vague suspicion that all was not well began to fill her mind, a suspicion bred of the old house, the musty smell which arose from the furniture, and the long absence of the strange little man whose domain it was. "Something," observed Miss Withers, "is distinctly up!"

Impulsively, she moved toward the door, and at that moment there came a crash which shook the house. Dashing through the doorway and down the front hall, she came upon a scene of wreckage.

The front door stood ajar, with its chain dangling, but the hall was blocked by the remains of the what-not which had fallen forward on its face, amid a shattering of broken glass. Drawers were flung aside, wood splintered, castors gone, and beneath it all the frightened school-teacher saw the body of Jonas Lindst.

By some inexplicable power born of her fright, she managed to lift the cumbersome piece of furniture from the man. Much to her amazement, she found that he was bound, with his own belt, to one of the deer antlers designed as hatracks. The leather had cut deeply into his throat, but he was still alive, gasping and choking, as she loosened the improvised noose and dragged him free.

The fiendish ingenuity of the plan struck her on the instant. The mysterious person who had rung the doorbell had overpowered Lindst and somehow managed to hang him, as he suffocated, to his own hatrack! Then, as the would-be murderer had fled, Lindst's struggles had overturned the heavy piece of furniture, saving his life by summoning aid!

He was not badly hurt. Slowly he came back to consciousness. Miss Withers could hardly wait. Here, at last, was an eye-witness — here she would receive a description of the murderer!

But it was not to be. Jonas Lindst shook his head as she pressed him. He had not seen his mysterious caller, but as he opened the door a hand had come through and caught his throat, bringing darkness ...

"You're positive that it was one hand, not two?" Miss Withers demanded.

He was positive. That was all he knew.

They both went out, through the front door, and stared at the empty street. It was not more than five minutes since Miss Withers had heard the crash of the what-not, but no one was in sight except a solitary cab-driver tinkering with his machine.

She rushed down the sidewalk. "Did you see anyone leave that brick house in the last ten minutes?" she demanded.

The driver shook his head. "No, lady. I didn't see nothin'."

Inwardly she cursed his lack of perception. She returned to the house. "You saved my life!" Lindst was saying. "If you had not come, I —"

There was a lot more of the same, but Miss Withers was thinking of something else. No matter who had come to this door tonight, bent upon murder, it had not been Sheila Thorne. Sheila broadcast between eleven and twelve. It was not for nothing that Hildegarde had read her newspapers carefully that day. She had proved the point which she had set out to prove, but she was extremely dissatisfied.

She had no ears for the breathless posturings of Lindst. She watched while the little man painfully replaced the what-not in its niche, and picked up the glass. Drawers had come out, and scattered their contents over the hall rug — drawers which appeared not to have been opened for years. From one of them had rolled a cheap clock, and by some freak of the crash it had started ticking again.

Miss Withers had no interest in that clock. Yet in spite of herself, its ticking was to echo in the back of her mind all through the rest of that night. The loud ticking, like the beat of steel upon tin, was not to be silenced until an amazing and impossible possibility forced itself upon her. And then it was almost too late.

† † †

The Inspector was more difficult than usual. She spent almost all of the next forenoon with him before he promised to fall in line with her plans. But finally she convinced him that she knew what she was doing.

"But are you going to tell Abe Radin?" he wanted to know.

"Why not? I want everyone to know. I want this to be one of those secret meetings that everybody knows about. Radin, and Sheila, and Sven Nord — and everybody else."

Piper shrugged his shoulders. "Go ahead," he said. "You're putting all your sheep into one basket, and then walking out among the wolves and saying — 'here you are!' But it might work."

"It will work," promised Miss Withers — "if you'll stand by."

She did not tell him that since the previous evening someone else had been standing by — that she had noticed, in the shadows across the street from the little remodelled brownstone in which she lived, the lurking figure of a tall man whose left arm hung rather stiffly his shoulder. He had been there when she returned from her brief adventure in the Village with Lindst, and he was there next morning when she set out for Piper's office.

"I must remember to pull down my shades," she told herself quietly. That night she gave a party, according to the plans which she had discussed with the Inspector.

There were seven guests in all at the party. Five of them were the remaining Nord jurors, drawn from their homes by a cryptic telegram which Miss Withers had spent some time in composing. "Be at West 74th Street tonight at nine," she had written, "and you will receive important information regarding the so-called Suicide Circle."

† † †

The five were average New Yorkers, who might have been impanelled from a subway train at rush hour. There was Johnson, a broker, Wassvogel, a furrier; Satterlee, a grocer; Dirk, a druggist, and Lindst, the notary. Their ages varied from thirty-five to sixty, and their weights and complexions as widely, but they were united by the most common bond, and the strongest — abject fear.

These men, almost a year ago, after a long disagreement had brought in a verdict of guilty against Don Nord, the ghost whose presence haunted the meeting. Four of their number had paid a terrible price for that verdict, and the end was not yet.

All had been eager to come, eager to unite against the invisible foe. Miss Withers saw that they were seated comfortably in a circle in her living room, and rapped sharply on a table, much as she would have done when bringing her third-graders to attention.

"Gentlemen, we are gathered together in the hope of making some concerted action against the shapeless, nameless horror which is slowly striking you down, one by one," began Miss Withers. "My position is largely unofficial, but I may be better able to help you, for all of that."

As she spoke, she could not help noticing the suggestion of veiled animosity and suspicion with which the guests regarded one another, and her, too. Most particularly did little Lindst skulk in a corner.

"Has any one of you a suggestion as to who the killer may be?" she went on. "Look back at the trial, for in that lies the roots of all that has happened."

Dirk, the druggist, leaned his bulk forward. "Say—" he began. "I just got an idea. That lawyer fellow who led the defense for Nord, Radin or whatever his name was, he got mighty angry at us when we brought in a verdict against his client. You don't suppose —" He stopped, and shook his head. "No, I must be going crazy," he said. "It's too far-fetched."

Miss Withers spoke up. "The strain you gentlemen have been going through must be enough to make all of you doubt your sanity. Isn't that so?"

Everybody agreed with her — except little Lindst. He shook his head stoutly. "I'm not crazy," he maintained. "Though the rest of you may be..."

"Let him alone," counselled broker Johnson, who knew Lindst of old. "He's always on the other side, just to be different. The lady's right. We got to keep our heads. Somebody's trying to kill us all off, and I think I know pretty well who it is —"

They were interrupted by a ring at the buzzer, and Miss Withers admitted the two remaining guests — Lawyer Abe Radin and his lovely client, Miss Sheila Thorne. She found them seats, introduced them.

"Absolute frankness is the only way out of our situation," Miss Withers went on. "Now we're all together, and we're all of one mind about our aim — to find and put out of commission the murderer of four jurymen. Miss Thorne, gentlemen, has a particular reason to get at the truth —"

Sheila flashed a glance at the school teacher, but Miss Withers did not notice it. Radin started to speak, but she cut him off.

"Let me handle this," she said calmly. "We've got to put our heads together and figure out who the mysterious killer can be. So far he has struck unseen without leaving a trace. Never a fingerprint, never a clue. There is just one victim, found hanging from some article of his own clothing in what could be suicide — but *isn't.*"

Abe Radin spoke up. "Well said, dear lady." He glanced around the room. "But is this sort of thing wise? Have you thought that perhaps the murderer is one of us, sitting right here in this room, and waiting for a chance to perform another of his — er — miracles? Just now it occurred to me that the key to this entire problem might be —"

He stopped short as the lights went out, throwing the room into inky blackness. By some mischance, Miss Withers had left every shade drawn tightly, and not a bit of glow came in from the street.

There was a low scream from Sheila, and then the crashing of furniture and the bewildered, angry cursing of the men. Someone lit a match, and someone else knocked it, and the striker, out.

Miss Withers, mildly perplexed, counted fifteen and then blew shrilly upon a borrowed police whistle. Nothing happened except that the sound increased the pandemonium of the room. She found her way, not without minor mishaps in the milling, trampling crowd, to the hall door. "Oscar!" she raised her voice. "Don't you hear me? That's enough!"

"Yeah?" she heard a familiar and reassuring voice from the upper stair head. The glow of a police flash outlined her angular figure.

"Turn the lights back on!" ordered Miss Withers.

"Damn it, I didn't turn 'em off," protested Piper. "It was ten minutes before the time you set... "

And then Miss Withers *was* worried!

But Piper and his aides, with their flashlights, soon got to the root of the trouble. A main fuse had blown out, though what blew it was a complete mystery. Replaced, all the lights came on, and the other tenants of the building went back into their own apartments. Miss Withers knew that she would hear from the landlord next morning, but she had other and more immediate worries.

She found most of the furniture of her living room overturned, but nothing else very wrong. Sheila Thorne crouched beneath the library table, her gown half torn from her shoulders. But she was otherwise unhurt. Abe Radin, surprisingly enough, stood on the table with his glasses off and a small pearl-handled, gun in his fist. He produced his permit and put it away.

Everybody wanted to know if this was a practical joke, or if Miss Withers had gone completely mad. But that lady stood amid the wreck of her carefully laid plot to trap the "Suicide Club" murderer, shaking her head. She had told the Inspector to put out the lights — but someone had beaten him to it. But why?

Sheila Thorne answered the question. She was staring across the room. "Why —" she gasped — "where's the musty little man who sat in the corner?"

The girl was right. Jonas Lindst had disappeared into thin air. The remaining members of the party made a concerted rush for the door, but found it blocked with uniformed officers.

"Search the place!" gasped Miss Withers.

But she knew now the truth of this fantastic affair — knew what she must find somewhere. While a sergeant guarded the frightened group in the living room, and while Piper and his men scoured her little apartment and the stairs both up and down in the hall, she stepped into the kitchen. She looked in the rear entryway, she looked behind the gas range and in the little closet under the stair.

She met the Inspector in the doorway. "But a man can't disappear into thin air!" that worthy was exclaiming. He stopped suddenly, and brought forward a chair. "Here, you sit down," he ordered. "You're white as a sheet. I'll finish searching the kitchen... "

"I've looked everywhere," said Miss Withers quickly. There was an oddly strained expression about her mouth. In spite of her pallor, she never looked more determined, more formidable,

She took the chair he offered, waving away a glass of water. Her lips were very thin, and her clear blue eyes were as hard as stones. She might have worn, above her neat dark hair, the black cap of an English judge to pronounce sentence of death.

† † †

The Inspector was vaguely puzzled by her expression, but he had other worries. "There wasn't time for anyone to open a window and shove that man out, was there?" He sent his men down to the street, just in case. They returned almost immediately. They had seen no sign of Lindst, but across the street they had seen the shadow of a man standing behind a doorway. He was a young and handsome man, though his left arm hung stiffly at his side.

"Mr. Sven Nord," began Miss Withers.

But the Inspector cut her short. "Well, young man, suppose you come clean and tell us just what in blazes you know about this?"

"I don't know a thing," Nord returned. "I've been hanging around trying to find out what you people knew. I wanted to —"

There was a little gasp behind them. "Sven! Oh, no — you didn't, you couldn't have... " It was Sheila Thorne, blank and very incredulous.

"Of course he couldn't have!" snapped Miss Withers. "Oh, are you all determined to be fools?" She stepped between the Inspector and his quarry, and caught Nord by his shoulder. "Go make love to her," she ordered. "Or something. Go on!"

Nord crossed to Sheila's side, and as the fear and horror melted from her face he put his good arm about her shoulders.

Miss Withers stole a glance at her watch. Fifteen minutes since the lights had gone out. The seconds passed more slowly than hours.

But the Inspector, pacing up and down the floor beside her, suddenly stopped short. "What's that?"

"What's what?"

"I hear a knocking — in there," he said. He pointed toward the kitchen. Before Miss Withers could stop him he was through the door. She shook her head, and stood in the doorway as he made a tour of the room, coming at last to the little closet under the stair. He opened the door, and his "Good God Almighty!" could have been heard as far south as Columbus Circle.

Policemen shouldered past Miss Withers, and helped their chief take down from a hook in the closet the limp body of little Jonas Lindst. Quick fingers tore from his neck the smooth and silken noose, and strong arms forced his flat diaphragm into slow, painful breathing.

"We've saved him!" cried the Inspector.

Then he saw the expression on Miss Withers' face. "Yes," she said bitterly. "You've saved him — for the *chair*. Oscar, why *couldn't* you let well enough alone?"

† † †

That was all there was to the famous party at Hildegarde Withers'. Sheila Thorne, taking French leave from her night-club contract at Miss Withers' motherly advice, left for a long deferred honeymoon trip to Niagara with Sven Nord, the young man to whom she had been married for weeks. "That was the trip which wasn't to take her out of the state," Miss Withers explained to the Inspector when it was all over. "I should have smelled a rat when I found out that Nord married one Sally Thompson. When people pick aliases or stage names they usually keep their old initials. You've told me that yourself... "

"You've got plenty of explaining to do," said Piper almost savagely. "One of these days, Hildegarde, you'll go too far. Do you realize that you've been an accessory after the fact?"

"An accessory to a fake suicide?" She smiled grimly. "I only tried to save the state the expense of a trial and execution. To make the punishment fit the crime, as the song has it. But I'll begin at the beginning, in words of one syllable.

"Do you remember, Oscar, my saying that a murderer who would come back and re-hang his victim with the police in the next room must be mad? Well, it was true. Lindst is mad, quite mad."

"You mean insane? But why?"

"He went on that Nord jury full of the dignity of his position as a notary public," she began. "But being an odd little person, he didn't see eye to eye with his fellows. He was the only one convinced of Don Nord's innocence — convinced, no doubt, by Sheila Thorne's testimony. The other jurors complained tonight that he was always disagreeing, just to be different. It was Lindst who kept that jury in disagreement for four days, and nearly got a mistrial. But the others didn't want to wait around that jury-room. They wanted to get home, and if the truth were known I'm afraid they brought considerable pressure to bear upon Lindst. I've read that sometimes there's a black eye or two when the jury came out to give their verdict, and if you'll study the newspaper photographs of the jury you'll see that Lindst has a cut on his forehead ... They roughed him, Oscar — and it rankled.

"That was no motive for killing the others, I know. But his mind couldn't have been very strong, and the tremendous pressure of the trial and the resulting newspaper publicity completely unhinged him. The suicide of Nord at Sing Sing suggested the means and Lindst set out on a wild trail of vengeance. He is a little man — but madness gives superhuman strength. With a silk noose he strangled his victims, and then while they lay unconscious he slipped off the noose and substituted an article of their own clothing — because that was what Nord, the condemned man, had used! And it left no trace... "

Miss Withers smiled. "I knew that Sheila didn't do it as soon as I realized that all she had to hide from me — and from the public — was the fact that she had married the brother of her dead sweetheart a little sooner than would be considered respectful to the dead man's memory. Then I called on Lindst, and he staged a little show for me. It was too nice a coincidence that the murderer should strike while I was in the house."

"But the ring at the bell?" protested Piper. "You told me he answered the door?"

"He had previously set an alarm clock in the hall, when he made a trip to see who was at the back door. The alarm went off in ten minutes or so, and he rushed out to answer it, as I thought. Actually he made a noose of his own belt and hung himself to the hat-tree, having first put the door ajar to imply that someone had just left. He meant to make a noise with his heels which would summon me and thus "save" him, and the fact that the what-not tipped over only made the fake seem more real.

"However, there was a taxi-driver outside, and I never saw a driver yet who would fail to see a person leaving a nearby house at such a late hour. They're trained actually to smell out fares in these times. And the fact that Sheila was on the air during that hour was the best alibi in the world for her."

"Go on," ordered Piper. "You've got plenty to cover yet."

"Well, I only suspected Lindst at the time," she explained. "It seemed such a thin motive, somehow. But I got all the figures in this case together in my apartment, and planned to have you turn out the lights. I was sure that the murderer, if it was Lindst, would certainly make an attempt to kill another of the jurymen while such a golden opportunity existed. I planned it so that he could be intercepted before any real harm was done... "

"But he fooled you, and put out the lights for himself!" The Inspector was almost smiling. "It's easy enough to do, by putting a piece of metal such as a knife blade into a light socket. Lindst sat in the corner near the bridge lamp, didn't he?"

† † †

She nodded. "When I saw him missing I thought at first that either I had been terribly wrong or else he had simply broken and fled. I felt sure that he was mad, you see, because he alone out of all the persons in the room refused to admit the possibility of not being sane. That is supposed to be typical of the mad, Oscar. The whole world may be crazy but they are sane."

"But I still don't see... "

"You will. He was growing afraid that someone suspected him, particularly when Radin said the murderer might be one of us. The same instinct which makes the writer of poison-pen letters always send one to himself or herself, made Lindst seek to prove his innocence by having an attack made upon himself. His first trial was a fiasco, but this he meant to be perfect. He used his original noose, for there was no chance to change it for his necktie or scarf. He meant really to choke himself, Oscar —"

"But why? Why should he kill himself to prove his innocence?"

Miss Withers smiled. "He didn't plan to *die*, Oscar. He knew that one passed through from twenty to forty minutes of unconsciousness before strangling, having had plenty of what you might call laboratory experience. He knew that the place would be searched at once, and with a madman's cunning he counted on being found and cut down — and dragged back to life!"

The Inspector let go a long breath. "And you found him there — and *left* him?"

She nodded. "I thought it the best way, you see. For everybody concerned. There would have been no murder trial, with its bad effect upon jurors and public alike. There would have been no horrible day up at Sing Sing, with a gurgling, pitiable animal strapped to a chair. If I could have kept you from finding him for ten minutes more, Jonas Lindst would have got just what he asked for, and deserved."

Piper shook his head. "Hildegarde, you like to monkey with dynamite, don't you? You like to put your own whims above —"

"Common sense above nonsense," she cut in. "Yes, I do. And as usual, you may have the credit for solving the Suicide Circle murders." Inspector Piper looked as disgusted as he felt.

The Riddle of the Marble Blade

In order to love her fellow man as she felt in duty bound to do, Miss Hildegarde Withers found it necessary to avoid humanity en masse whenever possible. Had her inclinations led her otherwise, she might possibly have stood shoulder to shoulder with a thousand or so fellow Manhattanites in solemn conclave one bright October afternoon. In that case, one chapter in the history of criminology would have been considerably shorter.

As it happened, she spent most of the Saturday in her little West Side apartment with a stack of uncorrected examination papers beside her, reading. By the time she was dragged rudely back to the present century by the shrilling of her telephone, the fat was most completely in the fire.

"All Hades is broke loose in Central Park!" was the way Inspector Oscar Piper put it. "You see, they were unveiling a blasted statue or something... "

Properly speaking, the unveiling was completely in the firm white hands of Deirdre Bryan, daughter of the Commissioner of Parks. She had been given the name because of old Mike Bryan's desire thus to honor the grandest and most unhappy queen who ever graced ancient Gaeldom, but nobody ever called her anything but "Dee."

At a few minutes before two o'clock that afternoon Miss Dee Bryan, looking better than her best for the benefit crowd and the massed newsreel cameras, was holding a rope. That rope, if properly and briskly tugged, would uncover from its drapes of flags and canvas the latest representation of the father of his country. Now the statue loomed shapeless and muffled against the sky, and thus it must remain until the last tune had been played and the last speech gasped.

The minutes dragged for Dee Bryan. His Honor the Mayor, looking even more like an angry sparrow than usual, was working himself up toward a climax. He had already disposed of politics, slum clearance, the widening of Broadway, and the five cent fare. Now he was in the middle of "the City Beautiful... "

When he finished, if ever, Dee would go into action with the rope, while the band struck up "The Stars and Stripes Forever" and the mayor shook hands with Dravid, the sculptor.

And then the mighty marble Washington, which the city of New York had just purchased for five thousand dollars as part of its program of encouraging the fine arts, would stand forth in impassive magnificence above the as yet uncompleted hole which was to be George Washington Uptown Pool Number Two.

Dee sensed by the Mayor's delivery that he was nearing the wind-up. She tightened her grasp of the rope, and cast a glance at the two newsreel cameras which were perched upon a nearby sedan. The news director, a bored little fat man in a leather jacket, waved at her to look up at the statue.

Then there was a commotion behind her. The brisk young secretary from City Hall who was acting as master of ceremonies had caught her father by the arm and led him out of a cluster of aldermen.

"Commissioner!" his voice came clearly to the excited girl. "There's been an upset. Dravid hasn't shown up — so you've got to stand beside the Mayor and let him shake hands with you instead."

"Me?" The Commissioner of Parks looked unhappy. It was bad enough dressing up in cut-away and striped trousers. "But I had nothing to do with the statue," he protested. Then he pointed past his daughter. "That's Dravid's wife, the big handsome woman in white standing near the newsreel truck. Why not let His Honor shake hands with her?"

"There isn't time!" hissed the master of ceremonies. He leaned toward Dee. "Understand the change? When His Honor shakes hands with your dad, haul on the rope!"

Dee nodded. Her father shrugged his shoulders. "All right," he said. "But it's a shame that Dravid isn't here."

† † †

The Mayor was coming at last to his finale. "To dedicate this statue of the father of his country in the spirit of reverence, and to honor a true genius which has grown and flowered in our own fair city, the great Manuel Dravid..."

He half-turned, with his hand out — and caught the frantic signals of the secretary from City Hall. His Honor blinked, and managed a graceful about face. "Manuel Dravid, New York City's own, who is unfortunately unable to be with us today, but — but —"

The Mayor's hand went to his breast pocket, and brought forth a yellow bit of paper. — "but who has telegraphed to ask that his statue which is shortly to be displayed before you be accepted and understood as a true affirmation of his artistic faith! Ladies and gentlemen, in behalf of the people of the city of New York, I accept the Dravid Washington!"

He turned, as the band blared forth in Sousa's most stirring march, and grasped the outstretched hand of the Commissioner of Parks. There was an instant's delay, for the improvised twist in the end of the speech had caught Dee unprepared. She was staring for all her blue eyes were worth at a man who stood against the newsreel truck — a tall and bearded young man whose mouth was open.

He was gazing up at the veiled statue, with an expression of fascinated horror on his face. Then, as Dee was recalled to her duty by a hiss from the master of ceremonies, he seemed to melt into the crowd.

She gave a vigorous heave at the rope. Something stuck, and she tried again. Finally one of the aldermen gave a hand, and the rope loosened ...

There was a faint burst of applause from the crowd, which died away in a low moan of horror.

There stood the Dravid Washington, twice the size of life, dignified, handsome, and glistening with the white of eternal marble — the father of his country, one hand outstretched as if holding a torch.

But he was not alone. Caught in the crook of his great bended arm was the crumpled body of a man, a spare, roughly clad person whose face wore a look of blank surprise!

His head, with its shock of white hair, was bent forward and from the back of his neck the life blood had gushed forth to stain the immaculate marble of the monument in a long brown cascade.

The first thought that Dee had was: "I mustn't faint in front of the cameras — I really mustn't!"

The cameras were clicking still, with an expression of pure and unalloyed delight upon the faces of the newsreel men. They'd come for another speech and a statue — and got this!

But there was more to come. The Mayor, speechless for the first time in his life, was pointing up at the body. He barked, cleared his throat, and finally managed — "But — that's Dravid!"

And then, for a full minute, there was no sound but the widow's horrible hysterical laughter.

† † †

"So I thought you might possibly be interested," the Inspector finished.

"You mean you're stuck and you want me to lend you a hand!" Miss Withers told him over the telephone. "But it's a fine time to tell me about it — the body was discovered a little after two, you say. It's after five-thirty now."

"I know it," Piper admitted testily. "But there're no phone booths in the middle of Central Park. And you have no idea what it is to try to investigate a murder with His Honor the Mayor screaming for an arrest. I haven't had a second to slip away and call you until now. I'm on my way to have a look at Dravid's studio in the Village, and I thought you might like to go... "

"I'll be ready when you get here," she cut him off. True to her word, the angular schoolma'am was pacing restlessly up and down the sidewalk outside her flat when the Inspector, traveling incognito in a taxi, pulled up.

He started to give the man an address downtown, but Miss Withers vetoed the suggestion. "You can give me five minutes to look at the scene of the crime," she snapped. "You've had all afternoon." The taxi obediently headed up Central Park West and into the park.

There was still a good-sized crowd held back from the statue by a squadron of officers. George Washington had been covered with canvas again, but Piper lifted the drape to show her the tell-tale brown stain. The body, of course, had been taken away for an autopsy.

"He was killed with some sort of a stone hammer or arrow," Piper admitted. "Part of it stuck out of the back of his neck. Dead since sometime in the night, Doc Bloom said."

"Between twelve and one, I imagine," Miss Withers murmured.

"What? How did you know?"

"Because the park is quite crowded until twelve — and while I was waiting for you I called the weather bureau and found that there was bright moonlight last night — except for that one cloudy hour. The murderer would hardly risk working except in the dark."

"Oh, I see." Piper nodded. "Yeah, guess you're right."

"Elementary, my dear Watson," Miss Withers murmured softly. "By the way, Oscar, when was the statue set up here?"

"Yesterday — which was Friday," he told her. "Owen, Dravid's young assistant and a bunch of workmen got it into place; the newspapers took a few photos and then Dravid was handed his money from the city. Today's unveiling was just the usual official splurge."

"I didn't know," Miss Withers admitted. "I suppose the sculptor was in a last minute rush to finish the thing?"

"Rush?" Piper laughed. "Why, the statue has been finished for weeks. It was chosen from a dozen others in a competition, you know."

"Hmm," observed Miss Withers, "I was just wondering why there are so many marble chips around the base, that's all. Unless the workmen had an accident setting it up."

She had gathered up a hatful of odd-shaped fragments. "For my rockery," she told the Inspector.

A stepladder leaning against a pile of scaffolding told how the body must have been lifted to its oddly macabre position in the crooked arm of the massive statue. "Cases like this usually are broken pretty easily," the Inspector was saying. "Contrary to usual ideas on the part of the public, the more unusual the crime and the weapon, the more easily it's solved. The whole situation here comes down to one point — the *how* of the crime. Why was Dravid killed with a piece of sharpened stone?"

"No doubt," agreed Miss Withers. She was thinking of something else, as usual. For most of her career as a sleuth she had been most successful when she set her course as far as possible from the Inspector's reasoning. "Well, I'm ready to go with you to the studio," she decided.

The taxi swirled southward with the incessant howling of newsboys rising at every corner. It was not often that the papers got hold of a story like this. "HIS HONOR FINDS CORPSE" was the way the tabloids handled it.

"His Honor finds corpse and ye dicks find murderer — or go back to walking a beat somewhere in Queens," Piper remarked.

"They say the suburbs are much more healthful," Miss Withers retorted wickedly. And then they pulled down a narrow street beneath the Ninth Avenue El, in a noisy, dirty world of garages, rooming-houses, and lofts.

They finally stopped before what appeared to be an ancient stable. In spite of the neat brass plaque which read "Atelier Dravid" Miss Withers looked dubious. But the Inspector swung out of the taxi.

An exceedingly unemployed-looking person, in rusty clothing, casually detached himself from a railing and walked past. "Nobody come in since I got here," he grunted out of one corner of his mouth.

"Swell!" said Piper. He led the way to the big double door, and tried a key in the padlock. It worked.

"Stole it from the stiff's pocket," he informed her. "Come on in — it's only housebreaking."

† † †

There were mingled smells of clay, rockdust, cooking and decay at which Miss Withers wrinkled her nose. Piper closed the door behind them and cast his flash around the rudely furnished hall.

There was a stairway at the left, and a locked door directly ahead of them. "Let's see what's in here," Piper suggested. He tried another key, and then led the way down a long passage. The place still looked more like a barn or ware-house than a dwelling, in spite of the overalls and other rough clothing which hung here and there. At the far end the hallway made an abrupt turn to the right, and opened through a doorway into what at first seemed to be a starless and skyless outdoors. From somewhere came a cool draft ...

Piper cast his flash ahead, and Miss Withers squealed. It shone full in the face of a black and evil giant who was crouched as if ready to spring down upon them. A second glance told the school-teacher that the giant was cut of black stone, and eternally unable to move.

All around them loomed the vast, monstrous creatures which spoke of the odd genius of Dravid, the sculptor. Some of them, like the black giant, were roughly shaped. Others, most of them in ghostly white marble, were finished and ready for exhibition. Farther on were various smaller projects, some of them barely begun — models in clay and the like.

Walking softly, almost unwilling to speak for fear of disturbing the massive and brooding figures, Miss Withers and the Inspector pushed farther and farther into the vast studio.

Once Miss Withers paused to admire a fanciful interpretation marked with a brass placard — "The Fates," which consisted of four crouching female figures completely hooded in marble drapery. A moment later the Inspector, stepping back suddenly from an unlovely model of Judas Iscariot writhing beneath a thorn tree, lost his balance on a pile of rock chips and staggered into the outstretched arms of a vast and naked lady who leered back at him …

"Oh!" he gasped. Then, to Miss Withers, "You know, I almost said 'pardon me'!"

He raised his flash, and they both stared at the voluptuous, Junoesque figure — truly a caricature of desirable womanhood. Her robe had just slipped to her feet and her face wore an expression of invitation, of evil knowledge — all in all, here was sculptured with all the clear cold hardness of marble, a woman perfect in her fleshliness.

"Isn't she something!" Piper remarked gaily. But Miss Withers was frowning.

"Hussy!" she accused the marble figure. Then — "He must have known some woman — much too well," she analyzed.

But they were not to spend the evening in admiration of the murdered sculptor's genius. From somewhere in the upper regions of the place sounded the shrill ringing of a telephone.

"Say — I'd like to answer that!" Piper told her. "Maybe if we hurry… "

They ran back past the Fates, past the Judas and the black crouching giant, and came into the little hallway again.

Here both stopped short, and Miss Withers, who was normally a person of calm and restrained temperament, gave her second squeal of the night.

Coming toward them was the white marble woman which they had just left in the studio!

She seemed smaller, and she was wearing a white negligee which hardly concealed her large and Junoesque figure — but it was the same woman. Even though this woman had red lips, and walked smoothly …

She was not surprised to see them. "I am Mrs. Gretchen Dravid," she said. "If you're the detective, you're wanted on the phone!"

Piper gurgled a bit. "But — but my man said you hadn't come home!"

† † †

She pointed past them. "Perhaps your spies don't know of the studio entrance — it opens on another street," she explained. "I heard you come in the front door, and I'm sure I don't mind your poking about. But I wish you'd have your telephone calls somewhere else. I've stood all I can today!"

Without a word, the Inspector followed her back down the hall, through the front entryway, and up the stairs. Miss Withers, taking one look over her shoulder at the looming black giant, threw her dignity to the winds and scampered after them.

"The telephone is in here," said Gretchen Dravid, leading the way to a chaste and modernistic bedroom. She sprawled out on the bed, where she had evidently been comforting herself with smelling salts, a gay looking novel, and a bottle of wine.

"She's the type of woman who never sits down," Miss Withers told herself. Piper was looking for the telephone. "Lucky I left word where I was going," he remarked, "for this must be a matter of life or death."

Gretchen had to point out to him the location of the phone, which was reached by lifting the silken skirts of a saucy French doll. The Inspector looked somewhat abashed, but he finally got the instrument in his grip.

"Hello!" he barked. There was a long pause, after which he said "Yes" five times and "My God" twice. Then he put down the phone and stared at Miss Withers with bewildered eyes.

"They've found the murderer?" Miss Withers prompted.

He shook his head. "It's Dee Bryan, the girl who unveiled the statue," he told her. "She's been kidnapped!"

At which, for no particular reason, Mrs. Dravid was hysterical again.

† † †

It was not until five that afternoon that Park Commissioner Bryan was able to leave the blood-smeared statue in Central Park. Miss Deirdre Bryan had waited, in spite of his efforts to make her drive on home without him.

"It's a terrible thing for a girl your age," old Mike had told her.

"It's the most thrilling thing that ever happened to me," Dee insisted. "And if you make me go home I'll disown you." Dee had stayed, all through the fruitless questioning of the crowd, the preliminary examination by Dr. Bloom, and the removal of the body.

Then, and not until then, she drove her father along the boulevard in a smart new Packard roadster. They came out of the park onto Fifth Avenue, and headed downtown.

"I've got to phone my office," Bryan told her. "Pull up here a moment, and have a cigarette."

Dee was surprised at this, which was a breach of discipline. "Your driving shows that you need a sedative," her father told her. He gave her a cigarette, and then headed down 59th Street to where a Childs' gleamed whitely.

Bryan was barely in the phone booth when Dee caught a glimpse of the tall young man with the beard. He was walking very fast down Fifth Avenue. Instantly she remembered something.

This was the man who had stood near the newsreel sedan at the unveiling — the man who before the unveiling had stared up at the hooded statue with a wild and fascinated horror on his face. He must have known, then, what was hidden from the rest of them!

Suddenly she knew what she must do! Though her knees trembled and she found difficulty in breathing, she slipped from the car. Her rouge-stained cigarette dropped to the leather upholstery; she left the motor running and the door open ... but Dee Bryan had no thoughts for such minor matters.

The young man who was hurrying away into the twilight was either a clairvoyant — or a murderer! And Dee Bryan was going to find out which.

Tense as a steel spring, eager as a cat at a mouse-hole, Dee trailed her quarry. He stopped and looked cautiously around before he descended the stairs to the BMT subway station at the corner of the park, but Dee was actress enough to walk briskly across the street as if there were not a thought in her head except a desire for tea at Rumpelmayers.

Then, as he went out of sight, she doubled back and slipped down the farther stair. A southbound train swung past and stopped noisily. She saw the bearded young man enter the middle door, and she managed to slip into the end door of the same car.

He leaned against a pillar, though there were many seats. Dee crowded between a fat woman and a couple of stenographers and picked up a discarded extra which shrieked of "The Statue Murder." Casually she turned to the sports page, now and then peeking over the top at the man she was trailing.

He was not over thirty, she decided, in spite of the beard. Hatless, dressed in rumpled clothing of excellent cut, he looked lost, appealing, and exceedingly romantic. He stared constantly out of the windows at the bleak ugliness of the subway cavern which flashed past. At 42nd Street he suddenly left the car, and she almost had to tread on his heels to get out before the door closed. But he did not look back.

"I wonder if I have the nerve to ask him —" Dee breathed. But he was already hurrying up the stairs. At the top he turned left and made for the IRT turnstiles. Luckily she had another nickel, and got through in time to see him go down the downtown stair of the other subway.

† † †

Here the platform was crowded with homeward bound office workers. Dee saw the bearded young man buy a tabloid and stuff it into his pocket. Then he moved along.

He was standing on the express side of the platform, but as a local train pulled in he turned suddenly and slipped through a closing door. For a moment Dee imagined that he cast a triumphant backward glance at her, and then she realized that if her suspicions were correct he was running away, not from her, but from everybody.

She managed to get her arm in the door of the last car, and the automatic release flung it open long enough for her to crowd inside. The man with the beard was two cars ahead, and there was too much of a crowd for her to force her way forward even if she had dared to risk being noticed again.

But she thought of another idea. There was room on the rear platform, and she paid no attention to signs forbidding passengers to ride there. Shoving the door open, she took her stand at the gate, where she could at least see if her intended quarry got out on the platform.

Penn Station ... 28th Street ... 23rd ... 18th ... 14th ... slowly the train emptied, and was refilled, but still no sign of the man with the beard. Sheridan Square came next, the heart of Greenwich Village. But this was another blank. The train started forward with a jerk, and then she saw him!

The young man with the beard and the hunted eyes had concealed himself behind a pillar on the platform. Now he was hurrying toward the stair which led to the street.

He knew, then! Yet he was not looking back toward Dee. "It must be the police he fears," she told herself,

There was nothing for it now — he was gone, with his terrible secret. Yet Dee's Irish was up. She had followed him this far, and she was going to track him down.

Climbing up on the gate, she balanced herself a moment and then sprang toward the platform from the rapidly accelerating train. She landed sprawling, overturned a tin container full of old newspapers, and then rose dizzily to her feet. The train roared into the tunnel.

"Me and Tarzan!" said Dee Bryan proudly. And then, as the straggling crowd stared open-mouthed, she ran briskly past them and up the stairs.

Her quarry was luckily in sight, walking fast in the direction of the North River. "Now to see where you live," Dee remarked, not without triumph, "and then a phone call to daddy and the cops... "

He went on, with Dee keeping as close behind as she dared — one block, two, three ... and yet another. They were coming into an odorous and unsavory region, the borderland of the Hudson waterfront. Overhead the elevated roared deafeningly.

The man with the beard hurried past a building where Dee caught a glimpse of a sign "Atelier Dravid." There was a lounger across the street, but Dee did not realize the significance of his hump-toed shoes. To her all policemen wore bright cheerful brass buttons and carried nightsticks.

Around the corner and along a side street went the bearded man — and then suddenly he disappeared into thin air.

Dee stopped, stared all around and up into the narrow lane of sky, but there was no sign of him.

She went ahead softly, and then she saw the door. It was a large door, almost large enough to permit the passage of a truck, and it was open. Everything would have been different if the door had been closed. But it was open, suggesting untold possibilities.

†††

Dee bolstered up her courage, and walked briskly past the door. Nothing happened. Yet the man she had pursued must have gone through that door! If she could only be sure!

It seemed so easy to her — just a peek at the door. After all, this was New York City. There was a taxi at the corner, and some children were noisily playing cards on a nearby stoop. And an open door isn't like a closed one. It's so easy just to take a step inside, and as long as the door is open, a person can turn around and come right out again ...

Dee took a deep breath, and peeked in at the door. In the murky twilight she caught a glimpse of looming marble figures. "Why!" she told herself, "this must be a side door to the studio!"

Drawn in unsophisticated wonder by the mystery of the mighty stone images, she took a step inside ... and then another ...

She knew that it was madness as soon as she heard the soft closing of the great door behind her. She turned, and her red mouth opened in a silent scream as the darkness engulfed her, rising like water over her head ...

†††

"What are you going to do?" demanded Miss Withers.

"Blanked if I know," admitted the Inspector. "But I've got to drop this murder case and do what I can on the Bryan kidnapping. That girl has to be found! I suppose the Federal detectives will be horning in any minute... "

"Fiddlesticks," Miss Withers came back. "Can't you see? The kidnapping of that girl is part of your murder case! She must have known something or seen something... "

"What?" demanded Piper, not without reason.

Miss Withers admitted that she didn't know. "But while Miss Dee Bryan was holding that rope at the unveiling, she must have involved herself somehow... "

"But what could she see that a thousand others didn't see?"

Miss Withers shrugged. "If I'd been there, I could tell you, no doubt. Saving that, I'll have to have a talk with an eye-witness. Can you suggest anybody?"

"The Mayor — but he's hard to reach. Her father — but the Commissioner is so upset at losing his daughter he can't think straight. Says he left her in her roadster and came back five minutes later to find her wiped off the face of the earth —"

Miss Withers shook her head. "No, I don't want to talk to any of the official personages involved. You don't happen to know any newspapermen who were there? They usually see what's to be seen... "

She was suddenly cut short by a bellow from the Inspector, who turned and burst back into Gretchen Dravid's bedroom. Rudely he seized the telephone from beneath the skirts of the French doll, and barked a number. In a moment he was back, jubilant.

"It's all fixed," he said. "And I've got you an eye-witness that is an eye-witness. Just wait!"

As Gretchen Dravid, widow of the sculptor, watched with wide and slightly bleary eyes, the two oddly-matched sleuths went scurrying out of the studio and into the street, where a taxicab was noisily summoned. Fifteen minutes later Miss Withers was hustled into the Times Square offices of the Paradox News Service. She was whisked to an upper floor, elbowed into a pitch-dark room which seemed to be well provided with leather chairs, and after a brief delay the Inspector joined her.

"Just out of the drying racks," said a voice somewhere above and behind them. "No cutting done yet, but here goes... "

Then a great white square appeared before them, and a moment later the projection machine cast upon the screen a flickering picture of a public gathering. With a gasp Miss Withers recognized the Mayor, who was beginning his speech — and beyond him, a great draped figure, and a pretty dark-haired girl nearby who clutched the release cord. Everywhere else there were people, crowding up against the base of the statue, even a line of heads before and below the camera ... in the background were the trees of the park and, far to one side, the spires of Manhattan.

Miss Withers and the Inspector listened to the Mayor's speech — they noted the last minute bustling of the master of ceremonies and saw, but could not hear, his hurried change of instructions to the Commissioner and to his daughter.

They watched, spell-bound, while Dee Bryan nodded to show that she understood her instructions. They saw her glance right at the camera, and then up at the muffled statue.

† † †

They heard the Mayor make his clever recovery of the climax of his speech, and heard him read again the telegram "from Manuel Dravid" ... expressing his regrets at not being able to attend the unveiling.

"That was a quickly thought-up lie of His Honor," said Piper. "You got to hand it to him."

Miss Withers did not answer. She was staring with wide blue eyes at the white, glaring screen. If there was a detail she missed, it must have been a very slight one indeed.

Directly before the camera, and somewhat out of focus, she could see the back of Gretchen Dravid's head. That head, and the full neck and shoulders, were unforgettable ... The Mayor was winding up his speech now, but Gretchen Dravid still was calmly staring straight ahead.

At that moment Miss Withers realized that the woman could not, by any possible chance, have had the slightest premonition of what hidden thing lay beneath the covered statue.

Yet Dee Bryan, the lovely black-haired colleen who held the rope, was staring in the direction of the Dravid woman with an expression of incredulous wonder on her face. She began to tug at the rope.

"Stop it!" shouted Miss Withers. And suddenly the moving figures on the screen were frozen into immobility.

"She isn't looking at Mrs. Dravid!" Miss Withers told the Inspector excitedly. "She's looking at the young man beside the Dravid woman — the hatless young man with the rumpled coat!"

Only the back of his head and his ears could be seen, and those none too clearly because the camera had been focused some distance further off. But even now, it was clear enough that he was staring up at the statue as if he expected the thing to topple over and crush him beneath its weight — cringing away a little —

"And that," declared Miss Withers, as the screen became alive again, "that is what Miss Bryan happened to see."

They watched the end of the film — saw the canvas fall from the statue, and disclose the fearful crumpled burden which grotesquely was held in the arm of the sculptured Washington.

"You're wrong, Oscar," said Miss Withers softly. "The answer to this puzzle isn't How — it's Where!"

"You mean the setting for the murder? But maybe Dravid was killed somewhere else, and brought to the statue..." Piper stopped. "No, because the blood was on the marble. Bodies don't bleed after death, so Dravid was killed while climbing on his own statue. But I don't see... "

"You will," Miss Withers told him.

The film was ending — but not before they both saw the young man who had stood beside Gretchen Dravid as he turned quickly and melted out of range — and not before they both saw that he wore a soft brown beard!

They came out of the projection room, and Piper thanked the official who had arranged for the preview. "I hope that we'll get permission to release the film tomorrow," the man was saying. "It'll be the biggest scoop since we caught the death plunge of those men from the Macon... "

The Inspector said that he had to call his office. Miss Withers suggested another telephone call that he might make.

"But that was only a graceful way out for the Mayor... " Piper began. "He didn't really have any telegram from Dravid."

"Ask him, anyway," Miss Withers insisted. He hurried away to the telephone, and for the first time that day the school-teacher had an opportunity to study the marble fragments which she had lugged around with so much difficulty. It was very much like working a jigsaw puzzle, one of her minor vices, and by the time the Inspector returned she was surveying her results with considerable triumph.

† † †

There was a little table in the waiting room of the newsreel offices, and upon this table Miss Hildegarde Withers had spread out her bits of rock. The Inspector stared at them. "Well — whatever have you got there?'

"The weapon," she told him.

"Weapon? But I just talked to Doc Bloom. Dravid was killed by being stabbed with a marble blade, which Bloom just took out of his neck. A nasty weapon, too... "

"Exactly." Miss Withers nodded in agreement. "And that blade fitted right on the end of this!" She pointed to her joined fragments, with a few gaps representing a stone hammer and a stone sickle with the end of the blade missing.

"When Dravid was struck, the blade broke off in his neck and the rest of the weapon, along with its hammer, fell to the base of the statue and shattered. The murderer didn't have time to hunt for the pieces, or else he thought they didn't matter... "

"Good Lord!" But still Piper didn't understand. "The statue was complete as it stood, wasn't it? Anyway, forget that! I just talked to His Honor, as you suggested — and he says yes, that telegram was on the level. He'd forgotten clean about it until Dravid didn't show up — but it really was delivered to him this morning. So Dravid never meant to be on the scene."

"*If* he sent the wire," Miss Withers reminded him.

"But he did! I called the Western Union at Penn Station office and got a description of the sender. It was Dravid — at eleven o'clock last night. Luckily the night staff have just gone on duty again, and one girl remembered seeing a young man with a beard standing in the doorway last night waiting, while Dravid wrote the wire. They went away together... "

Miss Withers nodded. "And just when was Dravid seen last — alive?"

"His wife told one of my men that he left home late in the evening without saying where he was going. He had a bundle under his arm, and he seemed very excited and almost gay ... as if he was up to something."

"So he was," Miss Withers agreed. "Let's get out of here. I don't suppose there's any news about the missing girl?"

"Well, she has been reported seen eloping on the Chicago plane, and she's been noticed driving a taxi on Staten Island and walking across a road in Bronxville. But I'm afraid it's the usual thing... "

"There's nothing about this case which is unusual," Miss Withers retorted. "I'm beginning to see part of it, but it's that girl who worries me. And another thing — I don't remember my mythology as I should. How many Fates were there, according to the ancient Greeks?"

"Eh? How should I know?" Piper looked blank. "Four, I guess. Yes, there were four... "

"And their names were —"

"Athos, Porthos, and Aramis," the Inspector surprised her by answering. "Or something like that... "

"Oscar! They're the three musketeers," she snapped back. "The real Fates were Atropos, Clotho and Lachesis, if I'm not mistaken. But there were only *three* Fates!"

"Four!" insisted Piper stoutly. "Why, there were four figures in the statuary group that we saw a little while ago in Dravid's studio!" He stopped short. "Hildegarde! What's the matter?"

For Miss Withers was having some difficulty keeping her teeth from chattering. "Three Fates," she repeated dully. "One who spins, one who holds the thread, and one who cuts with the dreadful shears... "

Piper shook her by the shoulder. "Lord, woman, you're hysterical!"

But she shook her head. "Not quite, Oscar! Not hysterical, just a blind, silly old woman." She suddenly turned and ran, like some strange, long-legged bird of prey. "Come on!"

"But where?" insisted the Inspector as they burst out into the lights of Times Square. Miss Withers told him, with a voice which sounded weary.

"In that case, we need the boys," said Piper reasonably. There was a police signal box on the corner, and he unlocked it and spoke into the mouthpiece. "Emergency, and I mean emergency," he said.

† † †

Then they climbed into a taxi, but before it had gone two blocks in the direction of Greenwich Village, the wail of squad car sirens sounded behind them, and from then on they raced through town like Admiral Byrd returning from the Antarctic, only much faster. There was no deluge of ticker tape and scrap paper, but a driving squall of rain made up for that.

The sirens were stilled as they raced down Ninth Avenue and came to a stop outside the studio of Manuel Dravid. Miss Withers made for the door.

The Inspector caught her arm, and pointed out a light in an upper window. It was the widow's bedroom.

"I know," Miss Withers came back. "She doesn't matter, though I suppose she was really the cause of the whole thing. But women like her make their own hell on earth, given time enough. You'll never get anything on her. But come on — unlock the door or break it in. I want to find the Bryan girl — or what's left of her!"

They raced down the long hallway, and came at last into the high-vaulted studio with its grim looming figures. Even a hard-boiled copper might well wince as his flashlight struck the grinning face of the black, crouching giant, or the tortured figure of Judas in the thorn tree. But it was before the statue group labelled "The Fates" that Miss Withers paused.

"I'll be something!" gasped Piper. "There were only three figures, after all!"

"There *are* only three," Miss Withers corrected. "Which means that we are too late!"

Then she felt a draft across her ankles — just as she had done on their other visit to this world of the stone figures. But this time there was the faint sound of a closing door.

"Quick!" she gasped. "There's another way out of here — find the door!"

Blue-clad officers scurried like fire flies among the great implacable figures, their flashlights slashing the darkness in frenzied and futile endeavor. It was five minutes, at least, before the great doorway was discovered and flung open.

They plunged out into the street, and stopped short. Across the way was a lounging figure in an old over coat.

"Mullins!" yelled the Inspector. The plainclothes cop snapped to attention. "What are you doing here?"

"Why — nothing. But I had an idea that maybe this studio place had an exit on the side street here, so I was just having a look... "

"All right ... but who did you see leave by this door?"

Mullins shook his head. "Why, nobody, Inspector. Nobody that doesn't belong here, that is... "

"For God's sake, man, speak up! Who did you see?"

"Why, there was nobody but a guy named Owens, who works for the sculptor. A nice young guy with a beard."

"You saw him leave, just now?" Miss Withers pressed on.

† † †

Mullins nodded. "He come out of there with a big white statue on his back, and dumped it into an old car that was waiting at the curb. I figured he had to deliver it somewhere... "

"Remind me to recommend Mullins for promotion to a school for the feeble-minded," gasped Piper, as he led the way in a race for the squad cars. "If we only knew which way the fellow went... "

"North — to the Bridge!" Miss Withers breathed. "Can't you see? He'll throw it over the rail!"

"Can't you go any faster?" demanded Piper of the driver, who was already doing seventy through crowded West Side streets. But it was fast enough, all the same.

At the foot of 57th Street a ramp leads up to the elevated auto highway, later connecting with Riverside Drive. As the squad car raced up this ramp Miss Withers screamed, and pointed ahead.

There in an ancient open touring car, she had glimpsed a single young man who was driving like a maniac — and there was a white bundle in the rear seat.

The squad car leaped forward, sirens howling — and the lone driver knew that the long trail was over. He turned back for one glance, showing a face paper-white above his beard, and then suddenly jerked the wheel in a reckless death leap toward the thin wooden railing and the street fifty feet below ...

There was a crash of wood as the touring car plunged through. The police car slowed, with a terrific screech of brakes, and Miss Withers shut her eyes.

But she opened them again — for the fugitive car was hanging awkwardly halfway through the railing, with its front wheels spinning in thin air.

The bearded young driver stood up suddenly, his face a mask of defiance and desperation. Then he turned and dived over the side of the car — down, down, down.

"Best thing he could have done," the Inspector was saying, as his men worked the touring car back from its perilous position. "With two murders on his conscience... "

Deft hands were unwrapping the cleverly draped sheets which had given the soft young form of Deirdre Bryan the semblance of a draped marble statue. Then somebody yelled, a shrill exclamation of amazement and glory. "She's breathing!"

And so she was. "You can't kill the Irish with one whack on the back of the head," Piper told Miss Withers proudly after the ambulance had borne Dee Bryan away. "She's been knocked cold for two hours or more, but the doctor says she'll be right as rain in a couple of days."

"It'll teach her not to follow murderers home," Miss Withers agreed. "Well, Oscar, it wasn't as bad a tangle as I feared... "

"Bad enough so I'm still entangled," he returned. "I catch on that Owens killed his boss Dravid, but why?"

Miss Withers didn't try to tell him until they were in a nearby Coffee Pot. Then she spread out her rock samples on the counter. "You didn't study these sufficiently, Oscar."

"Study them? Just broken pieces of some statue or other... "

Miss Withers rearranged the roughly assembled fragments, so that the head of the hammer came inside the curve of the sickle. "Does this mean anything more to you?"

"Huh? No — why, yeah! That's the symbol or whatever you call it of the Young Communist party. Only the other day there was great excitement because one of the CWA mural artists tried to slip it into the design of a wall painting he was doing for the new building on Ellis Island!"

Miss Withers nodded, in triumph. "Right! Well, Dravid was trying to perform the same sort of practical joke on the city — by slipping a marble sickle and hammer into the hand of his own statue of George Washington! It would be great publicity, too, on account of the newsreels and the Mayor's speech. But he couldn't risk being there, so he sent a wire begging off, and then sneaked up to the park last night with his assistant to help him. It was no easy job to get those extra pieces of carved marble into the outstretched hand of the statue... "

"And Owen, being patriotic and all that, hit him in the back of the neck with the sickle? And then just walked off and left the body there under the canvas?" Piper looked dubious.

"I told you that the important part of this case was the location of the murder, and not the weapon. Why was Dravid stabbed while mounted on his own statue — why, unless he was making a last minute change?" Miss Withers took a large bite of ham and egg. "But I wonder about the motive, Oscar. Perhaps young Owen thought he was being a patriot when he seized the opportunity and killed Dravid. A little overemphasis on the patriotism, perhaps. But my own idea is that his motive was that big white woman who was married to Dravid. Remember the statue that her husband made of her? It was a terrible revelation of her true nature — and I'm very much afraid that, whether Owen admitted it to himself or not, that woman was really the reason why it happened that a great surge of hatred swept over him when he was alone with Dravid at the statue last night."

† † †

"Jealousy causing a rush of righteousness to the head, eh? When it was really only a rather silly practical joke that Dravid was trying to play on the city." The Inspector finished his coffee, reached for a toothpick, and then tossed it away under Miss Withers' disapproving stare. "Seems a lot of shooting over small potatoes, to me."

The school-teacher agreed. "The only lucky one is Miss Dee Bryan," she pointed out. "When that inquisitive and charming Miss gets out of the hospital she'll have the unique memory of having been fourth among the Three Fates!"

"She won't remember much, she was out cold all the time," objected Piper.

Miss Withers' blue eyes twinkled.   "I have an idea that, being Irish, Dee Bryan will have a grand rousing story to tell, all the same — one that will get better as she grows older."

And again Miss Withers was right.

The Riddle of the Whirling Lights

Somehow it had always happened that Miss Hildegarde Withers came upon the trail of murder in the most unlikely places and at the most unlikely times. A grinning porter was now handing her a telegram while she was in the midst of re-reading Dickens' *Christmas Carol!*

She had slipped the immortal classic into her suitcase as a proper preparation for a holiday visit with her married sister in Dubuque, but her perusal of the adventures of the remarkable Mr. Scrooge were cut short as she tore open the yellow envelope.

The message was from her old friend and sparring partner, Inspector Oscar Piper of Centre Street.

"URGENT DROP EVERYTHING INVESTIGATE MURDER IN CHICAGO PLANETARIUM ANTHONY LASSITER HELD AS MATERIAL WITNESS PARENTS AUTHORIZE ANY EXPENSE... "

"Any answer, lady?" The porter offered a well-chewed pencil.

Miss Withers produced her own fountain pen and even as she puzzled over the proper manner in which to inform the Inspector that what he asked was absolutely impossible, she found herself writing a terse "CERTAINLY WHY NOT?"

"Send this at once," she told the porter. "Send it collect and get me the Chicago papers as soon as you can!"

†††

Since early that fateful morning the wind had been howling along the lakefront as wind can howl only in a Chicago December. There was not a taxi to be seen anywhere on the esplanade, a long and bleak expanse drenched with spray and icy with frozen spume. To the north Lake Michigan howled and raged at its breakwater, and by noon there was a glistening of icy spray upon the steps of the planetarium itself.

That doomed pill-box of a building, standing like a squat lighthouse on the farthest corner of the land recently reclaimed by a growing city from the lake depths, became a beacon for young Tony Lassiter. Stranded in Chicago between trains, without a single girl to call up on the telephone, he had wandered for a look at what remained of the fantastic structures of the recent Century of Progress. But the wind steadily increased, and Tony found himself wet and chilled and miserable. The skyscrapers of lower Michigan Avenue were a mile behind him — Tony headed out along the esplanade hoping for the comforting sight of a rank of taxicabs outside the building.

There were only a dozen or so parked private cars and a long and very deserted looking Greyhound bus. Tony shrugged and hurried toward the steps under the legend "Adler Planetarium and Astronomical Museum." ...

It was then that the girl plunged out of the revolving doors and came skidding down the steps. She was blonde and curving, and her expression of gayety changed suddenly as the full force of the wind struck her.

"Oh!" she cried, fighting to keep her balance. But the wind was gusty, and there was glare ice under her feet. Tony braced himself and caught her in his arms just in time to keep her from hurtling headlong into one of the decorative mosaic pools which center the esplanade.

He very neatly went over backwards, for she was something of an armful. But he hung on.

A capful of spray flung itself in their faces, and the wind beat with redoubled fury. His arm around her, Tony helped her back up the steps and they burst through the doors into the warm interior.

Her eyes were wide and of fathomless gray. "Thank you," she breathed. "I — I guess that after all I'll have to wait for the bus to take me back to town." She made a pouting *moue*. "Such a blowy day!"

"I'm waiting, too," Tony told her. "When does the bus go?"

"Not until after the lecture," the girl informed him. They were standing in a narrow and overheated foyer, hustled and jostled by couples and finally groups who seemed to be making a determined and weary tour of the museum.

"We're stranded here together, then," Tony ventured. He was about to inquire if the lecture was nearly over when a guard in the uniform of a French gendarme approached, announcing through a small megaphone that the next lecture demonstration would take place at 2 P. M.

A frown crossed the tanned forehead of the girl, and she drew the fur collar of her light blue cloak more tightly around her neck.

"I hate to wait," she said. "I want to get the first train for New York."

Tony told her that the next Manhattan bound train left the I. C. station at five — he knew, because he was booked through on it. The girl didn't say anything.

"Well," Tony remarked, "sorry I can't get you a taxi or anything. I'd say I hoped to see you on the train if you wouldn't think I was just being fresh." He prepared to leave her.

The gay eyes surveyed him, and then looked up and down the long hall. She took his arm. "No — don't go. Please don't — let's be bored together, as long as we have to be bored." And that was that.

They walked slowly around the outer hall, past cleverly illumined photographs of the more distant parts of the universe, and between showcases filled with what looked like ancient instruments of torture, but which were variously labelled "astrolabe," "quadrant," "nocturnal" and so forth.

A crowd began forming before the closed inner doors above which a red warning light burned. Tony looked at his watch. "They start in ten minutes," he said. "We might as well hear all about the stars as long as we can't possibly get away until it's over."

The girl's eyes clouded, and cleared. "Why not?" she said gaily. "Maybe it will be fun." She began to chatter brightly, and in the next few minutes Tony learned that her name was Avis — Avis Le Glare — and that she had arrived from Los Angeles just a week ago. "A week of Chicago weather is enough for me," she told him. "I'm going to the Big Town to seek my fortune, or something... "

Ahead of them was an information counter covered with postcards and photographs, over which a bored and sulky-looking young woman presided. She was at the moment rearranging her hair, which she wore in a becoming Greek knot.

"Buy you some picture post-cards to send to your sweetie back in Los Angeles," Tony offered cheerfully.

But Avis Le Glare gripped his arm more tightly. "Let's — let's get in line," she said. She half turned him around. "We don't want to stand up, do we?"

They pushed in through the wide inner doors on the heels of the crowd, but Tony found that the big planetarium room was hardly half filled. They sank into a seat in the middle of the fourth row from the rear, and Avis opened her neat little suede bag and spread raspberry across her lips.

The room was like no lecture room that Tony Lassiter had ever seen, for the ceiling was a silver dome, the lecture platform was in the rear instead of in the front, and in the exact center of the place stood an instrument which looked like a working model of Mr. H. G. Wells' Time Machine. It was in the shape of a monstrous dumbbell mounted upon a movable frame, but the instrument was almost completely covered with tiny glistening facets like the eyes of a fly under the microscope.

As soon as the crowd had settled, a small door in the rear of the room opened and two men came through. The foremost was very tall and straight, with a mop of unruly white hair and the face of an ascetic.

"Professor Ames, the director," whispered the girl, as if Tony had asked. "I've seen his pictures in the papers."

The second man came into the light, a lean and handsome young man with a softly poetical face. He stepped upon the platform and made last-minute adjustments to a microphone which was fastened to the control board before him. He then stood aside and let his superior speak.

"Ladies and gentlemen!" began the professor, his voice through the amplifier seeming at once to come from every quarter of the room. "I welcome you to the planetarium — and bid you *bon voyage* upon a journey which will transport you to the farthest bounds of uttermost space. The subject of this afternoon's lecture is The Architecture of the Heavens, and your speaker will be Mr. Grant Bell ... all right, Mr. Bell... "

His voice trailed away, and he turned toward the younger man, who had been busily engaged in closing the room's high ventilators by means of a window pole, so that the ceiling was now a clear unbroken expanse of silver.

The professor departed, and in the small doorway through which he had left immediately appeared a young lady in uniform — a sullen, almost sulky young woman bearing an armful of booklets.

Mr. Bell touched a button on the control board, and the lights of the room began slowly to diminish. "I shall waste no time this afternoon in a description of the wonderful mathematical instrument which you see before you. The planetarium instrument is well described in the booklet which you may purchase from the young lady at twenty-five cents, either as she passes among you now or at the close of the lecture."

"Want one?" Tony asked his companion. She shook her head, and the girl from the information counter passed them with her wares.

The lights grew dim ... and the rich and resonant voice of Mr. Grant Bell boomed forth. He spoke of the magic and mystery of the sky, and as he spoke, through the pitchy darkness there sprang forth upon the domed ceiling the entire firmament of heaven — the stars as seen through a good telescope on the brightest night that ever shone.

The great dumbbell of the planetarium instrument began to swing upon its axis — and suddenly the people in that room were hurled out of their chairs and transported into the open air beneath a sky which spun past as never a sky had spun before.

"We are now seeing the heavens perform in one minute the circle which to us on earth appears to take place in one day!" came in honeyed accents from the microphone. "In the track of the sun and moon pass our sister planets of the solar system... "

Through the magic of the projection machine the planets began to perform their yearly orbits around the sun in the space of a few minutes, and then Jupiter and Venus and Mars and Saturn faded away and the constellations of the nearer stars came out one by one to illumine the dome. From Polaris in the north to the very Southern Cross the lecturer chanted his story of the vastness of space, and from an invisible flashlight in his hand a blue arrow darted across the ceiling to point out now a cluster or galaxy of stars, and now the vicinity of some great spiral nebula — a world in the making ...

"On and on and as far as the greatest telescope can take us there are ever more stars and solar systems," the lecturer was saying. "It may be true that some day, when man learns to make greater lenses for his telescopes, we may be able to find the jumping-off place of the universe — the utter end of all things beyond which there is only absolute void! Try to imagine it with me — an unending eternity of Nothingness!"

Tony Lassiter shivered a little at the thought, and he fancied that the girl beside him shivered likewise. Then she leaned over against his shoulder.

The lecturer was speaking a little faster now, as if hurrying toward the end of his talk. He spoke of the estimated number of the stars in the Milky Way, which now swung slowly over their heads in shimmering loveliness. He told of the number of light years between those twinkling points of light and this earth — so great a distance that many of them may have been dead as ashes these many centuries and yet the final flare of their passing not yet reached us! The crowd was tense now — not even a whisper or a cough. Across the room somebody dropped what sounded like a metal vanity-case. The speaker went on ...

But Tony was deathly tired of astronomy and its facts and figures. He remembered, being twenty, that he was in a pitch-dark room with a very pretty girl who had let him pick her up on the planetarium steps. She was leaning a little against him — and slowly he let his arm pass across the back of her chair.

What else was darkness and starlight for? Yet — as his hand touched her cool, smooth neck and the mass of tangled yellow curls, it stopped short.

Ice water seemed to gush through his veins, and he opened his mouth in a silent nightmare scream ...

Avis Le Clare's head rolled limply and horribly on his shoulder, and there was something warm and sticky ebbing from the back of her neck!

Somehow Tony Lassiter stumbled to his feet, crying out above the voice of the lecturer — "Lights! For God's sake, turn on the lights!"

There was the briefest of pauses, and then the lights began to come on, almost as slowly as they had gone off. The heavens paled, the Milky Way dissolved, and the room came through a terrible twilight into bright noonday.

The face of the young man on the high control platform was white as chalk. The crowd surged and yammered, and young Tony Lassiter stared into the contorted face of her who had been pretty Avis Le Clare.

A woman screamed chokingly. But someone was still in control. As the crowd pushed and surged away from that huddled figure in the chair next to Tony Lassiter, the man on the platform turned suddenly to the girl who stood by the little doorway, her arms still full of booklets.

"Get the Professor!" he shouted. "Get Murphy, too!" He leaned toward the microphone. "Nobody move!" he shouted, his voice cracking with excitement.

Bell leaped down from the platform, came up the aisle and forced his way to Tony's side. For a moment he leaned over the body, his fingers pressing back the eye-lid, touching the chilling temple ...

He stood up, his face calm. He looked at Tony Lassiter.

"Give me the knife," he demanded.

"Knife?" That was all Tony could say. "Knife?"

A guard appeared in the doorway, blocking the exit of the frightened crowd. "Nobody leaves, Murphy!" shouted the lecturer. "I'm going to call the police." The door slammed behind him.

Ten minutes later two grim-visaged radio cops found the "knife" — in the shape of one half of a pair of scissors, lying twenty feet away beneath a row of seats at the front of the hall. The slender steel blade at first appeared to be painted crimson.

And it was then that young Tony Lassiter found that his troubles had just begun.

† † †

The door marked "District Attorney — Cook County" opened, and three men came out. Two were burly, self-satisfied deputies, and the one in the center was a boy of twenty. Tie awry, hair plastered over his forehead, young Tony Lassiter looked so much like the "thrill-killer" which the news papers had already dubbed him that any jury would have hanged him on sight. Then a small personage appeared in the inner doorway — none other than the great Mr. Alton Coe himself, who nodded genially at the reporters and other hangers-on who ornamented his outer office. He held up a well-manicured hand.

"He hasn't confessed — yet!" said Mr. Coe. "But stick around, I'll try to break him before the forms are locked up."

With that cheering pronouncement, Mr. Coe returned to his private sanctum, as he thought, closing the door behind him. But he looked up from his desk to see the slightly equine face of a determined looking spinster, who shook a black cotton umbrella in his face.

"Young man!" she challenged.

Mr. Alton Coe had been a member of the bar for more than eighteen years, and the opening remark of this apparition stopped him short. Then Miss Withers laid upon his desk a bright silver badge ornamented with the arms of the City of New York. "Doesn't mean a thing," she admitted. "Purely honorary — but I've been asked to do what I can for this Lassiter boy. At least until his parents and attorneys and so forth can get here by plane." She sniffed. "I suppose that you realize you haven't the slightest case against him?"

Mr. Coe glared and choked, and then burst into gusts of laughter. Wiping his eyes, he shook hands with his uninvited guest. "Welcome to Chicago," he said. "You'll find that I'm as anxious to get to the bottom of this planetarium thing as you are. But it's open and shut. Young Lassiter, over-brilliant student, while *en route* to his home in New York for the Christmas holidays, suddenly goes hay-wire and decides to pull a murder for the fun of it. He picks up an ordinary pair of scissors somewhere, throws away one blade, and uses the other to stab the first pretty girl he meets."

"Were his fingerprints on the blade?" Miss Withers queried.

Coe shook his head. "Wiped them off. But we've got enough on him without that. His story won't hold molasses."

"Clever case," Miss Withers admitted calmly. "But you don't believe it."

Coe frowned. "Well, what else? We've checked on this Avis Le Glare. She's only been in town a week — a stranger in Chicago. Lassiter says he picked her up — or she him — because they were both lonesome. Cock and bull story."

"How'd you find out her name?"

"Funny thing about that," said the D.A. "There was nothing on the body to identify the girl, but when we searched the planetarium we found her handbag under one of the showcases devoted to astrolabes or whatever they call those old-fashioned astronomical instruments on display. Looks like she dropped it — or maybe she was scared that somebody was after her and hid it. She had sixty dollars and a gold vanity in the bag — also a little address book. There was her name and a Santa Monica address in the front. That's another reason we know Lassiter is lying — he says he saw her bring the bag inside the planetarium room."

"He lies — or he is mistaken — or somebody snatched the handbag after killing the girl," Miss Withers decided in judicial tones.

The D.A. stood up. "Anyway, we'll prove this case," he promised. "And now, if you'll come with me, I have a little further questioning to do — some of the planetarium employees that I ordered brought up here to complete their preliminary statements that Lieutenant Titus took down."

Coe led the way into an adjoining conference room and Miss Withers found herself face to face with four of the actors in this drama of blood and stars.

Around a long mahogany table were seated three men and a woman, all of whom were showing something of the strain they had been under all afternoon. Introductions were brief — Miss Withers learned that the elderly ascetic with white hair was Professor Ames, the director, that the young man with the narrow shoulders and the deep voice was Grant Bell, lecturer, and that the sulky young woman in the tight uniform was Miss Vida Hooper, who presided at the information counter and sold postcards and booklets. Last of all was Guard Walter Murphy, still in his ridiculous blue and red uniform.

"We'll only take a few minutes," Coe began. "You people have been under surveillance since the murder, but I promise that very shortly you'll be permitted to go home. This lady here —" He had seen Miss Withers ostentatiously preparing notebook and pencils — "this lady here will take a few short-hand notes for the record."

Professor Ames came first, as was his due. The Professor expressed himself as being most tremendously bewildered by the whole affair — and almost in tears because a scandal had attached itself to the astronomical museum, first of its kind in the world. But Professor Ames was a poor witness.

He was unable to say whether or not he had noticed the girl Avis Le Glare when he came into the planetarium room that afternoon to make his usual speech of introduction. "You see, I have so much on my mind... "

Miss Withers' eyebrows went up. So far, it seemed to her that there was nothing upon the Professor's mind except for Miss Hooper's neckline, which happened to be a trifle peek-a-booish.

"I'm preparing a monograph upon the Variations in the Transit of Venus," he explained.

"The what?" demanded Coe. "Oh, astronomy. Well, skip that. At any rate, you have said that at about two o'clock this afternoon you left the planetarium room just as Miss Hooper here entered with her booklets — that you returned to your private office and the — er — Variations of Venus. You were there when the crime was discovered at approximately two-twenty-five. Alone?"

"Of course!" said the Professor indignantly. "Quite alone,"

"And you have never seen the deceased except when the alarm was given and you ran into the lecture room?" Coe went on.

The Professor thought not, but he would not swear. "I meet so many people," he said.

Mr. Grant Bell came into the limelight. "I noticed nothing out of the way this afternoon," he said. "But I couldn't help noticing the girl who — who died. I noticed her when I came into the room, because she was very pretty and she seemed very interested in the young man who sat beside her — that was before the lights went low. But I'd never seen her before... "

"Did you hear the tinkle of the blade as it fell?"

Mr. Bell thought not. "My attention is on the microphone and the control board," he explained. "And I have my hands full."

Mr. Coe said he was anxious to learn just how many exits there were to the planetarium room.

Bell frowned. "Only one main exit, for the use of the visitors. That can't be opened when the red light is burning. Then there is the little door near the speaker's stand in the rear of the room, for the use of the staff... "

Miss Withers cut in. "Would it have been possible for someone to have come through that little door when the lights were out — and to have slipped away after murdering the Le Clare girl?"

Bell was smiling now, a friendly, open smile. "You ought to ask Miss Hooper that question, not me."

Vida Hooper was standing up, her brown eyes almost black pin-points. "Why, what do you mean, you —"

"Only that you usually stand near the doorway, waiting in case someone wants to buy a booklet at the end of the lecture," Bell added hastily. "If anyone had come in, they'd have had to push past you."

"Oh!" said Vida Hooper. "Well, nobody did."

The District Attorney cut in. "No matter. Avis Le Clare was not murdered by a mysterious invader, for she and the prisoner sat in the fourth row from the rear — in the middle. Nobody could have stabbed her without climbing over the feet of the nice old ladies in the row behind them, so it must have been Lassiter. Unless the killer wore wings, or had arms ten feet long."

"That's an idea," observed Miss Withers. But nobody heard her.

"And in case I'm under suspicion," put in Bell belligerently, "remember that my alibi is the best in the world, for everybody in that room heard my voice coming through the microphone."

"According to your statement to Lieutenant Titus," Coe went on, "you said that you had only been with the planetarium for a few weeks?"

Bell nodded. "I worked at the Century of Progress for a while last Summer, and when it was over I heard of this job through a friend of mine —" (he glanced briefly at Vida Hooper, who was sulkily toying with one of Miss Withers' pencils) — "so I learned the speeches and got the place."

Miss Withers put in a question. "By the way, Mr. Bell, when you examined the body of the girl before turning in the alarm, did you happen to notice a handbag on her lap or nearby?"

Bell blinked and stared fixedly at the table. "Handbag? No, I didn't see any handbag. But I wasn't looking for —"

"Never mind," Miss Withers told him. Her notebook gained a few more meaningless scribbles.

† † †

The session dragged on. Vida Hooper denied that she had ever seen the girl Avis Le Clare before she was killed, although she admitted that she had sold picture postcards to a large number of people before the lecture began. No, she had not heard the tinkle of the knife. Or maybe she had, only she hadn't thought it was a knife. Or scissors, or whatever it was. Miss Hooper was almost hysterical, and the District Attorney passed hastily on to Guard Murphy. Murphy heavily reiterated his earlier statements as to the position of the body when he came on the scene.

"She was slumped over against the chair where the murderin' young man had been sitting," he explained, "with the blood all over her neck. And him with his hands all red..."

Mr. Bell wiped his forehead, and Miss Vida Hooper stirred restlessly. "Can we go now?"

Mr. Alton Coe stood up, but Miss Withers flounced out of her chair and spoke intense words in his ear. He frowned, nodded, and stepped for a moment into his private office, from which he reappeared bearing a large brown envelope from which he took a woman's small suede handbag.

"This was Avis Le Clare's," he said doubtfully. "But its contents were quite intact. Money and vanity, handkerchief and all. So I don't see —"

"I'm beginning to," said Miss Withers. "That bag held something that somebody wanted badly. Letters, perhaps, or photographs. And that certain somebody got them, and then tossed aside the handbag. So you can forget about young Lassiter." She drew a deep breath. "You four have been under police scrutiny since the alarm was given, and presumably have had no opportunity to get rid of anything you might have — borrowed from the bag. In the light of possible future developments, wouldn't it be a good idea if you — well, if you permitted... "

Grant Bell cut in. "If you think we ought to submit to a search, start with me."

† † †

Much to Miss Withers' disgust there was no opposition from any one of the four. The Professor's pockets brought forth, among the usual keys and gadgets, a small photograph of a voluptuous movie star, well thumbed. There was nothing of interest on the person of Mr. Grant Bell with the possible exception of one thousand dollars in crisp new bills.

"I always like the feel of some cash on me," he explained. Miss Hooper, oddly enough carried a vanity case, a hotel key, and a tangle of strong light string on her person. Guard Murphy produced the makings of home-made cigarettes, a dollar and something in silver, and a pair of dice.

On the whole, it was a disappointing collection. The Professor rose to his feet. "After this, I presume that we will be permitted to leave so that we may hold our usual evening lecture without police interference?"

"Lecture — tonight?" Alton Coe started to shake his head, but Miss Withers caught his eye and nodded heavily. Then, as he gave grudging consent, she returned to her scrutiny of the dead girl's handbag.

The four who had been questioned pushed out into the hallway, and Miss Withers noticed that Vida Hooper lingered as if to speak to someone. But the Professor and Grant Bell were deep in a discussion of the best manner in which to handle the unfortunate publicity arising from the case, and Guard Murphy hurried away.

Impulsively, Miss Withers dropped the handbag and approached the other woman. She saw an opportunity for a little inside work.

"My dear," began the schoolteacher, "there was just one little addition I wanted to make to my shorthand notes... "

Vida Hooper laughed, shrilly. "You better learn more than two or three hen tracks before you try to pass yourself off as a shorthand expert, lady — I was looking over your shoulder!"

With that sally she departed, leaving Miss Withers a little deflated.

The school-teacher returned to Mr. Coe's office, to find the D.A. rubbing toothache remedy on his gums.

"Gaw!" he managed. Then — "Well, Hawkshaw, ready to give up after your fiasco with the handbag and the frisking?"

"In the bright lexicon of some thing or other there is no such word as 'fail'," she told him. "I want to ask you a few questions. First, was Miss Le Clare *enciente* — or haven't you heard from the medical examiner?"

"I have — and she wasn't," said Coe.

"No incipient motherhood, no letters or photos," Miss Withers remarked. "Motives are getting scarcer — but I still don't think it was a thrill motive." She rifled the pages of the little address book which had been part of the contents of the dead girl's bag. "Not as long as the alphabet continues to be ABCDE, etc."

"Eh?" said Coe testily, wishing she would go away.

"This address book is alphabetized," Miss Withers said. She showed it to him. "But didn't you notice that the alphabet is spelled A-B-C-D-E-F-H-I-etc."

"Minus 'G'?" asked Mr. Coe blankly.

"Minus 'G'," Miss Withers agreed. "One question more. Do you have a method of sending photographs by telegraph?"

"Between police stations, yes... "

"As far as Los Angeles?" she demanded.

Coe nodded. "But it costs money. And I don't see what difference it makes if Avis Le Clare... "

"I wasn't referring to Avis Le Clare's photograph," said Miss Withers calmly. And she explained what she did mean.

"My theory won't hold molasses," she explained. "But before the evening is over I'll plug the holes. Will you do as I suggested?"

"It means I'll miss my appointment with the dentist," complained Coe. But he finally gave in, in the face of Miss Wither's insistence.

"All right, I'll dig up the picture from the newspaper files and send it along," he said. "You've certainly upset things, my dear lady; but contrary to common belief, a District Attorney is no more anxious to convict an innocent man than anybody else. I'll give this Lassiter every chance — but where are you bound for?"

Miss Withers sniffed. "I'm looking for the other half of that pair of scissors," she told him. "And until it's found this case will not be solved."

††††

But if the maiden school-teacher was on the track of the remainder of the murder scissors, she chose a strange manner of search, for the next two hours of the winter evening she spent on the telephone in her modest Loop hotel.

There are something more than 1,200 hotels in the city of Chicago, and Miss Withers faced the necessity of calling them one by one. She shuddered at the thought of her expense account, in spite of the word that the Lassiter family would guarantee any costs. Then she decided to call only those hotels listed as being within the Loop itself.

"Avis Le Clare, would hardly have been the type to have lived in the suburbs during her stay in Chicago," the school teacher decided.

She phoned hotel after hotel, monotonously working down the columns of the phone book. Everywhere she drew a blank. Miss Withers was beginning to think that the girl had used an alias, after all, when suddenly as she gave the one hundred and something number to the weary girl at her own switchboard, the operator interrupted.

"I couldn't help listening in on your call, ma'am — and if it's a Miss Le Clare you're looking for, she's registered in this very hotel!"

"Oh!" said Miss Withers blankly. She hadn't thought of that. In a moment she was downstairs and bestowing modest largess upon the helpful girl.

"And the police — you told them of this when you read tonight's extras?"

The girl at the switchboard shook her head. "They didn't ask," she admitted. "But there's a Miss Le Clare in room 1216... "

"Good!" Miss Withers marched calmly over to the desk and rapped with her knuckles. "My key, young man — 1216!"

The ruse worked, and a sleepy clerk handed over the key.

It seemed that the elevator would never take her to the twelfth floor, and Miss Withers was sure that the operator stared at her in wonderment as she passed her own floor, the sixth. But finally she was down the hall, and inside of room 1216.

† † †

It was oddly lacking in character, this last abode of Avis Le Clare. There was a bathroom cabinet crammed with creams, shampoo lotions, and fingernail polishes, a dresser mirror with a photograph of a bungalow which Miss Withers recognized as standing in one of the more unlovely sections of Santa Monica, California — one suitcase filled mostly with evening dresses —

That was all. There were no letters, no burned scraps in a fireplace, no scrawls on a blotter. Miss Withers felt a little ashamed of herself at her heartless invasion of the privacy of the dead. She locked the door and started down the hallway. Then suddenly she made an about face and entered the room again. There must be something here — she felt one of her strongest hunches. Idly she lifted pillows, poked at the nondescript rugs and pictures. Then, on an impulse, she picked up the telephone book which lay on a table by the bedside. It fell open where someone had inserted a folded newspaper page — part of a Sunday supplement which, to Miss Withers' amazed delight, dealt with the new Chicago planetarium. It was from a Los Angeles paper — and bore the photograph of Professor Ames standing beside his beloved planetarium instrument, with a grinning Grant Bell in the background toying with his microphone.

Miss Withers tucked it into her handbag and was about to steal from the room when she thought of something else. The clipping must have marked a page. It did — halfway down a column someone had made a pencil dash after the entry "Grubb, Mrs. Frank V. r. 3540 Ellis Drexel 5525." ...

About to call the number, Miss Withers thought better of it. She hurried down the hall, paused in the room long enough to pick up her handbag, and descended to the street and a taxicab.

The residence of Mrs. Frank V. Grubb turned out to be a five story brownstone in the heart of the South Side rooming house section. Outside was a sign "Apartments — double single rooms — with or without board."

Miss Withers pressed the bell. Nothing happened. She pressed it again, hard. Still no response. There was a key in her bag, but she did not dare to use it.

Finally a light flashed on at the end of the hall, and a round waddling figure approached. The door was flung unceremoniously open.

"Always forgetting your key, Miss... " began the squeaky voice. Then Mrs. Grubb realized that this was not one of her tenants after all. "You want a room?" she demanded.

"Er — no," admitted Miss Withers, getting her foot into the door in case of a peremptory dismissal. "Does Professor Ames live here?"

Mrs. Grubb shook a wrinkled face, wise with the bitter wisdom of the landlady.

"Then could I see Miss Hooper?"

"None of them folks lives here," said Mrs. Grubb. "And I'll be asking you to go and leave decent people... "

"I'd like to see Mr. Bell, Mr. Grant Bell," Miss Withers tried finally. The door swung wider.

"Ain't here — he works nights," said Mrs. Grubb. "Come back tomorrow... "

"But I'm his aunt ... from Buffalo," Miss Withers lied calmly. "Can't I come in and wait for him?"

† † †

It was the wrong approach. "Aunt, eh? Another of Mr. Bell's relatives, eh?" Mrs. Grubb seemed to have a grievance. "Only last week it was a wife — and he already living upstairs in my best suit with one wife! Now be off, and think of a better one... "

"Last week a wife, you say?" Miss Withers produced a dollar. "Couldn't you let me see his wife, please?"

Mrs. Grubb took the dollar. But she shook her head. "She moved out," said she. "They had a fight you could hear for blocks. If Mr. Bell didn't pay regular every Saturday I'd 'a' thrown him out. Seems as how she wasn't his wife — the second one. Maybe neither of 'em, for all I know. Anyway, she packed and left and that's the end of the women for Mr. Bell, except for the phone calls he gets every day... "

Mrs. Grubb evidently felt that she had given a dollar's worth. "Good-night to you," she said shortly, and Miss Withers took her foot out of the door just in time to save it. The door slammed, and Mrs. Grubb retired to her fastnesses. All the same, Miss Hildegarde Withers tiptoed softly up the steps when the lights were out again, and tried a key in the lock. It worked —

She closed the door again, and departed, half-intoxicated with the realization that the key she had palmed while searching Miss Vida Hooper fitted the lock of Mrs. Grubb's rooming house.

Which was enough sleuthing for one day. As Miss Withers entered her hotel she heard newsboys crying that Tony Lassiter had confessed, but the report cost her not one minute's loss of sleep.

† † †

It was nearly noon when Miss Withers stalked into the office of the District Attorney of Cook County, and this time she waited barely ten minutes outside his door.

"Well," he greeted her — "Did you find your scissors?"

"I did not," she confessed. "I've had to spend the morning comforting the hysterical parents of your prisoner. About this confession, young man... "

"Oh, yes," said the D.A. "The confession... "

"I can't believe that a college sophomore would be able to dictate a document as illiterate as that one," she went on. "It sounds more like the work of one of your masterminds of the force... "

Coe grinned sheepishly. "I spoke to Lieutenant Titus about that. Seems that he told young Lassiter he could have a cigarette and some sleep if he signed it. The kid gave in — but it doesn't look so good, does it?"

"Then why don't you announce that it isn't on the level?" Miss Withers demanded.

"Elementary, my dear Watson," crowed the D.A. "Because it would put the real murderer on his guard." He shoved a typed message across the desk. "I got this from Chief Davis of Los Angeles this morning."

Miss Withers read the teletype message, and raised her eyebrows. "So! Mr. Grant Bell is really Mr. Lucian Grant of Long Beach, California — formerly wanted by the police!"

"Formerly, but not now," Coe reminded her. "Seems that it all happened after the earthquake out there. Bell — or Grant — was a smooth-tongued promoter who built a lot of those stucco houses and a public school building all of which fell down when the quake jiggled the ground a little. Mostly because there wasn't enough cement in the mortar. There was an indictment out against him for a dozen different counts, but Chief Davis says it fell through and that they wouldn't bother to extradite him now. And that's that."

"Isn't it!" agreed Miss Withers.

Coe stared at her. "You don't think that this Le Clare dame had a grudge against Bell on some count or other arising out of that disaster, and came after him — only to get it in the neck first?"

"Um," observed Miss Withers, noncommittally. She rose and paced the soft carpet of Mr. Alton Coe's office. Then she stopped short. "I wish I could find the other half of that scissors," she said. Then — "Busy this afternoon, Mr. Coe?"

The D.A. still had a swollen jaw. "I had a dentist appointment for two," he complained. "Don't tell me you're going to talk me into breaking this one!"

But that was just what Miss Withers did.

It was, as it happened, the day before Christmas of the year 1934, and due to impending holiday festivities the afternoon crowd at the planetarium was much smaller than usual. For that reason Mr. District Attorney Alton Coe and Police Lieutenant Waldo Titus, two persons ordinarily too busy to indulge in research into the ways of the heavens, felt exceedingly prominent and uncomfortable as they took their places in the fourth row from the rear of the planetarium lecture hall.

"I looked at the microphone," whispered the lieutenant, "and the blasted thing is screwed tight to the instrument panel!"

The D.A. rubbed his jaw. "Don't suppose there could be a recording of that lecture, hooked up so he could play it vita-phone fashion? It just occurred to me that a guy who worked in here most of the time would be able to see pretty well in the dark... "

"Maybe the schoolma'am from New York has found the rest of her scissors," said the D.A. He seemed to think the idea funny.

"That dame? She's plum loco," the lieutenant insisted. "Why —"

Coe hushed him as the small door in the rear opened, and Professor Ames entered, followed by Grant Bell. Both men looked as if they were very tightly wound up and feared to fly to pieces at any moment. Vida Hooper kept close behind with her booklets, very tense.

The main door was being closed by a guard, but suddenly a determined feminine figure thrust its way through and flounced in.

Miss Withers came straight to the District Attorney, her face alight with an unholy joy. "Eureka!" she cried, in a voice that was perhaps louder than she meant. She lowered her voice to a stage whisper. "I'm positive that I know who did it! I've no real proof, but you can arrest the party and try the third degree... "

Using every particle of a histrionic ability that had been highly praised in the past, Miss Hildegarde Withers cast over her shoulder a glance that was at once accusing and fatuous.   She prayed fervently that she created the proper impression of a meddling busybody who had somehow stumbled upon the truth. And as her mild blue eyes caught a glance from one who stood near the control desk, she knew that she had struck fire.

Those eyes were starkly terrible — filled with hate and fury and fear...

But Mr. Alton Coe shook his head at her. "See me afterward!" he said loudly.

As it happened, there was no vacant seat beside him, and Miss Withers sank down into a place which she realized must be either the seat where Avis Le Clare had died or else very close to it. It took all her courage to turn her back to what was behind her, especially as the Professor made his somewhat breathless introductory speech and the lights went low ... nobody cared to buy Miss Hooper's booklets today ...

Grant Bell spoke into the microphone, telling of the magic and mystery of the sky — and the heavens sprang forth overhead, the entire firmament as seen on the brightest night that ever shone.

Word for word as he had given it on the preceding afternoon, the man who called himself Grant Bell spoke of The Architecture of the Heavens. He told of the planets, of the nearer stars, and of the immensity of the Milky Way. At last he spoke of the possibility of some day an astronomer's seeing, through an as yet undreamed-of lens, the jumping-off place of the universe ... the vast Nowhere filled with Nothing ...

Then it happened, as the heavens turned on the silver ceiling — there was a scream from Miss Withers, who lay prone on the floor between the rows of seats, and two police flashlights cut through the gloom.

One fell on the white face of Grant Bell, poised above his instrument board, with both nerveless hands gripped around the microphone. He fumbled interminably for the main light switch, and Mr. Alton Coe, who held the flash, gasped in wonderment. For this — this had been the man he suspected.

Then he saw that, caught in the glare of the lieutenant's flash, was the muscular figure of Vida Hooper, who was vainly trying to draw back a strange weapon which she had used all too well ...

The lights went on, and Miss Hildegarde Withers climbed to her feet. Pinned to the back of the seat in front of her was her overcoat topped by her Queen Maryish hat — pinned by a deadly spear which had pierced them as they stood propped by her umbrella where she had been sitting when the lights went out.

††††

There was turmoil and confusion as the crowd was forced back and as the lieutenant laid heavy hands upon the cursing, struggling woman.

From her maniac hands he took the long window pole used to open the room's ventilators — but now, around the projecting knob, had been slipped the handle of the missing half of the murder scissors, bound fast with strong cord!

It was a spear which reached easily across the heads of the people in the rear seats, striking down from the height of the rear platform.

The first one to speak was Mr. Grant Bell. "I — I was afraid of that," he said. Then he would say no more.

"He doesn't need to say any more," Miss Withers told the D.A. as Vida Hooper was dragged away to wait for the police car. "It's clear enough, you see."

Mr. Coe didn't see, and said so.

"Young Lassiter, whom you'll have to release as soon as possible, told too weak a story to be lying," she explained. "The weakest part of it was that the girl let him pick her up so easily. She had to wait for a taxi, and she was a little nervous to stick around this place after what she had just done ... she wanted male protection ...

"And what had she just done?"

"Blackmailed Grant Bell, of course. He was hiding out from that Long Beach indictment, not knowing it had fallen through. The girl, who may or may not have been his wife in California, recognized his picture in the newspaper story, and decided to shake him down to get money enough to get to New York. Everybody in California wants to get to New York, and vice versa. She wrote him and wired him and finally she showed up at the rooming house where Bell was living with the Hooper woman.

"Vida Hooper was a terribly jealous type, Mr. Coe. She didn't know what the Le Glare girl had come for, and naturally Bell couldn't tell her. She thought he was going to take up with her rival again — maybe she knew that Bell and the girl had been more than friends in the past. So they had a fight and she moved out. I found that out from Bell's landlady... "

"Yes, but... "

"But nothing. Bell raised a thousand dollars and paid off the girl here yesterday, before the lecture. But there was no bus back to the city and it was a stormy day, so the Le Clare girl waited. Maybe she thought she could make some future use of young Lassiter — everybody knows how much money his father has. Anyway, she went into the lecture room to kill time and Vida Hooper saw her. She must have seen Miss Le Clare in the hall in order to have time to get the scissors and the string — for to her insanely jealous mind had occurred a diabolical scheme. She was going to put Avis Le Clare out of Bell's life — and get him back.

"So, when the lights went out Miss Hooper put down her booklets and put her spear together. Used to the darkness and not blinded by staring up at the lights of the sky as was everyone else in the room including Bell, she took good aim at the back of Miss Le Clare's neck — and struck!

"Luckily for her, there was no cry, as the knife severed the cervical vertebrae. She drew it back, hurled it in the general direction of the girl, and pocketed the string. There was very little blood at first... "

"Aha!" objected Coe. "But you say Bell paid the thousand dollars blackmail money? How did he get it back in his own pocket if he wasn't mixed up in it?"

"He was mixed up in it to the extent that he pocketed her handbag while looking at the body. Not for the money so much as to make sure she carried nothing to incriminate him. At the time he must have thought some stranger had done the girl in — before he turned in the alarm he tore out the page from the address book which had his real name and his Chicago address — and no doubt swallowed it before calling the police! Naturally he took back the money the girl had extorted — it was his by rights."

Mr. Alton Coe nodded slowly. "It all seems to fit. Bell thought he was a fugitive from justice, and his girlfriend Miss Hooper thought he was two-timing her, and the Le Clare wench thought she was putting one over on everybody —" He stopped short. "But look here — you didn't figure out where Vida Hooper cached the other half of the scissors. Remember, you searched her yourself in my office... "

Miss Withers gave him a bright smile. "The answer to that just occurred to me, Mr. Coe. She had it well hidden — yet it was where she could reach it at any time. Perhaps she kept it to kill herself if she thought she was trapped. Anyway, when I searched her I was led astray by the fact that most young women today have short curls and bobs. Yet Vida Hooper wears her hair in a very becoming knot at the back of her head. And that's where she kept the scissor blade!"

They came out of the planetarium and into the icy sunshine.

"Great Scott!" cried the District Attorney suddenly.

"What's the trouble with you?" Miss Withers demanded.

"My toothache's gone!" he told her, in wonderment.

"It's an ill wind," said Miss Withers sagely, "that butters no parsnips." And she walked away in the teeth of the breeze.

The Riddle of the Jack of Diamonds

The doorbell shrilled for a long minute, and then followed impetuous pounding of small hard fists upon the door of Miss Hildegarde Withers' modest little west side apartment. The middle-aged school teacher sat up suddenly in bed. By the pale grey light which filtered through her windows she saw that her alarm clock, set for eight, would not ring for another hour.

"Whatever in the world —"

Drowsily she found her slippers and dressing-gown, and swung open the door. It was a girl in her middle twenties, beautiful in a coldly perfect manner, and dressed in a soft coat which more than a hundred brown mink had died to make possible. Yet the dark hair was a little disarranged — the arrogant mouth frightened beneath its subtle smears of rouge.

The dark eyes flashed, without hesitancy. "You are Miss Withers? The one I've read about? I'm in terrible trouble!"

The school teacher swung the door wider, and offered her best chair to this perfumed and exquisite visitor. The slender gloved hands gripped together. "You will — you must help me!"

"I'm Lorna Davies — Lorna *Gault* Davies," said the young woman, as if that explained everything. She hesitated, and then plunged on. "It's about Rich — Richie Davies, my husband. They've arrested him. The police, you know. He's just an unworldly artist, and heaven knows what they'll make him do or say. It was all because the man who has an apartment on the floor above us was — died last night. A man named Merlin — Jack Merlin." She leaned forward, and the mink coat opened to show that she was still wearing an evening gown daringly designed of white satin. "Richie didn't have anything to do with it, of course. But he's got himself terribly involved. He works late at night at his painting, and last night or rather this morning he went out for a walk. When he came back the elevator boy made a silly mistake and took him to the ninth floor instead of the eighth. Richie never noticed — the apartments are similarly located, and he found the door of Merlin's apartment open and walked in thinking he was home.

"Then —" Lorna was staring at Miss Withers' slipper — "then he noticed that there was a dead body in front of the fireplace. He rushed out to call for help, and some people got out of the elevator and saw him. When the police got there they arrested Richie. They wouldn't believe his story, and of course the elevator boy swore up and down that he hadn't made such a mistake... "

"Of course!" agreed Miss Withers. She was growing interested.

"So you see? It's all a mistake, but Richie musn't stay in jail. If you'll only explain to the police!"

Miss Withers was thoughtful. "If what you say is true, your husband has nothing much to worry about. But I'll take the case. Only understand this, young woman. My aim will be not to protect any one person, but simply to find out the truth — and the chips fall where they may."

Lorna Davies hesitated only a moment. "Of course! That's what I want."

"I'd better go down there," Miss Withers decided. "Where did it happen?"

"Saxton Arms — 35 Park Avenue. I've my car here, but I can't wait while you dress. I must see some people before nine o'clock." She grasped Miss Withers' hand, in a clasp that was surprisingly firm. "I'm trusting you — take care of Richie —" She was gone.

Miss Withers frowned as she hastily dressed. She could understand why the young woman had other errands — there would be lawyers to see and all that — but why before nine o'clock?

A very few minutes later the schoolteacher was inside a taxi-cab and hurtling through the almost deserted streets of Manhattan. She was breathlessly deposited before one of the better apartment houses of lower Park Avenue.

She was trying to wheedle her way past the burly policeman at the door, when a dry voice behind her said, "Hullo! Here already?"

"Oscar!"

He took her arm and led her past the humbled guardians of the portal. "Only heard about this job half an hour ago," he remarked accusingly as they headed for the elevator. "Like to know how you got here ahead of me."

She told him, as they swept skyward, the bare facts of Lorna Davies' call. The Inspector looked rather stern. "You'll have a job of it, Hildegarde. It looks plenty bad for young Davies."

"But Oscar, coincidences do happen — and elevator boys can make mistakes!"

"Fish can wear water-wings, but they don't. Davies tells a pretty thin story — about his walking in upon Merlin's still-warm body by accident. Besides, he didn't rush out to turn in any alarm. He ducked down the stairs to his own apartment, and only the fact that some homeward bound merrymakers recognised him coming out of Merlin's door gave us the lead on him."

They were going down the ninth floor hall. "Then who did turn in the alarm?"

"Funny thing, that," admitted the Inspector. "The call came from an all-night drug store down the street. Man's voice, but wouldn't give his name. That was about four o'clock this morning. If it was Davies, why didn't he use his own phone?"

Miss Withers followed the Inspector down the hallway to the door of 9A, which was at the moment being propped up by the wide shoulders of Patrolman Doone.

"The medical examiner's just left, sir," he told the Inspector.

"This may be no sight for a lady," warned Piper. But Miss Withers marched stoutly through the door in his wake.

The Inspector was quite right. This was no sight for a lady. Through the open inner door of the wide foyer they could see flashes of blinding white light where the department photographers were taking pictures of the grim thing which lay sprawled face downwards upon the rumpled rug near the big living room fireplace. Mentally the schoolteacher checked down one point in favor of Richie Davies story.

A sergeant approached bearing a heavy iron poker — part of the set which lay overturned in the empty fireplace. "This did it," he announced. "Fits the hole in Merlin's skull. Not a print on it, either."

The Inspector nodded, and went over to scrutinise the corpse — a fattish, sleek man of perhaps forty or so dressed in a black robe and red silk pajamas. Piper thought he had seen that face somewhere before, though certainly not in the Lineup.

"What did the doctor say?"

Sergeant Dilling put down the poker. "Who, Levin? Nothing much. Death instantaneous, and could not have been self-inflicted. Probably happened about three o'clock this morning — maybe three thirty. That crack with the poker would have felled an ox," he said.

The Inspector spent the next half hour checking up on what had already been discovered about Jack Merlin and the apartment house. Merlin had lived here for two months — since February first. Two servants came in by the day — address unknown as yet. Entertained largely in the evening, both ladies and gentlemen of undoubted social standing. The elevator boys thought that there had been visitors last night, but they couldn't be sure, as Mr. Merlin's guests never sent up their names. A number of people had been taken up to the ninth floor.

At one o'clock, Piper learned, the doorman went off duty, and only one elevator boy remained. Guests had to use their own passkeys to enter the main door. Piper nodded. Then Davies could have walked down seven flights of stairs, phoned in the alarm from the drug store booth, and returned to his own apartment without being seen, particularly if he chose a time when the elevator boy was taking someone up or down. But why?

Pondering such problems, the Inspector sought his companion, and found her quietly playing solitaire on one side of the big round dining-room table. "Don't disturb me," she told him. "I don't often make Canfield, and it looks as if —"

She played out half a dozen more cards, and then stopped short. "If only I could have turned up the jack of diamonds, I'd have made it." She shook her head, and rose from the table. "Sorry to have kept you, Oscar — but there wasn't much to see in this place." The Inspector frowned, and then shrugged his shoulders.

Idly she lifted the buried card which had kept her from making the game. It was a queen. The jack of diamonds was not in evidence ... anywhere in the deck.

"Botheration!" said Hildegarde Withers. "For a man who keeps as many poker chips in his sideboard as the late Mr. Merlin, you'd have thought he'd have a complete deck of cards." She replaced the deck with the dozen others which rested in a drawer of the sideboard, and meekly followed the Inspector out into the living-room.

The schoolmistress pointed to a heavy brass stand, of the non-tippable variety which stood in the living-room near the foyer door. "Tell your blood-hounds not to neglect that," she advised.

The Inspector peered into it, and then suddenly went down on his knees. With a pencil from his pocket he proceeded to lift from the mess of ashes and stubs which clogged the tube several torn and twisted bits of paper. Miss Withers watched in silence while he pieced together the fragments of four cheques — amounts varying from fifty to four hundred dollars, all made out to cash, dated this same day, and signed with names straight out of the Social Register. Beneath them was a torn deposit slip for the Merchant's Uptown Bank, signed with the name "John Merlin" and dated to-day. Five cheques were listed — four with amounts varying from fifty to four hundred dollars — and a fifth to the amount of $2500! There was also a cash entry for six hundred and fifty.

Yet try as they would, the eager detectives did not light upon the missing cheque for the larger amount. Finally they gave up poking among the refuse.

"At least this gives us something to work on," Piper decided finally. Miss Withers sniffed, and led the way toward the door.

"I don't suppose," said Miss Withers casually, "that there's any use looking for the dead man's spectacles."

Piper stopped short. "Eh?"

"Of course you noticed that the corpse showed a red mark across the bridge of the nose, where glasses usually rest? Yet I didn't see any glasses."

"Neither did I," admitted Piper. He made hurried enquiries. "The sergeant didn't see any, either. He noticed the red mark and asked the elevator boys. They say Merlin never wore glasses."

"I wonder," said Hildegarde Withers. "Perhaps we'll find Merlin's spectacles along with the jack of diamonds."

Piper looked at his watch, and saw that it was barely eight. "How about some breakfast?" he demanded.

The schoolteacher shook her head. "Never let a trail get cold," she insisted. "Suppose we do a little breaking and entering?"

"If you mean Davies' apartment downstairs, the boys already gave it the once-over when they picked him up... "

"Then we'll give it the twice-over," said Hildegarde Withers. "Perhaps there is some tiny detail which your men overlooked."

With a master-key secured — no doubt illegally — from the building manager, they entered apartment 8A, first ringing long and loud to make sure that Lorna Davies had not returned from her errands. Except that the fur—nishings were of a distinctly Bohemian type, this apartment was a duplicate of the one upstairs — and Richie Davies' thin story was thus somewhat aided.

One end of the living-room, near the windows, had been transformed into a studio, and underneath a "daylight" lamp a large easel held an unfinished oil painting which the Inspector admired sardonically. It represented a purple triangle in the close embrace of seven orange and gold petzels. "Nude Descending a Staircase," Piper decided. Miss Withers sniffed. Then she leaned past him and touched the bright purple, which came off on a wide smear on her finger. She nodded. "I thought so!"

They wandered through the high-ceilinged rooms. "Plenty of dough," hazarded the Inspector. "Must cost a fortune."

"Hmm," Miss Withers interjected. "Must *have* cost a fortune, you mean. Notice the mend in the Persian rug, half-hidden by the coffee table? Notice that the curtains are sun-faded? All the same, the kitchen is in splendid order, and so is the bedroom. No twin beds here, either. Looks like a happy home, Oscar — run on a decreasing budget. Maid by the day, and dinners out."

"You're way ahead of me," protested the Inspector. "Now do we have breakfast? There's nothing more to see in this place."

But he was wrong. There was something more to see. It happened to be Lorna Davies, who spoke softly from the doorway behind them, as she removed her gloves.

"Mind if I come in?" she said.

"Er —" began the Inspector. "We just —"

"I'd love to show you around — some of Richie's paintings are considered quite good," Lorna continued. She placed her gloves and handbag on a table, and lit a cigarette with a steady hand. "Perhaps you wouldn't mind waiting while I slip into something more suitable than evening clothes?" She was still wearing the white satin gown.

"Thank you, my dear, but we only have a moment..." said Hildegarde Withers. Lorna Davies disappeared in the bedroom.

"Poker-face," observed Piper. "She was sore as — anything at finding us here, but she covered it."

"Eh?" said Miss Withers, startled out of her thoughts. "Poker-face! That's it." She said no more, but as the Inspector busied himself with lighting a cigar, the schoolteacher moved casually toward Lorna Davies' mesh handbag, shielding it from Piper's view. Her hands slid softly forward, and the bag opened without a snap. It was not robbery upon which the meddlesome lady was bent — indeed, exactly the contrary — but when she saw the interior of that handbag she changed her mind. Whatever she had expected to find there, it was not the missing jack of diamonds.

Coolly she pocketed it, and as coolly turned toward the Inspector. "Perhaps we'd better not wait, after all," she said — and they tip-toed out.

Downstairs Piper made a phone call. He had promised to be only a moment, but Miss Withers waited for ten minutes. He rejoined her with his cigar cold and dead between his teeth, and she knew at once that something had happened.

"A confession from Davies?" she asked.

"For once you're wrong," said Oscar Piper. "That young man isn't talking, though he seems plenty worried. There's..."

"By the way, Oscar," Miss Withers cut in, "do you happen to know how Davies was dressed when they arrested him?"

"Huh? Why, yeah. In a smock and old flannel trousers. The boys who picked him up had to wait while he dressed. Why?"

"Never mind why," he was told. "Now what's the rest of it?" Piper frowned. "It probably doesn't have anything to do with the case," he began, as they went out of the apartment house, "but they've made a funny discovery down at Centre Street. The fingerprint boys went through the Merlins' apartment a couple hours ago, and they found nothing. Or rather, they found so many prints that they didn't mean much. All the same, on a silver flask in Merlin's desk they found a print that checks up in our files with that of a gent who's been wanted for a long time ... a hood who goes by the name of Feets Titus. He's —"

"Aha!" said Hildegarde Withers.

"But he's not our man," continued the Inspector. "Because fingerprints age as the oil dries out of them, and this print was at least two weeks old. No fresh ones of the guy, so he didn't pull the job last night. It's not up his alley anyway — Feets is more the type to pull out an automatic or a machine gun and blow his victims to blazes."

"A public enemy, eh? Tell me more," insisted the schoolteacher, as they sat down to breakfast in a drug store on a little side street.

"More about Titus? Seattle wants him for homicide — he was driving away from the scene of a racketeer bombing and killed two kids in the street. New Orleans for dope running — Chicago for rape and attempted murder — Philadelphia for another hit-and-run gangster car job —" The Inspector patiently went on, from metropolis to metropolis, detailing the list of Feets Titus's escapades. "Here we've had him in the Lineup several times, but never pinned anything on him. He used to be Amy Rothstein's bodyguard and special messenger, that's how he got the nickname 'Feets.' "

The Inspector took a deep swig of his coffee. "Of course we'll try to pick him up, but it's like looking for a needle in a haystack."

"It can be done — with a magnet," said Hildegarde Withers. She pushed back her chair, very suddenly. "Oscar — arrest Feets Titus!"

"I'll do that — if you'll tell me where he is."

"I've got a good idea," said Hildegarde Withers tartly. She was thoughtful for another moment. "You just told me of the cities in which Mr. Titus had gotten himself into trouble — every large city in the United States *except* Boston. Gangsters never try to hide out in small towns, and I'll bet you anything you like that Titus is somewhere aboard a train bound for Boston this very minute — it stands to reason!"

The Inspector looked at his watch, and saw that it was half-past nine. "You think Titus did the job? If he did, and decided to lam in the way you suggest, he could have got a slow train at six this morning, and a fast one at eight-thirty. But —"

"Try it, anyway," begged the schoolteacher. "Wire his description ahead — or better still, doesn't the Boston plane leave in time to beat both trains into the city?"

"Wait a minute!" insisted the Inspector. "I tell you, there's no reason to suppose that Titus did this job. He wouldn't use a poker if he did. I'm convinced —"

"So am I," agreed Miss Withers. "Oscar, you aren't always as dumb as you are sometimes." She pushed at him eagerly. "Get to the phone and have them hold the plane — it leaves in half an hour, if I remember correctly, from Roosevelt Field."

They slid up into thin air twenty minutes late, but they were set down again at Boston Airport on schedule. Most of the trip Miss Withers had spent in a close and scientific study of the jack of diamonds which she had abstracted from Lorna Davies' purse, but neither the foolish smiling face of the knave nor the conventional bicycle back of the card told her what she needed to know. Oddly enough, tiny holes had been punched in each corner of the card, as if it had been pinned to a drawing board. It had been pinned there face downward, anyway — the holes showed that much.

"Anyway," Piper said, as they walked into South Station shortly before the slow train was due, "even if this is a wild goose chase, it isn't going to be as bad as if we had got in touch with the Boston police over nothing. We can sneak back home without anybody knowing... "

"Can't we!" Miss Withers agreed.

Then the train pulled in. Not more than a dozen passengers had arisen before daylight to make this trip — they straggled toward the gates in an unprepossessing line. First came two boys, bearing paper suitcases — all too evidently arriving homeward after an unsuccessful attempt to find jobs in New York. Then there was a young couple with a baby, a young couple with two babies, a frightened-looking young man with unbrushed hair and big glasses who clutched a violin case against his narrow chest, a faded fat blonde of forty, and a travelling salesman with two sample cases.

The Inspector turned to Miss Withers. "You see? I have seen Feets Titus often enough in the Lineup to know that none of these are him."

"*Is he*," corrected Miss Withers absently. Something bothered her, but she couldn't put her finger on it. She jerked her head. Finger — that was it.

"We may as well wait for the other train — though it'll be the same story," the Inspector said wearily. "Didn't I tell you... "

"Tell me later," she interrupted impolitely, and set off across the vast marble hall at a rapid trot. "Come *on*, Oscar!"

She raised her voice. "Wait a minute — Yoo hoo... "

The little violinist — whose hands were unmusical — stopped in wonderment. Then he darted away like a rabbit, dropping his violin case in his haste. It fell directly in front of Miss Withers, flying open and disgorging wearing apparel in every direction. Her foot struck something hard, and she collapsed in an undignified heap.

The Inspector helped her to her feet. They both looked down and saw that she had tripped over a nasty-looking automatic pistol.

"There he goes!" cried Miss Withers.

A yellow taxi whirled away from the curb. In a moment the Inspector and Miss Withers were in another, tearing like mad through the sedate streets of Boston.

"By heaven, it must be Feets Titus!" Piper roared. "Driver — stick to that car or I'll murder you." The driver clenched his teeth grimly and stuck.

Miss Withers clung to a strap and prayed. There was nothing else to do. A brilliant star with many facets appeared in the windshield as a white face showed itself for a moment in the rear window of the cab ahead and fired. At the next corner an officer ran out into the street and stood with his arms outstretched, but leaped aside as the first taxi swooped down on him. Along the sidewalks people were running ... screaming ...

Piper spoke to his driver, and their cab slowed. When it picked up again, it was loaded with two hundred pounds of bone and brawn on the running board. A service pistol cracked, and cracked again, but the bouncing of the cab was too severe for anything but pure shooting luck.

The cab ahead swerved. "Mother of God — the boy is driving him into a dead end street!" roared the new recruit. "He'll get killed for it... "

But nobody got killed for anything. The taxi ahead screeched to a stop with its headlights pressed against the low railing of a pier-head, and from its window a gun sailed lazily outward to splash in the water. The driver leaped out, hands upraised — for he knew the bad position he was in.

Then, as the Inspector and the Boston officer got their feet on the ground and came gingerly forward, the door of the other cab opened and a dapper young man stepped down, his hands busy lighting a cigarette.

"So you've got me," he observed politely. "So what?"

The Inspector slapped out the cigarette — men had killed themselves that way — and snatched off the big, lightly tinted glasses. They were a little large for Feets Titus, but he recognised the petty racketeer well enough now that his hair was combed back.

"Titus, you're under arrest for the murder of Jack Merlin," he announced. Feets Titus shrugged.

"Nice day for it," he observed. "Honest, Inspector, this is news to me. Poor old Jack — haven't seen him in a week."

"Then you might explain how you happen to be wearing his spectacles," cut in a shrewd and acidulous voice. Feets Titus said no more — by advice of counsel, as he put it. The Inspector turned to Miss Withers.

"That's that," he said. "We — you had the right hunch. Now, if you'll excuse me for a while, I'll go and arrange for this punk to waive extradition. Think we can argue him into it at the station. We ought to be able to catch the six o'clock train back."

"*You* ought to be able," said Miss Withers. "I'm not a deputy-sheriff. Besides, I happen to have five aunts in Boston, and this is a splendid time to pay a round of calls. See you tomorrow morning, Oscar."

She marched off toward the street. "Hey," cried the Inspector. "You've got those eye-glasses... " But she did not hear him.

The cop who had joined them on the running board was just finishing a quick and thorough frisking of the arrested man. "Six hundred and forty bucks in his poke," he announced. Piper remembered that there had been six hundred and fifty dollars entered on the bank deposit slip which was crammed into Merlin's ashstand, and he thought no more of the spectacles. By the time he put his prisoner aboard the six o'clock train for New York he had forgotten them entirely.

Miss Hildegarde Withers had a belated but pleasant luncheon in a tea-room on Milk Street, during which time something must have made her change her plans considerably, for she left the place only to take a taxicab for the airport again. This time she, and not the plane, had to wait, but all the same she arrived back in the magic island of Manhattan before the train bearing Piper and his prisoner southward was well out of the environs of Boston. The five aunts would have to wait.

"Thirty-five Park Avenue," Miss Withers told her cab-driver. She found herself ringing the bell outside the door marked "8A" before she had made up her mind as to what she intended to say.

A tense and silent Lorna Davies let her in.

"I've been busy —" Miss Withers began.

"But Richie is still in jail!" The young woman's voice was oddly high and nervous, for all her air of smoothness. "You haven't done anything about getting him out. You must! I'll do anything — pay anything."

"Anything?" Miss Withers leaned forward. "Would you be willing to confess to the killing of John Merlin to save your husband?"

There was a long and dreadful silence while Lorna tried to light a cigarette with a match held six inches from its tip. She stared at the wall. Finally she rose to her feet, gripping the back of her chair and twisting her tall curving body to face Miss Withers — or anything else.

"Yes!" she whispered. "I —"

"Never mind," said the schoolteacher, clearing her throat. She took a crumpled slip of paper from her purse, and handed it to the girl. "I think this is your signature?"

Lorma glanced at the cheque for $2500, and nodded.

"Your mysterious errands this morning had to do with stopping payment on it?"

Lorna shook her head. "No — I was raising funds to cover it. You see, I — I —"

Miss Withers understood. "It was more than you had in the bank? I didn't think of that. But my dear child, you ought to know better than to try to make money by playing cards."

Lorna's eyes narrowed. "You know everything, don't you?"

Miss Withers shrugged. "Almost everything. I know that you have been finding it more and more difficult to finance the lovable young artist you married — even the Gault bonds depreciate like everyone's else. Your friends were coming to Merlin's apartment to play, and you got in the habit of joining them. Perhaps you were lonely when your husband worked late — or perhaps you were lucky at first and made money."

Lorna nodded dully.

"Last night you went upstairs to play poker," Miss Withers continued. "You lost — and plunging, lost still more, until when you returned to your own apartment you left behind you a cheque for more money that you had in the bank. You brought along with you — this!"

Miss Withers produced the jack of diamonds. "*You* took it! I thought—"

"Let me finish. At the time you very wisely wondered if the game was a fair one. With your husband's help you discovered somehow that the back of this card — and presumably of the other face cards in the deck — was marked. Shaded, I think they call it."

Lorna nodded. "We pinned it on his drawing board, and studied it with a magnifying glass. The shading finally showed — when we tried a coloured glass —"

"It also showed through the spectacles that Jack Merlin wore when he played cards," Miss Withers explained. She patted her handbag. "But never mind that now. Up until your return from the card game, your husband had been painting, for oil paints dry quite quickly, and his work was still wet, this morning. When he realised the trick, he very rashly rushed upstairs — dressed just as he was — to face Merlin. The gambler tried to throw him out, and you heard them fighting up there and followed. You arrived to see your husband getting the worst of it —"

"Merlin was choking him," said Lorna Davies slowly. "Choking him and laughing. I used to be a six handicap golfer. I couldn't stand by — I snatched up the poker, and — I didn't mean to —"

Suddenly she broke, and fell to her knees. But her voice was even. "I *killed* him!"

"I know," Miss Withers said softly. "I know all the rest. You hurried out, with the card your husband had taken up to confront Merlin. Richie stayed behind to wipe away fingerprints, and was seen when he finally left. That is why he didn't telephone the police."

"I can't guess who did," said Lorna, as if she didn't really care.

"It was the other man who visited Merlin late at night," Miss Withers told her. "Perhaps because he hoped they'd find clues leading away from himself. He was a racketeer named Feets Titus, who acted as Merlin's bodyguard and messenger. He wouldn't have mixed well with the type of guests that Merlin had, so he only came in late at night to get the evening's receipts. Some banks, you know, have night boxes where deposits can be made at any hour. Titus came in this morning shortly after your husband was seen leaving Merlin's apartment, and found his employer dead. With a bad police record, and indeed, wanted in various cities and *de trop* almost everywhere, Titus knew he would be blamed for this murder or sent back to Chicago or elsewhere to face another charge, so he took the deposit which was ready for the bank, disposed of the cheques, and used the money for a getaway. He used a violin-case as part of his disguise, and at the last moment snatched the glasses from the dead man as an added precaution."

Miss Withers paused for breath. "He — he got away?" Lorna asked.

The schoolteacher nodded. "Miles away. And now —"

She was interrupted by a thunderous knocking upon the apartment door. Lorna Davies tried hard to breathe. "They've come — for me?"

"Lorna! Darling, let me in!" came a man's voice.

Lorna Davies gripped Miss Withers' arm, with icy fingers. "It's Rich! They've let him go!" She spoke swiftly in Miss Withers' ear. "May I have just an hour with him before — before —"

The schoolteacher nodded, and Lorna ran to the door. In a moment she was in the arms of a slim, rather handsome young man. "For heaven's sake, stop crying!" cried Richie Davies. "It's all right, I tell you. The police have got a man whom they say did it. We're —" Then he saw Miss Withers, watching.

"Oh—" He was introduced to Miss Withers.

"I was just leaving," said that lady. "My, it is getting late."

Lorna followed her to the door. "Then — I suppose I'll hear from — from your friends later in the evening."

"Before midnight," Miss Withers said. Her voice was hollow, though she tried to make it casual. As she went down the hall she realised that never before in her life had a triumph been so tasteless, so empty. She had unravelled the yarn — she had run the quarry to earth. And there was no savour in it.

"I'm a sentimental old fool," said Miss Withers to herself. "This is why women make bad detectives. Because they haven't the courage to —" She shook her shoulders, and set off for Centre Street.

At eleven fifteen that evening a sharp ring came at the door of the Davies' apartment. Lorna was just signing her name at the bottom of a long sheet of paper covered with smooth, even lines written with heart's blood and ink. Beside it lay a long envelope marked "To the Police..."

Her young husband, his face white and desperate, faced her. "Not yet!" he cried. "She said twelve —"

Lorna Davies raised her lips to his. "Kiss me, Rich," she said softly. "And — give me a drink, please."

Two pale yellow cocktails stood on a little tray beside her. But Richie shook his head. "She said twelve," he repeated stubbornly.

Another ring at the doorbell, and he crossed the room softly. "Who's there?"

"Western Union Messenger Service," came a squeaky voice. It was not that of a boy.

Lorna Davies took up her cocktail. "A stirrup-cup, Richie!"

"Wait," he whispered. He came closer to the door. "Push it underneath, there's a good chap."

A white envelope slid through the crack. "I'll wait and see if there's any answer," came the squeaky voice.

Lorna, the glass almost at her lips, watched her young husband tear open the message addressed to her. He read it — as he thought — aloud, his lips making no sound.

Then he tottered toward his wife, and she took it from his fingers. "Dear Lorna Davies," it began, "I have spent the evening reading up the police record of a Mr. Feets Titus, who — the authorities are convinced — killed Jack Merlin in your apartment house last night. They believe that he killed Merlin in a dispute, and took the money as an afterthought. They are also of the opinion that Merlin will plead guilty to second degree murder to escape worse charges elsewhere. It seems to me that a racketeer who has run down little children belongs behind bars much more than others I have in mind. Therefore I am not going to raise my voice against the wisdom of the Force ... signed, Hildegarde Withers." There was also a postcript. "As my fee in this case I am keeping the jack of diamonds. I suggest that you both take up the study of chess for these long spring evenings."

"Hey! Is there any answer?" Western Union was growing tired. Lorna Davies tore open the door and handed a twenty-dollar bill to the septuagenarian who waited there, and he hobbled off in blank amazement.

She found Richie pouring two pale yellow cocktails into the sink, with trembling hands. For a long time they did not speak.

At that moment, Miss Hildegarde Withers was standing in her own little west-side apartment, critically eyeing a playing card which she had slipped into a tiny wall-frame, wrong end up. The essential wrongness did not appear until you stared at the card through a pair of large spectacles, slightly tinted with amber — and then two spokes on the left side of the bicycle wheel design stood out bold and black above the rest.

Hands on her hips, Miss Withers surveyed the sole relic of her exciting day. She hummed softly the immortal line — "To make the punishment fit the crime… " With a sense of duty well done, she prepared for bed.

The Riddle of the Tired Bullet

"Oops, excuse me!" Like a ruffled Buff Orpington, Miss Hildegarde Withers backed hastily out of the Inspector's private office, where she had just surprised him in the embrace of a pretty red-head.

The spinster schoolma'am was deeply engrossed in a study of some old "Wanted for Murder" posters on the wall when Oscar Piper finally emerged to usher his fair visitor toward the corridor. She was thanking him effusively in a weak, brave voice. "And I'll take your advice, Inspector."

When the tap of her heels had died away, the Inspector came back toward Miss Withers, mopping his brow sheepishly. "Women!" he sighed.

Her sniff was pointed. "And at your age, too."

"And why not?" His Irish flared up. "You're jealous, maybe?"

"For some years," the schoolteacher told him gently, "my interest in you has been purely academic. I barely noticed the woman, except to see that she has suspiciously red-brown hair and that she was wearing a last-year's suit made over at home. Not exactly young, but still pretty if you like the type." Miss Withers paused for breath, and then noticed that the Inspector had turned back into his inner office. She rushed after him so fast that her hat, which resembled a bon-voyage basket a day after sailing, slid rakishly over one eye. "Wait, Oscar! Is it a new murder case?"

Oscar Piper poked painstakingly through his ashtray for a cigar butt recent enough to bear relighting. "Not yet it isn't," he admitted. "But the little lady was crying on my shoulder because she thinks she's going to be a widow.

"Something she dreamed, no doubt. Or is it astrology?"

"More to it than that. I had to agree with her that Ernest Hawkins is The Man of the Week Most Likely to Decorate a Marble Slab. Don't you recognize the name? Well, you'll be hearing more about him. Hawkins was secretary to old Amos Bigelow, ex-Senator Bigelow, of the Bigelow Buddy Fund Committee."

"But of course. They set out to raise money to send packages to the men in the armed forces, during the last year of the war. I was even asked to help them solicit, but the Grey Ladies work took up my spare time."

"Just as well. The Committee never got around to announcing how many packages ever got to the boys in uniform. The grand jury started to investigate them last week, and Hawkins blew the lid off when he promised to testify, under a promise of personal immunity."

"A tattle, eh?"

"None of your brats down at P.S. 38 are in his class, though. He did the stool-pigeon act up brown, dragging in a lot of supposedly important citizens.

He also admitted that fifteen or twenty thousand dollars of the money stuck to his own fingers, but he claims he dribbled it away in the night clubs and gambling."

"Fast women and slow horses, no doubt?"

"Yeh. He even named the bookie who took his bets, so now a tough Broadway character known as Track-odds Louie is out of business and under indictment. Which makes a sizable group of people who would like to cut Mr. Hawkins's throat."

"Oscar, something must be done at once!" Miss Withers nodded. "Think of his poor little wife."

"You think of her. Rena ought to be able to take care of herself — she used to be a tap-dancer around the 52nd Street spots before she married Hawkins and settled down. I told her that she ought to go home and look up a good private detective agency in the phone book if she wanted protection — the homicide bureau is only interested in murders after they've happened."

Miss Withers stood up suddenly. "But Oscar, you're like a doctor who doesn't try to cure his patient because he's so interested in how the autopsy comes out!"

"Now, my dear Hildegarde —"

"I'm not your dear anything. If you'll excuse me, I think I'll break our date for dinner and the movies tonight. I prefer the company of my tank full of tropical fish — they're so much warmer-blooded!" And she flounced out of the office.

In spite of what she had said, Miss Withers had no time for her aquarium and its miniature jeweled fish that evening. She dined very sketchily on what she would have called "cold nothings" out of the refrigerator, and then went out to sit through most of a double feature. But somehow between her and the screen drama there kept popping up the figure of little Rena Hawkins, who knew that her husband was going to be killed. "It's as bad as King Charles' head," Miss Withers murmured. The woman beside her turned blankly. "*David Copperfield*, by Dickens," the school teacher explained, and then fled in the midst of a chorus of annoyed hisses.

It was after ten o'clock, and she knew that she ought to go home and mind her own business. But somehow she was impelled to hurry through the drizzling rain to the nearest telephone booth, and then down into the bowels of the subway.

The house, when she finally located it on the wrong street in the wrong part of Queens, was a narrow three-story brick, stuck between a chain grocery and a used-car lot. It was dark and quiet, so quiet that the ringing of the doorbell under her thumb made the schoolteacher jump. But nobody answered, in spite of her repeated ringing.

Miss Withers went down the steps, hesitated a moment, and then picked her way back toward the alley, past the rusting heaps of unsold and unsaleable automobiles. From the rear the residence of the Hawkins family was even less attractive than from the front, and she paused to thank her lucky stars that she had never been inveigled, in her early days, into matrimony and a life amid these drab surroundings.

There was however one sign of life here — from a third floor window a lace curtain fluttered in the breeze and a soft light was shining. Someone must be at home, after all. Well, she had come miles and miles to bring aid and friendly counsel to a fellow human being in desperate straits, and she was determined to make delivery.

She turned in through the creaking back gate, past the looming bulk of ashcans, garbage containers, abandoned summer furniture and sagging clotheslines. The rain splattered on rusting tin and there were other sounds, like soft scurrying feet, which she tried not to hear. Hurrying a little, Miss Withers went up the steps and knocked on the door. There was no answer, nor had she expected any. Neither had she expected the door to swing silently inward.

In a way it was an invitation, like the bottle in *Alice* with the label on it that said "Drink Me." So she entered on tiptoe, and then jumped as the door closed quickly behind her. The beam of a flashlight caught and held her impaled. "Hel-lo!" cried a man's high nervous tenor. Then the kitchen light was turned on, and she blinked at a beefy, curled-haired man in his shirt-sleeves and stocking feet, an athlete just beginning to run to fat. There was the strap of a shoulder holster across his chest, and in his fist a business-like revolver. He looked jittery, competent, and — finally, puzzled.

Miss Withers heard her voice, breathlessly explaining that she had only come with the best of intentions and that if he would only dial Headquarters instead of shooting, why somebody would vouch for her, and if he himself was Mr. Hawkins then —

The man with the gun relaxed just a little. "Mr. Hawkins is asleep upstairs," he said, in a tone which plainly indicated that all other respectable citizens should be likewise. "And so is his missus. My name is Johnny Brannigan, from the Onyx Agency on Fourteenth Street."

"A private eye!" she cried impulsively.

"A what?" Brannigan stared at his prisoner with growing distaste. "Lady, you got a bad case of too many movie thrillers. I'm just an ex-cop that got out of the Marines a couple months ago and come back to help start up a new private agency. My job is to see nothing happens to Ernest Hawkins."

"I'm sure you are competent, but —" Miss Withers shook her head. "I learned about the situation quite by accident and got so worried that I just couldn't stay away. But nobody answered the door —"

He sighed. "Lady, would you answer a doorbell if you were in my shoes?" He caught her glance, and flushed slightly. "Anyway, I heard you out front. I heard you coming around to the back, so I left the door open and got ready —"

"So I see. And now that I'm here, could I have a word with Mr. Hawkins?"

"They both turned in for the night, lady. It's almost eleven o'clock, and I got orders not to bother them. They're paying me fifteen bucks a day and expenses to carry out orders."

"Of course. But —"

"Look," said Brannigan, with sarcastic patience. "Let's settle it this way. You leave me do my job, and you get back on your broomstick and fly away home, huh?" He held the door invitingly open.

She had no choice but to flounce out into the night and the rain, angry as a boil. But the anger was mostly at herself, for getting into a ridiculous situation. "Men!" she muttered, as she picked her way toward the alley. Then all of a sudden the night exploded, and she was paralyzed by a blinding light and a racking roar of sound, which turned out to be nothing more than a suburban train swinging around the curve of the railway embankment, which bordered the alley on the far side, a dike of dirt and cinders as high as the telephone poles.

"My nerves!" protested Miss Withers. Then she stopped, and looked up at that lighted window. It was odd that a frightened man would lie in a room with an open window and a fluttering curtain. The curtain must be soaked with rain, too. The school teacher took a deep breath and then began to pick her way up the steep side of the embankment, at considerable damage to her dignity, her shoes, and her gloves. But she finally made it, and then turned to look directly into the lighted window. She stood still for a long moment, and then started headlong down

† † †

Across the street from Headquarters stands the Criminal Courts Building, one wing of which is devoted to the activities of the District Attorney. In a reception room, furnished with uncomfortable modern chairs and decorated with photographs of municipal projects, six people were waiting — six nervous, unhappy persons guarded by an impersonal policeman.

Though the members of the group did not know it, they were at the moment being carefully studied through a one-way mirror set in the wall of Assistant D.A. Tom Minor's office. Minor himself was uneasier than any of them. "I still think we've over played our hand," he was saying. "These people are big shots, and they can make a lot of trouble."

"I'm used to trouble," Inspector Piper told him. "Who is which?"

"The old man with the jowls and the flowing hair is ex-Senator Bigelow, professional do-gooder. The hag in mink and pearls is the actress, Maylah Raymond, who used to have Diamond Jim Brady drink orange juice out of her slipper back when she was the toast of Broadway. The fat man in tweeds is General Hector Fleming, National Guard, formerly a famous armchair hero. The tall guy with the lovely gray toupee is Waldemar Hull, world-traveler, author, and lecturer at women's clubs. Facing him is Matthew Gruber, used to be legal counsel for the Watch and Ward Society up in Boston. They say he has the world's finest collection of pornography. That's the entire Bigelow Committee... "

"What about the head-waiter with the big cigar, sitting all by himself?"

"Louis Margolis, the bookmaker. They say he has twenty dinner jackets."

"He may trade 'em for prison gray," Piper said. "Well, Tom, which is your candidate? Who looks like a potential murderer?"

Minor hesitated. "Well, now, Inspector ... this was your idea, not ours."

"Okay." Piper looked at his watch. "Five of eleven. Not bad work, considering the order to pick 'em up didn't go out until ten. Come on, let's give 'em the business."

A moment later they faced the group and Tom Minor cleared his throat apologetically. "Ladies and gentlemen," he began. "You have been asked to come down here —"

"Asked!" shrieked Maylah Raymond. "I was dragged!"

Minor held up his hand. "— come down here in connection with certain threats said to have been made against the life of one Ernest Hawkins." Behind him the door opened and a uniformed man came in to hand a teletype to Piper, but the Assistant D.A. did not notice it. "You will be allowed to return home very shortly, as soon as you have put up a peace bond. But first I want to introduce you to a gentleman who has a few words to say. Inspector Oscar Piper, of homicide... "

Minor paused, and waved his hand. He felt a crumpled sheet of paper shoved into his sweating fingers, and heard the door slam. Then he too read the message, and gulped. "The — the Inspector asks me to apologize for him," he continued automatically. "He's just been called to take over the investigation into the murder of Ernest Hawkins. *Hawkins!*" he repeated, staring blankly at the six people who had every reason in the world to want that name on a tombstone. And they all stared back at him. Somebody in the room — was it Margolis the bookmaker? — let go a long, heartfelt sigh.

† † †

By the time the Inspector reached the Hawkins house, the complex machinery of homicide investigation was already whirring. The place was blazing with lights, and everywhere detectives, uniformed officers, ballistics, fingerprint and cameramen scurried like ants in a disturbed ant-hill. It was a picture to bring satisfaction to the heart of any homicide squad skipper, with only one jarring note — the gaunt and unhappy figure which rose to greet him on the front porch.

"Oscar!" cried Miss Hildegarde Withers. "They won't even let me inside, and I'm the one who discovered the body!"

He blinked at her. "But how —"

"I just happened to be climbing the railroad embankment across the alley from the rear of the house, so I could take a peak into the third floor bed room window. I looked in and saw a man lying in bed, under a reading-lamp. Only he wasn't reading at all — his face was covered with blood. Quite dead, I could see that. So I turned in the alarm."

She followed him inside, still talking about her adventures of the evening. "Wait here, will you?" he said finally, and left her. When he returned his face was very grave. "The body —?" she began hopefully.

"Dr. Gavin, the Assistant Medical Examiner, is upstairs now," Piper said. "If he needs your help he'll send for you."

"But Oscar —"

"This case has been a headache from the very beginning," he snapped. "Come with me." And Miss Withers found herself hustled unceremoniously into the living room, where Mr. Brannigan, the private detective, was sweating copiously under the stern gaze of a Headquarters sergeant. On the couch lay Rena Hawkins, her reddish hair disheveled and her eyes looking like two burnt holes in a blanket. She wore a man's woolen bathrobe.

"Oh, it's you," the woman cried, when she saw the Inspector. Her voice was thin and brittle. "Didn't I tell you so? Didn't I beg you to do something? You and your advice to go look up a good private detective — as if this clumsy ox was any protection —" She gave the private detective a look that could have curled his hair.

"Hold it," Piper said. "Brannigan, according to your story somebody tried to sneak into the house last night just before eleven o'clock?"

"Yes, sir." Brannigan pointed accusingly toward Miss Withers. "It was her. I figured she was just a harmless nut, so I let her go."

"Why, of all things, when I was merely trying —" Miss Withers was gasping. "How dare you say that?"

"Okay, okay, I'll ask the questions," Piper said wearily. "Brannigan, after you got rid of the lady, what next?"

"I began to worry about Mr. Hawkins. I tiptoed upstairs to see if he was all right, and there was a streak of light under his door. Only he didn't answer my knock. I went and tried to wake up his wife, only she was dead to the world. I got really worried then, because he was locked in and I didn't have a key. So I kicked in a panel of the door, and there he was, stiffer'n a mackerel. It looked like a .45 calibre hole in his head."

"The Medical Examiner bears that out. What did you do next?"

"Me? I went downstairs to let the police radio car boys in, before they smashed the door down. Somebody already called 'em... "

"What was the last time you saw Hawkins alive?"

Brannigan frowned. "Shortly after I got on the job, about nine-thirty, when he went up to bed."

"And you stick to your story that you didn't hear the shot?"

"Not even a loud noise. Nothing."

"How do you account for a man in this house being killed with a large-caliber pistol and you not hearing it?"

The man shook his head miserably. "Honest, Inspector, I don't."

Piper's face wore an expression of deep disgust, but he turned quickly to Rena Hawkins. "Well, are you deaf too?"

She was dry-eyed, but Miss Withers thought the woman not far from hysteria. "I didn't hear a thing," Rena said dully. "But there were two doors between me and Ernest. I was in our regular bedroom on the second floor front. You see, I just had to get some sleep, and Ernest has been tossing around so much at night, I made him go upstairs to the spare bedroom where he could lock himself in."

Miss Withers whispered in the Inspector's ear. "Oscar, I have an idea! Suppose we make a test — I'll lie down in Mrs. Hawkins' bedroom and you close the doors and then fire off a pistol in the murder room, to see if I can hear it?"

He was unimpressed. "No good, unless we had the same gun."

"Oh, yes!" said the schoolteacher happily. "*The same gun*! I wonder if it could have been the weapon Mr. Brannigan was waving in my face earlier this evening? He wore one of those gangster strap things around his shoulder... "

The private operative flushed beet-red. "Ask Sergeant Mertz about that," he said sulkily.

"Sure," said the sergeant. "We took the roscoe off him when we got here. Ballistics has it now, but I can tell you beforehand that it's a new .38, never fired, and too small for the hole in Hawkins's head."

Rena Hawkins said, through dry lips: "There wouldn't be any use in the test of whether I heard the shot or not, unless Miss Whatshername here took a couple of stiff slugs of whisky and a double dose of veronal, like I did when I went to bed last night."

"She was still groggy when we got here," Mertz put in. "The radio car boys say they had to pour water on her to wake her up."

"Okay for now," the Inspector said. Rena Hawkins subsided upon the couch, biting her handkerchief, but Brannigan stood up hopefully. At the look in Piper's face he sat down again. Miss Withers felt herself impelled out into the hall.

"Oscar," she cried hopefully, "I have another idea! Couldn't somebody have sneaked into the house and picked the lock of Hawkins's bedroom, or else climbed up to the window on a ladder and then shot him using a silencer?"

Piper shook his head wearily. "A silencer is no damn good except on a rifle, though the general public doesn't know it. Moreover, there's a Yale-type lock on the bedroom door, practically unpickable. No ladder marks in the soft mud of the yard, either."

She shrugged, "Well, I was only trying —"

"Trying to make a mystery out of what must be a simple inside job. That Brannigan fellow is lying like a rug. Only —"

"Only why should an ex-policeman, with so much experience along these lines, and with intelligence enough to start his own detective agency when he left the service, tell such an obvious lie?"

It was close enough to nettle the Inspector. "Maybe —"

"And with all those people on the Bigelow Committee wanting Hawkins dead —"

Wearily the Inspector gave a resume of his evening. "I was only trying to follow your suggestions," he said. "Preventive detection, and all that. But we can cancel out the lot of them. Dr. Gavin says that Hawkins died shortly after ten. None of the suspects could have been out here murdering Hawkins and got home in time to be picked up when the order went out. So forget it."

"But Oscar," she cried. "There must be some mistake... "

"You're making it," he snapped. "Nobody asked you to come out here and solve the mystery of the locked room. You're off base. Suppose you just sit here a while and let men do men's work, huh?" He pointed to the bench, and hurried upstairs again.

When the Inspector finally came back downstairs, he found her studying the pile of tattered phone books on the bench. His mood, she sensed, had mysteriously improved. "Trying to look up the answers in the back of the book, Hildegarde?"

"Not quite. But I did have an idea. Only none of the suspects seems to live out here on Long Island. Of course, these phone books are a year old. They're titled *Summer-Fall 1946*, and people might have moved."

"So what?"

"The murder was committed between nine-forty, when he went to bed, and a little after eleven, when I first saw the body. The Medical Examiner says shortly after ten. Suppose the killer lived only a few minutes from here — he could have still got home in time to be picked up. Maybe he was laughing up his sleeve, or quaking in his boots, down in the District Attorney's office?"

"Relax," Piper told her. "They all live in Manhattan. But we're way ahead of you. Now that the case is all over but the shouting, come on up and I'll show you how it was done."

"And by whom?"

"That part'll be easy. You see, Dr. Gavin says Hawkins was killed by a .45 bullet that only went an inch or so into his brain."

" 'Not so deep as a well, nor so wide as a church door, but 'tis enough'," she quoted. "Shakespeare."

"You don't get the point. The shot couldn't possibly have been fired in the bedroom at all, or it would have gone through him and buried itself in the wall. A gun that size can put a bullet through four inches of hard wood. The slug that killed him was a spent bullet, just about at the limit of its effective range." They came to the third floor and along the hall, through the door with the smashed panel and into the room where at the moment Ernest Hawkins was posing for his last photographs. Miss Withers took another look at the lifeless, sagging body, one hand still loosely holding a copy of *Turf and Paddock Magazine*, sniffed at the empty brandy bottle on the bedside table, and then turned quickly away. It was a relief to rejoin the Inspector, who was pointing out the window.

"Nobody heard the shot," he said, "because it wasn't fired inside the house. What noise there was was drowned out by the roar of a passing train. You see that the embankment is almost at this level? The eastbound trains go by like a bat out of hell, but the ones headed toward Manhattan have to slow down along here for a signal block ahead. The killer must have been standing on the rear platform, where he'd be alone. Luck was with him — it was a good two hundred and fifty feet, but you yourself know how the open window and the bed-lamp made a target out of the victim. And if the shot had only winged Hawkins, it would still have scared him out of testifying at the trial."

Miss Withers admitted all that. She had more to say, but the Inspector was suddenly called downstairs to the phone. A few moments later he came back up the stairs, his face wreathed in a wide grin. At the landing he stopped, frowned, and then turned back and went into Rena Hawkins's bedroom, where he surprised Miss Withers poking around among the boxes and bottles on the vanity table.

"Look, Oscar," she cried, displaying a sphinx-marked box. "She does use henna!"

"Okay. So you were right about one thing, anyway! But you have no business to go snooping around. What do you suppose you could find that we didn't notice when we officially searched the place, huh?"

She hesitated. "Sometimes I think that the police only see the things that are there, instead of noticing the things that should be and aren't." She gestured, vaguely.

The Inspector looked at the bottles and jars on the vanity. "Looks like ordinary dime store stuff to me."

But Miss Withers turned her attention to the heavy, steel money box on the bureau. "Oh, if that's it, I've got the key," Piper said. "Wanta peek?" He opened it, dumping out a sheaf of old pari-mutuel tickets. "Proving that Hawkins made some very unlucky fifty dollar bets when he went to the track. Probably saved them so he could prove his losses against his gains, for the income-tax people."

With feminine contrariness, Miss Withers had lost interest in the strong box and was peering into the closet. "Bedroom slippers, three pairs of oxfords, a pair of opera pumps run down at the heel, and one pair of overshoes," she enumerated.

"No Seven-League boots?"

"I was thinking," Miss Withers announced cryptically, "of glass slippers — the kind that Cinderella wore to the ball."

The Inspector said he had had enough of fairy stories and urged her toward the door. "I've got work to do," he said.

"You have your work cut out for you, if you're going to try to prove that theory about the shot being fired from a train," she insisted. "I've been thinking it over and —"

"And the shot that killed Hawkins was fired from a westbound train which passed this point at exactly ten-five p.m.," he told her.

"Just got a report that a maintenance man in the Pennsy yards stumbled on a .45 automatic, recently fired, one shell gone, on the rear platform of a suburban train that ended its last run at ten-fourteen. I'll bet you all the tea in China that the slug in Hawkins's head fits that gun."

Miss Withers was opposed to betting. "I don't see why you're so elated, Oscar. That puts us right back where we started. Because any of the suspects could have been aboard that train, perhaps as a round-trip passenger, and still have had time enough to get home to his residence anywhere in midtown Manhattan and be picked up by your detectives at ten-forty or before. It re-opens the case —"

"Sure. But now we've got some things to work on. We've washed out the possibility of an inside job. The shot was fired from outside, and neither Brannigan nor Rena were outside last night, because I personally looked for traces of mud on their shoes. We've got the murder gun and we'll start checking it. We know the killer was a good shot, and that he was on that train. We'll have men check with every ticket-seller, every conductor, every taxi driver... "

"It sounds like a lot of trouble," she said. "But I've noticed that nothing is too much trouble for the Department — after a murder is committed. Except to sit down quietly and think about things."

He grinned. "You mean the things that aren't there?"

"Perhaps I do. Oscar, are you still holding the members of the Bigelow Committee?"

"Only for the nitrate test. And the killer was probably smart enough to hold the gun with a glove and then toss it overboard immediately after the shot. First thing in the morning we'll comb the right of way, naturally."

"Naturally." Miss Withers started down the stair. "Oscar, will you excuse me? I hate to remind you, but it'll be daylight soon."

"Huh? So it will. Come on." They came down into the lower hall of the Hawkins house. Miss Withers peered into the living room, where Rena Hawkins was alone, sleeping sprawled out on the couch and snoring faintly.

Miss Withers gently drew the dressing gown over the woman's knees and turned out the glaring overhead light. "I suppose you have already released Mr. Brannigan?" she asked.

"Sure. He was glad to get out of it, even if she wouldn't give him his pay for the job. Last thing he said was that he thought he'd try to get back on the Force, and I'll help him." Piper turned. "Hey, Sam!" After a short wait Sergeant Mertz came toward them from the kitchen, wiping his mouth. "Sam, will you be a good guy and run Miss Withers home? She has to teach geography to a bunch of little hoodlums tomorrow."

"Sure!" the sergeant said. "Glad to."

"Thank you," said the school teacher. "But it's just that I want to get away from all this confusion to some place where it's quiet." And she stalked out of the door.

† † †

Promptly at nine o'clock next morning Miss Hildegarde Withers accepted the two red apples which were her day's offering, and then called to attention her third grade class at P.S. 38. At nine-ten the last of her pupils disappeared down the hall, headed for an unexpected half-holiday. " 'All work and no play,' " she said to herself, and reached for her hat again.

But it was rising noon when she walked into the office of her old friend and sparring-partner, to find the Inspector taking aspirin and chasing it with black coffee out of a paper cup. "Oscar!" she cried. "I just dropped in to congratulate you. Because it says in the afternoon papers that the police have the Hawkins case well in hand and an arrest is expected at any moment!"

"Don't rub it in," he said bitterly. "As you very well know, that's the standard press handout when we are completely up a tree."

"Dear me! You mean to tell me that even with the entire Bigelow Committee as ready-made suspects, you haven't arrested anybody? Do they all have perfect alibis?"

Slowly Piper shook his head. "Worse than that. They don't have any alibis that you can check. They all had motive and opportunity — at least opportunity to be aboard that train, though the railroad employees don't seem to be able to identify anybody. We've more or less narrowed it down to General Fleming, Waldemar Hull, and Track-odds Louie, just because an army officer, an explorer, and a gambler should each have had some experience with firearms. But they all deny it. No luck tracing the pistol, either — it was listed as stolen eleven years ago."

"How sad," she murmured, "to have the wonderful, efficient, infallible detective machinery bog down."

"We found the glove, anyway!" he blurted out. "On the right of way, not fifty feet from the Hawkins house. Only —"

"Only it was probably cheap cotton, untraceable, and large enough to fit any suspect, man or woman?"

Piper nodded, his shoulders sagging. "I guess that was to be expected." Then he cocked his head, suspiciously. "All right, why are you needling me this way? What are you up to?"

"I? Why, nothing at all. I just gave my pupils a half-holiday this morning, so I could play hookey. I made several phone calls, too. One of them was to the Onyx Agency, after I first got the number from Information. Mr. Brannigan answered the phone, and I asked if he remembered me. He said he didn't think he ever could forget, but that he would try. Very bitter, he was. But he did brighten up when I asked him to help me solve the Hawkins case, and told him my theory..."

"Wait a minute," put in the Inspector testily. "Whose side are you on?"

"I am," she said, "interested only in getting at the truth, through any available door. That was why I made another phone call this morning — to Mr. Margolis, the bookmaker. Did it ever occur to anybody to ask just how much money the late Mr. Hawkins lost playing the races?"

"No, and I don't give a hoot."

"But you should. I did ask, and I found that Hawkins didn't lose — he won. Thousands and thousands of dollars. The devil takes care of his own, they say. Anyway, his winnings must have constituted the money that was in the strong-box in the Hawkins bed room, before the murderer took it and substituted old pari-mutuel tickets. There had to be something for you to find inside."

"So what?" Patience had never been the Inspector's long suit. "Will you get to the point of all this, if there is any point?"

"By all means. I made still another phone call — to Rena Hawkins. I wanted to ask her who it was that suggested the Onyx Agency to her."

"She said she looked it up in the phone book —" Piper began.

"I know she said that. But the phone book was put out a year before the agency was opened. I wanted to ask Rena if maybe she hadn't known Brannigan when she was a dancer around the hot-spots, and when he was a policeman assigned to the Times Square area. In fact, I did ask her, but she only hung up on me."

The Inspector was rigid. "Brannigan!" he whispered.

"An inside job," Miss Withers agreed. "And you have no idea just how much of an inside job it was."

Piper wasn't listening. "Brannigan," he said again. "Somebody got to him, hired him to do the job. Why, that —"

"We really ought to make Mrs. Hawkins answer the question," Miss Withers suggested again. "Perhaps if we went out there ...?"

"Never mind that. *Brannigan* — and you actually phoned him and tipped him off?" Without waiting for an answer the Inspector pressed the switch of the inter-office communicator, roaring orders to pick up Thomas Brannigan on a charge of murder.

It was some time before Miss Withers could repeat her request for a trip out to Queens. "That can wait," Piper told her. "Lucky thing we've got a man stationed in the Hawkins house." He reached for the phone, and dialed a number.

"No answer?" Miss Withers nodded. "It doesn't surprise me at all." The Inspector grabbed his hat and headed out of the office, but she kept close behind him. The departmental sedan, siren screaming, cut across the bridge and eastward into the depths of Queens County. During a lull Miss Withers said gently, "Oscar, if you shot somebody from the rear platform of a train what would you do with the gun? Would you put it down gently beside you, or would you hurl it as far as you could? Also, why couldn't the gun have been tossed onto the train, by someone standing on the embankment out in back?"

He didn't answer. Finally they drew up before the Hawkins house and for a while everything was confusion. The door had to be forced and then they found the policeman on duty there. He had not left his post after all, but he lay on the kitchen floor cold as a Christmas goose, a lump on his head and a broken beer bottle beside him. Of red-haired Rena Hawkins there was no sign whatever.

The Inspector was on the phone, directing the laying of a dragnet, the complicated operations of a manhunt that would extend all over the metropolitan area of New York. "And put all available men on the railroad stations, the bus depots... " Miss Withers plucked at his sleeve, but he jerked away angrily. "You and your meddling," he growled.

"Shh," she whispered. "Watch your language. Little pitchers, you know— "

He suddenly realized that she had brought a veritable horde of small boys into the house with her, thirty or more round little faces staring at him, smiling through missing teeth, breathing heavily

"My class," she explained. "But Oscar, before you hang up, I suggest that you forget about the stations and the airports and look for a 1931 gray-Maxwell coupe, probably headed south for Mexico."

He only stared at her.

"You see," she hastily went on, "while you were running around in circles in here I went out and had a chat with the nice man who runs the used car lot next door. I had noticed that one car that was there last night was missing now, and it occurred to me that if somebody was in a hurry to hide some money last night, in a safe place *outside* the house... "

"Are you saying Rena stole the car?"

"Oh, no. The man said it was sold over the phone this morning, to a Mr. Smith. It's being delivered to him out in Jersey City right this minute — the buyer promised to pay cash and I wonder if perhaps he doesn't plan to pay it out of the money that was stuffed under the cushions or somewhere last night just after the murder was committed?"

The Inspector was already giving quick orders over the telephone, orders that were eventually to result in the New Jersey state police swooping down on their motorcycles to pick up Brannigan and Rena Hawkins before they had even had their first flat tire. Which was a good thing, because there was no air in the spare tire — only eighteen thousand dollars, in a neat package.

"They're guilty all right," the Inspector was saying. "But we've no valid case against them. Because neither one of them left the house last night, to fire the shot or to stash the money. I checked their shoes —"

"Feet," pointed out Miss Withers, "were made before shoes. I mean bare feet. And moreover, I keep trying to tell you — the shot wasn't fired from outside, either from the platform or the railroad embankment. It was fired *in the bedroom!*"

"And I keep trying to tell you," Piper shouted, "that it couldn't have happened that way, because the bullet would have gone right through Hawkins's head at close range!"

The thirty little boys still waited. Miss Withers pushed two of them forward. "Inspector, this is Sigismund and this is Walter — two of my best pupils. When I gave my class a half-holiday, I suggested that they might use their bright little eyes in searching the alley and the railroad tracks back of this house. Boys, please show the nice Inspector what you found?"

Walter nudged Sigismund, who gulped and then started to prospect in the recesses of his clothing. With some assistance the urchin finally produced a piece of oak two-by-four. "There, you see?" cried Miss Withers, in modest pride. "That will do, boys. The Inspector will reward each of you with a dollar, and everybody else gets money for ice cream."

In a daze the Inspector found himself paying off. The little boys disappeared, whooping like Comanches.

"This piece of wood," Miss Withers promised the Inspector, "is worth every cent it cost you. Do you remember saying to me that the gun which killed Hawkins could shoot through a four-inch plank? Well, it immediately occurred to me that if there actually had been a plank held against the forehead of a sleeping man, and if the muzzle of the gun were pressed tight against the plank... " She gestured.

"Judas Priest in a whirlwind!" muttered the Inspector. He rubbed his thumb against the powder-blackening on one surface of the two-by-four, and then poked a finger into the hole drilled clean through the wood.

"It was a spent bullet, Oscar, just as you said — even though it had to travel only a few inches."

The Inspector had to admit that she was right. He wrapped up the piece of wood in his handkerchief and put it into his pocket. "This will be Exhibit A in the case of the State of New York versus Thomas Brannigan and Rena Hawkins."

Miss Withers nodded. "Hell," she said, "hath no fury like a wife who finds that while she has been sitting home her husband has been gallivanting around the night clubs. Exhibit B should be a pair of new evening slippers."

"Huh?" Oscar Piper blinked. "What slippers?"

"The ones he never bought her," said Hildegarde Withers.

HILDEGARDE WITHERS: SHORT STORIES

Collections:

The Riddles of Hildegarde Withers, ed. Ellery Queen. New York: Lawrence E. Spivak (Jonathan Press), 1947.
The Monkey Murder and Other Hildegarde Withers Stories, ed. Ellery Queen. New York: Lawrence E. Spivak (Bestseller Mystery), 1950.
People vs. Withers and Malone, with Craig Rice. New York: Simon and Schuster, 1963.
Hildegarde Withers: Uncollected Riddles. Norfolk: Crippen & Landru, 2002.

Individual Stories:

"The Riddle of the Dangling Pearl," *Mystery*, November 1933 [Collected in *Hildegarde Withers: Uncollected Riddles*, 2002]
"The Riddle of the Flea Circus," *Mystery*, December 1933 [Collected in *Hildegarde Withers: Uncollected Riddles*, 2002]
"The Riddle of the Forty Costumes," *Mystery*, January 1934 [Collected in *Hildegarde Withers: Uncollected Riddles*, 2002]
"The Riddle of the Brass Band," *Mystery*, March 1934 [Collected in *Hildegarde Withers: Uncollected Riddles*, 2002]
"The Riddle of the Yellow Canary," *Mystery*, April 1934 [Collected in *The Riddles of Hildegarde Withers*,1947]
"The Riddle of the Blueblood Murders," *Mystery*, June 1934 [Collected in *Hildegarde Withers: Uncollected Riddles*, 2002]
"The Riddle of Forty Naughty Girls," *Mystery*, July 1934 [Collected in *Hildegarde Withers: Uncollected Riddles*, 2002]
"The Riddle of the Hanging Men," *Mystery*, September 1934 [Collected in *Hildegarde Withers: Uncollected Riddles*, 2002]
"The Riddle of the Black Spade," *Mystery*, October 1934
"The Riddle of the Marble Blade," *Mystery*, November 1934 [Collected in *Hildegarde Withers: Uncollected Riddles*, 2002]
"The Riddle of the Whirling Lights," *Mystery*, January 1935 [Collected in *Hildegarde Withers: Uncollected Riddles*, 2002]
"The Doctor's Double," 1st publication unknown, 1937; reprinted in *Ellery Queen's Mystery Magazine* [hereafter, *EQMM*], August 1946 [Collected as "The Riddle of the Doctor's Double" in *The Riddles of Hildegarde Withers*, 1947]
"The Riddle of the Jack of Diamonds," 1st publication unknown; reprinted in *Fifty Famous Detectives of Fiction*, 1938 [Collected in *Hildegarde Withers: Uncollected Riddles*, 2002]
"A Fingerprint in Cobalt," *New York Sunday News*, 1938; reprinted as "The Blue Fingerprint," *EQMM*, May 1942 [Collected as "The Riddle of the Blue Fingerprint" in *The Riddles of Hildegarde Withers*, 1947]
"The Purple Postcards," 1st publication unknown, 1939 [Collected in *The Monkey Murder*, 1950]
"Tomorrow's Murder," 1st publication unknown, 1940 [Collected in *The Monkey Murder*, 1950]

"Miss Withers and the Unicorn," 1st publication unknown, 1941 [Collected in *The Monkey Murder*, 1950]

"Green Ice," *EQMM*, Winter 1942 [Collected as "The Riddle of the Green Ice" in *The Riddles of Hildegarde Withers*, 1947]

"The Puzzle of the Scorned Woman," *New York Sunday News*, 1942; reprinted as "The Lady from Dubuque," *EQMM*, March 1944 [Collected as "The Riddle of the Lady from Dubuque" in *The Riddles of Hildegarde Withers*, 1947]

"The Hungry Hippo," 1st publication unknown, 1943 [Collected in *The Monkey Murder*, 1950]

"The Riddle of the Twelve Amethysts," *EQMM*, March 1945 [Collected in *The Riddles of Hildegarde Withers*, 1947]

"Snafu Murder," *EQMM*, November 1945 [Collected as "The Riddle of the Snafu Murder" in *The Riddles of Hildegarde Withers*, 1947]

"The Riddle of the Black Museum," *EQMM*, March 1946 [Collected in *The Riddles of Hildegarde Withers*, 1947]

"The Monkey Murder," *EQMM*, January 1947 [Collected in *The Monkey Murder*, 1950]

"The Riddle of the Double Negative," *EQMM*, March 1947 [Collected in *The Monkey Murder*, 1950]

"The Long Worm," *EQMM*, October 1947 [Collected in *The Monkey Murder*, 1950]

"Fingerprints Don't Lie," *EQMM*, November 1947 [Collected in *The Monkey Murder*, 1950]

"The Riddle of the Tired Bullet," *EQMM*, March 1948 [Collected in *Hildegarde Withers: Uncollected Riddles*, 2002]

"Once Upon a Train," with Craig Rice, *EQMM*, October 1950 [Collected in *People vs. Withers and Malone*, 1963]

"Where Angels Fear to Tread," *EQMM*, February 1951

"Cherchez la Frame," with Craig Rice, *EQMM*, June 1951 [Collected in *People vs. Withers and Malone*, 1963]

"The Jinx Man," *EQMM*, December 1952

"Autopsy and Eva," with Craig Rice, *EQMM*, August 1954 [Collected in *People vs. Withers and Malone*, 1963]

"Rift in the Loot," with Craig Rice, *EQMM*, April 1955 [Collected in *People vs. Withers and Malone*, 1963]

"Hildegarde and the Spanish Cavalier," *EQMM*, December 1955

"You Bet Your Life," *EQMM*, May 1957

"Withers and Malone, Brain-Stormers," with Craig Rice, *EQMM*, February 1959 [Collected in *People vs. Withers and Malone*, 1963]

"Who is Sylvia?" *EQMM*, July 1961

"Withers and Malone, Crime-Busters," with Craig Rice, *EQMM*, November 1963 [Collected in *People vs. Withers and Malone*, 1963]

"The Return of Hildegarde Withers," *EQMM*, July 1964

"Hildegarde Withers Is Back," *EQMM*, April 1968

"Hildegarde Plays It Calm," *EQMM*, April 1969

In 1952, Stuart Palmer wrote that there were about 50 Withers stories to that point; but we have notes on only about 30 through that year (32 including the collaborations with Craig Rice). Therefore, twenty or so remain unrecorded, perhaps from the period 1937-1942 when at least some were appearing in newspapers. The publishers will be grateful for any further information.

Hildegarde Withers: Uncollected Stories

Hildegarde Withers: Uncollected Stories by Stuart Palmer is set in 11-point AmeriGaramond font and printed on 60 pound natural shade opaque acid-free paper. The cover illustration is by Gail Cross and the Lost Classics design is by Deborah Miller. *Hildegarde Withers: Uncollected Stories* was published in August 2002 by Crippen & Landru, Publishers, Norfolk, Virginia.

CRIPPEN & LANDRU LOST CLASSICS

Crippen & Landru announces a new series of new short story collections by great authors of the past who specialized in traditional mysteries. All first editions, each book collects stories from crumbling pulp, digest, and slick magazines, and from collectors and the estates of the authors. Each is published in cloth and trade softcover.

The following books are in print:

Peter Godfrey, *The Newtonian Egg and Other Cases of Rolf le Roux*
Craig Rice, *Murder, Mystery and Malone*, edited by Jeffrey A. Marks
Charles B. Child, *The Sleuth of Baghdad: The Inspector Chafik Stories*
Stuart Palmer, *Hildegarde Withers: Uncollected Riddles*, introduction
    by Mrs. Stuart Palmer

The following are in preparation:

Christianna Brand, *The Spotted Cat and Other Mysteries from the
    Casebook of Inspector Cockrill*, edited by Tony Medawar
William Campbell Gault, *Marksman and Other Stories*, edited by Bill
    Pronzini
Gerald Kersh, *Karmesin: The World's Greatest Crook — Or Most
    Outrageous Liar*, edited by Paul Duncan
Joseph Commings, *Banner Deadlines*, edited by Robert Adey
Margaret Millar, *The Couple Next Door: Collected Short Mysteries*,
    edited by Tom Nolan
William L. DeAndrea, *Murder — All Kinds*, introduction by Jane
    Haddam

Lost Classics